Under a Starry Sky

LAURA KEMP

ORION

An Orion paperback

First published in paperback in Great Britain in 2020
by Orion Fiction
an imprint of The Orion Publishing Group Ltd
Carmelite House, 50 Victoria Embankment
London EC4Y 0DZ

An Hachette UK Company

3 5 7 9 10 8 6 4 2

A CIP catalogue record for this book
is available from the British Library.

ISBN (Mass Market Paperback) 978 1 4091 8918 3
ISBN (eBook) 978 1 4091 8919 0

Typeset by Deltatype Ltd, Birkenhead, Merseyside

Printed in Great Britain by Clays Ltd, Elcograf S.p.A.

MIX
Paper from
responsible sources
FSC® C104740

www.orionbooks.co.uk

To my beloved rambling club tribe,
Paddy, Reuben, Ceri and Ollie

Prologue

Finally, Wanda Williams was getting out of here.

Punching the air as she tore off her dirties, her last Saturday shift at the family campsite was over.

Next week was the official start of her gap year – she'd spend six months working at Get Lost travel agents to save up for a backpacking adventure Down Under, starting in February, before uni the following September.

She'd had it all planned since she could walk, according to Dad, who'd fed her globetrotting tales from his navy days. Wanda by name, wander by nature, he always said. Mam didn't get why anyone would leave the village: 'We've got a chemist and the pub does a lovely Sunday roast – everything you could ever want is here!' If you were after incontinence pants and gravy dinners, that was. 'Plus, everyone knows one another!' Precisely. Gobaith was a claustrophobic cauldron hemmed in by the mountain: a speck on the map, in an area known as the Desert of Wales. Remote, inward-looking and smack bang in the middle of the country, people here were vastly outnumbered by sheep. There was nothing to stay for. Particularly as the unrequited love of Wanda's life was leaving too. Not that she'd stay for him, obviously, because she was an independent woman with a future.

I

As the shower water drummed down on her she told herself, as she had told herself before, that had anything ever happened between her and Lewis Jones, she'd feel far worse about him going away. Her heart would be broken rather than bruised. And it was aching enough already at the thought of saying goodbye to him tonight ...

Dry, dressed and her freckles toned down with foundation, Wanda dropped a kiss on her mother's head in the kitchen.

'But there's tea, here,' Mam said. 'Your favourite, lasagne.'

'Ah! Plate me one up, I'll have it later. No idea when I'll be back.'

Carrying the scent of canvas on his weathered skin, Dad appeared from the back door, rubbing his huge hands with glee at the sight of a laid table. 'Another August bank holiday is nearly over, then. Best one yet, I reckon.'

Towering over her, he came behind Mam to give her a squeeze and she turned her adoring face to his for a peck. It brought a lump to Wanda's throat to see they were still in love after all these years when their hair was turning grey. 'All down to you,' Mam cooed like the little bird she resembled.

'Us, you mean, Lyn,' he said, nodding at the Best Small Campsite 2004 trophy gleaming alongside another five from the previous years, which commanded a shelf of their own on the dresser. 'We all earned that. Even you, Wanda! I don't know what I'll do without you when it comes to cleaning the loo block.'

Their laughter was interrupted by the screech of a chair pulled back on the centuries-old stone floor. Wanda's

2

sister Carys gave her a hormonal once-over. 'I prefer your hair when it's natural and wavy. God, and the sisterhood, love you for who you are, not as you think you should be.'

Wanda tossed her straightened-till-it-was-singed ginger mane at her. Fourteen-year-old Carys was in the middle of a Christian feminist phase and any reply would lead to a lecture of letting love wait. Abstinence was, unfortunately, enforced on Wanda rather than a choice.

'Right, I'm off,' she said, as casually as she could.

Slipping out of the farmhouse, the night was warm, but Wanda still shivered as she made her way through the twilit campsite. Beyond the bustle of barbecues and the hushed voices of parents getting their kids ready for bed, she could feel something in the air tonight. She didn't want to go all Phil Collins about it but what if, what if it was something she'd been waiting for all her life? Yet again she wondered why she and Lew had never got it on. Five years ago, aged thirteen, she had woken up one morning and suddenly seen him no longer as a boy with a waft of feet about him but as her destiny. Now, even more so, she felt they had such a connection – their in-jokes, their shared love of hikes up the mountain and pints in the pub.

Stop it, she commanded herself, *you're just lopsided with love and prone to high emotion. That feeling, of being unsettled, is because things are about to change, that's all. This is the end of the summer, no, your childhood, and the beginning of the rest of your amazing life. Work your Kate Moss Glastonbury chic instead.*

Breathing in the sweet smell of grass, she ran a mental inventory of her little waistcoat and cut-off denim shorts, but when she got to her wellies, she could only hear the whoosh of air as she trod the path. Then her insides began to bubble because there he was, sat on the steps of Dad's shepherd's hut, a corrugated-iron shed on wheels, at the far end of the silvery lake, in the shadow of the mountain. So gorgeous with that messy dark mop of curls; he was big and broad, a proper farmer's son, with ripe biceps and chunky thighs straining his black T-shirt and camo shorts. That face of his, oh my days, eyes the colour of spring ferns; those full lips, all wrapped up in olive skin and scaffolded with proud cheekbones and a jaw you could crack conkers on. Yet inside he was soft as anything, bottle-feeding abandoned lambs and feeling no embarrassment when his mother asked him to get some pink loo roll from Blod's Shop.

As she got closer, she was grateful her feelings didn't leap out of her chest in a throbbing cartoon heart. People had teased her over the years about their 'friendship' but the mud hadn't ever stuck. She'd gone out with other boys to prove it – and also to herself, because maybe she'd just go off him if she tried. It never happened. If Lew got it in the neck, he would pull a face which said 'as if I fancy her!' and he'd had girlfriends, the lucky, lucky cows. She'd never told anyone how much she adored him in case it got out and ruined everything. The vibes between them, claimed by some to be completely and obviously a sign of their attraction, were simply platonic or else he'd have made a move. And he never had. At least with his departure she could get over him.

'I can't stay long, sorry,' Lew sighed, his brow heavy with sadness. 'Dad wants to take me for a beer.'

''Course,' Wanda said cheerfully, but really thrown by

how little time they actually had. 'You're leaving crack of anyway ...'

'Yeah, he wants an early night. Long drive tomorrow.'

He was off to Scotland on an intensive six-month course to train as an outdoors instructor. When they'd next see one another had been floated many times over coffees, smoothies and beers and he'd say *soon*, *Christmas*, *next year*, maybe he'd join her abroad when he'd finished, as if it was inevitable and besides, they could call and email. But with the inevitability now seeming flimsy, she steeled herself for their farewell.

'And I've got loads to do too.'

He made a show of budging up for her but she couldn't let her naked leg touch his. So she went inside the rickety old hut to give herself some space, switched on the cosy gas lamp and sank down on one of the sheepskin rugs on the wooden floor. Lew didn't take the hint though and joined her, laying back on an arm so his body curled around hers.

'How was it then? Your last day?' He blinked slowly with his thick black eyelashes and smiled that wonky smile of his which turned her to jelly. Dazed, she drank him in, trying to save some for a rainy day. Or a very sunny one in Australia. Words wouldn't come to her: she felt sick now that the reality of her loss loomed. 'Can't be worse than mine. Had a hand up a sheep's bum. Unless you were on bog duty again?'

In spite of herself, she laughed. But it only reminded her how much she'd miss their familiarity.

Lew tilted his head, sensing her unusual restraint. 'You okay?'

Yeah. I'm just feeling a bit devastated that this is it and

I've loved you forever and nothing will be the same again. No biggie.

'Fine,' she lied. Wanda wrapped a strand of hair around her finger to busy herself, but there it was again, a kind of buzzing just out of reach of her fingertips.

'I'll call as soon as I get there. This won't change anything, will it?' He gave her a plucky grin, but she couldn't match it and before she could stop it, the tumult of her yearning and grief came out as tears. 'What is it?' he said, concerned, taking her hand. His touch melted her defences.

'It's just … I know we've talked about this the whole summer but now it's here … I can't process it,' she sniffed. 'That I won't see you tomorrow or the next day or the day after that.'

He dropped his head. 'I know,' he said, quietly. 'It's horrible.'

She waited for his breezy 'but it'll all be fine!' as he lifted his chin. But instead he looked as haunted as she felt.

'Well, this is fun!' she croaked.

She saw his Adam's apple rise then fall as his eyes wandered the hut. Then they fell on hers and that something she'd been sensing seemed to come into focus. His cheeks were pink and he looked unsure.

'Look …' he gulped.

'Don't, honestly. We'll be over this by tomorrow.'

'No. Listen to me …' he said. 'We've never been … available at the same time, have we?'

'Really?' She pretended to wonder, as if it had never occurred to her. But she knew the cyclical pattern of Lew dates girl, Wanda pines, Wanda dates boy, Lew dumps girl, Wanda dumps boy, Lew dates girl and on and on.

'Not till now, no.' He pressed his lips together, looking nervous. She wouldn't let herself even think where this was going. But that thing that was coming in the air, well, it was kind of giving her a nudge. 'I've always wanted to ... be with you, Wanda. Stupid of me to say it now, I wish I'd been brave enough to tell you before ...'

Wanda's breathing went shallow. 'Lew? You serious?' She wondered if he was just saying this as if he'd heard her most private of thoughts and was doing it out of kindness. Through the little square window of the corrugated-iron hut she saw the sky was at its finest, dressed in sapphire velvet studded with diamonds. Were those stars aligning? No. They couldn't be. 'Even if we ... where would we go from here?'

'I'd meet you on the other side of the world if I had to.'

Was this real? Was he trying it on, maybe? Yet he looked as if he meant it and he was no player. Wanda couldn't think straight and she hesitated. Could she start something only to have to let him go? Agonisingly, he read her silence all wrong.

'Ha! Forget it!' He ruffled his hair awkwardly and cleared his throat. She couldn't bear this misunderstanding: her heart, her overjoyed heart, overruled her head.

'No, Lew ...' She inched towards him.

His eyes widened and then desire tumbled in, dragging them under, and their lips were almost touching. Wanda heard nothing but their breathing; only they existed in this moment. But then another face appeared and it took her seconds to register that their friend Annie Hughes was at the doorway, looking panicked and saying their names over and over.

7

'Have you seen my brother? Have you seen Ryan?' Annie's black eyes were flashing with fear.

Their intimacy forgotten, Lew swivelled round and got to his haunches, poised for action, while Wanda went to Annie's side. A bit of a tearaway, Ryan was one for going walkabout, but this time Wanda sensed it was different.

'He's in a bad way, a falling out with his dad, I had to get in between them. I've looked and looked, but nothing.'

'Have you been up the mountain?' Lew asked. The pair of them, in fact the four of them, had spent hours up there all of their lives. It was their backyard, their playground: as kids, sledging in winter and surfing the slopes on flat pieces of cardboard in spring and summer and making dens; then, as adolescents, they'd sneak away from prying eyes, taking cans to The Bunkhouse, a dilapidated old stone barn, and play truth or dare.

Annie shook her head. 'I've been all around the village.'

'I'll go,' Lew volunteered, knowing its every rock and crevice.

'We can look round the campsite,' Wanda said and then to Lew, 'Come back, to say goodbye.'

''Course,' he said, placing his hand on his chest.

They bundled out, Lew disappearing up the mountain path into the darkness, and there was Annie's scrawny boyfriend Dean sucking on a fag. His small eyes travelled up and down Wanda's body as he declared, 'Let the little shit stew.'

Wanda grabbed Annie and led her away. They checked every hedge and tree, the outhouses and storehouses on the land, asking campers if they'd seen a skinny thing of a young man in tatty skateboarder clothes, but after half an hour there was no sign. As they worked out what to do next, Annie suddenly cried out in anguish, pointing to the silhouette of the mountain.

A strip of orange, the colour of furious lava, was glowering above them – and streaking along the tinderbox of dry scrub. Grass fires weren't unusual: at school, they'd had regular visits from the fire service to warn of the dangers of 'arson for fun' carried out by yobs who claimed it was just harmless entertainment when there was nothing else to do. Sometimes you'd see smoke rising or small circles burning, but they'd either fade or be put out. This blaze, though, looked different: aggressive and hungry. Within minutes, it was zipping down towards them and thick smoke rolled onto the site.

Mesmerised by its speed, Wanda's feet at first couldn't move. She and Annie could only grip one another, her friend wondering aloud, aghast, if Ryan and Lew were safe. It was Dad running out of the house, with Mam and Carys, shouting into a phone, waving arms to evacuate that kicked them into action. Wanda banged on caravan doors and stormed the ladies and gents, yelling into tents to get out and run to the lane. Crying children in sleeping bags were carried away; there was coughing from the thick acrid fumes, people were scattering, terrified. Blue lights, yellow helmets, breathing masks and oxygen tanks, the crackle of walkie-talkies and villagers running in to help. Blod Evans from the shop directing the way to the community hall; Glanmor Hopkins, her boss from Get Lost and Dad's best mate, gathering extinguishers from the fire points; faces she recognised from the bakery, the curry house and the café lining up with buckets by the lake but being shooed away from danger.

9

It was all pointless as the flames licked the fringe of the house. Wanda scanned the crowd desperately, where the hell was her family? Then, among them, as close to the searing heat of the farmhouse as they could bear, were Mam and Carys, both sobbing and shaking.

'We couldn't find you!' Mam grabbed hold of her. 'Dad's gone inside to see if you're in there!' Mam covered her mouth but the scream ripped through Wanda's heart.

The fire was devouring the roof. Wanda broke free and began to run towards their home. A fireman setting up a cordon caught her and held her back and she struggled in vain to fight him off. From the pit of her soul, she howled 'No!' just as the top windows blew. The curtains were alight, then incinerated to ash. And the front door exploded in a blast of raging flames.

Life didn't happen here, she'd thought today. Now she was certain that death had come to prove her wrong.

I

Fifteen Years Later ...

Very clean but basic. A satisfactory four-night stay.
An answerphone and online booking system would
be helpful as we found it very difficult to make a
reservation.

The Smiths, Birmingham
Campsite Visitors' Book

Wanda Williams was doing the Right Thing.
Everyone had said so. In their own particular
way, of course, not missing the chance to point out her
round-the-world trip had been delayed by fifteen years.

'About bloody time,' Blod Evans had bellowed across
the counter of Blod's Shop. 'You're not getting any
younger!' With arms aloft, she'd come at Wanda in a
blur of cerise lipstick, red glasses, spiky silver hair tipped
peacock blue and a dazzling gold-sequinned plus-size
jumper, repeating it at volume in her ear in a huge *cwtch*
of a cuddle. Telling the matriarch of Gobaith before
anyone else had meant news of Wanda's solo adventure
raced up and down the bustling one-road high street
faster than Usain Bolt, saving her the job of breaking the
story.

And so she'd been on the receiving end of good wishes wherever she'd turned. Alis at Coffee on the Corner had cried, 'At last! Don't you go getting fancy tastes, mind. I've only just got the hang of soya lattes!'. Geoffrey at GoBooks had quoted something in Latin at her, but with a smile, so she'd guessed it was congrats. Only one was less than convincing: Phil the Pill, so-called because he was the pharmacist, who, along with a pair of deep vein thrombosis socks for the flight, gave her a wet-eyed 'Well done!' because he'd finally realised she would never say yes to a date.

Whether it was the charity-shop volunteers calling to her as she passed, Amir from Keep Calm and Curry On asking who'd be his best customer now, the butcher boys giving her the thumbs up or the staff at Oh My Cod parcelling up her fish and chips, the support was enormous. Partly because life was quite samey here and this was out of the ordinary, it was also because her ambition to travel was part of their version of Wanda. These people, who were both shopkeepers and friends, saw it as inevitable; like a feel-good next chapter of her story. It was meant to be: after all, it had been in the making for years.

It had been inconceivable that she would go away after she'd lost her father and her home in the fire. Mam and Carys had fallen to pieces and Wanda had somehow propelled herself through it to take care of them. She'd kept tears at bay, busying herself with funeral arrangements, and had watched the entire village overcome with grief when it emerged that Ryan had been found dead and red-handed at the scene. Worrying about money while the insurance was processed, Wanda had abandoned backpacking and uni to stay at Get Lost. As Carys got on with her education and Mam worked herself into the ground to rebuild the campsite, Wanda got her travelling kicks from booking others' holidays. Still she wouldn't leave, though – her sister and mother needed her. The years flew and before she knew it, she was shop manager and a mortgage payer with a flat in the village. The desire to see the world remained, though – so when Glanmor retired to Spain two months ago, selling up the once-thriving, now-dying business because the industry no longer relied on footfall but internet sales, she decided this was her opportunity. 'It's what Dad would've wanted,' she'd say, echoed by Glanmor, who had encouraged her to fulfil her dream. Inside, Wanda's grief remained a rock in her belly. Anger too, at Annie, who refused to condemn her brother, and at Lew.

She'd never seen him again after the fire – he hadn't come back to say goodbye that night and he'd left the next morning. He had messaged and tried to call, but in the fog of devastation, she'd been numb, wanting nothing to do with anyone. He'd sent his apologies for missing the funerals because he couldn't afford to fall behind on his course. Deeply hurt, she let time pass and reviewed his declaration of love as false; as him trying it on. As for Annie, she had married Dean and moved away, no doubt to escape the shame. Neither of Wanda's two oldest friends had figured in her adult life.

Back in January, around the time she'd discovered Get Lost was closing, Wanda had found out Annie was moving back to Gobaith and Lew had bought The Bunkhouse to turn it into a hostel for hikers, overseeing it from East Anglia, the flattest place you could get, which was ironic for a man of the mountains. Privately, that was another reason why Wanda had decided to follow her heart. The thought of seeing Annie or hearing about Lew's project was too painful. Publicly, though, she said nothing about them, merely that the time was right to go. Having badgered her for years to do it, Mam and Carys were thrilled for her: they were a team of their own. Carys, who still lived at home, ran the mud-and-wellies manual side of the business, while Mam did the books.

So tomorrow she was off. Wanda heaved her rucksack onto her back as she took a last look round her near-empty flat, which was up for rental from next week. She'd shifted her stuff into boxes and up to Mam's and there was nothing left to do but lock up. Down the stairs, she wobbled onto the pavement, where she nearly barged into Sara, who was shutting Gobaith Gifts, which sat below Wanda's place.

'You taking the kitchen sink then, lovely?' Sara said, gasping at Wanda's wide and heavy load.

'This, would you believe, is the pared down version of kit!' Wanda grimaced, her hips already aching from the weight of her bag.

'I think I'd die without my home comforts,' Sara said. Her straight blonde long bob, black jumper and skinny cigarette trousers made her look every inch the winner of the Most Stylish Shop in the annual high street awards – for six years running. 'I almost did during my year out.' She shuddered at the memory. 'The grubby hostels and strangers' pubes in the showers, they made me realise I wasn't cut out to be a bohemian artist. Glad I got it out of my system though, it's important to find these things out about yourself . . .'

How reassuring. Wanda had increasingly found herself awake at 3 a.m. wondering if her filtered fantasy would live up to the true grit of the experience. While she worked in travel, how prepared was she really when she'd only ever holidayed in Europe and most of her clients had been of a certain age, either heading to Whitby on a coach or a fortnight on the Algarve?

'Oh, I'm going to miss you!' Sara hugged her and gave a final squeeze of her hand. 'What am I going to do without our Wine and Woe Wednesdays upstairs? Who am I going to share a curry with and moan at about life, the universe and men?'

As much as she'd had a skinful of village life, Wanda was sad to be leaving Sara.

'I'll be back before you know it!' she sang. 'I've got to go; last supper at Mam's.'

Wanda set off up the high street. It was a typical early evening in March, the crisp and cold made her chest tight – and then the air was squeezed out of her when she saw what had become of Get Lost. The jaunty red sign, underlined with an aeroplane and its vapour trail, had gone last week and, ever since, workmen had been hammering away inside. Everyone knew it was going to be a hardware store; they'd all pictured an old-fashioned Aladdin's cave of drawers filled with hooks and nails and staff with waxed moustaches and aprons. But this … it looked like a discount pound shop! The windows were cluttered with a riot of colourful plastic tubs, garden pots, steel bins, pegs, brooms, cheap toys, T-shirts, camouflage netting and God knows what else. And why was it called Fork Handles? If this was a reflection of the owner, he was sure to be an absolute crazy mess of a man.

What would Glanmor make of it, she wondered. He'd be horrified ... then again, would he even care now he was in Spain with the early heat of spring, knowing Gobaith was still being bitten on the arse by winter? And really, why should she care either; she'd soon be in her flip-flops. Instead, she braced herself for the solid ten-minute uphill march to her Mam's house and went through her itinerary.

As the high street faded into fields and farms bathed in a glorious red sunset, Wanda laughed as she remembered how easy she'd thought it would be to pick a route. Stick her on the spot and she could reel them off – clockwise or anticlockwise, overland or by air. When it came to the reality, it hadn't been so straightforward. At eighteen, it had been simple: Australia, New Zealand and South East Asia for beaches, extreme sports and even more extreme drinking.

But now that she looked forward to nights in and drank wine priced more than a fiver, she couldn't think of anything worse.

Then there was the cost – she couldn't afford to go to one-hundred-and-eighty-odd countries, not without a private jet.

There was also the time factor: a year was the ideal, but within the week of Wanda's bombshell, Carys had had some news, so it was six months max. Wanda wasn't going to miss out on becoming an aunty. Especially when the father had no idea he was going to be one. Carys and dark-and-handsome Danny had met in December when a bunch of city lads from Manchester had come in a convoy of camper vans to the campsite for an outdoorsy stag do. After hitting it off at first sight, then over drinks in the pub, where they hogged the jukebox with their love of nineties grunge, they spent the night together and waved each other goodbye, promising to stay in touch. Only recently had Carys confessed the cock-up that followed – she felt embarrassed she'd tried to play it cool and she hadn't wanted to drop Mam in it. It turned out he'd tried to give her his number but because she hadn't wanted to seem too keen, she'd said she'd find it in the booking details. Except it wasn't there, and neither was his address or surname or anything. Just 'campervan x six'. Under questioning, it came to light that Mam hadn't been on top of things, what with Christmas coming and the end of the season. The adventure company wouldn't give out the party's details; Facebook threw up nothing, and where did you start looking when all the detail you had was Daniel Platt, call-centre worker, and, according to Carys, the perfect man? Carys had insisted she would keep the baby. Which turned into babies at the twelve-week scan, at which Carys nearly ripped Wanda's arm from her socket in disbelief when they heard two heartbeats. Wanda had refrained from asking if Carys regretted abandoning her 'let love wait' teenage days.

It had been a traumatic time for her, especially with morning sickness to contend with. But with the grainy ultrasound photos pinned to the fridge, and having named them Rock and Roll, Carys kept the faith – what was meant to be would be, and that included the hope that she'd find him. Wanda wasn't so sure; there were stories of people pretending to be somebody else, giving fake names and identities, just to get a leg over. She hadn't said as much, but she had told Carys that if she wanted her to stay around, she could delay her trip.

Carys wouldn't hear of it – she had Mam, and tons of friends.

With that law laid down, Wanda devoted herself to her expedition. And she encountered so much more than she'd bargained for. Did she go the way of a bucket list, ticking off all the big beasts of Niagara Falls and New York, the Taj Mahal and Thailand, the Great Wall of China and the Great Barrier Reef, the Sydney Opera House and Christ the Redeemer in Rio de Janeiro? Or did she go off the beaten track and look for hidden gems?

It became obvious over hours of self-examination – not to mention drunken chats with anyone who'd listen – that this wasn't about where to go but rather who she was and what she wanted out of it. To know that, she had to first work out what she *didn't* want. She wasn't eighteen any more, when she'd been set on happy hours, BFFs and sharing a dorm. Now, in her just-about early thirties, Wanda wanted to learn things, have an authentic journey – and snap a billion pictures to put up on her Instagram account, @WandaLust, which had zero posts so far because what was there to photograph round here?

And so tomorrow she'd fly to Colombia for a three-week course to learn Spanish, head down to Buenos Aires to be taught the tango, volunteer on a community project in Chile, hang out on a South Pacific beach, get to grips with yoga and surfing in Indonesia, take a class in Indian street food in Kerala and finish off in a last blast of shopping in Moroccan souks. And if the fancy took her, she could add on destinations and take a few detours. Perhaps she'd end up living somewhere exotic. Maybe the next time she was here she'd be packing up for a new life ... Wanda's heart pounded with excitement all the way to the turn in the narrow lane where a piece of wood against the hedgerow announced in Mam's painted handwriting, *Campsite This Way.* Coming here always caught in her throat. It was a place of laughter and life, where she and Carys had been born, the scene of long happy summers playing with the kids of campers and winters when the lake would freeze and the air nipped your nose. But still she saw Dad's ghost everywhere.

She went over the sheep grid and up the gravel drive, knowing now, at dusk, how the darkening sky would swallow the mountain, reducing it to its actual official status of just a hill – much to the locals' irritation, the peak fell short of two-thousand-foot mountain status by mere inches. She'd once loved those slopes, but after the fire, she had only ever viewed them with loathing.

Letting herself in to the restored grey-bricked farmhouse, she flopped her rucksack down in the hall and called out, 'It's me!' There was only silence though: no lights were on and neither was there the smell of Mam's lasagne. *How odd.* She went back out and saw the Land Rover was still there. *Where could they be?* She wandered into the garden, around the near-empty campsite field, where just two tents were pitched, past the shower block and found nothing. Back to the house she went and she began to run when she heard her phone ringing. She got there just in time to catch her sister's call. Carys was bound to be saying they'd only have been up the road feeding someone's cat or putting some chickens away for the night.

'Hiya, Caz!' Wanda said, moving into the kitchen and switching on the light. 'I'm here. At home. Where have you two—'

'Wanda,' Carys interrupted, 'don't panic, but we're in the hospital.'

'What? Oh God,' Wanda clutched her chest, 'is it the babies?'

'It's not me, Wanda. It's Mam.'

'Mam? Oh no!' Wild thoughts raced through her head – losing a parent in a tragedy made you doubly fearful for the surviving one.

'She had a fall at home, she was trying to change a light bulb, it's a suspected hip fracture. She's fine, on pain relief, we're waiting for X-rays then we'll know more probably tomorrow.'

Relief swept through her. 'So she's not dead?'

'No!'

Wanda was embarrassed that she'd revealed her default trait of expecting the worst; this was a hangover from Dad being taken from them too early. Feeling defensive, she went on the attack.

'Why didn't you leave a note? Or ring me?' she snapped.

'Because it all happened in a flash, the ambulance came and then off we went, and I didn't want you to do ... *this*.'

'Do what?' Wanda felt her hackles rising further.

'Go into a fluster, get all worked up, assume it would be the end of the world, as you tend to do.' Carys could be infuriatingly calm.

'Hang on ...' Wanda stopped. This wasn't the time to have a row about what she tended to do or not to do. She took a breath and then spoke. 'Never mind. I'll be there now.'

With that, Wanda grabbed Mam's nightie, toothbrush

and her bedside photo of Dad, then scooped up the keys to Mam's spluttering old 4x4 from the dusty silver bowl in the hall and left without giving a thought to her rucksack in the hall.

PS. It might be an idea to have someone on duty in the evenings as no one was around to help when the loo roll ran out.

The Smiths, Birmingham
Campsite Visitors' Book

'You can still go, you know,' Carys said over a midnight cup of tea at the kitchen table.

'I'm going nowhere. I told you.' Wanda rolled her shoulders, done in from the dash to hospital, the trauma of seeing Mam looking so vulnerable in a threadbare gown and the concentration of the ride home in the pitch black through wet, winding country roads in a downpour so heavy it had been raining knives and forks.

'But your trip ...' Carys said with anguish.

'What about it?' Wanda sighed.

'You've waited so long to go.' Carys's arm cradled her belly as if she was trying to protect her babies from the disappointment.

'It won't do any harm to wait a bit longer then, will it?' Wanda gave her a big-sister smile to convince her. 'It's all insured.'

'So you can go in a few weeks then! When Mam's better.' Satisfied with her conclusion, Carys tucked her blonde bob behind her ears, looking so much younger than twenty-nine.

'Yes! Now stop worrying and take yourself and Rock and Roll to bed. I'll tidy up here.'

Wanda held her calm composure until Carys had disappeared up the stairs and then dropped her head in her hands. A few weeks? There was no way she would be able to leave that soon. From the second she'd had the phone call, she'd known her plans were finished: not in a self-indulgent way but in a simple fact of acceptance, which was underlined when she'd seen her mother groggy from pain relief and heard the diagnosis.

Mam was going to need some time to recover from her broken hip – the operation would take its toll and there'd be months of physio. But that was just the shark's fin of it – Carys would need support too and Mam wouldn't be up to it while she was getting her strength back. Twins would take it out of Carys physically and then there was the emotional side of facing parenthood, most likely, alone.

Still smarting from Carys's accusation that she was a drama queen, Wanda had swallowed hard every time her heart raced up her throat, telling herself it was big-girl-pants time. But now she was alone she was overcome by the position she was in. And, damn it, her sense of catastrophe was having a riot. Because the campsite was in an absolute mess. That was the third and most troubling thing. Worst of all, Wanda hadn't even noticed it until now.

Mam's mistake over Danny Platt's booking details

should've flagged it up, but Wanda had put it down to the stress of the run-up to Christmas. She kept her nose out of the business, too, because it was Carys's and Mam's responsibility. Then, since January, she'd been preoccupied with organising her travels.

It was only when they'd come back to the farmhouse to find a note from the campers asking for loo roll – such an obvious requirement to be overlooked – that Wanda had stopped to look around her. The kitchen was in even more chaos than normal. Mam had never been a tidy person; she was too busy living. Yet now the paperwork pile was taller and stuffed with red bills, the dust on the cobwebs had grown fingers and no surface was visible beneath the clutter of odds and sods.

She'd thought back to when she'd gone looking for Mam and Carys and then it registered that the garden was overgrown, the campsite field wasn't clipped and tidy but sprawling with weeds. When she'd nipped out to replenish the toilet roll while Carys put the kettle on, she'd been stunned to see the showers were mouldy. A scroll through the visitors' book revealed that while everyone loved the big Welsh welcome, they were less than impressed with the facilities and surroundings.

Now, overtired and anxious about Mam, Wanda couldn't rein in her drama queen. The season started in a week's time and it would never be up to scratch. Her father would be mortified. How had her mother and sister let it get to this? And where did she start with what needed to be done to get it ready? Because it would fall to her, and quite rightly, because Carys wouldn't be up to it, the larger and more exhausted she got; her job would be to look after Mam.

Her agonising took her to a place Wanda had long ago buried – back to the darkness of being fresh with grief, blaming herself for Dad's death. He'd gone in to the house to look for her, so it was her fault. Her mind was hurtling back to the fire and forwards to Mam's accident, making a connection which would have to be shaken off in the light of day, but here, in the silence of the farmhouse, in the lonely hours of the night, she wondered if she was jinxed. Yes, it was self-pity, but it was also fear, and she couldn't stop herself wondering if there was something in her daring to leave that led to bad things happening.

Cross with herself for playing the victim, Wanda wiped away tears and turned off the lights. But the voice of common sense was drowning in the darkness and right now it felt as if she would forever be going nowhere.

3

A trickle of sweat ran down the small of Annie Hughes's back as she wielded her roaring two-metre strimmer through a jungle of brambles.

Sunrise was glinting off the blade and already her feet were sodden from the frost, she stank of petrol and her nails were black as coal.

Remind me again, she thought as her hot breath made clouds in the crisp air, *why do I call myself The Lady Gardener?*

That business card of hers, of a dainty hippy female silhouette among flowers, birds and bees, was as close to the reality of working life as her marriage had been to Mills & Boon. The name was also open to interpretation – one woman had rung asking if Annie 'did those waxes, you know, the South American ones'.

But she forgot the brutality of eight hours' physical labour as many days a week as she could manage to cover the costs of no income in winter. She set aside the beef of working in all weathers, in the finger-numbing cold, like today, and the blistering heat and the punishing wind and rain. She accepted the pain of injury, from her industrial lawnmower battering her arms, to thorns stuck deep in her skin. And she rose above the misunderstandings and cheap innuendoes about trimming bushes.

Because The Lady Gardener was hers and hers alone. It paid the bills and it had given her the security to afford the biggest decision of her life. It made Annie feel strong and capable: she had the muscles to show that. It was a defiant cry of self-respect and a very firm two fingers up at her ex, and anyone else who'd bad-mouthed her, and there'd been plenty. No one had ever called her a lady before. Ever.

Besides, it was all she had – she had no qualifications, contacts or family money to fall back on. Her sideline of herbal remedies, which soothed her own scrapes and aches and teased thorns out of her hands, was more of a hobby than a source of income. And when it came down to it, how many people were one hundred per cent happy at work? Despite the chill, the sunstroke and the back-breaking digging, Annie was blessed – she was her own boss and, as of two months ago, her own woman. Okay, she might have been forced to move back home to Gobaith, where she was still tagged as 'one of those Hugheses', to sleep on Blod's sofa for a while until the sale of the house went through. But The Lady Gardener had given her a second chance at life. And wow! Just as the shadow of the mountain retreated, Annie saw something. She cut out her power tool and lifted the scratched visor of her face shield to admire this gem: a long-abandoned nest, of spindly sticks and wispy feathers, damp moss and crunchy leaves, all useless apart but together, woven perfectly by a bird's beak, it had been a home.

The Lady Gardener also gave her this – moments of sheer wonder at Mother Nature. These magical surprises, which happened every time she went to work, could be anything from a wet spider's web twinkling like a chandelier dripping with diamonds or a single red poppy blossoming through a crack of patio, to a humble earthworm enriching the soil of a flowerbed or bulbs multiplying year after year.

The best things in life are free, her Nanna Perl had always said. When Annie was young, she'd only feel sad because it reminded her how poor they were. But now she could understand what she'd meant: joy was all around you if you looked for it. And it was here in abundance, she thought, wiping her brow with a gloved hand.

Spring was definitely on its way – bare branches were coming alive with shoots of green, sprays of wild garlic were carpeting the ground and swooping red kites had begun their aerial displays in search of a mate.

Annie took a huge lungful of countryside air and felt almost at peace: there was just one thing missing and that was Teg. She stared into the distance, imagining her sniffing the grass, lolloping after a squirrel or resting, tongue out, as she held her face to the sun. Her ghost was everywhere, a gust of wind disturbing a bush was her ferreting around for a lost ball and a brush of her knees against a damp plant was her nose asking if it was treat time yet.

Teg was her five-year-old mongrel with the skinny legs of a greyhound, the shaggy grey coat of a wolfhound and the purest grey eyes, which were as deep with loyalty as the lake. How she missed her constant companion, whether outside with her at work or curled up by her feet on her bed; but because of Blod's cats, Annie had had to put her in kennels. Huge, smelly and belonging to a

Hughes, no one would've had her and she hadn't even bothered asking. Yes, she could've brought her with her every day, but it killed her enough when she had to say goodbye at the end of her visits – it would only confuse her if she had to send her back every night. Teg was better off with a routine, in spite of the cost, but she'd halved it with an arrangement to maintain the kennel grounds. It wouldn't be forever; soon she'd be reunited with her best buddy, her comfort – and her protector, who, if she was here now, would be stood as still as a statue, bar her nostrils flaring to catch the scent of the woman coming towards her in order to detect whether she was friend or foe . . .

Annie's stomach dropped when she saw this one was definitely foe. Her warmth deserted her as a blue-eyed stare turned the space between them glacial.

The figure of Wanda Williams had been purposeful but non-threatening as she'd squelched through the mudbath of the clearing, but now she'd recognised Annie, her body language became hostile, with a stern chin and forceful shoulders. Well, of course it would be.

You idiot, Annie told herself, *why did you think it was a good idea to come to the campsite? Did you really think you could nip in and out unnoticed with a noisy strimmer and then go to work shining your halo?*

In what she saw now as a moment of madness, she'd decided last night to be a good Samaritan when Blod had told her Wanda's mam had had an accident. To her trained eye, every time she drove past the site she saw how overgrown it was. Wanting to do something for Lyn, she'd come up with a quick tidy-up of the hedges. But obviously now she looked like a trespassing nutter.

And that madness was actually desperation – of trying to make amends. Cutting a hedge uninvited was hardly going to make up for her brother's suspected hand in Gobaith's biggest ever tragedy, depriving a family of a husband and a father and a community of an upstanding man.

What had she been thinking? Even coming back to Gobaith at all – but then she'd had nowhere else to go. In the aftermath of the fire, her shameless extended ragtag family of cousins and aunties had upped and fled to the nearest benefits town on the coast. So thanks to Nanna Perl's lifelong friendship with her, Blod's it was, and she had stayed under the radar, up out and early to do her jobs across the valley in her old neck of the woods, only to return after dark and hole herself up to avoid ostracised silence or confrontation. But during the dark winter nights, when the fire was going and they pottered about, Blod doing her knitting and Annie making her ointments, Blod would fill her in on the goings-on of Gobaith and Annie felt herself being drawn back in. Every day for the last fifteen years she had felt loss: of Ryan's death and of her friendship with Wanda. Hearing about the comings and goings had exposed her old scars – of guilt on Ryan's behalf, the burden of being from ne'er-do-well stock. So she'd acted on it and with hindsight it was crazy. Like walking into a lion's lair.

'What are you doing here?' Wanda said tightly. Her cheeks were flushed though, and she looked as if she was struggling to keep a lid on her emotions. That was the Wanda Annie had known. She crossed the arms of a shabby padded wax jacket across her chest. The coat was obviously not hers, it was too big for her, as were those gaping wellies. How could someone who had lived outdoors as a child look so foreign to it now? *I suppose that's what comes from sitting in an office all day*, Annie thought. There was further evidence of Wanda's indoor lifestyle close up: her face had barely aged. Yes, there were a few crow's feet, and she looked tired. But her complexion was clear and her orange waves hung as if they'd been styled that way – as ever, she looked normal and loved and cared for. Annie was weathered beyond her years; her hair was a long dark tangle of black turning grey – she couldn't afford the hairdresser – and her hands were gnarled and blistered.

She shrank into her leaking boots and laid down her strimmer in submission.

Because Wanda had every reason to hate her. Never mind her attempt at living an honest life and doing the decent thing, Annie was the only reminder left of her younger brother Ryan. Their mother wanted nothing to do with her, hadn't done from the day she was born. Young and unable to cope, she'd handed Annie over to her own mam, Nanna Perl, who'd brought her up – but she had long since passed. Ryan's father was dead and Annie's had buggered off before she was born. That left Annie to face the music. She wouldn't have left Mid Wales anyway – memories of her brother were all around and as much as they hurt, they were all she had of him. Her soon-to-be-ex-husband's sneer, which he couldn't even hold in until the funeral was over, was in her ears: 'Good riddance to the little shit. He was only ever going to give you trouble.'

Ah, she thought, catching herself, *you don't have to listen to Dean Pincher any more*. Twenty years together with someone; it was a hard habit to break when you didn't feel like you deserved a good man or a good life.

But she had to, because she'd already wasted half her life – Annie owed it to herself to be herself. She was free; her ex had no idea she was here, he'd never think she'd return to this village. Her spine straightened a fraction because she was just forty and it would all come good ...

But probably not this second, she thought, as Wanda turned up the intensity of her contemptuous glare.

'Just tidying up the campsite; it's opening full-time from next week, isn't it?' Annie heard the tremble in her own voice.

'I know when the season starts, thank you,' Wanda said, oozing with sarcasm, as thick as Nanna Perl's jam on a doorstep of bread. The sub-zero temperature of this reception was the very least Annie could expect.

'I heard about your Mam, I'm sorry.'

Wanda twitched, catching but ignoring Annie's attempt at conciliation. 'I never asked you to come here.'

'I just wanted to help,' Annie said.

'Why would you do that?' Wanda asked, incredulous.

Annie wanted to blurt it all out: *I'm doing it to try to repair the damage caused by my brother.* But she'd only get a well-deserved whipping of words from Wanda.

'Because it needs doing. A quick job before my day starts ...'

Wanda looked suspicious; unsurprisingly, considering Annie's family history. She needed to explain that she wasn't here casing the joint.

'Because ... you know how things are for the campsite ...'

Wanda's eyebrows knitted together with fury at

32

Annie's clanger. Yes, it was run-down compared to its heyday of twenty years ago, but Wanda wouldn't want to be reminded of its decline. Annie braced herself for a verbal battering. What came out, though, was rather more desperate.

'Yes, well, I'm sorting it. It'll be ready.' Wanda nodded firmly. 'Now that I'm not going away.'

In an instant, Annie felt sorry for her. She'd heard Wanda was leaving – Annie had always kept her ear to the ground, hoping one day she'd learn that Wanda had gone to see the world as she'd once dreamed. It had continually amazed her that every snippet about Wanda had been mundane chatter of her life in Gobaith. So to know that she'd almost made her getaway but had been prevented at the eleventh hour filled Annie with sorrow. While Wanda was no longer a friend of hers, Annie wished no ill on anyone. Not even Dean Pincher. Acceptance and moving on was a straighter path to happiness than bitterness. There was also a tiny speck of hope that maybe she might be useful – she'd grab any opportunity to make amends to the Williamses.

'I can help out,' Annie offered. 'Ask around, too.'

Wanda looked at her as if she was mad and then stalked off back to the farmhouse. Annie understood why: she was tainted by association.

But Wanda hadn't said no. Annie would hold on to that. She had to believe in the power of good: Blod hadn't given a stuff about Annie's past when she had offered to put her up.

Getting this place back to its former glory, to the summers of bobbing dinghies on the lake and the sound of kids in the playground, could heal them all. Before that, though, this jungle of weeds, nettles and brambles needed to be cleared.

Annie lifted her hand to drop her visor and saw the sun rise above the mountain: it turned the lake a breathtaking blue, as if the curtains had been drawn. She took it as a sign – a smile from the heavens. And then she pulled hard on the cord of her strimmer and revved it up. You had to start somewhere, didn't you?

4

*Stunning landscape and the sky at night is a thing to
behold! It would've been lovely to go out on the lake
but the canoes were broken. Lovely welcome from
Lyn – we're very sorry to hear she is in hospital – but the
campsite could do with a freshen-up.*

Mr and Mrs Green, Devizes
Campsite Visitors' Book

It was bad enough with Mam in hospital and the mess
of the campsite. Chuck Annie on top and Wanda
couldn't think straight.

She saw her hand tremble as it turned the back door
handle to let herself in after the showdown with her
former friend. Today, she'd woken up determined to be
positive. Even though she'd slept fitfully in her room,
which had never felt like hers after the house was reno-
vated, she'd vowed there'd be no more 'poor me' after
last night's descent into self-pity.

And it'd been a good start, if a very early one. Over a
strong cup of coffee, she'd gone online to inform the insurance company, airline, Colombian B&B and language
school that she had to cancel. While her heart longed

to be at Mam's bedside, the practicalities meant Wanda needed to be here and so she'd seen Carys off to the hospital with a crack-of-dawn fry-up before beginning to tackle the pile of bills. But the nearby buzz of some kind of machinery had sent her outside to discover her former friend was on their land.

Shock that she would be here, of all places, after all these years, quickly gave way to anger and then disbelief as Annie stood there claiming she was cutting the hedgerows because she wanted to do Mam a favour. It was a blatant self-serving motive, that's what it was – she wanted to appease her guilty conscience, more like. How dare she try to take advantage of Mam's misfortune to wheedle her way back into the good books of Gobaith?

And the way she'd said she'd known how things were at the campsite had cut to Wanda's core – the absolute cheek of her. Yes, it was obvious things weren't fine and dandy; the cold light of day was unforgiving, but it wasn't Annie's place to say it.

How she'd managed to restrain herself, Wanda didn't know. Annie's offer to help out would absolutely never be taken up. So why hadn't she thrown her off the land?

Wanda didn't want to answer that because it suggested that perhaps a very small piece of her had registered a kindness, as if to say time had passed and here they both were: if they were going to be within the same village then they should be on the same side. *But that could never be, surely?*

Sunshine streamed in through the kitchen window and hit the dusty dresser where Dad's camping trophies should have been. A lump came to her throat – he'd be here if it wasn't for Ryan. The verdict at Dad's inquest had been 'open' – she felt the outrage anew that the finger of blame had never conclusively pointed at Ryan. No one could prove that he actually started the fire. But everyone knew the truth – that in a fit of rage he'd torched the mountain, seeking destruction. *Damn it*, she thought, screwing up her fists, pulsing with grief. Tears came again and her shoulders began to heave as if she was back in the past. After the fire, when they'd spent the night at a neighbour's, she and Carys had woken to Mam's gentle moans from downstairs. They'd tiptoed out to the landing to see a policewoman bowing her head, having delivered the news they'd dreaded. The funerals had been so different: Dad's was jam-packed and dignified, Ryan's apparently poorly attended and drunken. She remembered Mam holding her back, pleading for her to behave when she had clocked Annie at her father's service.

If only Mam hadn't had her accident … she'd be checked in at the airport, putting thousands of miles between herself and the past. Instead, she was distressed about her mother, at the helm of a failing campsite and an emotional wreck, all compounded by being up against the clock. Was she being dramatic? She thought back to the most recent comment from the departing guests this morning, who had suggested a 'freshen-up' as if nothing more than a wet wipe was required. They'd been nice people, though; they were obviously being polite because Wanda could see the enormity of the task at hand.

At least there were only a couple of single tent bookings until next week, so the coast was clear for Wanda to get going. She sank onto a chair at the kitchen table and flicked through the admin. Plenty of unpaid bills told her that Mam was struggling with the finances. Luckily, Wanda had her travel savings and she could pay them off. But would it be so easy to fix the campsite? Maybe she should close it down until she'd managed it. But dropping the curtain would mean no income at all – and for God knows how long. This business was all about the summer trade – they simply couldn't miss the season. Besides, there was a group arriving in a few days and it was too late, too unfair on them, to cancel. She had no other option but to grit her teeth and get on with it.

But where was she going to find help at such short notice? There was only one place to start – Blod's Shop. Wanda showered and found some of the clothes she'd boxed up because she wouldn't be needing them in the tropics – if she was staying here, she couldn't walk around in Dad's old waxed jacket and wellies. She must've seemed like a madwoman to Annie, who, she had noticed, while lean and muscular in her body, with her big hair tied back, appeared softer round the edges, having grown into her striking looks.

Then she was on her way on Cary's bike, taking big breaths and trying again to be upbeat. Because Blod would help anyone. There was no need for a community noticeboard because she *was* the community noticeboard and she embodied the English meaning of Gobaith, which translated as 'hope'. Barely had Wanda entered the gloriously old-fashioned parlour with its wooden shelves bursting with goodies than she found the Williams family was top-of-the-hour news.

'Terrible about your mam, Wanda,' Blod said, buzzing her way to her from the vintage till in a black-and-yellow bumble-bee mohair jumper dress to give her a hug.

'There's a hamper going her way, I put it together this morning with all her favourites, you know, that local honey she likes, better than that rubbish jam you get in hospital,' she chattered, boiling like pea soup, 'a couple of bars of that lovely Cambrian chocolate, a snifter of sherry ...' Meanwhile Wanda was suffocating under Blod's tickly woolly top. 'It'll be something nice to wake up to, you know, after her operation this afternoon.'

'This afternoon?' Wanda cried as she released herself from Blod's bosom. But Carys hadn't messaged yet!

'Yes, so Bronwen says.' Blod returned to her crow's nest and popped a boiled sweet. 'Welsh cake and custard,' she winked, offering a bulging paper bag to Wanda. 'New in, very popular.'

'But your sister's in Portugal!' Wanda said, waving away the distraction. She didn't need Blod to go off on a tangent now.

'Yes,' Blod said, smiling as if it was obvious, 'but her old neighbour, Diane, her cousin's son was visiting, out of hours, mind, but he knows someone who knows the sister on ward four, and he saw your mam this morning, see?' She gave a firm suck like it was a full stop.

'Wow. Well, thanks for telling me. I think.' This was the good-stroke-terrible thing – depending on what it was concerning – about Gobaith life. Secrets had to be buried deep to remain that way.

'Awful luck for you, Wanda, dear, with your travels.'

'Just a delay, that's all it is.'

'That's the spirit! No point lifting your petticoat after you've wet yourself, eh?' Trust Blod to use the plain-speaking local version of *no point crying over spilt milk*. But her straight-talking was part of her charm. And it came at Wanda again: 'So you've seen Annie then. She came back to grab her flask, told me all about it. Good to see you're talking at last.'

'I wouldn't say that, Blod.'

'In my long sixty-six years on this earth, Wanda, I've learned a thing or two about pain. If you hold on to it then it never stops hurting. She's not a bad person, Wanda. You know that. She wants to help you too. Your mother never tarred Annie with the brush used on Ryan.'

'I understand why you're on her side, you're like family to her. But I can't even go there.'

'Listen, I remember when she pinched a sausage roll from the shop, years ago. I could've given her a good hiding, but I heard her out. Ryan was hungry, there was nothing in for him at home. After that, I'd slip him something every now and then. She never did it again. The point is, people have reasons for doing things, everyone deserves a second chance.'

But Wanda could never imagine being close to Annie again. And she didn't want to discuss it any more – time was pressing on. 'Anyway, I'm here because I need to pick your brains.'

'Anything,' Blod said, and she meant it, she was the beating heart of Gobaith.

'I've got six days until the season starts. The campsite's a mess. I need some help. I can't do it by myself.'

'What about some of the farmer boys?'

'They'll want paying and we're skint.'

'It's going to be hard finding someone with so little warning. There is Spike at Fork Handles. He seems keen.' Blod raised her eyebrows.

Incomers, especially English ones, always wanted to

throw themselves into community life. It'd be very weird going back into her old office. But what option did she have? Phil the Pill, who'd be thrilled she wasn't leaving, would take it as a come-on if she asked.

'I'll try him then,' Wanda said.

Blod suddenly froze – had she had a lightbulb moment? Wanda waited expectantly, praying she'd recalled a twenty-four-hour crack squad of altruistic grafters. But Blod's eyes were aimed behind Wanda's left shoulder. She turned round just as Blod bellowed a name Wanda knew so well.

'Look who it is! Lewis Jones! As I live and breathe!'

Wanda's jaw flopped and he registered her at the same time, his face falling, taking a nervous step backwards. But it wasn't just his actual physical presence that shocked her but what had become of him. In a dirty fleece and holey trousers, he was completely dishevelled. Exhausted-looking, sallow and with baggy moss-coloured eyes, which quickly darted away from her to Blod.

Then it was as if the sun had come out when he smiled at Blod, his gaze turning to summer leaves. It was like seeing the old Lew and Wanda felt her stomach somersault. Her heart boomed too, filling her ears, and she watched with a dry mouth as Blod went to him and reached up to pinch his cheek of dark stubble to check it really was him, a long-lost child.

'Still so handsome!' Blod cooed. Wanda was startled to find herself agreeing. 'Well I never! It's you. I can't believe it!'

Neither could Wanda, especially hot on the heels of seeing Annie. Nothing of either of them for fifteen years, then both in the same morning. It felt like a conspiracy to her as her emotions rose in her chest. But where there had been anger with Annie, there was confusion instead - the memory of how much she'd loved him rushed in, their almost kiss, and then the emptiness of remembering he'd gone without saying a proper goodbye and how years of friendship she'd thought was stronger than steel had evaporated almost overnight.

Lew *cwtched* Blod hard. Wanda gulped as he shut his eyes, his defences down and she took the chance to take him all in as he towered taller and wider than he'd been as a young man, yet still soft too, with those still luxuriant cow's eyelashes of his.

As they parted, Lew looked again at Wanda and gave her a small nod of recognition, which she returned. She understood his gesture, even though she didn't understand who he was any more, because she couldn't find the words to speak to him either. How did you pick something back up which had been screwed into a ball and lobbed into the bin?

'I thought you were in Norfolk! Those builders you got in at The Bunkhouse giving you trouble?' Blod said.

'Got back a few days ago,' he said in a deeper, more gravelly voice than he used to have, 'I'm taking over the redevelopment for the foreseeable. I've signed up with the mountain rescue, too,' he said, pointing at the logo on his top. 'Thought I might as well while I'm around.'

Wanda lurched inside. It sounded like he was doing a Take That – back for good. Or at least a while.

Blod beamed. 'How lovely! Time for a cuppa?'

'No, lots to do. Just popped in for some caffeine. To prop my eyes open. Had a call-out last night, a sheep stuck in a ditch. Then it was impossible to get back to sleep.'

'We'll have a proper catch-up soon in that case. Coffee's between the nappies and cat food.'

He went off to the shelves and Blod elbowed Wanda. 'You could ask him to help.'

Wanda stared at her, stunned. You couldn't not see someone for fifteen years and then just ask if they minded saving your life. 'I don't think so,' she said, her pulse still galloping from the encounter.

'Life's too short,' Blod replied knowingly.

It was all too much. Wanda was glad of the excuse that enabled her to leave. 'I'm off to speak to Spike. Thanks, Blod. I'll leave you to it.'

Before Blod could protest, Wanda went, stopping herself from taking a look at Lew because it would only throw her even further – she could think about this later, and she knew she would. The important thing now was to recruit a helper.

As she approached Fork Handles she saw she'd have to get past the jumble of plastic wares that had belched its way onto the pavement. Luminous pink and green 'pow' shapes of cardboard in the window yelled 'Bargains galore!!!' and 'DIY tips!!!' and inside was heaving. Wanda plotted her way through the mops and spades, chairs and buckets, immediately identifying the proprietor – he had an energy around him, a kind of celestial light, like a beacon for those in need of home-improvement advice. Effortlessly, and in a very different accent to theirs, he dealt with one inquiry after another – 'you need a six-millimetre steel 'ex nut'; 'sandin' sponges go furver than sandpaper'; 'try a USB socket, you won't regret it, mate!' – and all with a smile. Wanda knew she'd found her man, or rather her cockney geezer.

He appeared at her side and held out a hand which was surprisingly smooth to the touch.

'Wotcher! I'm Spike. You're …Wanda, right?'

His blue eyes twinkled and she could have sworn he had a halo above his blond crew cut. Capable, manly and very pleasing to the eye, too. Plus he knew who she was and that told her he wanted to get along here.

'Hi, yes! I used to—'

'Work here? Must be weird seeing it all changed.' He folded his hefty arms across acres of chest and gave her the most understanding look. It was the polar opposite of that cool and muted scene with Lew and she felt liberated by his warmth and, for the first time that day, hopeful.

She thought back to the tick-tock of slow business, Glanmor's lunchtime dozes at his desk – and her own frustration. 'It is odd. But it's brilliant to see it busy in here. It's got a new life.'

'What can I say? People love a bargain!' Spike said. 'So … what can I 'elp you with?'

'Ah, I'm afraid I'm not here to buy anything. I'm on a begging mission.'

'If I can do anyfing, I will.' She couldn't help but notice his teeth were straight out of a Colgate advert, his tan was the healthy outdoors sort and his Fork Handles T-shirt strained over his biceps. How old was he? Late thirties? And no wedding ring. This Spike was going to be inundated with flirty requests for a screw. She filled him in, asking if he'd pop over to the campsite to have a look at what needed doing, see if he could show her what to do …

'I love a bit of *DIY SOS!*' he said. 'I always 'ave a cry at that on the telly.'

Oh, stop! He was bordering on Perfect Male!

44

'I'll bring the van up, some tools, 'ave a butcher's, see what we can do.'

'Amazing! Thank you so much, Spike! I don't know how to repay you!'

'A drink?' he said, instantly.

O-kaaay. That was forward. Was this nice-guy thing an act to cover up his inner sleaze?

Wanda took a step back. His face fell.

'Sorry!' He held up his hands and did a very good job of looking bashful. 'I ain't making myself clear ... Look, I'm new here and I just want to get to know some women. Oh Gawd, that came out wrong too. Let me explain, cards on the table. I want to make friends ... Lucy, my wife, she died two years ago, and Arthur, our eleven-year-old' – he pronounced it *Arfur* – 'he's struggling still, obviously, as you would. Misses her so much. Trouble is, the family is all over the place, there's no close aunties or grannies, one's in Scotland and the other is in Spain. We moved around a lot too, I was in the forces, and 'e was never anywhere long enough. So I saw this opportunity, to make a permanent 'ome for us here, in this beautiful part of the world, to settle, and ... I think he needs some female company in his life ...'

God love him, Wanda thought.

'I see, I'm sorry to hear that. Maybe bring him up with you when you come? Would that work?'

'Yeah! Nice one.' Relief was written all over his face.

He wasn't a sleazebag, far from it. Self-effacing and sweet, he just wanted the best for his boy. Wanda said goodbye, she had so much to do – she needed to ring Carys, get up to the hospital to see Mam and make a start on a plan of attack on the campsite, prioritising what was compulsory and what could wait. She watched as Spike was swallowed by a swarm of customers. *He'll fit in here,* she thought, mounting her bike. *Especially if he's willing to work up a sweat for nothing.* And who was she to argue, if he was going to be doing that for her benefit.

5

L ew's arms around her was the closest thing Annie had to having her brother back.

With the wind whipping around them, she squeezed him hard as tears of joy and sadness blurred the individual stones of The Bunkhouse, turning them into a slab of grey, segueing into the mountain which was yet to burst into spring.

It was the most bittersweet of moments. So harsh a reminder of what she had lost; Lew had been Ryan's best friend, his only friend in fact, and his defender. It made her imagine how Ryan would have looked now. He wouldn't have been as firm as Lew, but would he have filled out from his whippet frame and sunken chest? Would he have been nudging silver, like she was?

The regrets took the opportunity to barge their way in: if only she'd been able to protect him from his upbringing. If only she could have saved him ... Yet being with Lew again was a real thrill. He was a physical connection to Ryan, an anchor when she was adrift, here and now as well as in the past, when she knew he'd pick up if she rang. A good part of her past, and someone with whom she could be herself, free of hesitation and doubt. He was also the one person who had believed that there was a chance Ryan hadn't started the fire. Lew had never found him; he'd gone to the other side of the mountain, to an old haunt of theirs, then as the slopes breathed fire, he'd rushed home to check on his parents. Annie was crushed that he hadn't returned for Ryan's funeral, but then again the course had been a long way away and to miss a week or so would have set him back and she'd wanted nothing further bad to come of the fire.

'Fifteen years!' he laughed as they separated and their clothes rippled in the stiff breeze. 'You haven't changed!'

'I bloody well hope I have!' Annie said, blinking back her conflicting emotions to take him in just as a scud of cloud whooshed away, allowing the sun to light him up.

At thirty-four, he had aged – he'd spent his working life outdoors – but in the way men did, their skin maturing. With a thick head of dark hair and laughing green eyes, he was in his prime, or at least he would be if he didn't look so tired.

'You're not doing too bad yourself!' she said, pulling her Puffa closer and stamping her feet on the muddy gravel. It could be a nice day down in the village but up here where it was exposed and unsheltered, it was unforgiving.

'Only because I'm stood next to this pile of rubble!' he said, thumbing the scaffolded building. 'Makes anyone look half-decent.'

'Oh, *cer i grafu*!' she teased through her dancing hair. This had always been their way and she was chuffed it had come back to them so easily in person.

'Go and scratch? Charming!' He gave a harrumph of fake outrage.

'Fishing for compliments as ever, Lewis Jones!'

But that was unfair to him, really; he'd never been a

48

big-head about his looks, more confused actually about the attention he got from girls, who'd either sigh and part the way at Gobaith Community Hall youth club to allow him through, or else throw themselves in his path. He'd only ever had eyes for Wanda.

'Yeah, and look what good it's done me,' he said, suddenly looking battered and beaten. 'Exiled from Norfolk.'

It was an inkling of why he'd returned. But that'd come, there was no need to press him for details.

'Well, you'll be a wanted man here then, won't you, eh?' she said softly.

'Not getting involved with women, thanks very much.' So heartbreak was responsible for his reappearance. Wasn't it always? 'This is my life now. The Bunkhouse.' He nodded with determination, the cracks plastered over.

With the scrub of the forecourt littered with materials and rubbish, it was clear there was still much to do, but it was a vast improvement already on the decrepit barn that had been a hideaway for generations of kids, including her.

'To think we used to come up here for a sneaky can of cider! How long has this taken to do so far?'

'A month. The builders came in. Then I ran out of this,' he said, rubbing his fingers together. 'I'd used up all the money from my half of the house we owned. So I had to get down here a few days ago to finish it. Inside was pretty much sorted, actually, I was lucky, they did a tidy job. The last few bits are mainly cosmetic, painting and whatnot. Come and see.'

The door, towards the left of the large oblong building, was ajar, so he pushed it open and pulled back a dusty opaque industrial plastic curtain.

'Fantastic!' Annie gawped at the transformation – he

was right about it being a tidy job! Open plan in design, with arched windows, there was a simple kitchen of gleaming steel, a long distressed wooden table with benches and a lounge area with a wood-burning stove. The stairs led up to a bathroom, two double rooms and a dormitory, so the place could sleep up to fourteen.

'At the back, there's another loo, a drying room for boots,' he said, leading her round the corner, 'and this is me ...'

A squat stone extension sat back against the building but afforded him the most amazing bird's-eye view: she'd thought it was good from where they'd been standing before but here, the ground seemed to fall away from their feet. The lake was below, like a teardrop of glass, mirroring the clouds and the undulations of the hills, nestled in the curve of the land as if the earth had been scooped out by a spoon. Beyond Gobaith with its Monopoly-sized houses, the distance went on and on, dotted by sheep, weaving hedgerows and patchwork fields, a picture of isolation and peace. Above, the jagged top of the mountain seemed right there, but that was just an illusion, of course; the ridge ran like a fork of lightning for an hour's walk at least until you could see the trig point and claim it conquered.

'This is incredible. I must have seen this view a thousand times but ...' It still took your breath away. In fact, it was more affecting now because life experience gave you context.

'I know,' Lew said quietly, in awe. 'It's part of us, all of this. Sometimes you forget ... to take it all in.'

Annie understood. 'We're so busy keeping our heads down that we forget to look up.'

He turned to her and nodded slowly, smiling wistfully.

'Come inside,' he said, excusing the drop in standards from The Bunkhouse. 'The priority has been getting the barn ready for rental. I can sleep anywhere.'

Or not, Annie thought, as they stepped out of the light and into the dimness which threw the bags under his eyes into sharp relief. A lump formed in her throat at the bumpy rug spread on the cold concrete floor, the electric heater, stove and camp bed topped with a neatly laid out tapered downy sleeping bag and folded Welsh knitted blanket. Lining the bare brick walls were stuffed holdalls, boxes marked 'books', 'saucepans' and 'paperwork' and bundles of equipment including a red safety helmet, orange padded life jackets, canoe paddles, ropes, waterproof jackets and trousers, walking boots, maps, torches, a drone and harnesses. A couple of open doors led to empty rooms and the space echoed with their footsteps. Was this the sum of Lewis Jones's years? Yet she could hardly judge: if it weren't for Blod, she'd have less than this. And actually, he seemed content, like it was a blank canvas of opportunity. And if he was, then she was, because here she was with her old mate.

'Take a seat,' he said, pointing at a camping chair while he unfolded another and then switched on the gas and boiled a pan of water from the makeshift kitchen area of sink and still-packaged units.

'Isn't this weird, the timing of us both being here.' There was Wanda, too, but she needed to tread carefully with that one.

He gave a non-committal shrug. 'I just needed to get away. Had nowhere else to go. I didn't want to crash at Mam and Dad's, they've retired down west ... my sisters are all busy with work and kids.' He saw her nod and he laughed. 'Which you'd know, obviously.'

'Ha! Blod tells me everything!'

'So I saw this and thought, *why not?* I'm not sure how long I'm going to stay; it's kind of a project to keep me going, an investment too. I'll see how things go.'

When he saw her face drop, he added, 'But I'm around for a bit. We can hang out, smoke fags, chuck stones at hikers, just like the old days.'

'I'm forty now. I'm into gardening and herbal remedies.'

'You? The original wild child?'

She hadn't been that bad. Nicking a sausage roll from Blod's Shop for Ryan's tea and necking Bacardi Breezers – flogged by one of her cousins off the back of a van – was as mad as it got round here. And she could see why the younger kids would think she'd been proper crazy. They'd probably seen her trying to look 'hard' while she tried not to choke on the fizz. That was how it was: with not much to do and siblings to be looked after, kids from seven or eight would hang out with teenagers, maybe not in the same group but in the same street, the same park or on the mountain. They all knew each other through their families anyway; back then, children would run errands or go from house to house, the doors of which were left unlocked. While six years separated Annie from Lew and Wanda, this was how they'd become friends.

'And I go to bed early. Well, as soon as Blod goes up and I can stick my sleeping bag on the sofa.'

'But ... why? What happened with Dean?'

'I left him.' She had only ever told people about the split on a need-to-know basis.

'I'm sorry,' he said, full of sympathy.

'I'm not!'

'I should've asked earlier, there's me banging on and—'

She waved his apology away. 'As they say, he was a charmer to outsiders but a devil in the home. So tight with money he kept a hedgehog in his pocket. I could go on ...'

'But you're okay?'

'Yes. Completely. He doesn't know I'm here. I feel safe.'

'Hey, what's that?' she said, seeing an angry sore on his wrist.

'A burn. I was escorting a climber down yesterday, and on the way there was an abandoned fire smoking – kids, probably – and I put it out but got this in the process. It'll be fine.' He didn't look fine, though. He looked troubled. No wonder; the fire of fifteen years ago had left all of them scarred.

'You need some aloe vera. I can make you a pot to-night. My faithful aloe vera plant, I call him Alan, came with me to Blod's.'

'Cheers, you're a star! Here's to Alan,' he said, raising two mugs of coffee before handing hers over. 'And Ryan.'

'To Ryan,' she whispered. 'He wouldn't believe what you've done here. Probably rob it, though, if he saw it.'

In private, she could say this about him to Lew.

'He wasn't so bad. He'd have changed, you know, I bet you.'

She appreciated this so much but didn't believe it. 'I doubt it.' Annie blinked the pain away. 'God, what a pair we are, ending back here.' She paused, knowing she had to address the elephant in the room. 'And what about Wanda still being in the village? I never thought she'd stick around long-term.'

Lew's jaw clenched. 'Bit of a shock to see her yesterday, to be honest.'

'Same for me. Although I did ask for it, cutting back the campsite hedges uninvited. I was only trying to help out. The place is a wreck.' Lew shrugged with indifference. 'It must be a difficult time for her. About to finally leave and then she can't.'

'Yeah, I s'pose. But you know, she can't ask people she turned her back on, can she? She never contacted me after the fire. I tried to get through to her but she wouldn't talk to me.'

'She was grieving.'

'I know. But then why didn't she get in touch later?'

'I don't know, Lew, only she knows. But it felt good to help her. I'd like to do more.'

'Why, though?' he pressed her.

It was a good question: Wanda hated Annie's guts. 'Because I'm in the same position as she is. I'm here, back to square one, same as her.'

'She welcomed you back with open arms then?' he said, cynically.

'No. Obviously not. But that's not the point. I just want to stop all this nonsense about the past, heal the rift, because so much time has passed and if we're going to be neighbours then we should try to get on.'

'It's a nice idea, but ... too much has happened. Building bridges is all very well—'

'Actually, it's more about mending fences, clearing the rubbish and bringing back some joy to that bedraggled old site.'

'How are you okay with all of this?' he said, looking into his coffee.

'Because Blod let me back in, that's why. She could've turned her back on me like everyone else. I want to pass that forward. I'm not after forgiveness or anything, I just want acceptance. Plus, like Blod says, life's too short.'

'Sometimes it feels very long.'

'What's happened?'

'Breaking up isn't just the actual break-up, is it? It's the months leading up to it, when you know it's wrong but you stay because you don't want to hurt them and you try to convince yourself this is just a blip. It drags along and it's so painful and then, *boom*, it all explodes and you think you were hurting before ... It all boiled down to the question of kids. I didn't want them. I couldn't imagine them, not with her. And that's such a horrible thing to admit to.'

'I know that feeling,' Annie said, not to punish him but to give him an insight into her situation. 'Dean already had two girls, he was ten years older than me, remember? Already had a family. He didn't want to do it again. Maybe if he'd let me be their second mam then I'd have been okay. But I was never allowed to get close to them. He made it impossible, he was so horrible to his ex that she saw me as the wicked stepmother, the girls were always going to take her side. I don't blame them. I should've stayed well clear – he claimed he'd left her before I realised ... But then I was broken, coming from the Hugheses, I thought no one else would have me.'

Lew lifted his face and listened with his ears and eyes, his mask slipping as she spoke.

'I was okay for years, I just got on with it, bottled it up. The trouble came when I realised I needed an outlet. If I couldn't have babies, I'd have to make myself useful, give myself a purpose. Dean didn't like it, he saw my "gardening thing" as a way to meet new men. I wanted to do up the patch of garden too but he decked it, which was like a coffin lid slamming shut. Then along came Teg. My rescue dog, my "baby". But Dean was jealous. And when he lost his job, he exploded ...' She wasn't going to revisit that scene. '... And that was that. Now I'm happier than I've ever been.'

'In a funny way, I am too. Kirstine, my fiancée, she just wasn't the right one. I tried to feel it ...'

'That's brave that you tried, but it's braver to admit it.'

'Yeah. I started to feel physically sick whenever she brought up the wedding; it would've been next spring. I was in the wrong place. The kids thing on top, it was too much, she wanted a honeymoon baby. I wasn't sure if I wanted one at all. Kirstine was, is, lovely. Mad angry at me when I told her I couldn't go through with it, rightly so; we had a house, worked at the same outdoor pursuits centre, both of us instructors. It blew up her entire life. It was kinder to leave, make it clear there was no going back. I should've manned up sooner; we had five years together. Luckily she's just thirty, she's got bags of time. And,' he said, raising his eyebrows, 'so have I. Hours of it, every bloody day. I work my arse off with the building, I'm volunteering, I'm setting up a few courses here for hikers, I'm ordering bunk beds, sofas, all the bits and pieces to get it ready, and still I'm twiddling my thumbs, unable to sleep, up with the lark.'

'Well ... and don't give me a row about it,' Annie said, carefully. This was as close to the right moment as she'd get. 'Maybe you need to use that time to help Wanda.'

They stared at each other: Annie challenging him, Lew with disbelief.

'Are you off your rocker?'

'Have you listened to anything I've just said?' Annie asked him.

'I've got too much on.'

'Just an hour or two?'

'What's the point? It's not going to make us all best buddies again, is it?'

'We won't know unless we try. And it'd help Lyn, it'd be nice to do it in Wanda's father's memory too.' He had been such a can-do man, one of those people who'd dig cars out of the snow or help bring the sheep in from the mountain. 'Good for Gobaith too.'

'I just can't. You know what she's like, we'd do the work then she'd ditch us again. Then she'd bugger off round the world and forget us.'

'Well, that'd be a result then, wouldn't it? The sooner we help, the sooner she'll be gone,' Annie said, trying to call his bluff on how he really felt about making up with her. Because while he'd been dismissive about Wanda, the fact was he'd come back here. It was irrelevant that Wanda may or may not be around – there was clearly the same need in him to reconcile himself with the past.

'I'm sorry, Annie. But it's a no,' he said, taking her mug and getting to his feet. 'And you should think twice about getting back involved with her. Nothing good will come of it.'

The conversation was clearly over.

6

A lovely spot although the satnav had no idea where you were! Perhaps register it on GPS as a POI? Or give it a name that's identifiable rather than The Campsite?

Derek and Barbara McDonald, Bristol

Campsite Visitors' Book

'What the surgeons did, with all those screws, it's remarkable,' Mam said, trying to cover up a wince of pain as she reached across her hospital bed to the table to pour a beaker of water.

'Mam! I'll do it!' Wanda said, leaping up to take over.

'I'm not an invalid, you know.' She flapped the neck of her favourite Marksies floral nightie with indignation. 'I'm iron woman! More metal in me than AC/DC. I'm scared I'll set off the shoplifter alarm at the big supermarket, mind.'

Two days after her hip fracture operation and she was clearly back to her usual self. Or at least she was attempting to be. That was a relief, because since coming round from surgery on Tuesday night she had been flat on her back, wan and groggy. Today, her brown eyes were less frightened; she had managed to put some make-up on and style her short grey hair as if she was off to Blod's for supplies. But it was still a shock to see her with an oxygen nose pipe and a morphine pump.

'Stop fussing!' she said as Wanda plumped her pillows. 'Go and make yourself useful and get me a paper, will you?'

'But the physio is due any minute.'

'I'm the patient, not you!' she tutted, through a quick spray of perfume, ready for battle.

Wanda suspected Mam wanted to hear the extent of her rehab programme alone so as not to worry anyone. It was going to be a gruelling return to health. That's if she didn't have any complications in the hospital such as bed sores or blood clots or ...

'I've got my notebook, somewhere,' Mam said, patting the sheet around her to locate it. 'I'll write it all down so you two can supervise me, as you like to do.'

'I've googled it already,' Wanda said. 'You'll be home within a week or so, mobility needs assessed, we'll get you walking and swimming. You can get hip protectors, they're much better than they used to be, less bulky, apparently. I'll ring Age UK—'

'You won't, young lady! Age UK! I ask you!'

'Mam, you haven't just had a cold,' Wanda implored. 'You'll need looking after.'

'I don't think she wants to hear that,' Carys mumbled to Wanda. 'Mam, I'll go to the shop and see Wanda off.'

Then, with a 'Give Mam a peck on the cheek' to Wanda, she frogmarched her out of the ward.

'You're not about to accuse me of overdramatising, surely? I was just saying the facts, Caz!' Wanda said, pink with exasperation.

'I know, but just go at her pace, yeah? She knows she's had it bad. She doesn't need reminding.'

Wanda took it on the chin. Carys did know better in this instance: she was the one sitting with her all hours. And actually it was the best scenario, because Wanda didn't want Carys anywhere near the temptation of physical graft back at the campsite.

'How's it been going at home?' Carys asked as they walked down the corridor.

Wanda's sister only came back to the farmhouse to sleep – when she wasn't with Mam, her mind was elsewhere; her hands on her thickening waist indicated that. Wanda really didn't want to add the woes of having just four days left until opening day. Carys had enough going on. Wanda felt bad, too, that she'd been oblivious to the campsite's decline in the off-season.

'I mean, I know it's a bit of a mess,' Carys said. *Understatement of the year*, Wanda thought. But there she went again, molehills and mountains and all that. 'I feel terrible it's all down to you. You having to clear up after us. I kind of got distracted … I should've done something. I should've been watching Mam more closely. I thought I'd have time to get it ready. But then everything happened, didn't it?'

There was a tremor in Carys's voice – it was most unlike her, she was always one to keep her cool and trust in the universe.

'Are you all right?' Wanda slid her arm through Carys's, in solidarity.

'Hormones, I think,' said Carys, sounding ever so small, her heart-shaped face so childlike. 'I always heard pregnant women talking about them but I never thought I'd feel so … weepy.'

Wanda pulled her closer. 'Really, don't worry.'

'But we've got a group booked in for Monday.'

A roar of bikers had been promised twelve ready-erected tents. Twelve tents they didn't have.

'It's fine!' Wanda cried. 'It's under control. I'm dealing with it. I've got loads of people helping out.'

The lie sat like indigestion in her chest.

The reality was that nobody had come to her aid. Spike had seemed so willing, but maybe she hadn't made it clear that it was urgent. And of course she couldn't expect him to down his own tools when he had a new business to run. Annie had obviously had second thoughts, which Wanda couldn't blame her for: she hadn't mentioned her appearance to Mam or Carys either, for fear of adding more stress to the already difficult situation. Local farmers who might have had a spare hand had given her their apologies – they were already round-the-clock busy preparing for lambing. Electricians, plumbers, painters and handymen and women were all booked up too, although, bless them, a few had offered to come along for an hour or so at the weekend. But it'd be too late.

She'd never accuse the community of not caring. Wanda completely understood – people had busy lives and now was the time of year when they came out of their winter slumber to fix their own backyards. So Wanda had cracked on with it by herself, using every spare minute doing what she could. But everything was a battle. Mowing the grass with Mam's temperamental machine took forever just to cover a small area; clearing drains blocked with leaves revealed broken pipes, and bleaching toilets and grey-water points was all well and good, but she couldn't tackle the jobs of dodgy lights in the loos and flooding showers, of turning bogs back into pathways and testing electrical hook-ups. Today's delights included emptying the chemical loo disposal point and bagging up the rubbish and recycling in the bin area to take to the tip tomorrow. The reception kiosk needed a good clean and airing. If it was just that, though, maybe she could get through it. But the paperwork was heavy going, too. While she'd dealt with the water, gas and electric, there was still the insurance to renew and health and safety issues to appraise. Plus she had to make sure the guests had an up-to-date welcome pack of doctors' numbers, campsite rules, nearest petrol station; the list went on. And it panicked her. The more she achieved, the more she realised she had to do.

'I'd better go,' Wanda said, fighting the fluster.

'Take the Land Rover,' Carys said at the exit, 'I can get the bus.'

'No, honestly, can't have you doing that in the dark. The bus is due in five. It only takes half an hour.' *And the rest*, while the passengers took an age to get off because they were too busy chatting to the driver. Why didn't they just do the expected 'cheers, drive!' and bugger off? 'It'll give me time to make a few calls.'

On the journey home, though, Wanda dropped the positivity act and went full hippo, sinking down into a mudbath of misery, helped by the dirty windows. It felt as if time hadn't stopped so much as reversed – this was the same route she'd taken back from high school. The narrow country lanes felt claustrophobic. Living at the farmhouse, she was haunted by the world map on her bedroom wall, dotted with drawing pins marking where she'd been going to, which now were punctured dreams of places she'd never been. If only she could have gone back to her flat. She hadn't dared go near it since – a 'nice young man' had rented it out but she didn't want to see the actual person, to imagine him on her toilet seat or weeing in her shower. Sara had promised she'd keep an ear out for any problems. Her head was full of Annie and Lew, too; their reappearance had floored her and she was going to have to work out a way of coping, because avoiding them would be impossible. Trapped and drowning, she found herself empathising with pickled onions.

I shouldn't be here in this dank and dismal place, she thought. *I should be waking up in that Colombian B&B, my eyes adjusting to glorious sunlight, preparing to start my Spanish course. Walking the cobblestone streets of crumbling, baking Cartagena, breathing in the rich dark coffee from elegant cafés, drinking in the bright colonial buildings before arriving at the classroom, rolling my tongue around the language; making friends, who knows, even going to the beach in the afternoon before an al fresco dinner and dancing the night away in a sexy salsa bar.*

The itch became a scratching frenzy, consuming her entirely. She pressed her lips together hard to counter the creeping sensation and dug her nails into her palms, looking for cars to count to distract herself. Bare branches scrammed the windows of the bus, setting her teeth on edge.

She took out her phone, tapped the Instagram icon and there, immediately the aggravation subsided as she scrolled through her feed of travel influencers and tourist boards. A search of Cartagena took her to the powdery sand of Playa Blanca, the mangroves of Barú and the turquoise water of the Rosario Islands. By the time the bus pulled up in Gobaith, she was face down in sun-lounging hot-dog legs and pert bottoms in string bikinis. If only she could jack in all of this bother. A few emails and she could be away first thing ... Damn this travel envy. Her barren @WandaLust account should have been stuffed with photos by now. It was embarrassing and so disappointing. How was she going to get over this? When would she be able to pick up her rucksack and get out of this dead end? In a month, two? Hardly. It didn't look like she'd even get a week away in the summer, the way things were.

She kept her head down as she disembarked, praying not to see anyone she knew. The nosy parkers would badger her about Mam, or about how she was dealing with the biggest let-down of her life. And inevitably someone would have received a postcard from Glanmor and say, 'He's gone naked paragliding in the Pyrenees!' Shown up by a man twice her age. That scratch had left her with a bloody wound ... and *that* reminded her she had to write a list of things to get for the first aid kit and stock up on camping essentials for reception.

Back at the farmhouse, she threw herself into it, and by the time it was dark, she called it a day. Carys would be home any minute, so Wanda got going on a veggie curry, losing herself as she chopped away, savouring the gorgeous scent of spices mixed in with silky soft frying onion. Once the lentils, tomatoes and cauliflower were added, she let the pan bubble away and decided to open a bottle of wine at the kitchen table. As she sat down and let the chair take the strain off her aching legs, slowly the stress slipped away as she allowed herself to think she might actually make this all work. She'd got through the last few days and the site was looking less grim. Someone would come good, she'd just have to renew her begging mission tomorrow.

Her eyes glazed over and she played with the stem of her glass, trying to be mindful of the moment. A burning smell wafted her way and she got up, tutting at herself for forgetting to stir the pot. But on inspection, nothing was stuck to the bottom. She turned the gas off just in case. Had she put some toast on absent-mindedly? Or was there a hob ring alight under an empty saucepan? No and no. Her spine began to creep and her nostrils tingled. It could just be a trick of the nose; she had a peculiar thing sometimes when she could've sworn blind something was on fire. But that was just from the trauma of the fire, she knew that. But she'd always check.

Sniffing the air, she went to the back door, opened up and went into the cold dry night – and her stomach toppled over itself when she saw a cloud of smoke funnelling from a field across the way. Automatically, she held her hands over her nose and mouth to stop the taste of the acrid memory of the mountain breathing fire like a dragon. Her legs began to tremble and her heart was pounding. *Come on, come on, pull yourself together*, she thought, but her legs were stuck still. She patted her pockets for her phone, jabbing 999 to report the fire, stuttering as she explained where she was. With the fire engine on its way, she began to pace, wondering what the hell to do. *Where were the campsite extinguishers? Think, Wanda, think.* But she couldn't and all she wanted to do was get away: if she saw the flames she'd be frozen with fear and flashbacks. So she ran, heaving gulps of the black air, not knowing where she was going exactly, just trying to outrun the thudding in her chest. Who should she go to? It had to be Blod's, she'd know what to do, so she got to the shop and went down the alley and bashed at the door at the back, shouting her name over and over.

'What is it?' Blod said, reaching out to her, as Annie and then Lew appeared by her side, their faces etched with worry.

'Fire! It's fire. In the field. I …' Her mouth dried up and the three of them shot her yes/no questions.

'Have you called the fire brigade?' She nodded to Annie, struggling for breath. Her mind threw up an image of the charred, still-smoking black mountain the day after the fire.

'Is it up by you?' She nodded at Blod, still panting. Every day being reminded of losing Dad – their home while the farmhouse was rebuilt had been a damp static caravan on the site because Mam couldn't bear leaving the land where her beloved had died.

'Have you seen any kids?' She shook her head at Lew, her eyes wet with tears. Carys's education had gone to pot after the fire, she'd never fulfilled her potential.

Blod pulled her inside as Lew grabbed his jacket. She heard him murmur something to Annie about a grass fire in the village last night.

'Looks like the season's started,' he said with anger. 'And they call it fun.'

'Bloody kids,' Annie said. 'Has no one told them what happened last time? I'll come with you.'

'Keep her here, Blod,' Lew said, his eyes boring into Wanda's, full of concern.

'Will do. Take care, the pair of you.'

Then they were gone and Wanda was collapsing into Blod's arms. A siren was wailing in the distance and she was bracing herself, burrowing into Blod, and as it approached and got louder and louder, she clamped her hands over her ears and drowned it out with her own howl.

7

Annie sank back into the warm bubbles of Blod's avocado bath and groaned.

She was completely spent from a rollercoaster of a day.

From sunrise to sunset, she'd been on what she called her 'social services' rounds: the bread and butter of lonely old ladies and gents who lived for her visits. Her role was as much to brighten their day as it was weeding borders and forking compost over their vegetable patches. The kindest of souls they were, offering tea until her bladder threatened to burst, in return for a pair of listening ears and, more often than not, hands to help with add-on apologetic requests to lift a piece of furniture or take a bag to the charity shop. Their struggles were many and could be pitifully small, things which others didn't even think about: Enid Stokes depended on Annie to open a too-tight jar and Cyril Woods needed her eyes to read the small print on a bill. Stoic in spite of feeling bewildered, invisible or a burden on their families, they saw her as a connection to the outside world.

She'd been revived by a visit to see Teg, who gave her the full bum wiggle of excitement when she arrived. But Bonnie at The Hound Hotel had had some news. Annie's stomach pitched, thinking about it again. Teg had refused to go with a new dog walker, a man, which was no surprise – it was a learned response and had taken Annie back to the scene which had been the last straw with Dean. She'd never forget it, how he'd taken his anger out on her poor dog. The pressure she felt about failing Teg, by not providing her with a safe home, squeezed her temples.

Annie exhaled long and slowly, trying to let it all go. She shut her eyes, only to see Wanda's panic-stricken white face from last night. It had turned out to be a small grass fire, apparently started by kids, and had been out before Annie and Lew had got there. If Annie thought she carried the torment of the campsite blaze from fifteen years ago, Wanda was clearly buckling under it.

'That girl needs help,' Blod had said to Annie and Lew over brandy after Wanda had been picked up by Carys.

'I wish she'd let us,' Annie said as Lew quickly drained his glass and left. He'd been quiet; they'd all been hit by Wanda's reaction and Annie felt powerless. Warned off by Lew after Wanda's cold reception, Annie hadn't gone back to the campsite to continue the tidy-up because she didn't want to upset her.

Even though she'd soaked herself wrinkly, there was still a thorn stuck in her finger and she applied a few drops of her own homemade lavender oil onto a plaster to draw it out overnight. Then she got dressed and found the envelope she'd picked up from the doormat at her last job. The £7.50 inside would get fish and chips for her and Blod. It was a bittersweet thing, doing Mrs Jenkins's garden. Annie had turned her square of nettles on a down-at-heel estate, far away from the chocolate-box cottages photographed by tourists, into a beautiful patch of lavender, agapanthus, yellow daisy-like rudbeckia, leafy sedums and aquilegia which attracted bees and butterflies in the summer. Yet she never knew if Mrs Jenkins took any pleasure in it: she never saw her to speak to. It was said she suffered from nerves, but Annie understood how life was here and always left Mrs Jenkins's carrying her bags full of clinking bottles to recycle. Still, at least there was Pastor Pete to keep an eye on her and he understood too. A former drug addict with a couple of stretches inside, he'd been pals with Ryan, but after nearly overdosing, he'd got clean and done a theology degree before becoming their minister. The old scars were there: his skull and crossbones tattoo peered over his dog collar, but he said, for him, it was a reminder of how far he'd come and it gave him insight and empathy.

All in all, it had been a difficult day. And it was still all over Annie's face when she came downstairs.

'You look like you've swallowed a mule!' Blod said at the cleared table in the corner of her cosy lamp-lit lounge.

'I could eat a horse too, I'm starving!' Annie said, seeing a letter propped up against the carriage clock on the fireplace. 'Is that for me?'

'I'm afraid so.'

The thick envelope was official and she knew straight away it was from Dean's solicitor. With trembling fingers, she slit the envelope open and read then re-read its contents, in shock.

'He's accusing me of unreasonable behaviour!' she spat, handing it over to Blod. 'The gall of him! Look, it says "lack of intimacy", when I was ever the dutiful wife, "spending too much time out of the house" when I was working, and "verbal abuse", but that happened once. *Once!* And he deserved it.'

'It's just a process, Annie, that's all,' Blod soothed, over the click of her knitting needles.

'It's a stain on me! Why he has to do this, why we can't just sell the house and then divorce later, I don't know.'

'Because he wants to punish you. For leaving him.'

'And I'm supposed to sign up to these lies?' She slammed her palm down on the table.

'It'll be done then, at least. You'll be a free woman.'

Blod was right. But it hurt like hell. There was a dull thud of paws landing and tabby cat Shirley sat quite still, watching, as if she was on the jury. Her tortoiseshell brother Bassey joined her, jumping up on the table, but he stalked towards Blod for a stroke. 'You cheeky things,' Blod whispered at her pets.

Annie felt a wave of surrender crashing over her. This was Blod's home; she shouldn't be here in her space, filling up Blod's narrow terrace with tools and boots. She needed to agree to Dean's demands to get this over and done with. But on one condition – that the house went on the market straight away so she could get herself and Teg a roof of their own. She was so very tired, but she had to find the strength of character to change her way of thinking that she was giving in to him when really he was speeding up her liberty.

'All right,' she said, twisting her hands, 'I'll sign it.'

'I know you're hurting, but remember there's always someone worse off than you.'

She smiled at Blod, so grateful for her insight. Yes, in spite of everything, she did feel blessed to have her in her life.

'Thanks, Blod. You've no idea what you've done for me.'

'Get away with you!' Blod said, heading to the drawer for cutlery.

Annie was just on her way to the door when there was a knock. She opened up to find Lew stood on the step with a steaming parcel smelling of salt and vinegar in his arms.

'Hungry?' he asked with a grin.

'Lew! You angel!' Blod said, bustling round him, taking his coat and the food and gathering plates and ketchup.

'Well, we've hardly had a chance to catch up, have we?' Lew said. 'Our cuppa was interrupted last night, so I thought I'd try again.'

'There's lovely!' Blod said, beaming at the surprise, shooing the cats and getting everyone up to the table.

'And ... well, I've been thinking,' Lew said, heavily, playing with his fork. 'I think you were right, Annie. Wanda needs our help. How she was last night – I mean, I know she can be dramatic, but that was something else. Like, she looked haunted. She can't get that campsite ready by herself. We've got two days and I reckon we could do it. It's the right thing to do.'

A weight lifted off Annie's shoulders. There was so much crap around, it was a tonic to be able to come together and do some good. It might pave the way for reconciliation and rehabilitation too – she'd seen the way Lew had looked at Wanda when she'd turned up terrified yesterday. If you cared about someone then you could reverse the estrangement.

'I'm so happy you're up for it,' she said. 'And I don't think she'll push us away this time. I don't suppose she has the strength.'

'I checked on her this morning,' Blod said, giving a little shake of her head. 'Not good. Wan-looking.'

'So how shall we play it then?' Annie asked as she dished out the delicious fortifying spoils.

Blod speared a chip and winked. 'I'll spread the word after we've had this.'

Within the hour, Annie knew, Gobaith would be answering the call to arms.

8

The delicious aroma of baking greeted Wanda when she got up on the first official day of the season.

The sweet smell took her back to her childhood when Mam would welcome them home from school with a still-warm slab of *bara brith*, made from her own granny's recipe. Thanks to an overnight soaking of raisins in Welsh brew, the tea bread was so much moister than fruit cake. A stab of sadness came to her as she trod the stairs and found not her mother but Carys in a pinny.

'Morning! How are you?' her sister said brightly, her eyes searching Wanda for signs of a repeat of last week's breakdown over the world's smallest grass fire.

Carys had been an absolute gem in the days since, taking care of the cooking in between visiting Mam as well as her. Wanda had been surprised that a sniff of smoke had hurled her backwards to the fire which claimed her father, and embarrassed that she had been

74

so exposed, not just to her sister and Blod but to Annie and Lew. Carys had stroked her hair late into the night, listening to Wanda's tearful admission that she still felt responsible for Dad's death and repeating to her over and over that she wasn't to blame. Did Wanda believe it? Not completely, not yet, but Carys had taken her to a better place – to hear that she it wasn't Wanda's fault, that no one thought so, that things happened, and that while you couldn't change the past you could accept it, had been a revelation.

'I'm good,' Wanda said, truthfully. Being treated with kid gloves had been what she'd needed and because Carys had done that, she felt recharged.

The community had played a massive part in that, too. They'd sworn not to breathe a syllable of Wanda's upset to her mother, as she had developed an infection and was feeling very homesick.

They'd come in droves over the weekend to get the campsite ready for today. The hard work and determination of the volunteers to fix the electrics, the plumbing and the general bombsite appearance of the place had been humbling. Wanda was incredibly grateful, even to Annie and Lew; in fact, especially to Annie and Lew. They owed her nothing, but still they'd shown up. They hadn't exchanged words with her, partly because they were so busy but also because their actions were speaking much louder. And Carys took the chance to tell Wanda that her grudge against her two old friends was a self-defeating waste of energy.

'How have you got so wise?' Wanda had asked her sister last night.

'Don't take this the wrong way,' Carys had said, 'but

I don't think you ever really processed what happened to Dad. I was allowed to grieve, I was just a kid. I remember you being a mother to me and Mam afterwards. Perhaps you're a little bit stuck there still?'

Was that why she'd freaked out over the grass fire? And maybe it was time to let bygones be bygones. Annie and Lew had laid the foundations for reconciliation and now it was up to Wanda to build on them.

Carys proceeded to take a batch of bara brith out of the oven and Wanda's stomach grumbled.

'Five loaves? Are you baking for the whole ward?' Wanda said, eyeing up the perfect colour and rise in Mam's old tins.

'I'm doing another five too before I go up the hospital. They're not for Mam or the nurses, although that is a good idea,' Carys said. 'They're to welcome the guests. I can't do much to help you with the campsite, but I can do this.'

'That's lovely!'

'Go on, have a taste!' Carys said, slicing off the crust and slathering it with butter.

Wanda took a mouthful and her eyes widened. 'This is lush! There's something different in it, though ...'

'Yep!' Carys said. 'I've gone posh – it's Earl Grey flavour! There's also one with Welsh whisky, one with ale and one of the next lot is Cointreau.'

'Ha! Been raiding Mam's booze cabinet?'

'Closest I'll get to alcohol for a while,' Carys said mournfully. Last night she'd confessed that if she hadn't been pregnant, she'd have had a skinful after her latest fruitless Facebook search under the names of Daniel, Danny, Neil and Platt. Wanda had suggested a

'Where's Danny?' campaign, using social media and the *Manchester Evening News*, but Carys was afraid of what she'd discover, and perhaps it was better not to find him. What if he was married? Being a single mother was hard; being a rejected one was worse.

'Oh, come here,' Wanda said, giving her a *cwtch*. 'You've got me and Mam, you don't need anything else.'

Carys squeezed her back. 'Don't get me started,' she said. 'I'll ruin the bake if I cry into it!'

'Stand by for some tears from me too! I've got to go out and put twelve tents up!'

Wanda spent the next two hours bashing hundreds of pegs, and lots of her own fingers, into the ground. Her vision of a dozen identical low-impact, sink-into-nature two-berth tents was not to be, however. The nearest camping shop, an hour away, hadn't had enough in stock when she'd gone on Saturday morning. Ringing round, everywhere else was found wanting too: either they only had massively expensive geodesic ones or they'd just sold out of what she was looking for. She'd had to search online and by that point it was too late for a Sunday delivery, apart from one single website called InTents, which ominously boasted, 'we put the FUN in camping!' Near-delirious at this point, she'd clicked 'confirm order' – she had no other option – and so now what lay before her was a kaleidoscope of frankly ridiculous canvas.

She stood up, her knees creaking, walked to the edge of the field and then turned around to see them at full dazzle in the glorious and blinding beam of sunshine after a weekend of drizzle.

Oh God, it was like a psychedelic refugee camp crossed with a bonkers festival, resembling some kind of drug-induced hallucination so out of keeping with the backdrop that she wouldn't be surprised if a strongman in a leotard trotted in bareback on a unicorn.

She hoped these macho bikers had a sense of humour. Because she could see how it could come across as a 'camp' piss-take. A costly one, with a price tag taking another chunk from her savings. Twelve designs in two rows facing one another, shaped like a giant slice of red pipped watermelon, a line-up of white-sliced sandwich triangles and a wedge of yellow holey cheese. The rest featured varying designs of leopardskin, bricks and mortar, stripey circus tent, strawberries, rainbows, a Welsh dragon, flamingoes, cacti and lastly a silhouette of a couple snogging.

At least the site looked spotless. Spike had ripped out the rusty playground, recruited a scrappy to take it away and rebuilt a wooden area containing a balancing trail, a see-saw and a fort. Lew had made pathways out of chippings which hid the mud and created neat boundaries and Annie had trimmed back every branch and bush. And it was all done in time ... in the nick of time, as she heard a low rumble in the distance becoming a thunder of throttle which filled the basin of hills and lake, as if an earthquake was coming. That would be just her luck when she'd busted her all to get the tents up.

The first guests of the season were coming! In a cloud of mushrooming dust, twenty-four riders came up the driveway and ground to a halt, their polished silver handlebars and black helmets shining. Had they been cyclists, she'd have felt nothing but pity for their sore backsides. But the size of them in their bulky jackets and trousers, plus their manly chariots, some with 'Blood' stickers, made her feel suddenly vulnerable. What if they were Hells Angels? What if they were going to ransack the campsite?

The leader kicked back his side stand, dismounted and stomped towards her and she tried to swallow her fear, feeling her legs prime themselves in case she had to run.

He pulled off his helmet to reveal ... he was in fact a woman with long blonde hair and a lovely warm smile.

Of course they weren't Hells Angels. Outlaws wouldn't have paid a deposit, would they?

'All roight!' the lady said in a broad Brummie accent. 'I'm Babs, I did the booking so I've got our details. Oh, look at those tents! Aren't they jolly.'

Wanda gave an inner *phew*. 'So what brings you here?'

'We're doing a sponsored ride. We're all blood bikers from the Midlands, we bike blood and surgical equipment and so forth to hospitals on behalf of the NHS.'

Ha! Blood bikers! Wanda's having feared the worst was so preposterous. When would she learn?

'It's a volunteer thing, we don't get paid, but the fuel and upkeep of the bikes has to be paid for somehow. So we're raising money with this, the Wales Wide Ride. Some of the best motorcycle roads in the world around here.'

'Well, that's amazing!' Wanda cried, as positivity took her over. The group clearly weren't glampers expecting luxury. This place was just a stop-off for them – a hot shower would be all they needed. What was there to worry about? She felt herself relax and began to hum as she took payment. *Here we go*, the first step of the climb to scale the mountain of woes. *And, look!* she noticed some shoots and buds on the hedgerows, signalling spring had bloomed overnight.

'The sleeping bags, they're in the tents then, are they?' Babs said, expectantly.

'Sorry?' Wanda was just sorting out the receipt in the reception kiosk. She could've sworn Babs was asking if there were sleeping bags inside the tents.

'Er ... no.' She looked up, confused.

'Oh. The thing is, when we booked, the lady said it'd be no problem. We could hire them. It wasn't the norm, but when I told her about us, how we need to keep the load down on the bikes, she said she'd help, because it's for charity.'

No! Mam! She had forgotten to put this bit of vital information down on the booking. Bless her for being kind and all that, but details were kind of essential. *See?* Wanda thought, she had been right to fear the worst.

She couldn't mess this up, though. Not least because she had no idea how to perform a refund on the machine. Where else would these people go at such short notice? But where the flaming heck was she going to get twenty-four sleeping bags? Her mind raced ... her mouth opened ...

'... So, silly me, when I said no, the sleeping bags weren't in the tents, I meant I've got them, obviously, well, they're waiting to be picked up from the dry-cleaners.'

Babs was overjoyed. She backed out of the cubicle and Wanda quickstepped it in pursuit.

'I wanted to make sure they were spotless for you,' she added, trying to work out her plan of attack. 'In the meantime ...'

'Ooh! Cake!' Babs clapped her hands with delight. 'That's what I call a consolation!'

Cake? What?

Carys was stood at the rear of the Land Rover's car boot, handing out vintage saucers of bara brith and milking tea from a catering urn in dainty chintz cups. It was like a scene from the Ritz as bikers drank with cocked little fingers and pulled '*Mmm, delicious*' faces.

'You star!' Wanda said into Carys's ear, before she cleared her throat to point out where the bikers would find the bathroom block, the kitchen area and the bins. Then it was time to locate twenty-four sleeping bags, so off she dashed into Gobaith. She could ask the local scout group or Pastor Pete, as she remembered he did an annual sleep-out for the homeless. But there'd be no time to wash and dry them. What was she going to do? Then miracle upon miracles, she saw Spike setting up a display of camping chairs and billy cans outside Fork Handles.

'Spike!' she called. 'This is a long shot but ...'

Fifteen minutes later, she was heading back with the goodies. And a date, well a sort-of one. Overwhelmed with thanks, she'd asked him if he fancied that drink.

'It'll 'ave to be at mine,' he'd said, 'Arthur's grounded and I need to make sure he doesn't go AWOL.'

And so, after delivering on Mam's promise, helping wash down dirty boots from the bikers' mountain climb and giving instructions on how to find the Travellers' Rest, she had a quick shower, put on some make-up for the first time in days, threw some casserole down her neck which Carys had left for her and, with a bottle of white wine, made her way to Spike's place.

The five-minute meander along a narrow lane gave her a chance to recap. She'd survived the day and Mam was stable. But she couldn't help thinking her adventure would have been one week old today. She imagined how it would feel for her skin to be tingling from the sun and her tongue rolling with Latino *rrr*'s. But what was the point in torturing herself? She tried to soak up the sound of the evening chorus and admire the pink blancmange sunset, but wasn't really feeling it.

Spike's handsome smile and his contagious enthusiasm for his eighteenth-century semi-detached cottage made all the difference.

'We've got original beams and our own bit of river at the back. It's 'eaven!' he said, welcoming her in. 'Can you believe we swapped a tiny two-bed terrace on an A-road for this and the shop! You get a lot for your money round 'ere. Arthur's got a goal in the garden and I'm going to teach him to fish. Best of all, no one's next door, it's empty. It's like our own kingdom. We're frilled to bits!'

He showed her in to the cluttered hallway stuffed with boxes and boys' stuff, only to knock his head on the low ceiling. 'Still getting used to it,' he grinned, rubbing his scalp.

Wanda presented her bottle with a heartfelt thanks. 'You did a brilliant job on the playground. And those picnic tables were a stroke of genius.'

'My pleasure. I got to meet the gang, lovely bunch, especially Annie and Lew. You've got some proper friends 'ere, haven't you?'

She nodded, and then again with more feeling because perhaps she could get over her demons and see them once more as mates.

'Right, let's crack this open! You go in the sitting room – I have an actual sitting room! – and I'll get some glasses.'

Wanda prepared herself for a classic country snug with *cwtchy* chairs and throws and brass and bellows by the fireside.

Instead, she was overwhelmed by a huge telly showing a very fighty computer game. Sat in one of two enormous lazy-boy chairs was who had to be Arthur in headphones, his fingers in a frenzy on his console. Dusk had fallen but no lights were on, leaving the flickering explosion of colour from the screen to lash out at the room. Plates of TV dinners, one with untouched peas, broccoli and carrots, plus cups and crisp packets lay on the threadbare carpet, but everything else was empty – the walls, the shelves, the corners, the windowsills. And there was a smell of feet and farts.

This wasn't a home for an eleven-year-old boy who needed a mother. This was a bachelor pad of extreme angular male proportions devoid of any femininity. Not even a photo of his mam was anywhere to be seen.

'Turn that off, Arthur!' Spike said, entering the room with a bowl of nibbles and two tumblers. Then he confessed, 'Haven't quite unpacked yet. It's not easy running your own business and raising a kid on your own. Arthur! Wanda's here!'

The boy turned round and pity rose in her chest when she saw ketchup on his school shirt.

'Hi, Arthur!' She was such an idiot for not bringing him anything. Even if it had been a bar of chocolate, it would've felt like she was including him. This child urgently needed a female influence. But she had no idea where to start. How did you cross into a confused and grieving and defensive boy's life when you were a stranger?

'Stay for a chat, yeah?' Spike asked his son kindly. 'I've got a smoothie for you, keep you regular!'

'I've got homework,' Arthur said, angrily switching off his game and pushing past his dad.

''Ave a shower when you're done, stinker!' Wanda could tell Spike didn't mean it the way it came across – to a woman's ear, the directness of blokey speech was always rather harsh. He was trying to care for his son, it was obvious from the fruit and veg count. 'And put that shirt in the wash!'

Footsteps crashed up the stairs and a door slammed.

'He's just not fitting in, that's the problem,' Spike confided, as Wanda poured the wine. 'Detention today. His first ever. I feel like I'm letting him down.'

'It must be hard for him.'

'He's turned into some patriotic English nutter. Says 'e hates Wales. He was never like this before ... Lucy was all about talking about feelins and all that, but I just can't seem to get through to 'im.' Spike rubbed his stubbly chin and sighed, offering Wanda a seat.

'Look, I know we only just met but—'

'Steady on!' he joked. 'I thought I'd made it clear to you I wasn't after a new mum for my son or anything,' he said, cringing. It was a self-deprecating flag to remind her he was aware of his clumsy behaviour on their first meeting.

'Forget it. What I mean is ... maybe be mam and dad for a while. Think of something that'll bond you together. I'm no expert, but perhaps he thinks it's a weakness to show he misses her? Like you're putting on this front, and I get why, you have to get on with it, earn a wage, but you could, say, do something to show she's still there in the front of your mind. I dunno, maybe make a collage of your favourite photos of her together?'

Spike stared at her intently, his cogs working away, as if she'd tripped a switch. An hour whizzed by: she found out about his beloved wife, her work as a nurse, his decision to leave the army to care for her. How devastating it had been. And how still he couldn't bear to unwrap the photographs ... But he was determined to do it to make the cottage more homely.

When she announced through a yawn that the day had caught up with her, he immediately offered to walk her back.

'Shuddup! This isn't London! Thanks for tonight and for the sleeping bags, you're a legend.' She meant it – it would've been impossible without him.

'The power of Fork Handles!' he beamed.

'Yeah, what is that, by the way?'

Spike waggled a pair of imaginary glasses and waited for her to get it with a huge, wide-eyed grin.

'Sorry, I haven't got a clue what you're on about.'

'The *Two Ronnies* sketch! You know, Ronnie Barker goes in to the hardware shop and asks Ronnie Corbett for four candles, but what he really means is fork handles! Classic comedy, one of my favourites.'

'Oh yes! My dad loved that! How didn't I realise!'

As she left, she caught sight of Arthur's face at the top of the landing, the way she and Carys used to eavesdrop when Mam and Dad had people over. He was in a onesie with wet hair and looked so very young. She hoped she'd got it right with what she'd said about his mam. Tentatively, she waved and he nodded, which was a breakthrough of sorts.

The path home was lit up by a swathe of stars in the Milky Way. *Like God had sprinkled some diamonds from heaven*, Dad would say, to give us something to look up at when times are dark. Her feet took her past the back door to the old shepherd's hut, her father's beloved sanctuary. Other dads had sheds and garages to retreat to; he'd had this. With a nip of whisky on a cold day, he'd sit for five minutes on the wooden steps. He called it communing with the elders – the hut had belonged to his great-grandfather, who would roam the vast lonely acres of farmland, and he'd always wanted to restore it. He'd do it in his retirement, but he'd never got the chance ... In the years that followed, it had become even more decrepit.

Taller and longer than a camper van, twice as wide, with two tiny windows and a domed roof, it was made almost entirely of corrugated sheet iron, shaped like a shed with a padlocked door at one end. It had four cast-iron wheels, but they hadn't ever worked, not in her lifetime anyway, and it sat on sleepers. Inside, she remembered, there had been a wooden ledge for sleeping, a stove, small table, a rocking chair and a cage for poorly lambs. Dad had kept bits and pieces in there, nothing valuable, just a few spanners, a book of crosswords, a pack of cards. He'd make it cosy with hay and sometimes he'd let Carys and Wanda sleep out there until the dark and the barking of foxes and *what-if-they're-wolves?* would send them in hysterical. She touched the rusty metal and even though it was cold, she could feel her father's beating heart and it gave her a shot of strength.

She didn't have much to moan about, she knew that. Not when she compared herself to Spike bringing up a lost little kid. Her funny turn about the grass fire, it was a one-off blip.

This latest episode in her life, it wasn't the end point.

Instead, beneath the blanket of the night sky, she realised this was just a detour.

9

With Teg trotting alongside her, Annie was holding her head up high on Gobaith's main street.

It was the first time since she could remember that she felt able to meet people's eyes and face the world.

To go out on a busy Saturday had once been to run the gauntlet of judgement, earning daggers as if she'd been a witch. Someone had even compared her to Gwen Ellis, from the sixteenth century, Wales's first woman to be hanged for witchcraft, because they'd both had healing potions in common. It didn't help that Annie was going through her adolescent goth phase at the time.

But today, the first warm and sunny weekend of the year, felt different. A few, of course, still dropped their eyes to the pavement – including former Travellers' Rest barmaid Rita Griffiths, who'd never been repaid the tenner she'd lent Mam for Ryan's tea, which had ended up down his dad's throat in liquid form in 1994. But in the main her little smile was returned, no doubt helped by Teg's waggy tail and grin. Blod, though, would have spread the word that Annie had helped lead the campsite clean-up. As a respected member of the town, her support was priceless. It meant everything to belong. And it paved the way to reconnect with Wanda. But she'd only do that when Wanda was ready. They hadn't spoken during the renovations – there were too many jobs to do and lots of people around – but Wanda had accepted the community efforts with grace. It was a start, and Annie would take that.

Gobaith hadn't changed much since she was tiny. The indie shops were still thriving; this town was too far out of the way for chains. Not many kids around, though, she noticed: probably inside on Xboxes. In her bag, Annie had a warm granary loaf, parsnip soup and a good strong cheese from the bakery deli Bread and Butter. Next, she would pop into Fork Handles for a new pair of secateurs. She had a spare and hadn't intended on replacing her missing ones, but it was a chance to say hello to Spike, whom she'd met at the campsite call to arms.

''Ello, Annie!' he said, immediately coming over to her. Muscle memory kicked in and she waited for Teg to duck behind her, afraid of this man. But Spike knelt down, held his knuckles out for her to sniff and, incredibly, Teg stayed put.

'Who's this then?' he said softly, ruffling Teg's ears before getting up.

'Teg. It means beautiful in Welsh. My baby girl!' she said.

'She is beautiful! I love dogs.' What a gentle giant Spike was! 'I've got some treats be'ind the counter if you're stopping?'

She nodded as Teg's ears pricked up at the mention of food.

'What can I do you for, then?' His blue eyes were the colour of cornflowers and she felt herself glow in his presence.

'I'm after secateurs.'

'Follow me!' he beamed. 'What about these? They look your size, ergonomic, a lightweight aluminium chassis, they're nice and snappy.'

Her heart jumped a little when his hands touched hers. His warmth and, yes, good looks, had found a small chink in her armour. In fact, he'd found a soft spot inside of her, and while she had no romantic illusions, it had been so long since a man made her feel like a person, she couldn't deny this simple pleasure. But even though he seemed genuine, was he? Dean had started off a gent, with gifts and kindness, then as soon as she'd fallen in love, he'd treated her like an object, a thing to paw if he desired or as a verbal punchbag. She still felt the echoes of that now.

'You goin' to the community hall for the Big Smoke-Out later?' he said, taking payment and giving Teg a biscuit or three. 'I've got some chops you can 'elp me polish off, if you fancy?'

Surprise, surprise, she had always avoided the fire service's annual spring barbecue. Could she make an exception? She found herself wanting to so she could get to know him. But who was she kidding? Her past would come out – he'd run a mile when he saw she had more baggage than an aeroplane.

'Maybe,' she lied. 'I've got a few things I need to do.'

It's better that way, she thought, waving goodbye, *you won't be disappointed then when he backs off.* Annie drove Teg back to the kennel, showering her in kisses and burying her nose in her neck, then stopped on the way home to pick some splendid-looking dandelions. People were sniffy about them but they were like little rays of sunshine to Annie – and useful. She'd let the flowers wilt, stick them in a jar, top with olive oil, rest them on the windowsill for two weeks when she'd strain them out and the ointment would be good to go for Blod's joints.

Once she'd made lunch, she called to Blod, who left her Saturday girl at the till to hold the fort.

'Ooh, parsnip! I do love a sweet vegetable!' Blod said, slurping away at her soup and dunking hunks of bread into her bowl. 'Fancy the do at the hall later? I'm going to close early today. No point being your own boss if you can't mitch off every now and again, is there?'

Annie gave her a stare which said *as if!*

'Well, tough,' Blod replied. 'I need your help to take some burgers, fizzy pop, baps and trestle tables down. I promised the fire service I'd contribute.'

It was an obvious ruse to get Annie there. But she agreed because she couldn't say no to her. 'I won't stay, though.'

'But there's a nice young man going,' Blod winked. 'My second cousin, her great-nephew is the new fire service education officer. He's the one who's moved into Wanda's flat.'

'Oh, great. I can definitely see me and a fireman getting together!' Annie tutted and Blod went innocent-eyed.

'Just to give him a crowd, that's all I mean.'

Blod was transparent – the barbecue was always popular, but it would be especially so today, after the spate of grass fires in Gobaith. No one wanted a repeat of fifteen years ago.

'And you have every right to be there.' Blod's faith in her couldn't be argued with.

So, a few hours later, she found herself nervously

taking in the car park outside the hall, where a fire engine was being clambered on by kids, young and old. There was a tombola, hook a duck, a bouncy castle and a giant dressed-up Fireman Sam whose foam hands were being tugged by toddlers. The poor bugger inside took off his cartoon head and puffed out his ruddy cheeks and waddled to the little stage.

Wholesome and innocent-looking as a little lamb, he cleared his throat and almost jumped out of his skin when the engine gave a *Whoop!* of its siren to call everyone's attention.

'Welcome, everyone, to the Big Smoke-Out! I'm the new education co-ordinator for the fire service.

'As we all know, this is the time of year when our mountains are ablaze. Lighter evenings, dry grassland and kids, whether they're bored, they've been brought up to see it as fun or they're simply fascinated with fire – it's a dangerous combination.

'Wales has eight times as many deliberate grass fires as England. Nowhere is safe, not even Gobaith, where we've seen rising call-outs.'

The crowd muttered their disgust.

'Our colleagues over at Mountain Rescue ...' Lew stepped forward at this point and held aloft a drone, '... have footage of a fire that was started recently. It was small this time and no one was hurt. But we have to nip this in the bud. We don't want what happened fifteen years ago to happen again.'

Annie took a self-conscious step back and wished she hadn't come.

'Of course, you here today understand that arson is not thrilling or harmless. You know it's criminal, devastating for wildlife and could not just injure a firefighter but take them away from a genuine call ...'

Was it her imagination or were people shrinking back from her? She didn't wait to check, but quietly melted away, looking for a hole to climb into. But instead she bumped into Spike and Arthur.

'This whole place deserves to be torched,' the boy said. 'It's so boring.'

'Arthur!' Spike hissed, giving Annie an apologetic look.

'It's okay,' she whispered. 'Some kids don't know how to respect the land. They used to roam free round here, but now with their screens on the one hand and protective parents on the other, they're kind of hemmed in.'

Arthur rolled his eyes.

'We had nothing else, Arthur,' she said. 'We'd have to make dens, set up assault courses, go swimming in the lake, play hide-and-seek, we'd use whatever nature had blessed us with.'

Arthur sized it up. 'That sounds—'

'Watch your mouth!' Spike growled.

'I wasn't going to say *crap*,' Arthur said, enjoying the chance to say it anyway. 'I was going to say better than being here or at school. Although, if I did go and do all that stuff no one would do it with me anyway. They hate me.'

Spike put an arm around his boy and Annie knew she'd inspired something when he didn't shrug it off. 'They don't, son. They've just seen you acting out. If you lash out at them, no one will want to go near you.'

Poor kid. It was horrible being the odd one out. 'That used to be me,' she said, daring to reveal a bit of who she was to Spike – better it came from her than someone else. But before she could say anything more, the siren signalled the speech was finished and the giant barbie was to be lit.

It was all that was needed to kick off the party. Annie's attempts to leave were halted by drinks and plates appearing under her nose and, in the collective hug of Lew, Blod and Spike, she began to feel part of things. As the evening rolled in, they took to a table in the Victorian hall, where she was included in the chit-chat of people coming to say hello to Lew and Blod. 'He who steals an egg steals more' might have legs as a saying round here, but no one treated her as one of the Hugheses or mentioned Ryan: Blod had been right, Annie had earned her right to be here.

Soon she relaxed into it, helped by the booze – although she'd declined the rounds of shots which had sent Blod weepy about missing Lyn, which was so sweet. Annie was enjoying Spike's attention too. If he wasn't the real thing, he was a very good actor. Lew liked him too – they both knew the Brecon Beacons, Spike from his army training and Lew from his wild camping exploits back in the day. They were guffawing about wild toilets when Wanda appeared in a yellow firefighting helmet a few feet away. Bump-first, Carys was guiding her through the hall because her sister was weaving in the style of a few too many sherbets. It was slow progress because she stopped to talk to everyone, receiving hugs as she went, particularly a long one from Phil the Pill. When she saw Annie and Lew, she halted, swaying on the spot. With her inhibitions down, it was easy to see her uncertainty as to what she did next. Annie was willing her over because now was as good a time as any – in fact, it was probably the best way to start again because everyone was merry and the ice had been broken by the booze. Carys said something to Wanda and she hesitated before giving an enthusiastic jab of the air with her finger.

'Hi,' she sang to the group. But her confidence a split second ago had turned to apprehension and she wasn't yet sure if she was doing the right thing.

'Hi, Wanda! Carys, you want a seat?' Spike said, ever the gent, rising before he was waved back down.

'I'll not be long,' Carys said, rubbing her tummy and yawning. 'We've just come over to say thank you.'

'Yes, we have!' Wanda said as if she'd been reminded of why she was here. 'Thank you sho mush,' she said, slurring.

'We couldn't have done it without your help, could we, Wanda?'

'Nope.' Wanda's glassy eyes went round the table, probably unaware how long they lingered on Lew.

His smile had gone behind a cloud. Annie had assumed he'd parked the past by helping Wanda last weekend. Clearly not. He was looking everywhere but at Wanda and the atmosphere felt chilly. Annie had to do something.

'Did it all go off okay, this week, for you?' Annie was nervous too because this would be their first interaction since their showdown.

'Yes!' Wanda cried. Then her face dropped. 'Well, sort of ... you know. No campers at all actually since the bikers.'

Spike got up; he was off to take Arthur home. Annie's stomach dropped in disappointment. And when he went round giving everyone a farewell *cwtch*, she realised she was holding her breath, hoping, waiting for her turn.

When it came, she savoured his strong arms around her and returned it with feeling before she thought better of it, she wouldn't let him go otherwise. She made a note to self to put it down to a drunken crush: it was just because he was the opposite of Dean, with his open face rather than an angry brow, a doer rather than a taker.

'I think we should go too,' Carys said, draining her J20. They'd always been inseparable. Even when they were kids, when the older-younger sibling dynamic had been played out, they were a unit. Losing their father would've consolidated that and with their Mam in hospital and Carys a single mum-to-be, their bond would be even tighter. Annie and Ryan hadn't had that, partly because they lived in different houses but also because he seemed so vulnerable. The closest thing she'd had to a sister had been Wanda.

'Go? I'm not going anywhere!' Wanda said with horror and then defiance. 'Ha! I'm really not going anywhere, am I? I can't seem to get out of Gobaith!'

It was a joke, but an awkward one.

'Right, well, I'm taking Rock and Roll home,' Carys said with a sober sigh.

Oh Christ, that'd leave just Annie, Lew and Wanda. It was hard to believe they'd once been a gang: relying on each other, sharing stuff. Those two had been Annie's only ever real friends with whom she had felt an equal. In her year, her pals had been odd-bod losers like her, clinging together for safety against the bullies, only to disband when they'd left school. In her working life, she'd had the kind of jobs which didn't make it easy to get to know anyone: either shifts or solitary positions at the till of the petrol station or after-hours cleaning. The job she'd always wanted, working at Gobaith garden centre, among nature and kindred spirits, never came up. Then she had met and married Dean and WAGs of his friends had become hers. Finally, she'd had some women to hang out with down the pub on a Friday night. But over the years he'd become possessive, developing mystery ailments if she had something planned or belittling her wanting to sign up to evening classes or keep fit: he'd accuse her of having ideas above her station or wanting an affair, and eventually her world had shrivelled and she'd learned to live in isolation. It was less draining than arguing. That's why it was so great to have Lew here again. But it would be even better if Wanda was in the circle again too.

'Going to join us?' Annie asked, tentatively. Lew gave her a look of disdain, which she ignored. Those two needed to sort out whatever it was between them and they could only do that if they were in the same airspace.

'Thanks,' Wanda said, quieter, as if she'd woken up to where she actually was – alone with people who'd known her intimately but were now strangers.

'How've you been?' Annie asked.

'Really good,' she said, not very convincingly. 'No idea what happened to me the other night, the grass fire thing, totally ridiculous!'

Annie had a feeling she knew – unresolved trauma from years of burying it deep down, only for it to rise to the surface because Annie and Lew had come back into her life. But she could hardly say that. It was hard to judge Wanda's mood, too. Annie looked to Lew for support, but he was finding a beer mat very interesting.

'So … you okay?' Wanda asked, taking a glug of her pint, watching both of them over the rim of the glass.

97

'Yes! Had a good night actually, haven't we, Lew?'

He nodded and sank his nose into his beer to avoid talking.

God, this was painful. Pretending the past had never happened wouldn't lead to reconciliation, yet they couldn't broach it here, now. And definitely not while they were pissed. Annie squirmed in her seat; this was such an uncomfortable situation. She saw Wanda gulp and hold her throat and then she was flapping her top, shifting around, and she went paler than normal. Was she going to puke? Her chest now heaving, Wanda placed her hands over her mouth and nose and began to struggle with her breathing.

'Are you all right?' Annie said. Wanda looked as if she was focusing on trying to control herself.

'Sorry, I don't ... know ... I feel really weird.' Wanda's eyes met hers, terrified.

'I think you're having a panic attack,' Annie said. 'Is it like the other night?'

She nodded. 'I can't ... believe this. Not again.'

'Come on, let's get some air.' Annie was surprised to see Lew joining them – if he'd been looking for a get-out then it would've been the perfect opportunity.

After a few minutes of sitting on the wall in the cool of the night, the colour came back to Wanda's cheeks, but she was still rocking slightly, holding herself when she felt able to speak again.

'I'm sorry,' she said. 'Maybe I'm just really tired. Not used to being physical; I sat down for years at work.' Her smile was weak.

'You must be under a lot of strain, too.'

Wanda's eyes watered. 'It's Mam, her infection hasn't

cleared up. Carys and the babies as well, I can't bear her brave little face. The campsite, worrying about money... it's all come to a head.'

Annie decided this was a chance to raise what else would be on Wanda's mind. Not to upset her, but to acknowledge it; it seemed the right moment, when the three of them were alone.

'It can't be easy seeing me and Lew again, either,' she said softly.

Wanda bit her lip. With tears streaming down her face, she admitted it. 'No.'

Lew produced a tissue. 'Here you go.'

It wasn't a groundbreaking start to rebuilding their relationship but at least he'd spoken to her now.

'Thanks,' she whispered, stealing a glance at him. 'I shouldn't have come out tonight. Stupid of me. When you've done one Big Smoke-Out, you've done them all, really,' she said, staring at her hands. 'This is self-indulgent of me and I'm trying to keep positive, but I just keep thinking I shouldn't be here any more, in Gobaith. It's like I'm trapped.'

'It's not forever,' Lew said. Annie heard a slight edge in his voice as if he thought she needed a dose of perspective, which was fair enough; but the timing wasn't great.

Wanda had caught it, though, and she lifted her chin to him.

'It feels like it,' she said in a hard voice.

Annie needed to calm this down. 'I know it must be disappointing. But it's not all bad, is it? You can still go away. Business will pick up, it's early days in the season.'

But Wanda threw her hands in the air. 'That's the trouble: the campsite looks much better, and I'm very thankful for that, to both of you, honestly,' she said, placing her palms on her heart, 'but it's not a patch on what it was. How are we supposed to compete when camping is all about bell tents and yurts? We'll be lucky if we get a couple of pensioners from Scarborough in their touring caravan.' She stood up and shook her head.

'God, when I think! There were so many things I wanted to do while I was away. I should be speaking Spanish in Colombia, being taught how to tango in Buenos Aires, volunteering in Chile, hanging out on a South Pacific beach, doing some yoga and surfing in Indonesia, cooking in Kerala and shopping till I'm dropping in Marrakech, taking photos left, right and centre.' She was going for it now, loudly and clearly. 'But no, here I am in nowheresville, with a mountain that isn't actually a mountain. Do you know something, I feel like I've failed my dad. He wanted me to travel. But I've let him down. And, what's more, I have never ever got round to doing up his shepherd's hut, like he wanted.'

Annie could see this was just frustration and loss tumbling out. 'All those things you wanted to do, well, do them here, then.'

'It won't bring my father back though, will it?' Wanda roared.

Annie froze.

'Wanda,' Lew said, firmly, 'don't do this.'

'What?' she spat. 'Every day I think how he died, looking for me in the house!' Then she swung round to point at Annie. 'In a fire Ryan started! And you reckon tidying up the campsite will make up for it!'

'You're being way too harsh, Wanda.' Lew lost it then. 'Can't you dial down the drama for once in your life?'

Enough was enough, Annie thought, staring at Wanda, who was pulsing with anger. 'What I'll say now, I will say one last time. Never again. I'm so sorry on behalf of my brother and for your dad's passing. Ryan was a victim in all of this too in his own way, whatever you think. But I am not responsible for it. Yes, I helped you out of guilt, I've carried it my entire bloody life. But I also did it because I wanted to be your friend again. We have to move on from this or we'll all be miserable.'

Annie turned her back on Wanda to find a crowd watching. It was kicking-out time and they must have heard the lot. And, oh, Spike was there with Arthur, they must've taken a while to say their goodbyes. For them to find out about everything like this sickened her. At least they'd heard it from the horse's mouth.

An arm came round her; it was Lew. 'Come on, let's go.'

But she calmly took his hand off her. So many times she had imagined this scene: to unload herself of her heavy heart and dirty conscience. She'd feared it would hurt her too much. Instead, having lanced the boil, she felt a stillness. It was done. She'd said her piece. And now she wasn't going to waste any more time on the past. She'd shed the skin of the last forty years.

Marching off, she decided that from now on she would only look to the future.

10

Wanda couldn't do enough for us! A brilliant host at a beautiful location. Shame we couldn't have a campfire, there's nothing like bangers cooked on an open flame!

Babs, The Blood Bikers
The Midlands

Wanda staggered down the stairs with what was probably the biggest hangover ever recorded in Wales.

If Lew considered her outpouring last night as dramatic then she was bloody well going to make her suffering Oscar-winning.

But that was just her shame talking. She'd lost the plot, her dignity and all sympathy – and she deserved it.

Obviously, the news had reached Carys, judging by the look of disapproval thrown her way from the hob when Wanda slumped down at the kitchen table. Then, to make it certain how she felt, Carys banged a drawer shut to make Wanda's head pound even harder. She had every right to, to be fair.

Wanda laid her forehead on the cool of the country-scene place mat and waited for what was coming.

'What the fudge was last night about then?'

Wanda looked up and met daggers. 'I'm sorry. I'm so sorry.'

'Apparently, you were quite the entertainment, you were. You put the gob in Gobaith, Blod said. Fair enough you're frustrated and sad, but to behave like that! It's so ungrateful, considering what people have done for us.'

'I know. I'm mortified.'

Carys plonked a coffee in front of her. 'Get this down you. I'll do some rarebit.'

'I'm not sure … I feel a bit sick.'

'I spent the last few months feeling sick, not just in the morning, but during the afternoon and evening too.' Carys put her hands on her hips and a crescent of stomach peeked out from under her now too-tight Nirvana T-shirt. 'So suck it up.'

Pass her a straw and Wanda would've done, even though she was full to the brim with self-loathing.

'I shouldn't have drunk so much,' she said to Carys's back as she prepared their ultimate comfort food: cheese, butter, flour, mustard, pepper and Worcestershire sauce all whisked in a pan, then grilled on doorsteps until it bubbled.

'It wasn't the drink though, was it?' Carys said, over her shoulder. The clink of the fork dulled as the mixture melted. She flipped the bread, spooned on the rarebit and popped it back under the heat to brown. 'It came out not because of the booze but because it's all in there. You've never really dealt with the fire or Dad or Lew or Annie.'

Then she softened. 'I get it, Wanda. It's all on you. You must feel like you're back where you were then, shouldering everything.'

Wanda didn't deserve understanding, but Carys's insight was spot-on.

'I didn't handle life well when Dad died. I messed it all up, my exams, remember the resits I put us all through: *life wasn't fair* and all that? But you were there for me, I could crumble because you were strong, you let me heal. But you were never allowed to do that. Do you think this is what it's all about?'

'It's hardly convenient now though, is it? For me to have a crisis? You and Mam need me to be—'

'We're fine,' Carys interrupted. 'Well, what I mean is, we'll get through it, you don't need to carry us.'

She dished up two plates of carbs plus cheese, basically God's own food. Wanda realised her nausea was down to hunger. She'd hardly eaten yesterday, she'd been so busy with campsite admin.

'I've got my babies, Mam'll be back on her feet any day, you'll be away soon.' She said it as if it was that simple. 'We'll find a way through it. Like people do.'

Carys was already two-thirds done on her first slice – she was delighted that twins meant she needed to eat for three.

'How? It'll take months for Mam to get fully mobile and you'll have your hands full.'

'We'll manage. Because we have to.'

There was an alternative, something Wanda hadn't thought of until now. 'We could sell up.'

Carys flinched. 'Now you're just talking stupid.'

'No, listen. Mam could retire, you'd both be able to afford a place each, no mortgage. You could get a job when the babies are older.'

There, that was simple.

'I don't want that!' Her sister's face was flushed now. 'Stop deciding what you think is best for everyone! It's not up to you! I want my children growing up on this land beneath this mountain – and it is a bloody mountain, by the way.' It wasn't, but now was not the time to argue. 'If you want to go, then go! No one has ever stopped you from leaving. No one apart from you.'

Wanda could barely breathe. Because ultimately, God damn it, Carys was right. She could book her trip and be gone within a few months. It was totally doable. So why wasn't she doing it? Immediately, the reasons reared their heads again, but now Wanda saw they were her own excuses, not actual reasons. They circled her head as she prepared for the day, dressing in scruffs and heading out for campsite duties. A gentle breeze caressed her cheeks and the warm midday sunshine echoed Carys's belief that there was a better way – just as Annie had said last night. Could Wanda sign up to it, though?

It would mean turning her version of things upside down. Was she brave enough to move forward? Could she stop blaming herself for her father's death? Could she forgive Annie and accept that her brother had been a victim too? Could she try again with Lew? Would that bridge that she had destroyed last night be fit for repair?

She dumped her bucket of cleaning equipment beside the bathroom block and dared herself to look up, not down.

As ever, it started with the mountain. Wanda gave herself a three, two, one countdown and she lifted her face to try to stare it out. The challenge was on as it soared on high, distant and intimidating. She blinked first, the brightness of the day making her head bang once more, and defeated, she dropped her chin to her chest. *Come on*, she willed, and so she tried once more, walking to the lake, the tear of liquid blue which sat in the curve of the hillside. It was clean and clear and, whether it was a hot or a cold day, always exhilarating, when you'd got past the shock to the ankles, knees, thighs, stomach and shoulders. But once you were in, it made you laugh and shriek and you'd stare down, wondering if there was any truth in its tale of the Lady of the Lake. Many a time her toe had brushed a mossy stone and she'd shiver as if the legend herself had brushed Wanda with her own fingertips.

Her smile began to spread then as she took in the treeline which had blossomed overnight, turning the woodland path into a low-level cloud of flowers. Then, by one path or another, the scramble up the stepping stones, which feet had rubbed smooth, then up the hillside which was beginning to turn green with life. Beyond, the crags and the brooks, the sheep and the moor grass, her eye followed the sweeping terrain higher and higher, which would soon burst into colour. Then the zig-zag of ascent, exposed but pure, to the jagged peak, its trig point and three-hundred-and-sixty-degree view for miles and miles. Yes, the mountain could be brutal and barren, but its calm and peace could also be euphoric.

Wanda hadn't been up it in years.

This time the mountain didn't stare her down, but it seemed to bask under her gaze. It was utterly, breathtakingly beautiful . . .

Do all the things you want to do but do them here, Annie had said. Wanda could start, by way of a warm-up, with a photograph for her Instagram account. It might also lead her to the unthinkable: apologising to Annie and Lew for her meltdown.

She took her phone, went onto the app but didn't look at her feed of foreign escapes. She went straight to the camera and took a shot of sheer wonder, no filter and no editing required.

As she posted the picture, she felt something release inside of her. Everything she wanted to do, she could do here until she managed to leave.

The surf of Indonesia may be continents away, maybe she could canoe on the lake instead? As for speaking Spanish, she could help Arthur with his Welsh. But cooking in India, dancing in Argentina and volunteering in Chile . . . hmm, where did she start with that?

She was interrupted by a notification on her screen. And another. Then another. These were names of people she knew in the travel industry, the ones whose perfect images of oceans and beaches, exotic foods and cultures had fed her soul. Only this time, they were giving her their love. Her eyes ran down the comments: *This place looks amazing! Where is it? What a find! Where are you?* It was only her back garden, she scoffed, smiling at the far-flung locations people were guessing at: was she in South America? Was it New Zealand? Europe? Africa? The Himalayas?

No, instead she was in a land of light and air, which wasn't claustrophobic but a breathing space. She hadn't left it over all these years because she hadn't been ready to. She had a mountain to climb, apologies to deliver, business to resolve and a resolution not to let the past happen again. Now, she realised, it was time to get on with this choice she had made: and enjoy it.

II

J ust when you thought the biting winds and driving rain of winter had gone, spring came and chucked a load of weather at you.

April showers, people called them. But in this part of the world they were more deluges. An icy gust straight off the knife-edge of the mountain sliced Annie's fingers, which were bloody and raw from today's jobs. Thick waterproof gloves were no good when it came to weeding, it slowed you down and in this kind of temperature, you wanted to whip in and out of every garden.

She let herself in to her van, which rocked from the gale, found her flask, then hugged her metal mug of four o'clock coffee for warmth. Not for the first time, she wondered how long she could keep this up. It wasn't a useful thought and most of the time she would think she just had to get through today, this very wet Wednesday. But could she still see herself doing this physical work for the next five years? A torrent of hailstones suddenly hammered the windscreen. Right now, she couldn't see herself doing it for the rest of the week.

Parked up in Gobaith just beyond the high street, the heater inside was broken – she had no money to get it fixed. Her breath and the steam from her drink misted up the windows and she felt her eyes relax into a trance. Imagine if the next call on her phone was the garden centre ... imagine if she was offered a position ... Annie would accept on the spot. There'd be someone younger than her, and just as desperate as she had been to be her own boss, to take on her clients.

Gobaith Gardening was a haven of all things bright and beautiful. With its decked walkway in a walled court-yard, it was as far as you could get from the polytunnelled plastic and rickety old tables of its poorer rivals. An ex-haustive range of shiny leaves, blowsy flowers and healthy branches sat in big wooden planters. *The hothouse, oh my God*, she could do with being inside that now, inhaling the humidity as the blood returned to her numb toes. The café, with a living wall of tumbling ivy, sold hearty lunches, some made from the nursery's own kitchen garden, and the farm shop bulged with local produce.

That job offer coming, though? She'd more likely bump into Ryan in the pub. The boss there would always give her a sad nod when Annie went in for supplies. 'Still nothing,' she'd say. And no wonder, because her staff were looked after, given free lunches and a good discount – people who worked there stayed there.

That left her one other option. The one nobody knew of, and that was even more elusive than her ex's manners. If she told anyone, they'd laugh her off the mountain. She knew it was a daydream, but still, when she was soggier than a slug's bottom, it was a seductive fantasy.

A little store of her own, of succulents and cacti, with an apothecary feel, selling herbal remedies, maybe her own, in little jars of this and pipette bottles of that, or-ganics and candles and a tea room offering fresh infusions of mint, nettles, turmeric and ginger. Yet without finance and support, this would never be on the knitting needles. But she was sure there had to be some other way for her to earn a living.

Her phone buzzed. Of course now would be the time for it to ring, to rub in the fact that it wasn't Gobaith Gardening or a solicitor saying she was the sole beneficiary of a long-lost wealthy relative. It was April the first, after all.

'Annie, it's Bonnie from the Hound Hotel. Don't panic, Teg's fine!'

Lovely Bonnie! She instinctively knew to calm an owner's fear.

'What it is, it's something a bit strange to be honest. There was a man come in just now, said he'd come to pick up Teg.'

'A man?' Annie's heart was in her throat.

'Yes. Didn't know him. Said he was here on your behalf.'

Annie knew who it would be. She just knew it. She'd thought she was safe from him, but somehow he'd tracked her down.

'You didn't ...' She couldn't bear it if she'd been taken.

'No, of course not. Teg's safe and sound.'

Thank God.

'Was he lanky? This man? Long thin face and a—' She would choke if she had to keep describing that streak of piss.

'Skinhead. Cruel grey eyes.'

Annie couldn't have summed him up better herself. 'My ex, Dean Pincher.'

'That makes sense. Teg started barking like mad when

he was here. Didn't see him, but she got a whiff of him, obviously. *Cwtched* in right behind me when I went to see her after.'

'Oh no!' Annie was breaking inside.

'It's okay, I gave her a good smooth; she calmed down.'

'Oh, Bonnie! Thank you so much. How did you get him to go?'

'I said I'd ring you. Wouldn't say his name. Very suspicious, I thought.'

'The gall of him. Listen, keep Teg close. Keep her on a lead if you have to.'

'Sure?'

Annie was sickened that she'd have to curb Teg's freedom. But she couldn't risk Dean getting his hands on her. While Teg wouldn't go to him, if there was food or a trap of some sorts, she might fall for it.

'Do you think I should come up? I should, shouldn't I?'

'I'm not sure, lovely, she's sleeping now, I think it took it out of her. She had quite a reaction to him.'

'Yes, of course.' How selfish of her to seek comfort without thinking about Teg's upset. There was no way she'd want her to suffer any more.

'Tomorrow, I'll come then,' she said, ringing off, seeing the drawn white of her cheeks in the rear-view mirror. How the heck had he found out where Teg was staying? Did this mean he knew where she was too? What the hell did he want from her? She'd agreed to the divorce on his terms. Why would he want to take the most precious thing she had away from her? Did this mean he would never let her go? Would he always punish her for having the courage to leave him? She had to get Teg out of there.

But how? She began to cry, softly at first, but then waves of distress at her own impotence brought judders to her chest and shoulders. Dean Pincher was a sicko, a psycho and—

A rap on the door made her jump in her seat. She wouldn't put it past him to confront her in broad daylight to show he was afraid of no one, or their judgement. But it was Wanda. *Oh no. What now?*

Annie opened the window an inch and switched on the engine as if she was about to go. She couldn't face this, whatever it was.

'Hi, I was wondering if you ... er ... had a second?' Wanda said through a mop of soaking red hair.

Annie was about to say no, but Wanda was peering in, all big blue eyes of concern.

'What's up?' Wanda asked, 'Are you okay?'

Great. Annie's face was puffier than a winter robin.

Another torrent of rain descended and Wanda disappeared, only to open the passenger door and ask if she could jump in.

Annie hesitated. She couldn't deal with this now.

'Look,' she said, her hands gripping the steering wheel. 'I think we said enough on Saturday night. I'm not up to—'

'I'm sorry!' Wanda cried. 'I'm so sorry. I want to apologise. Please?'

'Oh ...' Annie hadn't expected this. She turned to her, examined Wanda – and she looked like she meant it.

'It's ... er ... raining old ladies and walking sticks out here.'

All right, she'd let her have her say, they'd put it behind them and then they'd part and pretend everything was just hunky-dory between them. Such was village life.

'Fine,' Annie said, sighing, laying back on the headrest, trying to gather herself. Because, really, after their row at the community hall, they were never going to make it up properly.

'Thanks, Annie,' Wanda said. She flapped her wet coat about, wiped her face, shook her hair and then dried her hands on her lap. 'I was wrong. You were right. You *are* right. I've had my head stuck up my arse and I've finally plucked it out.'

'O-kay ...' That was pretty honest of her. It couldn't have been easy.

'You don't need to say anything. I don't want you to forgive me or say it's forgotten. Because I know I'm the one who's got to show you I mean it. That I can make the best of things here and move on and that I don't blame you and I just want to thank you for everything.'

Whoa, she really was going for it.

'I've been round everyone too, explaining myself. Blod, Spike ...'

Annie had avoided him – she'd dropped any designs she'd had on having him as a new mate. At least now she didn't look like a madwoman to him.

'I'd like to ask you up for a cup of tea soon, if you'd consider it? I'm off the drink, obvs.'

'Yeah ... maybe.' Annie had to give her something.

'In fact, how about now?' Wanda's voice was high with hope.

'Want a lift home, is it?' Annie was thawing slowly. She couldn't help but tease her.

'No! No!'

'I'm only messing about.' She gave Wanda a little smile.

Annie had had enough of this. Acceptance was every-thing – and what kind of hypocrite would she be if she didn't follow up on her own advice to Wanda?

'Yes. Let's do it. Come on.' She pushed off in first gear and drove them to the campsite without an atmosphere, focusing on the lane, which could be treacherous in a downpour.

But as she pulled in to the drive, the last drops of the rain had been squeezed from the clouds and the sun came out with a warmth that reached your bones.

Inside the farmhouse, Annie's heart had a pang when she saw nothing she recognised – of course, the fire had claimed all of the little bits and pieces which made up a family's history. But then they would have memories, like Annie had of Nanna's home, of crochet and coal, *cawl* stew and *cwtches*. And it was a lovely domestic scene here of life with cookbooks, a fruit bowl and on the fridge a grainy blown-up photo of two babies curled up together in the womb. Out of nowhere Annie felt a blow to her stomach. Even though she'd accepted long ago she would never be blessed with children, sometimes the fact still took her breath away. So she was pleased when Wanda brewed up and suggested they went outside.

'What a day! Four seasons at once!' Wanda said as they ambled towards the lake.

'Typical Wales,' Annie said, soothed again.

'I've got some bara brith if you fancy? Carys made it but from Mam's recipe. With a twist, knowing her.'

It was an offering, Annie knew. Wanda's mam's tea bread was legendary and had been a post-school reviver when they'd tumble in from the bus and slob out on the sofa together.

'What kind of twist?'

Wanda pulled a foil parcel out of her pocket and gave it a sniff. 'Ooh, smells like coconut! Definitely not arsenic.'

Annie let out a laugh and felt it ripple through her body.

Suddenly, Wanda stopped and gasped. 'Look!' she said, nodding towards the shepherd's hut nestled in the trees and hedges, cocooned from the rest of the campsite. 'What on earth? It's been done up!'

She gave Annie a huge grin and they picked up the pace until they were up close, where the hut was gleaming in the sunshine. Not quite looking brand new, but the vast russet of rust had been scoured away, exposing the original grey of the corrugated iron, leaving battered patches like dimples. The steps were varnished, the windows clean and the wheels painted black. It looked like a piece of art of the landscape.

'The padlock's gone, there's a silver keyhole instead!' Wanda said with excitement, trying the handle, but it was locked. 'Someone's got the key to this! But who? Who did this?'

'No idea! Did you mention it to anyone during the clean-up?'

Wanda shook her head. 'I was only down here the other day. It's been done since then. Oh my,' she whispered. 'It's beautiful.'

They both peeked through the window and saw a few tools, some vinegar and scouring pads.

'Could it have been Spike? Sara? One of your Dad's pals?'

'God knows … but it's a little miracle! A sign!'

'It is!' Annie said, as they perched side by side on the steps.

'It's like the hut has got a second chance … like us, I hope.'

Annie's heart bloomed at that.

'Sorry, again,' Wanda said, handing her some bara brith.

'Forget it. I'm all in for second chances. Come on, let's have a taste of this.'

The cake crumbled on her tongue, the sweetness reaching her tastebuds, followed by coconut and a light tea, and the raisins were soft and succulent. 'Delish!'

'Isn't it! I never knew Carys was a baker. I don't s'pose Mam let her.'

'How is she?'

'She's weak, her rehab programme isn't going to schedule because of that. And she's a thrombosis risk because she's immobile. Poor thing, she's going stir crazy now.'

'How long will it be before she's home?'

'Depends on her mobility. The doctors are very wary about sending her back. They know Carys can't help with anything requiring physical support and that I'm working. Friends have offered to have her in the meantime, but she won't be a burden on anyone.'

'Sounds like the Lyn I know!'

'How's life with you?' Wanda asked.

Annie felt the pressure of the moment: if she said everything was fine, then this friendship would never really recover. Wanda had made the first move with her apology and Annie wanted to show her she appreciated it. This was also the chance to fill her in on what had happened to her since the fire. Why she'd come back. Who she was now. And to have someone familiar willing to listen … well, that hadn't happened in a long time.

'Hard,' she said. 'My back's aching from the sofa. I miss my dog. And Dean tried to take her from the kennel today. God knows how he found out where Teg was.'

'What? Such a bastard!'

'I know. All to show he's got power over me.'

'Was it his dog then?'

'*Pfft*. No! He hated her.'

'Why?'

'Because she took my attention away from Dean, that's what he said.' Annie felt tears rush in and Wanda placed a hand on her arm. 'He wants to hurt me in the worst way. He'd know that I'd be beside myself at what he'd do to her.'

'How do you mean?'

'The night I left, the final straw ...' Annie squeezed her eyes shut at the horror. She'd told nobody about this. No one. But it was a relief to let it out. 'He'd got the sack from work, he was in a rage, he kicked the dog so hard I thought he'd killed her. I wish it had been me. I realised it would be me next.'

'That's despicable. What a coward.'

'Teg was in the vet's a while. I didn't say Dean had done it, I was too terrified. She had a cracked rib, luckily it didn't pierce her lungs; it could've done. Blod let me keep her at hers while she recovered; she wasn't interested in the cats then, she was too poorly. But once she was better, then I had to put her in the kennel. I need to work out a way to get her out.'

'She could come here?' Wanda offered.

Annie was touched. 'Thanks, but her next step needs to be back with me. It might confuse her, she might try to escape to find me, I just can't risk it.'

'It will all work out, you know.'

'It has to ...'

'It will do. It has for me. You reach a tipping point. You and Caz, you made it happen. All that stuff about leaving, it was just denial. I saw escape as ... well, my escape and I thought that was the end point. Now I see when I do eventually go away I will have to come back – the problems will still be there and probably more ingrained and I'll be in an even bigger pickle. I need to sort everything out now so I have something good to come back to.'

'And what about Lew?' Annie asked, softly. Because he was part of her rehabilitation.

'Yes. I'm working up to that. Sat here, this was where we were all last together, wasn't it, the night of the fire. It feels like he's missing.'

'He's missing out, that's what he's missing.' Annie gave Wanda a playful barge with her elbow.

'I dunno, I haven't got my head round all that, still. How do you think I should play it?'

Annie didn't want to be the vessel through which the pair communicated: the pair of them had to do so face to face, yet she knew them both and the back story. She hesitated, trying to work out how to put it politely and in a manner that wouldn't deter Wanda from trying, that Lew appeared to think she wasn't worth much at all.

'I don't want you to betray his confidence. If he's said anything to you, though ...?'

At least she could be truthful about this. 'He hasn't said much.'

'I don't even know why he's back. No one does, not really.'

'You've been asking, then?'

'Of course!'

'He saw The Bunkhouse as a way to run his own show in an area he knew.'

'And?'

'You'll have to ask him. I'm sorry.'

'I understand.'

'What I will say is, I get the sense he's seeking some kind of resolution.'

'I wish I knew where to start. I mean, I've blamed him for us losing contact, but now I'm wondering if I read things wrong and I didn't try hard enough to keep in touch.'

'How about dropping the blame altogether?' Annie said, astonished the old intimacy had come back to them so naturally.

Wanda considered it and then turned her head to Annie. 'Isn't it amazing, we've had no contact for fifteen years and now, I feel like you're back in my life. I've missed you,' she said, unable to stop her chin from trembling.

'Me too.'

They rested their heads together and sat in silence for a while.

Wanda was the first to speak. 'I've been thinking about Ryan a lot.'

Annie stiffened and *hmmm*ed her acknowledgement.

Wanda touched her hand to tell her she meant well. 'Yeah, I guess I grew up in this happy family, with all the love in the world and a mam who'd not just do the basics but the extras too, redoing my ponytail if it was too tight or listening to me kicking off and still giving me a hug after. And my dad, he'd sit and play princesses with me, and that stuff matters, doesn't it? It gives you wings and hope. But if that isn't there, then you've been let down, haven't you? And if there's violence and neglect, you might go under ...'

'Yep. I was so lucky. It could've been me, not Ryan. I had my grandparents, they protected me. He had a bully of a father and our mam was frightened and she couldn't find it in herself to stick up for him. It took me years to be that charitable to her – she didn't give a toss about me; she still doesn't.'

'Do you ever see her?'

'She lives locally, but no. There was a time when I did, but she'd turn up a wreck, asking to borrow money, or else she'd cancel. I thought she just needed to dig a bit deeper and she'd find some love for me. She managed to fit three men in her life – she remarried after Ryan died. But there was none left for me. I think she's spent her whole life numb. Maybe that's why I ended up with Dean: I wanted the love I never had from her from him. And it's complicated, because she was brought up by my grandparents, she was given everything, but at a young age, younger than Ryan was, she'd got in with the wrong crowd, my father for one, and I guess she found the instant rewards of that kind of life more satisfying than having to work hard. Then maybe she got trapped there.'

'It's not black or white, is it?'

'Never is. Listen, I need to go, there's a tree that needs lopping.'

'Thanks, Annie. You've made me see sense.'

'About bloody time!' Annie laughed, getting up and taking a last long thirsty look at the beauty around her.

'Looks like we'll be in for a sunset-and-a-half. The streaks of cloud, they look as if a dragon's clawed the sky.'

'I'll stay here for a bit, I think. Take some photos, enjoy the view. See you soon?'

That hopeful question would have been unthinkable an hour ago.

'Definitely,' she said, with a wave.

She might have been heading off back to work, but Annie's footsteps felt lighter than they had all day.

12

We came to Mid Wales for an off-grid back-to-nature
retreat but it was cancelled after the wifi went down.
Wanda very kindly put us up and let us use her internet
to upload photos to our @LifestyleInfluencers platforms.
We leave cleansed and re-energised.

Ra-Ra and Rik Wilson-Smyth, North London
Campsite Visitors' Book

There were so many 'get well' cards on Mam's hospital cabinet, Wanda felt like she was walking into a branch of Clintons.

'She's just powdering her nose,' Elsie said from the opposite bed.

'How is she?' Wanda asked conspiratorially, to see how it would tally with Mam's version, who had claimed to her daughters several times she was fine and dandy despite a temperature and swelling.

'Much brighter today.'

Talk of the devil, Mam slowly entered the ward – with a stick! Lately, she had been taken everywhere in a wheelchair, she was so poorly.

'You're up and about!' Wanda cried, overjoyed to see

her out of a nightie, in a comfy pair of cotton trousers and blouse and with some colour in her cheeks.

'No more bedpan for me!' Mam cackled, cuddling into Wanda. 'I'm proud of you, you know.'

'Me? What have I done?' Wanda stepped back, feeling unworthy. 'You should be proud of yourself. Look at you!'

'If I keep this up,' Mam said, reversing into a chair and patting the one next to her for Wanda, 'the physio says I'll be kicked out soon. They want to make sure I'm fully mobile before I go.'

'It's so good to see you doing so well. How's the pain?' Wanda popped a clean set of clothes into the cabinet drawer, then joined her.

'Bearable with the drugs. And I've started my exercises. The stairs, though, they're a bit of a killer. Can you believe it's been three weeks I've been here? Most people come in for a week at most. But your mam? She has to make a performance out of it.' She rolled her eyes at herself. 'Anyway, back to you. I can't wait to see the campsite!'

'Don't get too excited. But yes, it's a hell of a lot better than it was …' That came out the wrong way. 'I didn't mean it like that, I just mean—'

'Oh, I know it was in a state, I just didn't realise how bad it'd got. Funnily enough, this has been a bit of a life-changer, all this spare time and being forced to think a lot … I was sinking, I couldn't see it, but I suppose … I was lonely.'

'You? Look at all these cards! You've so many friends.'

'Indeed, but … being alone, without Dad, it still gets to me every now and again. I lost interest in everything: I was going through the motions, but not very well!'

'Oh, Mam, I wish you'd said, or I'd noticed.'

'Not your job to mother your mother,' she said sternly. 'Now, though, I can't wait to get back to it all. And to see the shepherd's hut! Did you find out who was behind it?'

'Not yet. No one's owned up to it.' There was one person she hadn't asked, but it was impossible to think they would be responsible.

'Well, it's a lovely little mystery, isn't it?' She gave a wistful smile. 'Oh, Wanda, what I'd give to be in my own bed, in my own kitchen, pottering in the garden! But there's so much to be excited about: the babies for a start, your travels, and, so a little bird tells me, you talking to Annie again. Well done.'

'Blod been on the blower, has she?' But she didn't mind, because Wanda's wobbles had been kept from her mother, such was the kindness of the community. 'Yes, me and Annie are talking again, which is lovely. I mean, like you, I've lots of friends, but I'd always missed her. Obviously it's early days, but ...'

'What about Lew?' Mam said evenly. She definitely hadn't heard about the scene at the Smoke-Out – she'd have been all over it if she'd been tipped off.

'I haven't really had a chance to speak to him.' *Shout at him, yes.* 'It's on my to-do list.'

The tinkle of cups and saucers gave her an out and Mam was content to share tea and gossip for a while before her eyes grew heavy.

'Carys will be up later,' she said, gathering Mam's washing and some thank-you cards to post, but her mother had already dropped off.

Back home, Wanda was delighted to deliver some good

news for a change to her sister. Carys repaid the courtesy, having just booked in a couple of groups of campers for the weekend. And there wasn't a suggestion of hipster beard about them! Social media influencers Ra-Ra and Rik had turned up late last night with their first-world problem of flat juice packs and had asked if there was a clean-eating restaurant nearby. The thought of them made her giggle: imagine planning to go off-grid in one breath while asking if they could charge up their phones in another.

'Our followers are expecting an Insta story – you know, a 'this is our final contact with the outside world for two days' update, namaste hands emoji, hashtag free yourself,' Ra-Ra had cried.

She'd told them they were in luck: she could put them up, plug them in and give them some *cawl* made with veggies so fresh they'd taste the fox poo.

Lew would find that funny, she thought. She'd tried to find him to apologise this week but wherever she went she'd just missed him. With a couple of hours spare now, she set off, determined to do this properly. No wailing, no throwing herself at his mercy, just a sincere apology, a thank you for his help and hopefully that would start the process of crossing the chasm between them. Just as Annie and she had resolved things, so they would too, surely? Because their bond was even deeper.

Turning right out of the campsite, she went up the lane and as it curved she got her first glimpse of The Bunkhouse, set against a bright blue sky. The tumble-down crumbling stone walls had been restored, the roof was shiny with slate and a big barn door, thrown wide open, gave it a homely, welcoming look. A few cars were parked up on the bank of grass beside the building and there were two men fiddling with carabiners and ropes and a woman testing a climbing harness. No one had said he'd officially opened; perhaps they were just test-running the place? She peeked inside, impressed at the mix of rustic bare brick and modern steel. A cork board to her left listed sunrise and sunset times, weather forecasts, mountain path routes and emergency details. A sign for 'sleep' pointed up the stairs, another directed 'drying room' towards the back. A man and a woman were sat at a huge canteen-style table in the kitchen area.

'Hi! Is Lew around, do you know?' she called out.

'On an abseiling recce. Can I help?' the woman said in a burr she didn't recognise.

'Know whereabouts?' Wanda asked.

'Up the mountain.'

Well, of course he would be. Wanda hadn't been up there since before the fire and it was the last place she wanted to go. Excuses tapped her on the shoulder: she was in the wrong shoes and what if the weather suddenly turned. But she had to do this. It was part of her rehabilitation. She eyed up the hillside, her guts in knots, and reminded herself it had been where she'd spent happy times with Lew, hanging out, sharing cans, lying flat on their backs at the top, watching the clouds scud along seemingly almost within their fingertips' reach.

It was a hard trail, especially if he was where she thought he'd be – in a small cave to the right of the slope which overlooked the lake. That was the only place where you could abseil from. She weighed it up: it would take half an hour to get there. If not now, when? *Just do it,* she said to herself; get it over with – think of the view, think of him. So she took the shrubby line which led to a stile, went through the woodland, and began the ascent, wishing she'd brought some water. She knew to take her fleece off in the bowl of hill which was protected from the breeze and to put it back on when she climbed the stones which took her onto a ridge that would lead her to Lew. Past the landmarks they'd given names, like Frog Rock, and White Water Point where the stream bubbled up. Meanwhile, the old mental battle of the climb returned: thoughts of *this is too hard, turn back* versus the quiet, the red kites at eye level and the sudden drop of land which gave a view down to the campsite. It really was an incredible sight, an ocean of beige and green undulations stretching out for miles without a sign of civilisation. She stopped a few times to catch her breath and, on each occasion, she was more blown away by the size of the sky, which became vaster the higher she went. Finally, she saw a figure by the cave, deep in concentration as he flew a buzzing spider-shaped drone in to land.

Wanda went slowly closer until he registered she was there and her heart leapt as their eyes met. It was more than nerves, it was something awakening deep inside her, an energy only he could generate.

'Hey,' she said through strands of hair dancing in the wind as she reached him.

He sat back on a rock, watching her with eyes the colour of soft spring ferns in the sunshine, fitting in as if he was part of the landscape.

'Hi,' he said, his face neutral, giving her room to speak.

'I've come to say sorry for blowing my top the other night.' Despite her inner tremble, her voice was calm and clear.

He nodded a few times.

'I was out of order. I should never have gone off on one at Annie or you. Things have been hard, but that's not an acceptable reason to—'

'It's done. Don't beat yourself up about it.'

Lew turned his face to the view. And Wanda shifted uncertainly on her feet. Was that it? Was that all he was going to say? All that he was going to give her? Realistically, what else could she expect. But emotionally, it fell way short, considering their history.

He'd drawn a close to this moment, she could tell, but there was still another matter to bring up.

'Lew,' she said, feeling ridiculous, but no one else had claimed it as their own work, 'about the shepherd's hut … was it you?'

'It was just a lick of paint, no biggie.' He shrugged and then messed up his dark chocolate waves, just like he used to when he was embarrassed.

She gasped – and grasped at it as if it was a piece of straw. As if it had more meaning. As if he was admitting that there was something between them, a kiss that they'd almost shared. 'But why?'

Lew recovered himself and crossed his arms. 'For your dad. For your mam to come home to.'

But not for her. She swallowed back her self-pity. 'Well, it looks amazing. Thank you. Mam is chuffed to bits. When did you do it?'

'Early morning. I don't sleep much,' he said, giving her a small sad smile, which she took as a way in. He fiddled in his pocked and threw her the key to the hut, which she clutched to her heart.

'I suppose you're on call a lot too with the mountain

rescue. Plus The Bunkhouse, lots going on for you … I didn't realise you'd be running it yourself …'

But her invitation to him to open up fell flat.

'When are you leaving then?' he said, and she could hear hope in his voice.

Slightly stung, she said, 'Soon. Once the campsite is earning again. When Mam is well enough to take over.'

'Won't be long.'

It sounded like he couldn't wait. It sounded like he couldn't wait to get rid of her. She kicked at the scrub and decided she should wrap this up. Lew wanted to keep a distance, it was obvious.

'I mean, it all happened quite quickly with The Bunkhouse when everything was in place.'

Wanda was confused – did he want her to stay now? 'Is it open then? There were some people there when I called in.'

'Not properly, they're my mates from Norfolk, they've come up to give it a go, see if I've forgotten anything. So far, they reckon it's all good. Can't be bad, though, when you've got this as your back garden, can it? I mean, Norfolk is amazing for the space, that endless horizon, but you can't beat this.'

'Is that why you came back then?' she ventured.

'Kind of.' He reached down to the brown earth with his fingers to feel the land beneath him. 'It's *hiraeth*, isn't it?'

He actually smiled at her then and it was like clouds parting. *Hiraeth*, the word people used up and down Wales to describe a sort of homesickness, a yearning and a love for the nation.

'I dunno, I've never been away, have I?' she said, daring

for the first time to relax. 'So what's with the drone then?'

'I'm taking aerial footage for the website. Little videos here and there, to show it all off.' He looked excited, like a kid, especially with those freckles, which would be running riot on his cheeks by September, just popping now.

'Very modern! It's a bit ironic, using the latest technology to lure in the tourists who want a get-away-from-it-all holiday. I had a pair of them last night. Two London types, double-barrelled, they were, rocked up because their off-grid retreat had been cancelled after the wifi went down.'

He laughed out loud and it made her insides swoop and fly. Emboldened, she went on.

'They came up, asking if anywhere did breakfast. I offered a bit of toast and they actually had a chat right in front of me about whether it was ethical that they ate something made using the mains electricity! I said, "I'll build a fire if you like, toast it like that!", and the bloke, Rik, he said it was a nice gesture but he was also concerned about global warming. So over a dippy egg and toast, they gave me a lecture about the benefits of living wild, being self-sufficient and connecting to the land, and there they were, sat on their arses eating food cooked for them and bought from Blod's Shop!'

'Brilliant! We used to get a few like that coming to survival days, absolute tools! Mind you, they were better than the Rambos who wanted to skin rabbits.'

Wanda shuddered. Then she had a lightbulb moment. 'There's a whole untapped market out there for quirky camping! That's what we could do! It's not "huge frame orange seventies' tents" anymore, is it? It's become a "thing", that idea of stripping life back, away from the screens and stresses of twenty-first-century living.'

Lew studied her through those thick lashes which she used to say were nicked from next door's herd of cows and she felt hot and shivery.

'You're spot on, I reckon.' He opened his mouth, shut it again, then decided to go for it. 'Look, I don't know if you want to but I'm doing an open house so people can have a tour of The Bunkhouse. Come along if you like? Share your ideas?'

It was a total breakthrough! The horses in her heart were on their hind legs, rearing to go, but she had to pull on the reins.

'Yeah, possibly. I'll have to check,' she said, as casually as she could. 'Wow, coming up here has given me some inspiration! Retro camping with a Welsh vibe! That's what we'll do. We could use the shepherd's hut, put a bed in, stick in a stove ...'

His eyes lit up and she felt the warmth of their glow. The years of uncertainty and waiting, the angry words last week, they'd been worth it to get back to this. It felt like a new start rather than a resolution to the whys and wherefores of fifteen years ago, but that was more than she'd expected. And she wasn't going to let this moment be ruined. She got up to leave on a high, feeling like she'd slayed a couple of dragons.

'Sounds great!' Lew said. 'Won't take much to get it going.'

Wanda grinned and waved goodbye. The mountain had looked after her! Lew was back in her life. She began her descent, taking care not to rush. But Lew wasn't done.

131

'The sooner you get the campsite finished, Wanda,' he called to her, 'the sooner you can go.'

Her foot slipped on some loose stones but her stomach had lurched before that. It was the second time he'd mentioned her leaving. Despite what she'd hoped, despite what she'd felt in her bones, he was making it quite clear how he felt: he'd be civil, but that was all.

13

The open evening had been one long 'ooh' and 'aah' as Lew showed people round The Bunkhouse.

Gobaith had turned up in its droves to have a nosey, opening cupboards to admire matching cups and plates and, once they'd necked enough prosecco, trying out the beds.

The stragglers gone, a few remained and Lew had invited them to stay for food. Annie was among them and feeling part of the gang. She'd arrived with a hand-picked bunch of wildflowers, she hadn't the cash spare for a fancy bouquet, but Lew had made her feel important by placing them centre stage on the long wooden table.

A wolf whistle made everyone turn when Lew appeared in an apron which made him look stark naked and otherwise engaged with a sheep.

'New girlfriend?' Annie asked him.

'Leaving do from the Norfolk lot.' He rolled his eyes at the cliché. 'But don't worry, I gave as good as I got with them, plenty of jokes about Alan Partridge and Bernard Matthews!'

'Please tell me that delicious smell isn't in fact Turkey Twizzlers?'

Lew guffawed with a 'Wait and see!' and again he'd

made her feel extra special. In fact, the rest did too, especially Spike, who had given Annie a big *cwtch* when he'd arrived. Did this mean he wasn't judging her after hearing about her past outside the community hall? Or maybe he was sticking by her because he didn't know anyone else. She didn't care – he was a breath of fresh air, as well as smelling like it. She knew only too well that after a day of sweating, grafters went overboard on the soap. Arthur was here too but was attached to his phone, earbuds in, blocking out the world. Annie could hardly believe she was here and included in the bosom of this beautiful stone building which embraced the very best of the village. Blod was gassing on with Pastor Pete while Sara from the gift shop was deep in conversation with Bowen, the education guy from the fire service. Best of all, Wanda was here, chatting away to Alis from Coffee on the Corner and Carys. Annie didn't know exactly what had happened between Wanda and Lew, only that they'd had a chat. Lew said he was doing it for everyone's benefit, he didn't want an atmosphere but Annie wondered if there was more to it. She'd caught him watching Wanda every now and again; then there was his revamp of the shepherd's hut – surely an old affection remained? But he insisted he just wanted the best for Gobaith, starting with The Bunkhouse.

The last time Annie had been here, it was still concrete and brick. Now it was fresh but cosy, with white-painted walls, low lighting, proper furniture and books on newly assembled shelves. A speaker was playing something folky and the air was thick with smiling, wine and beer while Lew cracked on in the kitchen area.

Annie went to the window and admired a sunset that

was throwing purples and reds above the mountain.

'It's not so bad here, is it?' Wanda said, joining her. 'You look hot, by the way.'

'Probably a flush from the wine!' Annie said, feeling her cheeks.

'Hot as in sexy!' Wanda leaned in.

'Oh. Do I?' Compliments may as well have been spoken in Russian, they were that foreign.

'Yes. Look at you!' Wanda said. 'All toned but with soft curves and your hair is amazing.'

'I ... er ... only washed it.' She held out a greying tendril, which sprang back into place when she moved her hand to her palm-leaf-printed tunic. It was a charity shop find and went well over leggings.

'Got your eye on anyone?' Wanda asked.

'No! I wouldn't know what to do.' Flirting was like a strange language too. She'd never got the hang of it, not even with Dean, who'd commandeered the chase and snapped her up before she'd realised it was happening. That had been his way, to engulf her rather than draw her out gently. She thought of Spike again then; he looked gorgeous tonight in a bright white T-shirt and jeans. 'What about you?'

'God no. My relationship history is pretty poor. A few boyfriends here and there, but mostly through work, you know, travel conference flings. I was always convincing myself I would be off any day so what was the point in having a steady thing going on?'

'You've got to live in the here and now though, some-times, haven't you?'

Wanda weighed it up. 'Yes, in life, but with men?'

Annie heard Lew calling her, so she went to him.

'Can you help me dish up?'

''Course. What have we got then?'

'Slow-roasted lamb shanks, braised leeks and potato pancakes. Carys brought some of her bara brith, chocolate chip and mint flavour. And cheese courtesy of Blod.'

'You know I said I'd do your garden, didn't you? I didn't want to bring anything crap.'

'Relax. I know money's tight.'

Money was very tight. The divorce costs on top of the kennel were taking her to the limit. Blod had offered a loan but there was no way she'd do that.

'A hand outside is worth more than a bottle of Lambrusco. Right, let's get these plates on the table!'

The meat was succulent, the leeks oh-so soft, the potato pancakes creamy but crisp and all that remained of the cake and cheese were crumbs. An hour later, everyone was happy, full and content, as well as up to date with everyone's news because they'd switched seats between courses. The headlines were that Bowen was settling in very well in his flat and was very tidy, much to Wanda's relief. Pastor Pete revealed one of his flock had caught a bunch of kids playing with matches at the foot of the mountain. Glanmor had started flamenco lessons and was surprisingly light on his feet. Blod's niece Belmira was coming from Portugal to see her. Best of all, Wanda's mam was in the clear and free to come home on Tuesday. Perhaps it was the booze, the Easter bank holiday or everyone's relief that Wanda and Lew had buried their public hatchet, but the atmosphere was so jolly and Annie hadn't laughed as much in ages. Friends really were the best. Their chattering was cut short when Lew tapped a glass with his spoon.

'So tonight isn't any old Friday night,' he began. He was beaming with joy – it was like seeing the old Lew. And Annie noticed the bags under his eyes had faded.

'No, it isn't! It's Good Friday!' Pastor Pete declared, making a sign of the cross.

'It seems the right time then to say a few words. About looking ahead, making the most of what we've got here in Gobaith. Wanda got me thinking,' he said, his eyes landing on her, which made her blush. Wanda had been her usual animated self while they were eating, her ginger waves dancing as she spoke with her hands, but now she sat quite still and contained, listening to what Lew had to say.

'I'd like to think The Bunkhouse is going to be good for Gobaith. It opens tomorrow properly and we've a group of walkers coming, so I hope they'll be down at your shop, Blod, or might need something from you, Spike; a coffee at yours, Alis; a souvenir from you, Sara.'

'Spiritual enlightenment from me?' Pastor Pete added.

'And that of course!' Lew said. 'Maybe if they have a good time, they might recommend us, drum up some trade for the campsite, too. I know Wanda has plans for that. We're not doing badly, this village, but there's always room to do better. And I've looked into what Wanda said about the mountain – I've had two independent surveyors come here in the week and they both calculated via GPS that it is actually an inch over two thousand feet.'

A murmur of impressed surprise went up – there was hope for Gobaith hill!

'I'm in contact with the Ordnance Survey people and they're going to have a look. It'd mean if it was officially a mountain then we'd have walkers and ramblers coming out of our ears!'

'I better get some mint cake in!' Blod cried.

'The International Dark Sky Association people, too, I've spoken to them; it takes a year or two to get formal designation but it's a start. That too would put us on the map.'

Lew's ideas had everyone agreeing like nodding dogs and it wasn't long before they added ideas of their own. Wanda, too.

'Annie gave me some very useful advice recently,' she said, which made Annie's heart surge at the name-check. 'She said to do all the things I wanted to do when I went travelling but to do them here. To embrace the now. I'd planned to do cooking, volunteering, dancing ... so how about ... Carys, you could do freshly baked bara brith for the campsite every morning. That's sort of cooking!'

Carys clapped and said yes straight away.

'We could have a disco, maybe, in the summer, at the hall, a fundraiser for the fire service? That'd be the dancing bit.'

'I can do the playlist!' Pastor Pete said. 'I love my dance classics!'

'Stick some Abba on there for me, please!' Blod put her hands together in prayer.

Annie suddenly found herself joining in. 'And the volunteering bit, I could do a gardening club for kids, you know, grow fruit and veg and ... make herb pizza pots with basil and oregano ... We can do seasonal stuff like grow pumpkins for Halloween ... sell our produce ... the time is right to do it, the last frost won't be long ...'

Doubt toppled in as she spoke – she was getting

carried away. Since when had anyone thought she'd had anything to contribute? But she was proved wrong.

'Yes! You can have a patch on the campsite!' Wanda said.

'You can have all my coffee grounds for the compost!' Alis offered.

'I'll help!' Spike said instantly. 'You'll come, won't you, Arthur?'

Arthur glanced up from his screen with scorn. She needed something to draw him out of himself. What did children go for these days? She had nothing else to offer but Teg – but canine therapy was brilliant for lost souls.

'I'll throw my dog in if that makes a difference?' she said.

He burst into a smile. 'I love dogs.' Then his expression darkened. 'Dad said we could get one, one day. Like that'll ever happen.'

'We will. I just need to get us settled 'ere first. How about the gardenin' club, then?'

'I'll go if I have to,' Arthur said, heavily, but Annie knew she was onto something.

There was one last contribution. But it wasn't a light-hearted suggestion. Bowen suggested someone went into the primary and secondary schools with him to talk about the danger of fire.

'I'd do it, but it'd look like a sermon,' Pastor Pete said. 'It's got to be someone the kids will look up to. It's mostly boys doing it too, perhaps someone … like you, Lew?'

Quickly, Lew ruled himself out. 'No, no. Not my area of expertise.'

He got up and threw himself into clearing the table.

139

Annie understood both sides of it: Bowen didn't know the weight his words had carried and Lew had drawn a line on the past.

The matter was dropped, the music was turned up and Blod boogied with Pastor Pete. But it wasn't long before big yawns broke out. Spike was the first to announce he had to leave to get Arthur home for bed. Annie found herself hungry for a hug – what was she like after a few glasses of wine! But she was disappointed when Arthur dragged his dad to the door. She consoled herself with a tentative plan to possibly ask Spike out for coffee to discuss the gardening club. He wasn't going anywhere … or was he? Because Wanda had sprung to her feet and had gone to him, holding out an overflowing bag.

'Before you go, Spike! Some throws, cushions, a few frames, charity stuff mainly, but some new things too. For your house. To make it a bit more *cwtchy*.'

Annie felt ever so small then: there she was getting excited about spending time with Spike in the garden and really, it was insignificant in the scheme of things. It was pure self-pity, but she wondered if Wanda had her eyes on him, having heard Annie's advice to live in the now. *And oh!* He was hugging her in thanks. Straight away, Annie got a grip of herself. With no home of her own, without Teg and flying solo after years of marriage, she was vulnerable. She had fought so hard to be free. She had to put it into perspective. Her priority was to learn to love herself before she was ready to reach out to anyone else.

14

We used to come here as kids way back when and my
brother, sister and I decided to bring our children for the
Easter weekend. It was quieter than we remembered but
then we made enough noise to make up for it. Wanda,
who recognised us from years ago would you believe, put
on an egg hunt. A lovely touch.

The Morris, Steel and Hill families. From all over!
Campsite Visitors' Book

'Welcome home!'
Carys pulled a party popper in the hall as
Mam arrived with Wanda in tow with her bags.

'What are you trying to do? Kill me?' Mam said,
holding her chest as sprays of pastel green, pink and blue
streamers gently landed on her new hairdo. A mobile
hairdresser had given her a textured and highlighted Jane
Fonda look and, with her make-up on, a smart Breton
top and jeans, she seemed determined to come back
fighting. It was as if she'd vowed she wouldn't let her
kids see her near-beaten again. There had been a brief
moment when her mother hesitated before the sliding
hospital doors discharged her back into the land of the

living – it must have been a shock to the system to leave the cocoon of care. But she'd made light work of her crutches to get to the Land Rover, where she'd reversed her backside into the passenger seat with determination, rolling down the window for lungfuls of air, declaring she couldn't wait for her own bed.

'Sorry I didn't come with Wanda to get you, Mam.' Carys led them into the kitchen. 'I was doing this,' she said, pointing out the afternoon tea she'd put together.

'I did phone ahead but the hospital said it didn't have a spare crane to hoist you out the car, Caz,' Wanda said, stroking her sister's blossoming sixteen-week bump. 'I don't mean it, you two, about your mother,' she said reassuringly to it. 'I love her really.'

Carys took Mam's coat while Wanda chucked the keys in the bowl and put the kettle on.

'What have you done with the place?' Mam tutted, surveying her kingdom. 'Where's all my rubbish?'

'Filed away safe.' Although Wanda had also binned a load, too. She hardly dared breathe as she awaited her mother's verdict.

'Well, I think it looks ... perfect!'

Wanda sighed with relief – after all, it was Mam's and Carys's home, while she herself had really only been holding the fort. Pleasure was all over Mam's face. She loved a do – any excuse and she'd put on a buffet, organise games, invite anyone within a radius of Wales to join them. But today was different and they all knew it. Not just a homecoming, but also a change from how things had been and both Wanda and Carys were nervous about what she'd make of it. The sisters had chatted about Wanda's ideas for the campsite and Carys was on board.

But as it was Mam's business, she was the one whose opinion mattered.

'Lovely, just the three of us,' Mam said, pulling her girls in for a group hug. 'Actually, there's five of us. Three generations!'

They stayed with her a while, reunited, Mam's soft cheeks sandwiched between her daughters, until Wanda gasped. 'Mam! Your hips! Are we hurting you?'

'No! I'm a bit wonky, but I'm in no pain. I'll show you my exercises later. Come on, this spread won't eat itself.'

And what a spread! Not just the tiered cake stands loaded with dainty crustless sandwiches of egg and cress and cucumber and shiny beef and horseradish brioches, nor Bread and Butter bakery's finest selection of mini eclairs, fruit tarts and Welsh cakes with sides of jam and cream. Mam's best china was out too and there was a vase of upstanding purple, yellow, red and orange tulips. It was topped off with a tablecloth of Welsh dragons and each of the three chairs had tied gold helium balloons which swayed with joy.

'So what's new?' Mam said, retaining her crown as mother with the pot of Welsh Brew. 'And don't pretend otherwise. The wheel has turned, it looks like, since I was here.'

'You go first, Caz,' Wanda said, because this was more important than anything to do with the campsite.

'I don't know how you feel about going back to the hospital, Mam, seeing as you've just left,' she said, piling her plate high, 'but I've had the date through for my next scan and I wanted you both to come.'

'You try and stop us!' Mam crowed.

'We can find out what they are. They think they

143

know, my last scan two weeks ago gave them an inkling, but this one it'll be confirmed. We can start thinking of names ...' Then Carys's mouth fell open. 'Oh my God, I think I just felt them move. The midwife said it'd be around now! Either that or it'll be a fart.' She stared ahead with her hands frozen.

'It'll be like a popping sensation,' Mam said in a hushed voice. 'I remember you, Carys, you were quite subtle to begin with. Wanda was like a cork going off.'

'There's a surprise!' Wanda laughed.

'I definitely felt something then. And then! Oh my word, it's like they're moshing in there! They must've heard me calling them Rock and Roll.'

Wanda got up and made a beeline for the bump.

'Too early for us to feel them,' Mam said.

Wanda felt a little sadness that she had no common ground in this situation. She'd never been anywhere near thinking about babies.

'But soon they'll be like a couple of fly-halves in there. Kicking away! You'll be thinking they'll be born wearing rugby boots. And boxing gloves, too!'

Her expression, her dramatics, made Wanda smile, though. In a moment of self-awareness, she realised this was where she got it from. And there she'd been thinking that Carys and Mam were the peas in a pod – homebirds with the same heart-shaped face and brown eyes. The family script had decreed Wanda was like Dad, with their baby blues, red hair and travelling tendencies. It was a bit of a revelation: maybe that was why she had been able to throw herself into the campsite revamp? Was she, dare she think it, not in fact a wandering soul at all? That might be the subconscious reason why she had never left;

And if that was the case ... *Dear Lord, no*, she couldn't bear going down that road because if she did, she'd be here for ever.

'Your turn, Wanda!' Mam took a slurp of her tea, announcing it to be heaven-sent, with apologies to Gloria, the hospital tea lady.

'Okay. Right ... So ... what it is ...'

'Hang on, before you say anything,' Mam interrupted, 'I need to get this out of the way. Because what you've done to the site is absolutely smashing. The confusion and so on, the state I let this place get in; I practically left Carys a single mother by not taking Daniel's details.'

'Mam!' Carys cried. 'I should've taken his number! I'm an adult! So silly of me to play it cool with him.'

She waved her daughter's words away. 'I've come to a decision. To let you two make the decisions. Whatever it is you want, I want too. Even if you want to sell up. I owe you both, leaving you to handle such a mess. So go on, Wanda ...'

'I want to make a real go of it here. We both do, me and Carys. I can do the main running of it, Carys can help you and you can do whatever you can manage, Mam. Soon we'll be five and they'll need a home.'

'But what about your travels, Wanda?' Mam said. 'I realise you must've been using your own money to keep this from sinking and you'll get every penny back, I swear. There's some savings, me and your father ring-fenced them off for you girls, but I can get hold of them—'

'Stop! Let's just give this a go. I can travel another time, maybe in a few months, once we know where we are. And, actually, I'm quite enjoying rediscovering Gobaith. I'm seeing it with new eyes.'

She had Annie to thank for that, and then there was Lew, who had kept his distance from her at the open evening but had made her feel welcome. The less said about how handsome he'd been that night and how she'd found herself staring at him over the table the better. Wanda got up to retrieve a plastic file from the clutter-free sideboard.

'I've been working on this,' she said, pulling out three stapled copies of a series of sheets of A4 and handing them out. 'Here are our main problems as you can see in the bullet points. First, identity, no one knows we're even here. Second, communication. And third, we have no unique selling point. So I propose we get ourselves a name, a website and an answerphone. And we look at what we've got that's unique to us, work out who wants it and then market it to them. The figures and trends and pie charts and all that, they're all in my report, you can peruse those at your leisure. I've detailed what I see as solutions to our USP on page two.'

They all turned over.

'This is not prescriptive and it's just a jumble of things, there's no real order to them, but ... We're at the foot of a soon-to-be, fingers crossed, official mountain. We have a lake. We are in one of the darkest, least light-polluted places in the world. We are under a starry sky! There's the shepherd's hut that we could turn into a place to stay; we could get bell tents, a yurt, make a treehouse, stick canoes on the lake, provide barbecue packs with marshmallows and sticks, we could give stargazing tours!'

'This is tremendous!' Mam cried. 'And, goodness, I forgot we had it, but our first caravan is in the barn. It's whatyoucallit ... vintage!'

'Brilliant! We can get one of the farmers to pull it out, we can do it up – Mam, you could sew some curtains while you're resting!'

'I'll sort out the website and answerphone,' Carys volunteered, bravely – if only they'd had one then, Danny might have been there with them now. It was clearly what her sister was thinking and she let out a sob.

'Oh, Caz,' Wanda said. 'Chin up.'

'Chins up, I'm so huge.'

'Look, we'll make sure this place is headline flaming news – it'll be impossible for him not to hear about it.'

Carys nodded and swallowed back her tears. 'Thank God for you two.'

'It's going to be all right, Caz. Mam's home now. I feel really positive, too.'

This felt like an opportunity to write a new version of herself.

It was definitely something to toast.

'Let's have a drink then, girls,' Mam said, raising her tea cup. 'To us! And to new names and new starts!'

15

What in the name of Wales had Annie done?

She had no experience with children, she wasn't a teacher and gardening was a solitary existence. Yet despite her glaring lack of qualifications with young people, here she was about to lead the much-promoted inaugural Grow Up club for the kids of Gobaith.

Remind me never to suggest anything ever again when I've had too much to drink, she thought, as she checked her watch, waiting for someone, anyone, to come along. At least she had Teg with her today. She narrowed her eyes across the campsite and saw her swimming in the lake – it was a sunny day with the gentlest of breezes but it would still be freezing in there. Teg loved the water, though – she especially loved coming out and shaking herself all over Annie, too.

The first Saturday of May had come around quickly. The preparation was behind her – she'd put up posters on street lamps, pinned up details in the community hall, Blod's Shop, Fork Handles and the Post Office and asked the primary and secondary school to give the eight-years-and-above club a plug. She was DBS-checked and Pastor Pete had secured funds to pay for insurance. Gobaith Gardening Centre had very kindly provided sponsorship in the form of a few tools, some compostable pots and lots of packets of seeds. And even though there was no legal requirement, Annie had paid out of her own pocket for a first aid course. If she was going to do this, she had to do it properly – it was a commitment; people had believed in her and it wouldn't do to let this piece of land be disturbed and then abandoned. She saw it as a challenge, not just to herself but to the people, to connect the Hughes family name with something good.

The grassy area was the size of a tennis court and there was a public footpath running alongside it so it would be accessible to all. In bloom, it would be a thing of wonder – a rival for the Hanging Gardens of Babylon, she reckoned. It sat to the right of the camping area, so it had a clear view down to the lake, as if they had their own infinity pool. The soil was good, it was south-west facing and if they worked hard it could be a legacy for the future. *Could be*, she thought, *could be* … Now, though, it was time to reap what she had sown.

Her phone buzzed. *Here we go*, she thought, *this would be the first of many excuses for a no-show.*

'Annie speaking, how can I help?'

There was a rustle on the line and she thought nothing of it until she heard the sound of someone breathing.

'Hello? Is everything okay?'

Still nothing.

'Are you in trouble?'

The breathing became heavier and with shock she suddenly realised it was a dirty call … She almost threw the phone on the floor. Disgusting, what did people get out of that?

She glanced at her watch. Ten a.m. on the dot and

there wasn't a soul to be seen. It was disappointing, but she was used to that. May as well get on with it, then. If anyone did turn up they could plant some seeds into little tubs, make labels and have a dig.

Annie had drawn a skeleton structure of a design: she checked it now and began to peg it out with string and stakes. The top half would be walled, with raised beds for quick-growing vegetables such as tomatoes, courgettes, lettuce and cucumbers. The borders would be full of wildflowers and colour, drama and fun. There would be a table in the middle for potting. The bottom half would have a barbecue of bricks on the left and opposite, in the right corner, would be an L-shaped sofa of pallets. Whatever could be painted would be – the children could choose the shade and there was space on the side middle sections for them to play with. There could be wellington boots of herbs, tyres of ferns, a living teepee of runner beans, crazy paving, stepping-stone circles of wood …

'Annie!'

She looked up with pleasure to see Spike carrying spades and forks, rakes and hoes. He had a huge khaki rucksack on his back as if he was on manoeuvres. Her face broke out into a huge grateful smile.

'Hiya!' she waved like a loon.

'Sorry we're late!' Spike said. 'I say we. Arthur and his mates are keepin' their distance; I'm embarrassin', obviously.'

Oh, you aren't, she thought, then stopped herself right there. She'd given herself a pep talk ahead of this: *enjoy his company but nothing more*, guiltily finding herself admiring his Action Man physique. She concentrated instead on his energy: the humming on his lips as he unpacked three flasks, some bottles of water and what looked like a shopping trolley of snacks.

'We the first, then?' he winked. 'Never mind, all the more for us! Tea, coffee and hot chocolate for the kids. I had to buy this lot to bribe Arthur.'

'Amazing!' All hope wasn't lost after all.

'I think they're in shock,' Spike whispered, 'bein' away from their screens.'

Arthur plus three other boys and a girl were scuffing the ground, their shoulders hunched, staring with tilted heads through defiant fringes.

'Morning!' Annie said, stepping forward to greet them, relaxing into her role with Spike as back-up. 'Great to see you, Arthur!' To the others she said, 'I'm Annie. Who are you then? And how old are you?'

Awkwardness seeped out of their adolescent pores.

'Joe. Thirteen,' the largest grunted in a low broken voice, shoving his hands into the pockets of a far-too-skinny-for-his-size pair of joggers. With spots and mousey greasy hair, puberty had started for him and he was head and shoulders above the others. She couldn't see this one *cwtching* up in the bean teepee.

'Nathan, eleven,' squeaked the smallest, a scrap of a thing, dark but with big blue wary eyes.

'I'm Mali, rhymes with Sally,' the girl said, all attitude, with a crop top, hoop earrings and a high brown ponytail. 'I'm twelve and I'm only here for the sweets.'

'George. I'm twelve.' This one, built like a barn, crossed his arms defensively. 'Mam made me come. I got kicked out of rugby and football. She needs the house on Saturdays to do her beauty salon.'

'And I'm bored out of my brains,' Arthur said to an applause of sniggers, which unsettled Annie.

Interestingly, Spike said nothing and Annie realised it was because this was her show. It was an awakening – and an empowering one. She decided to starve his cheek of oxygen and ignore him.

'You all know each other from school then?'

'Yeah,' Mali said, 'we met in detention.'

This was clearly going to be harder than Annie thought. Nevertheless, she had once been like them: suspicious of everything and everyone, difficult until she felt safe – but with good inside her, given the chance to show it. She launched into the benefits of less screen and more green – gardening connected you with the earth, there was a buzz in growing, harvesting and eating your own, and outdoor activity helped to deal with anxiety and stress. Next, she gave them a tour of the patch, feeling the heat of their resistance like a boiling radiator.

'Any questions?'

'What if we need the loo? Do we get to go commando?' Nathan asked, excited by the prospect.

'Nice try. There's a bathroom block just there.'

'How long is this going to last?' Joe huffed.

'An hour? Two?'

'Jeez.'

'Hang on, so you're saying this is ours then?' Mali said, distrustfully.

'Yes. It belongs to all of us.'

'What, so we can come up here at night and stuff?' She lit up at the prospect.

'Er ... that'd be up to your parents.' Mali rolled her eyes. 'We could do some early-evening sessions in the weeks to come as the nights get longer, perhaps. Cook up some sausages, toast marshmallows. If you'd like that?'

Mali gave a barely discernible nod and to Annie it felt like a victory.

'Two more! Eight o'clock,' Spike said, making fun of his military past.

A boy and a girl were on their way over, walking with confidence.

'Hi, is this the gardening club?' The girl was well spoken and had a graceful air about her.

'It is!' Annie's spirits lifted a fraction as she was seduced by the well-to-do look of them, probably Boden.

'I'm Primrose, I'm thirteen, and this is Benedict, he's my brother and he's eleven.' Both were in Hunter wellies and they didn't come cheap. 'I want to do horticulture when I leave university.'

They were like a different species, these two. Annie knew their parents – they were one of her clients, how lovely of them to support this. But, straight away, a divide opened up between the kids as the first lot sized up the incomers.

'Posh twats,' Arthur said in his best cockney gangster voice. The trouble was, at his age she would've thought exactly the same.

Oh dear. Quick! Do something!

'Everyone's equal here, Arthur,' she said, knowing some kids were more advantaged than others, but she was here to treat everyone the same. 'Right, time's pressing on, so how about we all do some digging. Let's start here,' she pointed at the ground in front of a section of string, 'along the line; planters will go behind, we can build them directly on top of the grass.'

Spike produced his tools and suddenly the prongs of the forks and the blade of the spades seemed hugely dangerous as Arthur's lot chopped divots into the ground. By contrast, Primrose and Benedict used theirs with expert precision. It wasn't long before Arthur was lobbing sods of turf around, culminating in Benedict getting a clump on the side of his head. And Arthur was about to go for him again ...

The little so-and-so. She had to be careful – not because Spike was here, he'd given her his blessing to do the disciplining, but because she knew if she got it wrong, he'd be even more confrontational. *Think: he's behaving like this probably because his dad is here, he's trying to fit in and he wants to be seen as cool.* Give him a bollocking and he'd feed off it as a badge of honour. However, go too soft and he'd think she was a walkover. He didn't know, though, that she was well and truly done with being a doormat. She thought back to what she used to say to Ryan when he played up. It wasn't very mature, but it had always embarrassed him enough to make him stop whatever he was doing.

'Arthur!' Her voice was hard to catch his attention.

He stopped mid-lob.

'Bit of life advice for you,' she said, softer now, but loud enough for everyone to hear. 'Don't be a dick.'

There were a couple of smirks at Arthur's expense, although the kids weren't laughing – they were interested to see how this would pan out.

He sized her up, weighing up what he'd do. She stared him out – she wasn't going to let him win this. Eventually, Arthur dropped the lump of mud by his feet and mumbled something, quite possibly swear words about her, but she didn't care. The tension was gone, but she wasn't done.

'That goes for all of you, by the way, just in case you're tempted.' She addressed every single child and each of them looked taken aback. 'If you don't want to do this, you can go home. If you stay now, you're here for the project and you'll have to put your best into it. Yes, it can be hard work, yes, it can feel monotonous and yes, you will get dirty.'

She paused, marvelling at how she had caught their attention. Worried she was too stern, she gave them a smile. 'But the reward will be creating something as a team that's your own, being proud of something you've done from scratch. If we get it right we can sell our veggies, use the money for more equipment or whatever it is you want – because this is all for you.'

One by one, their little faces softened into sweetness. Apart from Arthur. But she still had one last trick up her sleeve. She gave a piercing whistle, which made him jump. Poor lad looked terrified, but then he understood – and finally he was beaming as Teg bounded up, the pace of her run sending her ears flying and she was so desperate to meet her new friends she skidded on her face and tumbled over in a heap. While she was down there, Annie imagined her thinking she may as well stay on her back, wag her tail and hope someone would rub her belly. A chorus of 'Aaah!' went up.

Arthur raised his eyebrows, asking if he could go to her. Annie nodded and he was like a completely different child, gently approaching, cooing at Teg, asking the eternal question of 'Who's a good girl?'. He went down to his knees and let Teg smell his hand first, then smoothed her tummy, chattering away to her as if they were siblings, continuing way after everyone else had got their dig on. The children had abandoned their two opposing packs and were working as one.

'Nice job,' Spike said, coming over to her, wiping the sweat off his forehead.

'Nothing to do with me,' Annie said. 'I was bad cop, Teg's the good cop.'

Arthur was now in fits of giggles as he tried to navigate a wheelbarrow of turf to the compost area while Teg badgered him for a stroke.

'I'm thinking I can finish off the top section later and make a start on the planters. I've got a load of pallets in the van, so I may as well stick around.'

A little green monster suggested this might be an excuse for him to bump into Wanda.

'What about the shop?' she asked, hating herself for looking for a spoiler.

'I've got a Saturday boy. Good as gold, 'e is. He can ring if it gets busy. Arthur's got a Welsh lesson with Wanda later too … and … well, it'd be good to know what you wanted doing, if you're staying up 'ere? While the weather's decent.'

She was quite thrown. 'Oh … I don't know. I hadn't thought beyond this morning, really.' But she was also touched at his enthusiasm. 'But yes, that'd be great!'

Spike threw a look at Teg, who'd become Arthur's shadow. 'Dogs can't 'elp but spread the love, eh? I'll 'ave to 'ave a cuddle with her myself!'

'I'm afraid Teg's not one for strangers,' she said. Hearing her name, Teg began to trot over.

'We've met! She'll remember me.'

Annie suspected it wouldn't make a jot of difference. On cue, Teg suddenly stopped and, with a cocked paw, she sniffed the air.

'I dunno, she takes ages to warm to someone,' Annie said. 'She's frightened of men.'

'Oh, mate,' he said to Teg, crouching to his knees to appear less of a threat, 'I love dogs. Had 'em when I was small. Scruffbag mongrels.' Then he spoke to Teg. ''Ello, beauty, I won't hurt you.'

'She won't come to you, she's really afraid …'

Annie couldn't finish her sentence because Teg was actually on her way to him, cautiously taking one step here, another there, but not backing away, creeping closer until she had the measure of his scent and decided he wasn't a risk.

'You do remember him! Good girl, Teg!'

'I'm honoured!' Teg was letting him ruffle her ears. 'I wonder what it is about men she doesn't like?'

Because Teg had trusted him, Annie would too. It was as simple as that. She filled Spike in on her violent ex, her impending divorce, the kennels and her need to get her back by her side.

'I'm so sorry, Annie, 'ow can people be cruel to animals? To people, even! It's just …' he puffed his cheeks, '… incompre'ensible. Look, I've got a suggestion, and feel free to say no, but Teg needs a home, my boy needs a dog. Maybe we could help?'

'No! No! I couldn't, thank you so much though, I couldn't impose that on you and I'm not at the point where I'm panicking about it.' She was, but she couldn't accept this offer when Spike was already helping her with the gardening club. *Neither a lender nor borrower be*, that was how she had to live – if you had nothing to give, it was the only way to stay afloat.

'I've got you,' Spike said, sadly, 'but if you ever change your mind ...'

Annie felt herself welling up – this wasn't the place to cry. This was a place which shouldn't be contaminated by her emotional baggage. The strong smell of grass and earth brought her back to where she was: self-sufficient and fine with it. Being dependent on someone was not how she was going to live; she needed to be the one in the driving seat. Teg's situation was down to her to sort out. She was a loner. It was her armour and that determination, that autonomy, had got her away from Dean Pincher. She felt herself switch back to business, regretting saying anything about her old life.

'Snack time!' she shouted as she was immediately sur-rounded by hungry eyes. 'Spike's got the goodies, help yourself. What a difference you've made already! After this, we'll plant a sunflower each, do a bit more work and then it's games time!'

16

*Good luck with all the plans to revamp the site! We hope
the charm of the place isn't lost. Highly recommend
putting an order in of an evening for morning bara brith.
We thoroughly enjoyed eating ours with a flask up the
mountain.*

Dawn and Colin, Nottingham
Campsite Visitors' Book

Wanda wasn't being funny, right, but surely Carys
could've told her she was a bit of a whizz on the
old computer.

'You never asked,' her sister shrugged, her eyes fixed on
her laptop and her tongue poking out in concentration as
she tapped away.

'But since when did you start being so good at it?
Like, I knew you played Angry Birds and all that but we
could've sorted a website ages ago if we'd known.' Wanda
playfully squeezed one of her toes. Sat on the sofa, Carys
had her legs up on Wanda's lap, just like they used to
do as girls when they'd brushed their teeth and got into
their pyjamas for a special Saturday night film, tight like
herrings in salt between Mam and Dad.

'There was no need, was there. I just learned to do it as I went. It's only now that we've decided that we're moving with the times.'

How was she related to this woman? 'Did you not think to do it before it started going tits up?'

'Oh shut up, Alan Sugar. I'm doing it now, aren't I?' Carys glared at her then went cross-eyed to make Wanda laugh. Then she sighed. 'I was a kid back then.'

'It's not like you're ancient!'

'But I was just into my own thing, working here, seeing my friends, saving up for clothes and gigs and holidays.' She had been the baby of the family, that was true. 'You moved out as soon as you could. I liked staying here. And I was company for Mam. She liked making me tea and I liked eating it! And you have to admit, I've grown up a bit. I have to, for these two.'

'Ah, yeah.' Carys had taken out her belly-button piercing, for practical reasons, but she'd also postponed a longed-for Celtic cross tattoo and she'd started knitting tiny hats and mitts. 'And you'll be a fab mam. Think I'll be a good aunty?'

'Deffo!'

'I'll help with night feeds and nappies!'

'So you're staying around for a bit, are you?' Carys asked, her face full of hope, which kind of floored Wanda. Even though she was doing the adult bit, she still needed her big sister and it gave her a lump in her throat.

'I guess I am! Can't miss out on Rock and Roll making their big entrance! I reckon they'll come out screaming, "Good evening, Gobaith!" as if they're stadium rock stars.'

'I'll be the one screaming, I tell you that. I shouldn't

160

watch those birth videos. Terrifying.' Carys shuddered, and then remembered Wanda had a job to do. 'Come on, rub my feet, while I just do this ... and this ... and ... I think it's ready to go.'

Carys pressed a button, paused, then clapped with happiness.

'Here we go ... the website for our new campsite ... I present to you ...'

Wanda sat up to take the screen and at the same time they both cried, 'Under A Starry Sky!' They'd decided against naming the site anything like 'Gobaith Camping' because it would be misleadingly sensible. What they were after was something that would reflect where they were and who they were: remote but friendly, nestled in the wilds but with style. And the page did reflect that. A photo of the newly erected bell tent beside the shimmering silver lake, the soaring black mountain topped by the night sky full of stars. There were a few introductory words summing up the experience campers would have here, a gallery of photos of the facilities, plus some staggering footage of the area from Lew's drone.

'I love it!' Wanda pronounced. 'You've done an awesome job, Caz. It's all *cwtchy* cool.'

'*Cwtchy* cool! Good line! I'll stick that on the home page in a minute.'

There was a knock at the front door. Wanda leapt up. 'Mam, I'll get it!'

'Oh no you won't!' Mam's voice carried through the house – she was still stiff but she was down to a walking stick now and it was a job to get her to rest. By the time Wanda had got there, her mother had beaten her to it.

And there in the kitchen was Lew. Looking boyish,

with a sheen of perspiration on his cheekbones. What was he up to?

'Dilys is ready!' he said to Mam. They'd been waiting on him and his farmer mate to help, but they hadn't said a specific day, just that it'd be done.

His eyes flicked to Wanda and he gave her a little smile.

At The Bunkhouse open evening, they'd barely exchanged any words, he'd kept it professional. Yet that glance felt more intimate than anything they'd shared since he'd been back. As if he was opening the door a crack to her. Perhaps that was just familiarity though, that he had grown used to the idea of her being here for a while? Anyway, there was no time to dwell further on it because Mam was waggling her stick in excitement and so they went out to inspect the new addition to the family.

All three of them gasped in admiration when they saw her. Dilys translated from Welsh to English as *perfect* – and she was! Mam and Dad's vintage caravan, a two-tone 1970s classic of white and mint green with curved groovy edges, was in position, cosied up against a private bit of hedge.

'It looks like it's meant to be there!' Mam held her chest. 'Oh, thank you, Lewis! Again!' She'd been thrilled with what he'd done with the shepherd's hut.

'No problem! It took a while to get it to just-so.' The farmer's tractor was chuntering its way off the campsite now. 'But it's level, and I gave it a clean, so it's over to you now, ladies.'

Mam was in raptures and refused any help when she got to the door, the keys jangling in her trembling hands as she unlocked it, opened up and climbed the little steps.

'It's a time capsule!' she said, poking her head back out, then in again. Wanda pushed Carys up into the caravan and then joined her. It was a marvel! A homage to the seventies and eighties. It smelled musty, yes, but a good airing would sort that. The interior was pristine with its orange-and-white striped padded seating and matching tie-back curtains. Beige blinds sat above the plastic windows. A formica table sat between the sofas and the kitchen area was so cute with its little sink, stove and overhead open cupboards which still held crockery – matching mugs and plates with brown flowers, they'd set retro-lovers' hearts beating. It was like walking back into their childhood. So many trips ... only ever if it was quiet on the campsite in autumn and winter, but if they could get away to West Wales for a weekend, they would, their parents sleeping on the seats and Carys and Wanda on the floor below, bedded down on quilts and rugs.

Immediately the tears rolled down all three of their faces. For in here was Dad, and bits of their past they'd thought had been lost forever. The fire had destroyed every bit of their lives until that point. But this was like being with him again. Mam was opening cupboards and holding up his whisky tumblers, rustling around in drawers and finding one of his jumpers. Wanda remembered that yellow knit with diamonds. There were teabags too, an unopened bottle of Heinz tomato ketchup and a Gold Blend jar of solidified coffee. Books on the shelves – Delia Smith's *Complete Cookery Course*, three Stephen Kings, *Cosmos* by Carl Sagan, Madhur Jaffrey's *Invitation to Indian Cooking*, a few Roald Dahls, *The Color Purple* by Alice Walker – and Mam's old magazines in the rack with Princess Diana on the front. There was a box of toys, too. Wanda's headless Sindy in an air stewardess uniform – that's what she'd wanted to be when she grew up. And Carys's freaky battery-operated baby which cried to be fed and changed – like an omen, she said, of what would happen.

'We honeymooned in this!' Mam said, lovingly smoothing the worktop with her hand. 'We went to Abersoch up north. Such happy memories! In fact, you were conceived in here, Wanda!'

'Eurgh! Mam! No!' Wanda instantly felt fourteen again as Carys and her bump shook with laughter.

'And you, Carys!'

Now it was Wanda's turn to hoot, until they both realised that meant Wanda would have been asleep in the van at the time of conception.

'Gross!' the sisters chorused until Mam was cackling so hard she had to take a pew.

'This is wonderful,' she said. 'Truly wonderful.'

'We don't need to do much to it,' Carys said. 'New seat covers and curtains.'

'Do we keep it sickly seventies?' Wanda asked. 'Go with an eighties vibe? Or perhaps make it chintzy?'

'Not chintzy. It doesn't have that feel to it. Whatever we do, we should give the brown a swerve.'

'Agreed! I reckon a mish-mash of the best of both, then. Against a white backdrop. Go easy with the stripes and psychedelia.'

'Yes!'

'You girls choose, I'll do the sewing,' Mam threw in.

They all smiled at one another, sharing a moment,

buzzing at the project which had brought them together. Then it was time to step back into the present day, since Blod's larger-than-life presence was making itself heard as she talked to Lew outside.

'My God! This is a blast from the past, this van!' Blod said, her scarlet-tasselled earrings and fringed palm-leaf kaftan shaking from her excitement. 'That disco! We should have that as the theme. Blast from the Past!'

'Disco?' Mam asked.

'Oh, I didn't say, Mam,' Wanda said, gently, 'I didn't think you'd be up for it with your hips.'

'I beg your pardon! Everything Tom Jones knows about hips, I taught him! Come on, Blod, come and tell me all about it over a cuppa.'

'Oh good, for one minute when I turned up and no one was in, I thought you'd forgotten. It was in my diary, *Thursday, Lyn, three o'clock*,' Blod said, hooking her arm through Mam's, whose earlier vigour had taken its toll, on their way to the farmhouse. 'Then I saw Lew. Can't be long though, my niece Belmira has arrived. She's not staying with me, she's in a B and B up the road, didn't want to put Annie out, but I suspect she didn't fancy the sofa! So how are you, my love?'

Carys was making noises about following them too. 'I better go and check the ... uh ... bookings, see if anything's come in online.' She looked shifty – what she meant was that she was going to see if the new answerphone had any messages. From Danny. *The poor lamb*. Wanda had caught her virtually sitting on the machine this morning. How helpless she must feel. To be carrying his babies when he didn't even know. To be unable to gauge his reaction if he ever did return.

'Still a no to doing a story for the papers in Manchester?' Wanda asked.

'Yes, it's a no. I don't think I want to appear as the Welsh tart who dropped her drawers, got up the duff and has no idea where the dad is. You and me, we got this, yeah?'

It made Wanda's heart ache that she was included in the 'we'; it shouldn't be her, it should be Carys and that bloke. What an idiot he was for not getting in touch. Even if it was to say 'sorry, but ...' Then again, holiday romances and one-night stands happened. It was just a pity that he wasn't the decent bloke they'd thought he was. He'd been so keen. It just went to show people could fool you ...

That left Wanda and Lew alone and she braced herself for him to make his excuses and leave. But he kind of hovered around her and gave her another smile, even though it looked awkward.

'No campers tonight?' he asked, scratching his dark stubble, adding a mumble about needing a shave.

'Nope. A nice couple from Nottingham the other day. But ...'

'None coming later?' He ruffled his mop of curls and murmured about a shower, too.

'Nope.' Not until Saturday morning and that was just three tents for the night. 'Bunkhouse full?'

'Yep,' he said, looking guilty, finally stopping his physical inventory of what needed attending to. He looked fine to her – more than fine. 'Sorry.'

'I'm happy for you!' she said, happy too that he'd actually started a conversation with her. The crack of the door felt wider now. 'You've busted your gut, you deserve it.'

'Cheers. It'll pick up for you, you know.'

'I hope so.'

'It will! Just look at what you've got!' Lew said, spreading his arms, opening up his chest, which Wanda couldn't help but admire.

She did as he'd suggested. He was right: she couldn't expect immediate results.

Beside them was the caravan, which would be a real attraction once it was done. Beyond was the shepherd's hut.

'I'll help with that,' he said. 'Rip up and refurbish with white tongue-and-groove cladded walls ...'

'... distressed grey laminate flooring. Get a double bed, a junk-shop two-seater sofa, in velvet maybe, some Welsh tapestry throws, cushions and sheepskin rugs ...'

'... a metal bowl for a sink and a kettle on the stove. Nice and rustic.'

'Simple but gorgeous for it.'

Wanda felt a shot of embarrassment at this exchange: the wavelength they'd once shared seemed to be still there. Quickly she pointed at the latest attraction – the white circus-style bell tent. It wasn't offering luxury: just a decked floor, a double mattress, two singles, real pillows, duvets, deckchairs and some fairy lights were as posh as it got. But what it did have was a prime view of the lake – Wanda had experienced it for herself, sitting inside on her crossed legs with a morning cup of tea and an evening glass of wine, looking out through the swagged porch, the sunrise and sunsets framed picture-perfect. That was why people would come. For the crisp sweet air and the easel of sky. Wanda had canoes and a yurt on order, an appointment with a carpenter to quote her a price for a treehouse and she was thinking about putting a tent out on a fixed raft on the lake. That would be an incredible way to experience the beauty of the landscape.

It was like a little community of quirkiness, all under a starry sky.

'I need to get a load of shots in the bag so I can drip-feed them on Instagram,' she said, taking out her phone and crouching low to see if she could fit the bell tent, the lake and the mountain in the image. Yes, she could! The tent was bleached by the sun, the water reflected the sky; wild bluebells and soaring hillsides made it look heaven-sent.

'Have you had a sleep-out in it yet?'

Wanda was listening as she created a new account for @UnderAStarrySky, busy following all of her contacts in the biz who would realise it was her when she signed off this pic with her name.

'Oh ... no! I hadn't even thought about that.'

A few hashtags – *glamping*, *backtonature*, *wakeuptowildWales* – and then a Welsh flag emoji and a 'love, Wanda'...

'We should try it out!'

... *And, share!* Suddenly she heard again what he'd said. 'We' should try it out. There was a just-too-long silence at his slip of the tongue.

'Right!' she said, getting up, feeling a bit too warm, so she tied up her hair to get it off her neck. He was staring at her now and she checked her topknot for any sprigs which could make her look mad but finding none. What was he looking at, then?

'I'd love a night in the bell tent, to wake up to that. A refreshing dip before bacon butties.'

He was in a trance, his eyes were emerald and shining.

'You'd be very welcome,' she said.

'We can have a fire,' he said, rubbing his nose self-consciously. This was taking a bizarre turn – a fire? When he knew how she felt about fires? And again that 'we'… 'A bucket of sand and a watering can for safety.'

'But they're banned!' she said.

'Then you need to un-ban them. You can't have a campsite without campfires.'

She sized him up, searching for judgement, mockery or humour, but his face was soft. What was all this about? He was confusing her with this sudden reaching out to her, even if it was a bit Famous Five.

'Funny how we're here, isn't it? How things have turned out.' He had an intensity to him now and Wanda felt a spike of resistance. He'd changed the pace without warning and she didn't know where she stood. So she stayed silent.

'I'm sorry I've been a bit … distant.' *Distant?* She'd needed binoculars to keep up with him. Now they needed turning around, he was so close. 'I had no idea you'd be here and it threw me. But while we're in Gobaith, we might as well get on.'

She began to thaw but she couldn't resist testing him. 'And I'll be gone soon anyway, so …'

Lew had a long blink. 'Yeah, did I mention that at all?'

Wanda laughed. 'Just a bit.'

He put his hands on his head. 'I was just weirded out. I'm sorry. I meant that you have to go, you know, for you.'

'Don't worry about it,' she said, shrugging. But inside her heart was beating fast.

'Lots to catch up on, the pair of us … fifteen years, eh?'

The mention of fifteen years made her gulp – could they pick things up after so long when the last they'd seen one another was the moment they had almost kissed? Fifteen years ago they'd been teenagers, innocent and trying life out. Now they had been through things, she had no idea what he'd been up to and who he'd become. It all seemed so overwhelming.

'Things have changed,' she said, dropping her eyes.

'And yet here I am. And so are you.'

Wanda dared to look up and found he was appealing to her to go with him on this journey. It couldn't start now, the answers she sought wouldn't be revealed here in a field. But then he was biting his lip, looking pensive.

'Wanda …' he said quietly. There it was again, the attraction, the thing between them, like a rope pulling them towards each other.

Her feet tensed as if they were applying the brakes but still she could feel herself giving in, like it was the most natural thing in the world. What was he about to say?

'Yes …' she almost whispered, feeling ridiculous that something important was coming and here she was in flip-flops, cut-off denim shorts and a faded cerise T-shirt from a freebie trip which declared *What Happens in Benidorm Stays in Benidorm.*

'Wanda! Wanda!' Carys was waving both arms and waddling towards her.

Not now! Come on, Lew! But as her sister came closer, he swallowed and then shook his head.

'It's fine, it was nothing important,' he said.

No! Wanda wanted to throw herself at him, shake him by the shoulders and tell him to spit it out.

'Hang on a sec, Carys!'

'You won't believe this!' she was shouting, ignoring Wanda's request.

'Catch up later, Lew?' Wanda asked, hearing the desperation in her own voice.

'Er ... I can't actually. I'm out tonight.' He put his hands on the back of his neck.

'We've got our first booking off the website!' Carys screamed, launching herself at Wanda. The combined force of one bump and two big boobs almost winded her – so this was what it felt like to be a skittle hit by a trio of bowling balls.

'What?' This was great news! But still a part of Wanda wished Carys could have waited five minutes.

'I know! Come on up and I'll show you!' Carys started to drag Wanda away. And then she realised she was leaving Lew behind. 'I don't know why you're standing like a statue, Lewis Jones,' Carys said, 'Blod says you're on a date, you better get a move on!'

A date? Wanda let herself be pulled along, her head trailing back at Lew, watching him drop his chin and pat his pockets as if he was looking for his phone in a classic delaying tactic which put dead air between them. A torrent of thoughts came at her: *he was going on a date! But he'd only just got back to Gobaith! He hadn't wasted any time, had he?* She was jealous, she realised, and bewildered too because she'd thought they'd had a moment back there: he'd been on the verge of a declaration of some kind ... *or had he?* Her inner drama queen had read too much into it. God, he made her feel so frustrated, in every way possible. That wavelength of theirs was all jumbled up now. Her feet were tripping over themselves as she headed back to the farmhouse. That was life all right, not neat bows and tidy tying up of ends, but knots and fraying edges, laces that came undone and tried to floor you. Unravelled, that's how she felt, because in just a few minutes alone with him she'd discovered she wasn't over him. Those old feelings had bobbed back up, but larger – not merry like little boats in a harbour or sweet like a baby duckling on the water.

Hell, no. They were like floating turds in a flaming bath.

17

There wasn't much better in Annie's book than a glorious weekend weather forecast.

It was as if Mother Nature was smoothing her brow, apologising for the necessaries when it came to watering the Mid Wales department of her kingdom. And so Friday's drizzle was being mopped up by May's late-afternoon sun, heralding wall-to-wall blue skies and rising temperatures for the next two days. She could simply enjoy the outdoors with no work to spoil it. She'd turn off her phone, too – the ominous withheld-number calls were coming daily now and she was certain it was Dean.

Annie locked the van, which was stuffed with bargain-bucket goodies from Gobaith Garden Centre for tomorrow's Grow Up club. The less-than-perfect blooms which everyday folk overlooked just needed some TLC. She had cornflowers, dill and plucky red zinnia seeds in damaged packets which weren't good enough to sit on the shelves. Though the last frost was still a fortnight away, this lot were hardy enough to survive.

The familiar smell of Blod's lavender fabric conditioner greeted Annie as she let herself in. Shirley and Bassey circled her legs, meowing for food, doing a very convincing job of impending starvation. But she heard voices – those cats were just trying it on! Inside, she found Blod on the sofa alongside a jaw-dropping Mediterranean beauty.

'Annie! Meet my niece!'

'I'm Bel, nice to meet you!' The newcomer waved, shaking back a mane of long straight black hair and smiling with big brown eyes, all twenty-something lithe limbs and tiny-waisted, poured into a skinny pair of jeans and heels. Gobaith wasn't going to know what had hit it.

'Hi! How are you?'

'Stuffed!' Belmira laughed, patting her flat stomach. 'My aunty, she seems to think I need a-feeding up! Dinner at the pub last night and lunch out today. Now she's a-trying to give me Welsh cakes.' Her English was a strange mix of Welsh and Portuguese and it was very beguiling.

'How long are you around for? You know, if you want to stay here, I can very happily find somewhere else.' *God knows where.* Even though Blod had insisted Belmira would prefer her own space, Annie felt guilty they weren't under the same roof.

'It's really comfy in the pub, but thank you.' Belmira placed perfectly manicured hands on her chest to show she meant it. 'It's only a week so.'

'I don't think I'd have room for all her things, to be honest, anyway. Bel is a hand model back home.' That made sense. 'Carries all sorts of potions with her to keep them nice.' Blod rolled her eyes, but she was only teasing – pride was written all over her beaming face.

Annie stuffed her mitts in her pockets – her nails were a disgrace. 'What are your plans while you're here?'

Blod answered for her. 'I want to find her a nice Welsh

man, I do. Continue the family line here.' Belmira tutted playfully at her. 'I introduced her to Lew last night.'

Annie raised her eyebrows. *Lew! Wow.* She wondered what he'd made of her.

'Very nice. Charming.'

Blod winked. But Bel wagged a French-manicured tip at her. 'My mother, she'll have your, how do you say, guts for garters, when I tell her you want me here. I live in Lisboa and she already thinks I live in a different country. It's only two hours from her.'

'She can talk! She met your father on holiday and never came back. Deserted me, she did! This is payback. And she never visits. Says it's too cold. It's always me that has to go over there.'

'Worse places to go,' Annie said. 'Right, I'll leave you to it. I need a shower.'

'Post for you there.' Blod winced as she said it.

But Annie refused to take the blow. She had forty-eight mostly uncharted hours ahead of her, starting with a few beers tonight, a curry if she could persuade Lew; Teg tomorrow, gardening club, a walk, maybe a riverside tea room, arrange a roast for Sunday ... Nothing was going to ruin it. Not even the stiff white envelope which had divorce lawyer written all over it. It'd be paperwork, be-cause she'd given him what he wanted. Except it wasn't. And judging by its contents, repulsive and outrageous, it was purposely timed to arrive on a Friday so that she would spend the entire weekend worrying.

That bastard. She'd taken the blame. But it wasn't enough. He wanted more blood. Something switched in her head – he'd gone too far this time.

'What is it, love?' Blod said, getting up.

'Tell you later. I've got to go.'

Annie left and got into her van, revving hard when she took off to find him. She knew exactly where he'd be: at home getting ready for a night on the piss, preloading with cans from the shop next door, slapping on the spicy aftershave that had singed her nose hairs. It had taken her years to work out what that smell meant: it was denial in the main, because what it had spelled was trouble. A row with someone in the pub or an accusation the barman had short-changed him, kebab juice and fags on his breath, Annie hoping he'd fall asleep in the chair be-cause otherwise ... she felt a sour burn rise in her throat. The drive was determined despite her thumping heart. Crunching gears up narrow lanes, flying down the other side, until she came to the streets of her old life, which closed in on her as she got nearer. But this had to be done. It wasn't about her now. It was about something far more important.

Her fury didn't fail her: she pulled up outside the terraced two-up-two-down and noticed how shabby it looked. It hadn't been when she'd lived there – she'd had a reputation to disprove and she'd scrubbed that step clean every week. Now it had bird poo on it, there were fast-food leaflets stuck in the letter box and the curtains were drawn. The brass knocker of number 17 Jackson Street that she had religiously polished was dull with fingerprints and as she rapped it hard she felt tarnished. Belittled. Humiliated. But she had expected as much – she'd told herself on the journey that this is what he wanted her to feel, and it was how he'd got away with it for so long. She refused to be downtrodden any more.

Her heart was in her throat when the door flew open

and Dean Pincher stood there topless in jeans, his ribs exposed like knife blades. How had she allowed him to press them against her? His gunmetal-grey eyes flashed with victory and he tugged on the towel hanging round his neck as if he was a boxer, sending a waft of his stomach-churning scent towards her.

'Oh look!' he growled, sucking on a roll-up stuck to his bottom lip, 'it's the Lady of the Lake!'

The name he had given her long ago, which at first she had thought was mystical and special. Legend had it a farmer fell in love with a lady who emerged from a lake. After three attempts to woo her, she agreed to marry him on the condition she would leave if he struck her three times. But he accidentally tapped her three times and she had to return to the lake, heartbroken. By calling her that now, he was making a case for his innocence – that whatever wrong had been committed, he hadn't meant it maliciously.

'What the hell do you think you're doing?' Annie said in a low, slow voice.

'What?' he said, blowing smoke in her face and chucking the butt onto the pavement.

'Teg. You want custody of her. Are you for real?' Saying it out loud made it sound even more hideous.

'My solicitor says you're incapable of looking after her.' He scratched his groin and gave a leer that went right through Annie. 'Putting the poor dab into kennels.'

'I know what he said! You're out of your mind! You want me to tell my solicitor that you kicked seven bells out of her? Broke her bones? You can't even look after yourself, let alone a dog.'

'I never laid a finger on you,' he said, as if that was all

right then. 'No need for this, Annie …' his eyes darted to her body and his tongue darted out to lick his lips, 'I miss you.'

'Are you insane?' *The absolute gall of him.*

'Nice warm bed here, dog can have the run of the place.'

'It's for sale.'

'Yeah, we're having a right time of it trying to sell, we are. Someone keeps forgetting to flush the bog, the bathroom radiator is dripping through the ceiling and those fussy buggers apparently don't like smoking inside.'

He was disgusting.

'Keep dragging this out and it'll cost us both a fortune.'

'It's worth it, to see you upset about a fucking dog,' he sneered. 'Takes a walk every morning and every afternoon along the same path of the same woods. They've taken the lead off her again now. All it'd take would be a nice juicy steak, "Here, girl!" and she's mine. Court sees dogs as property in a marriage and you know what they say, possession is nine-tenths of the law.'

'You wouldn't dare!'

'Wouldn't I?' He snorted through his nose and rolled gob in his mouth.

'Why are you doing this? Why can't you just let me go?'

'Because,' he said, spitting it out so it landed by her feet, 'I can. Because you overreacted when you left. It was just a little kick. Deserting me.' So this was it: his pride was hurt. There was no mention of love. 'And for what? You look like you've been sleeping rough and you're worse off than when you were with me.'

She remembered she hadn't stopped to shower – she'd

have leaves in her hair. But so what? That was a sign of her independence. He was right about the money, though. Yet she was richer now than she'd ever been.

'Now listen to me, Dean Pincher, you drop this rubbish. You ring your solicitor now. And while you're at it, stop making those silent calls.'

He frowned at that, but then remembered what he was up to.

'Bye, Annie,' he said, giving her a sarcastic wave. 'Unless you, you know, want to ...' He raised his eyebrows lasciviously and she actually had the urge to punch him. Fighting to control her anger, incensed by him, she felt a tremble building up her calves, past her knees, shaking her thighs.

'This isn't over,' she hissed.

'Not until I get that dog, it isn't, no. Unless she has a terrible accident, running across a busy road. Whoops. Ta ta, Teg.'

And then he slammed the door on her, like a slap in the face. She hated him so much. For exploiting her Achilles heel, for trying to take away her best friend, for thinking she would even be tempted to go back to him, for delaying the sale of the house. For frightening her when she thought she could talk him round. And that tremor she had felt before was now in her arms and along her spine and she was gripped by a cold terror. She had to get Teg and she had to get her now. Into the van, *start the engine, seatbelt on*, she gave herself instructions to stop the panic taking her mind, *just get there, get to the kennels. Come on, come on*, she was gripping the steering wheel, shouting at slower drivers, swearing at a tractor, sticking her foot down to overtake and on and on until she screeched to a halt outside The Hound Hotel. Banging on Bonnie's door, calling her name until she had Teg back in her arms.

'She's coming with me,' Annie said, breathless.

'It's a bit sudden, Annie,' Bonnie said, kindly, full of concern. 'Are you sure? Can I help with anything?'

'No, no. Thanks,' she said, crouched with her face in her dog's ear. She felt better already, loved by this innocent creature, giving her everything she had in return. 'I'm sorry I didn't call ahead or come before during opening hours. It's just … complicated.'

'I'll get her bits and bobs, then,' Bonnie said, gathering her lead and bed, plus her favourite squeaky teddy.

'Can I settle up online? I'm kind of in a rush.'

'Of course. Text me tomorrow, I'll give you the bill then.'

'Thank you, Bonnie. Thank you.'

'It's time to take you home,' Annie told Teg, who was trotting beside her as if it was Christmas Day and there was a sausage for her under the tree.

But where was home? Where was she going to take her? Blod's was out of the question. Lew had enough going on with The Bunkhouse and being on call; Wanda too with her mother home. She was alone. Home would have to be wherever she could find it. A crazy idea came to her: that was how desperate she was. She'd make a bed in the van for Teg while she went and played normal with Blod. Then once it was dark and they'd said goodnight, she'd crawl unseen out of the house.

She had a sleeping bag and some blankets – and yes, Dean Pincher, she would sleep rough if she had to.

18

*We're seasoned glampers but nothing has ever compared
to our two nights here – it's not about John Lewis throws
and a wine fridge in your accommodation. It's about
where you wake up. Wanda took us out on a sunset
canoe cruise, served us prosecco from a bottle chilled in
the lake and then as night fell, we tracked the sky with
stargazing maps. I came back to shore a fiancée after my
boyfriend proposed!*

Reformed glamping wankers, Tunbridge Wells
Campsite Visitors' Book

The Williams women had so much mascara running
down their cheeks, they could have passed for an
Alice Cooper tribute band.

During the scan, they'd gone through half a box of
Kleenex between them. Now, as the sonographer wiped
ultrasound gel off the mountain of Carys's stomach, she
invited them to take the rest with them.

'So they're definitely fine, then,' Carys said, hitching
up her maternity jeans.

'Yes.' Trisha the technician smiled with confidence.
She had kept them guessing for ages as she went through

the checks of the organs and placenta, her brow low with concentration. The only sound had been the babies' racing, booming pulses. Then, at last, she had turned the monitor to Carys, Mam and Wanda, announcing a perfect pair of twins. And there they were! Two heads and a tangle of limbs in motion on a black-and-white screen as if they were floating in space.

'And they're definitely ... the sex, that's definite, is it?' Wanda couldn't help herself. This need to make sure of every bit of information they had was so overwhelming – seeing them both had brought it home to her that she was going to become an aunty to two new human beings. Of course, it had been evident there was something growing in there but, you know, it hadn't been real until now.

'As clear as day!'

Carys had jewels of tears in her eyes. 'They're fine!' she said, heaving herself up off the bed.

What a privilege it was to be here! 'Fancy some posh coffees and cake?' Wanda asked, wanting to keep the moment going.

'I think I'd rather go back to ours, I'm scared I'll blurt out what they are if we bump into anyone.' The trio had agreed to keep the boy/girl thing top secret – they wanted to hug it to themselves for as long as possible.

'I know what you mean,' Mam said. 'Mam's the word!' She mimed a zip across her mouth. 'If Blod finds out, then all of Wales will know.'

'Come on, let's go then.' Wanda ushered them out of the hospital, with Carys on one arm and Mam hobbling on the other, and into the Land Rover, apologising to Rock and Roll with every bump of the tarmac. All talk of Danny was off-limits – Carys simply said she believed that what would be would be. Wanda's heart ached that her sister was holding on to the hope that he'd suddenly appear as if by magic, but who was she to pop Carys's balloon? If she wanted to handle it that way, it was her prerogative. Food was a good distraction, too. Carys had a craving for an early tea of egg, chips and baked beans, so once they were back Mam got on it and shooed the sisters outside as if they were children.

'We've done good, Caz,' Wanda said, breathing in the lush grass in the late-afternoon sunshine as they wandered off, finding themselves en route to the gardening club plot.

'We have. The website is getting lots of traffic and we've got bookings coming in for half-term, that's less than two weeks away!'

'Things, dare I say it,' Wanda said, crossing her fingers, 'are looking up. About time, really. Our costs are going up. Those canoes, wetsuits and lifejackets didn't come cheap.'

'But worth it?'

'Definitely. That sunset cruise last night was magic. So romantic.'

Wanda had taken the reformed glamper wankers out for an hour at dusk, showing them the inlets and caves, as birds dipped onto the surface of the water before bats swooped overhead in the twilight. When the stars came out, they all lay back and let themselves sway on the lake as they gasped at the constellations. And it was good thinking tying a bottle of bubbles off the rear of her canoe: they were toasting the night in plastic wine glasses when the man only went and proposed to his girlfriend! It was a beautiful thing: he took the wire off the cork and turned it into a ring and they pulled their canoes together to seal it with a kiss. Wanda left them to it, paddling back to shore because she was approaching gooseberry status, but she was so happy that Under A Starry Sky would always be special to them. And they'd promised to spread the word about the campsite on glamping forums. The hearts on their engagement piccy had come in thick and fast on Instagram – as much as Wanda knew 'likes' weren't something to get too excited about, it was good to feel the love. She wasn't getting any herself, so that'd have to do.

Carys heard her sister sigh. 'You all right?'

'Yeah ...' She didn't want to moan, because Carys had it far worse.

'At least we can be spinster sisters together!' That was the drawback of psychic siblings, they could read your mind.

'We can crochet our own clothes and grow matching moustaches.'

Carys snorted. 'You'll find someone, you know.'

'What if I already have and he's off making wild love to a Portuguese chick?'

'Lew? Still? I had no idea!' she said, her eyes widening.

'I know, I know. I really should be over a teenage crush by now. But when I heard he was off on a date with her I felt so jealous. I still am.'

'It wasn't a proper date, Blod said she'd forced him to show Belmira round.' Bless Carys for backtracking.

'It doesn't matter what it was. The point is it's brought up all the feelings I had for him.'

'It could just be a reaction to seeing him again ...' Carys said gently.

'Yes, a reminder of adolescent infatuation. That's probably it.'

But Wanda had her doubts – because all it had taken for her to find herself weakening in his presence was one conversation. She'd examined it every which way but was no clearer in her mind about what he'd been going to say to her when Carys had interrupted them. It gave her a sense of madness; she hadn't been able to stop thinking about him. Ever. Was that why she'd never been in proper grown-up love? Was he the one? Or was she stuck in some time warp because her life had seemed to stop that night when they'd nearly kissed? For them to have never picked things up again though, that had to mean neither of them was actually bothered. You wouldn't drop someone from your life if you loved them, would you? Yet none of the notches on her bedpost had come close to Lew.

Three months, that's how long her relationships usually lasted. She knew she was guilty of sabotage; it wasn't them dumping her because they didn't like her, it was because she'd lose interest and talk incessantly of leaving – and they had no place in her plans. The most recent, Christos, had lasted nine months. A guy she'd met two years ago at a travel conference, he was Australian and heading home after ten years in London. He was the perfect man – tall, dark, handsome and she didn't have to commit to him. It was weekends only, lots of fun and laughs, but while he'd asked her again and again to visit him and his huge Cypriot family in Sydney, she'd always known she wouldn't.

Coming across Lew again, her heart had latched onto him rather too quickly. It couldn't be real, to feel so much for someone who was in actual fact a stranger. Why he'd come back, no one but Annie knew; she'd kept his confidence, but there was clearly no woman in tow. What had he done for the last fifteen years: had he come home to lick his wounds or was it always his long-term plan to return? Even the silly things she used to know – did he still have three sugars in his coffee? She didn't know him at all. Just look at how he'd knocked up a feast the other night, and he'd been barely capable of making eggs on toast. Wanda didn't know these things because she had never picked up the phone to call him. This had to be a kind of muscle memory of being around him and her fragile ego craved to hear him tell her how he'd thought of her every day and he'd never stopped loving her. But that stuff never happened. And what if he did say it? Maybe that's all she needed to hear and she'd move on. Wanda didn't trust her judgement when it came to matters of the heart.

She was much better when it came to work. That was where she had some control and, looking around her now, she felt so much pride. The camping area was neat, the motorhome hardstanding weeded and the all-natural playground smart with wood chippings. Even better, though, was the Grow Up garden. There were pallets and bags of compost and shingle and piles of earth and stones. Someone had been busy! Huge planters were already in place and there was a long, sturdy homemade wooden workbench too, topped with trays and pots. The borders were showing off gorgeous flowers of all colours – she had no idea what they were but they looked so bright, she felt a rush of optimism. After just two Saturday sessions, it was a credit to Annie and Spike.

'Isn't it fab?' Wanda said as she took out her phone to take some snaps.

'I'll use those,' Carys said, 'put them on our Facebook page, it'll show we've got a caring-sharing side to us.'

'Genius!' Wanda said, closing in on pink petals with the lake in the background. The click of the shutter set her mind racing. 'Tell you what else we can do ... get some hammocks to hang between the trees ... make a jumbo Jenga set from offcuts of wood for the play area ... put some solar-power storm lamps on the branches as night lights ... and,' she said, thinking of her sister's courage in the face of single motherhood, 'how would you feel if we got some fire pits too?'

The squeeze from Carys's hand told her all she needed to know – these sisters could and would do it, not just for themselves but for each other.

19

Annie had always been good at pretending, but a week in a sleeping bag on a hard floor was pushing her to her limits.

So tired, so achey, she was operating on her reserves and they were fast depleting. Asking for help wasn't who she was – instead, she was ruled by the shame of her situation. She had got herself into it, only she could get herself out of it.

But it was hard when you had only three or four hours' sleep each night. Her hot water bottle was Teg, who would begin the night curling up in the crook of her knees, then she'd wake up to find her the length of her body as if she was trying to stop the cold of pre-dawn seeping into her mistress's bones. Then the birds would start and the sun would rise and she would have to go back to Blod's, creeping in to shower and eat breakfast. Blod hadn't noticed – she'd been immersed in Belmira's visit. Yesterday had been her last night, though: Wanda had gone to the pub with them, plus Lew, who had been seated beside Belmira and hadn't complained. Was there anything between the two of them? Annie saw two people who were easy in each other's company and the occasional touching of arms, but she didn't know what to make of that when she was struggling to control an out-of-body feeling due to so much broken sleep. Everyone had laughed when she put sugar on her chips instead of salt – it didn't stop her from wolfing them down, though. An empty belly would keep her awake. She'd had to stay until the end, she couldn't slip off and get onto Blod's sofa because she couldn't leave Teg alone in the van. Paranoia had risen in her and made the most of her exhaustion. It'd been gone midnight before Blod had gone upstairs and she'd wondered if she could sneak Teg in, but she'd smell the cats and bark. Annie didn't think Blod would be cross, it was just that she didn't want to go behind her back. Waking up the house followed by an explanation of what Dean was up to would lead to tears and both of them had work in the morning. By the time she'd sneaked into the van and let it roll down the hill without starting the engine, found her secret spot where she couldn't be discovered and made up her bed, she'd lost the best hours already.

On her knees she was now, weeding at Mrs Jenkins's, with Teg snuffling around her, sensing she needed protection. Tidy up, collect more bottles and then she'd take them to the recycling point at the tip. She had a load of grass cuttings to get rid of, too.

Annie took a glug of her dark, strong coffee. Driving was the only time when she felt alert – she had to be, her livelihood depended on it. Even so, the motion of the van made Mrs Jenkins's empties chink as if they were laughing at her. She felt that paranoia again. It took her back to the times when she'd walk with her chin down to avoid people's judging eyes. She summoned up the energy to slam the steering wheel, she'd thought she'd left that behind.

Suddenly a battered white van came out of nowhere behind her and brought her to. *Focus,* she told herself, *there's a blind corner coming up here and then there's your turning. Don't miss it or you'll be unable to turn for miles.* Usually this shortcut was quiet and she would enjoy the peace of that feeling of being alone on the road. Her eyes flicked to the rear-view mirror, as the van seemed to get closer to her. With the next look, it was almost up on her bumper. She gasped at the aggression and then heard herself cry out when she saw that the driver looked like Dean. It was certainly his frame, she could see a close-cropped head looming over his dashboard, but her back window and his windscreen were both dirty. With the sun dappling through the trees, making her eyes squint, it was hard to know if it was really him. She didn't recognise the vehicle but he could be in someone else's, or it could even be nicked. How had he found her? Had he been following her? Had he been following her for weeks and she had no idea? It was just the kind of thing Dean would do, a cunning method of intimidation, out of sight and so easily brushed off on the pretext that he was on a legit journey. Should she pull over and let him past? But no other cars were around and he could block her in – she wouldn't put herself at risk.

'You utter bastard,' she shouted into the mirror, and the van began to flash its lights at her. *What the hell did he want?*

Teg began to whimper as she sensed the air charge with fear.

'Shhh,' she said, taking one hand off the wheel to stroke her ears. But she hadn't been watching properly and she had to swerve to avoid a branch in the road. *Just keep going, just get to your turning* ... Trying to resist the temptation to speed up, she went into third gear, hearing her engine roar, but this old thing didn't have the kick she needed. Counselling herself, she refused to look back at him and kept her eyes straight ahead, sticking to the speed limit, spying the turning on her left, beginning to breathe again when she got closer, applying the brakes with clenched teeth, hoping she wasn't about to get shunted from behind. Her indicator was ticking, calmly, and Annie tried to embrace that calm, because a car was coming out and she had to be in control. Her fingers were white from the pressure of gripping the wheel and her palms were sweaty; one false move and there'd be a pile-up. Exhaling through puffed cheeks, she left the main road and gave a quick glance at the van on her tail. How she wanted to roll down her window and scream at him cutting past her. She should go to the police after this: he'd put her in danger with reckless driving. But, at that second, sunlight streamed through the glass and she couldn't get a proper look at him or the registration number. She had no evidence at all that it was Dean. Perhaps all she had was proof that she was losing her mind.

20

We had a smashing time! If we'd known dogs were allowed, we'd have brought ours!

Mr and Mrs Timpson, Exeter
Campsite Visitors' Book

Wanda's CV was building nicely, she thought as she put her arm round the passenger seat of a guest's car and prepared to reverse their caravan into their pitch.

Toilet cleaner and photographer were already on her list of talents and now she could add marriage guidance counsellor.

The husband and wife were on the verge of divorce when Wanda stepped in with her best 'don't panic' face. It was an actual popcorn moment, with other visitors spectating from their camping chairs as the air got thicker with expletives. This was a family campsite after all, so Wanda had to do something – not that she'd ever manoeuvred a caravan before, but she remembered her dad's advice to similarly spatially challenged campers: *the back of the caravan will always go the opposite way to the back of the car. Go slow and keep an eye on the wing mirrors.* Swinging left, then right, she managed to get it into position on her first attempt, admittedly at a snail's pace, and it was with relief more than pleasure that she accepted their thanks. It was their inaugural outing with their baby, they'd always dreamed of getting away for long weekends with all the home comforts. Wanda had a feeling it'd be a case of 'careful for what you wish for', as they revealed they'd never erected David's awning before.

'Give me a shout if you can't get it up, David!' Wanda said, cheerily, until she'd realised what she'd just said. She scurried off quickly and giggled when she was safely out of earshot. It occurred to her that after only a short time, she was beginning to enjoy herself. She was doing things she'd never done, including laying laminate flooring with Lew in the shepherd's hut. It had felt weird at first being in there together, in the place where they'd been so close as teenagers. But the job had been about making the best of the old, sanding down the wood, and adding in new features, marrying them to make something beautiful again. That was kind of what this whole experience was about: repairing her own damage and coming back stronger than ever.

The visitors' book was always an education, too. It got her to thinking about the latest comment concerning dogs – perhaps they did need to reconsider that; she'd have a word with Carys and Mam and see if they minded. As long as they were well behaved, then why not? Although what dog had the guest been on about? Dusk was falling, so she decided to have a look around before it was dark – no one had arrived with one and surely she'd have noticed if one had been snuck in ...

After a trek round, Wanda found nothing. Perhaps it had just been a local dog in the community garden – that was open to the public, after all. There was nothing of note so she took a few snaps of the sunset. Crouching down, she was trying to fit in tendrils of leaves, the lake and the mountain, but she needed to go back a bit, a bit more and ... she backed into something solid, her feet went from under her and she landed right on top of a lump of something covered in tarpaulin. Curiosity got the better of her and she peeked beneath it, only to find a tent packed away in its bag. There was also a metal bowl and a saucepan. *How odd.* None of it belonged to the campsite. She looked around in confusion – who'd be storing their stuff here? And why? But here came Annie, maybe she'd know. Yet as soon as their eyes met, Wanda understood the sheepish look on Annie's face: it was obviously her tent and saucepan. Teg, bless her, went straight to the bowl, sad to find it empty, betraying the fact it belonged to her and solving the mystery of the dog on site.

Her face crumpled in agony, Annie did away with pleasantries and went straight in with an explanation.

'Oh God, I'm so sorry, Wanda.' Annie was actually shaking. 'I've been so stupid, taking advantage of you behind your back. I'm no better than my name, am I? I'll pay you for being on your land. I just didn't know where else to go.'

Wanda couldn't bear it. She'd been sleeping out here? 'What is it? What's happened?'

'I'm so sorry. I've ruined everything. This, you and me, how will you ever trust me again?'

'Hang on, hang on.' Wanda held Annie's shoulders to still her. 'Explain it to me. I'm not angry. Why aren't you at Blod's?'

It all tumbled out. Her ex wanting custody of Teg, threatening to take the dog; being unable to stay at Blod's, leaving hers as soon as she went to bed, pitching the tent in the dark, grabbing a few hours sleep fully clothed, *cwtched* up for warmth with Teg; making tea on her stove first thing before packing the tent away and sneaking back before Blod was up. Wanda counted her blessings all at once – Annie's whole life had been suffering: this dog of hers was her baby, the one she'd raised when her dickhead of a husband wouldn't let her have kids. And she'd come to this little piece of garden, a place she was pouring her heart into, seeing it as her only sanctuary.

'Why didn't you say anything? I'd have put you up. My God, I can't believe you felt like you had no other options.'

'I cause so much trouble, wherever I go.' Annie was sobbing silently now, as if she'd be a pain to cry out loud.

'You don't! You've never caused any! Not you, never you! You need to let people help.'

'But I can't.'

'Why not?'

'Because … I don't know how to. Nanna and Bampy looked after me lovely, they did, but I was a burden to them; when they were done with raising their daughter, my mam, they had to do it all again with me. I can't be a burden to anyone else.'

'Right, well, tonight, you and Teg, you're coming in with me and we'll work this out. When I think of you out here …'

Wanda took her into the living room, away from Mam and Carys, who, once they'd been briefed, rallied

195

round to make a bed and find a nightie. Teg was offered some ham and cheese, and she sat so very nicely that she convinced everyone that Under A Starry Sky should be immediately dog-friendly. Then, after Wanda had knocked up a quick pasta and Annie had made a phone call to Blod to say she was staying the night, the pair hit the wine to chew over the day.

'Bloody men,' Wanda sighed, kicking back on the sofa.

'Aye, bloody men,' Annie agreed from the armchair with a roll of her eyes. 'I'm off them for life.'

'Good luck with that! Because ...' Wanda hesitated, wondering if she should go there. But damn it, it'd give Annie a boost. '... I think you and Spike could be good together.'

'Spike? No. No way.' Annie shook her head rather too emphatically. 'I thought he was into you!'

'I don't think I'm his type – or Arthur's! Not worldly enough. I don't fancy him anyway, he's lush but ...' He wasn't Lew. Wanda caught a flicker of something like relief on Annie's face. Ha! She knew it! She did like him. But she didn't want to embarrass her so she carried on. 'I don't have a clue about kids. Arthur's quite the education when it comes to our Welsh lessons, he keeps looking up rude words in the dictionary. I'll have to practise motherhood on the twins. That'll be as close as I ever get.'

'Yeah, well, I've given up on kids myself.'

Wanda felt an idiot for bringing that up. But hang on ... 'You're only forty. Women have them much later than that.'

Annie shook her head far more convincingly now. 'You have to meet someone first, get to know them, prove you're not just after impregnation and that can take years.'

'God, the age-old biological clock thing.'

'I know. But at least I've got my Teg.' Teg heard her name and sat her chin on Annie's knees for a bit of spoiling. 'What about you then, Wanda?'

'Oh well, you know ...' She shifted in her chair and tried to ignore the quickening inside her when she automatically thought of a certain someone. 'I've got commitment problems, I think.'

Annie stared into her glass for a moment, then looked up at her as she fought to control a lazy smile.

'What?' Wanda said, not liking this at all.

'I wouldn't say that.' Annie gave her a knowing look. 'I'd say you're very loyal and in for the long haul.'

'Or stupid and delusional.'

'Lewis Jones, eh?'

'What about him?' Wanda failed spectacularly to keep a straight face. This was ridiculous! Just his name made her go all funny. But then she remembered where she was at with him and her face fell. 'We're only just friends again. And he's currently lined up to become Blod's nephew-in-law.'

'Don't assume anything.'

'Right, so he's said something to you about me, has he?' She said it knowing the answer would be a 'no' – but that didn't stop a tiny bud of hope that he had.

Annie see-sawed her head on her shoulders.

'No, I didn't think so.'

'But he's different around you than he is round me.'

'But that's because of Ryan.' It felt weird saying his name and realising she didn't feel that old hatred.

'That's true, we are like brother and sister. But still ... he wouldn't have helped you if he didn't feel something.'

197

'He's helping because he wants me to go travelling! To leave! He said so himself. Several times.'

'Maybe that's because he can't be around you if he can't be friends with you. Maybe he thinks you wouldn't take a chance on him.'

'That's quite a stretch, Annie. And I'm not sure it'd do me any good to hold on to that. Maybe it's best I fantasise about hooking up with my Spanish tutor or tango teacher. Or both.'

Wanda and Annie shared a tipsy cackle.

'Anyway, what about the love of your life? What are you going to do with Teg? The offer of having her here stands.'

'I know and I appreciate it, but I've had a think and there's someone who might need her more than I do. I'll sleep on it.'

'In a lush comfy warm bed!' Wanda said, holding up her glass.

'All thanks to you,' Annie replied, raising hers Wanda's way. 'It means everything to me to have you as my friend again.'

'Same here,' Wanda said, really meaning it. 'You've made me see my world through new eyes and that's been a gift to get me through it. You've dug me out of a massive hole, Annie, and it's about bloody time you had some help back.'

21

The glow of the best sleep Annie had had for ages lasted all day.

Waking up in a proper bed with rosy cheeks instead of in a tent damp with dew had revived her spirits. Teg's too, judging by her enthusiasm on her gardening rounds today – she'd detached herself from Annie's side to roll outstretched belly-up onto her half of the duvet this morning because she was so cosy.

It wasn't just the physical comfort though – it was the warmth of Wanda's care: of picking Annie up, feeding her and welcoming her into her inner sanctum. Accepting help hadn't been humiliating or degrading, she'd discovered. Neither had it meant relinquishing control. It had been meaningful for Wanda herself to step in, giving her a chance to pay back Annie's efforts. And that gave the two friends an even deeper connection.

She'd carried it with her on today's jobs: during the hedge-cutting at the high school, where she spied through a classroom window Arthur sat right under the teacher's nose; and later during the weeding and trimming for her divorce lawyer, who'd scoffed at Dean's brinkmanship and reassured her a judge would laugh his claim on Teg out of court. It was a profound revelation: accepting help was a strength, not a weakness, because she was no longer an island, there were bridges she could cross. When she'd wondered last night who could have Teg until she had her own place, her gut had suggested one person. That suggestion, after all the hours of thinking, had now become a no-brainer.

So here she was at their door, uninvited, which was a challenge in itself. Annie had quickly learned as a kid that turning up unannounced didn't inspire 'well, this is a nice surprise!' but a 'what do you want?' Yet she had a reason: to ask for help here would also enable her to help somebody else. She hoped they'd see it as she did – as a win-win situation.

As she knocked, she noticed the wreck of the semi next door – it had the most beautiful waterfall of lilac wisteria over the porch. A classic sign that it was mid-May, it needed to be cut back, but she could imagine it re-sembling a draped stage curtain, a subtle introduction to what could be a lovely little cottage. Someone would spot the potential behind its cracked single-pane windows and sprawling ivy, the lucky so-and-sos ...

'Hey! This is a nice surprise!'

Annie was gobsmacked at the reception and almost forgot her lines as happiness threatened to burst out into laughter. But she squashed it down just in time – put-ting her index finger to her lips, she gave a 'shush' and beckoned 'follow me' to her van. Once she'd outlined her plan, she waited for the verdict. And it was a heart-bursting: 'You better bring Teg in, then!'

In the hall, Annie was given permission to unveil the surprise – with a nod directing her to the left, she crept into the lounge and let her baby go to her new master.

'Teg! Hello! What's this label on your collar? *Please look after this dog … until she can live with her Mam again.*' Arthur's face was a picture! 'Teg! You're mine!'

'Just until Annie gets a place of 'er own,' Spike reminded him, but then he too was down on his knees with his son and cuddling the new addition to their family.

'What d'you say—' Spike began, but Arthur was already grinning up at Annie, shouting '*Diolch!*', which was thank you in Welsh, and which had to mean he was settling.

'So here's her bag: she gets a dental chew in the morning, a crust of toast if she's lucky; ideally she'll need a walk first thing but don't worry if you can't, just throw her a ball in the garden. I'll be along to get her if I can take her to work, then after school you'll need to take her out, give her her tea about six p.m. and then she'll flop out after that.'

'Can she sleep with me, Dad? Can she? Please!'

''Course! If it means you stop creepin' in to me in the night and wakin' me up with your snorin'!'

Bless that little boy – he needed so much love and so much comfort. Spike had leapt at the opportunity: it would never fill the gap Arthur's mother had left, but Teg would give him some company – and get him off that bloody screen! It wasn't only that; Annie had mentioned how dogs were an outlet – a way to express love easily when it was hard to do it to a person. Spike understood that; it was like having a fire burning in the home, a focus that pulled you in and warmed you right through. Teg had already unlocked Arthur's heart and they were on the floor wrestling as giggles and barking mingled in a scene of sheer delight.

This was exactly what that boy needed. This was the icing on top of the *cwtchy* space Wanda had created with her cushions and throws and photo frames which had lovely pictures of Arthur and his super-smiley mam, Lucy, arms around each other on a hot beach somewhere. Annie put a hand to her throat at the injustice of Arthur's and Spike's loss, the tragedy that Lucy would never see her son grow up and that Annie's own mother had walked away from her daughter, from all this, from a role that other people would kill to have. Including Annie.

'Stay for tea if you'd like,' Spike said. 'Just a spag bol, but there's some red wine goin'.'

Spag bol was her favourite – it smelled delicious. But was this too much to accept? Would she be outstaying her welcome?

He saw her waver. 'You're stayin'! Five minutes and it'll be ready.'

'You sure?' she asked shyly.

'Yes, don't go now, Teg needs you to bed 'er in.'

How could she refuse!

Over a lush bowl of pasta, all three of them at the table, Spike praised Arthur for sitting up.

'You'd rather have it in front of the telly, wouldn't you?'

'Yeah but this is ... all right,' Arthur said, giving Annie a smile before glancing down at Teg, who was by his side like a sentry – not least because she was hoping for a titbit.

It was strange, but sat here she felt as if she fitted in amid the colour of the kitchen, with its fridge magnets of holiday destinations – Turkey, Spain and France – holding up mementoes of a younger Arthur's stick-man drawings, a photo of a uniformed Spike holding his baby son and a thumbs-up selfie of Arthur with a trophy. There were schoolbooks on the counter, a couple of spanners on the windowsill and the washing machine was rumbling away. It was just how her home would feel, not messy but a sign of work and life entwined. Wanda didn't fancy him and she'd said Annie and Spike could be good together ... maybe she was right? And yet it felt unfamiliar to Annie to have any such expectations. *Hope for the best but prepare yourself for the worst*, that had always served her well. To have him as a friend would be more than enough; she should stick with that, she decided. How could she think anything more – it would be inappropriate, obscene, to think beyond that ... Lucy was irreplaceable.

'Anything good 'appen at school today?' Spike said, crunching on some garlic bread.

'Nah.' Arthur kept his head down, twirling a huge fork of spaghetti and shovelling it into his mouth.

'I saw you through the window today, I was up at the school doing some hedge-trimming,' Annie said.

He shot her a nervous look mid-munch. She suddenly realised why – being put at the front of the class was something that had happened to her. It was so the teacher could keep an eye on you. She wouldn't say anything. In fact she wished she hadn't mentioned it just now. His barriers had gone back up and she felt responsible. How stupid and clumsy of her. She needed to make it up to him.

'Saw you playing football in the yard after, you're a natural attacking midfielder.'

Arthur rolled his eyes, unconvinced.

Ha! But what Arthur didn't know was that Annie had grown up watching *Match of the Day* with Bampy and she knew a bit. 'You cut the defence open and that goal was pretty good. Reminded me of Maradona against England in the 1986 World Cup. Some say it was the best goal of all time.'

He flicked his eyes up at her from under his fringe. 'Was that the Hand of God goal?'

'No. That one was the first he scored in that game. I'm talking about his second: he won the ball in his half then dribbled it past everyone and went round the keeper.'

He gave her a look of surprised respect. 'Cool! I've seen that on YouTube.'

'I would've been … a bit younger than you are now … we watched it and back then, everyone here in Wales supported whoever was playing England – some still do! But it's just harmless rivalry. I remember my grandfather shot up out of his chair and shouted his head off! He called Diego *Dai-ego*; Dai's the shorthand for David here.'

'It's like Arsenal against Spurs! We're Spurs, aren't we, Dad?' The excitement lifted his defences, revealing the sweet little boy he really was.

'Oh yes! Come on you Spurs!' boomed Spike. 'You should join the school team, mate.'

'Maybe. Trouble is, they go in for me on the tackles. They don't like me.'

'Because you're good, son. If you were in the squad, they'd love you.'

Arthur was rolling his trouser leg up, but even as he did so, Annie wondered if he might understand that there was a way he could make friends of them.

'Look at this bruise! This is what they do to me!'

Ouch. Annie winced at the angry purple and green bang on his shin bone.

'Got any vinegar?' she asked.

'You a zombie? You want to eat my leg?' Arthur joked as his father went to the cupboard.

'No!' she laughed. 'Kitchen roll?'

Spike handed her the Sarson's with quizzical eyes, and then the kitchen paper. She folded a few sheets into a compress, doused it in vinegar and then told Arthur to elevate his leg.

'On the table?'

'Yep.'

He couldn't believe he was being permitted to do something outlawed.

'There,' she said, 'just lay this on the bruise and it's like magic. It encourages blood flow to the skin and breaks down the bruise. Keep it there while I clear the table – no arguments, Spike! – and then wash it off when you have your shower. Arnica, aloe vera, witch hazel, they work too; my Nanna Perl used to stick cabbage leaves on mine! I've got a whole apothecary's shop at home with potions and homemade remedies ... lots are plant-based, very handy when you're getting knocks on the job.'

Spike was agog – she thought it was at his son's compliance, but it turned out to be at her.

'You're a healer!' he said, not taking his eyes off her as she made trips to and from the table for plates and a wipe-down of the surface.

'Hardly!' she said over her shoulder as she ran the taps to fill the washing-up bowl.

'This is like the Lady of the Lake legend!'

She felt her spirits lower at the memory of Dean's so-called term of endearment. Trust Pincher to invade her happiness. But then Spike began to tell the tale, and as she listened … *Yes!* Now she understood what he was getting at.

'So, the Lady of the Lake and her 'usband, they had three sons and they were endowed with magical powers. They could've become great warriors, but instead they chose to be healers, using what they could get 'old of from the land. They were known as the Physicians of Myddfai. Just like our Annie!'

'Oh yeah!' Arthur said.

There was so much to be thrilled about. The comparison was complimentary and – *and!* – he'd called her 'our Annie'. It was like having a new identity, away from the abused wife: she was soaring, onwards and upwards.

'Tell you what, son, this one, she's a woman of many talents. So many layers,' Spike said with admiration. No one had ever said that to her before.

'Dad!' Arthur suddenly cried. 'Can we play that game?'

'What game?'

'The layers one. With the bobble hat and gloves. Have we got any of that Dairy Milk left?' Arthur was as animated as a cartoon.

Annie swung round from the worktop, drying her hands on a tea towel. 'I love that game! I used to play that. The one where you roll a dice and if you get a six you have to put on the hat, scarf and gloves, then try to cut off a piece of chocolate with a knife and fork and eat it but if someone gets another six you have to take it all off—'

'And you might be just about to eat the chocolate and you can't!' Arthur cried.

'Yes!'

'Go on then, I'll get the stuff together. Then we could take a walk with Teg? Fancy it, Annie? It's a nice night, we could pop in the pub for a swift one.'

'There's a meeting in the Travellers' Rest tonight, seven p.m., ideas for the disco.'

'Oh yes! It's Friday, isn't it? I forgot it was tonight.'

'We could show our faces.' She had thought about going. Even though she had become a part of the village again, she still had the age-old insecurity and reservations about turning up alone. 'Arthur, you could help with the playlist – we don't want it to be all old fogey music, do we?'

Right on cue, Spike got up and did some truly cringey dad dancing as he opened the cutlery drawer and the broom cupboard to find a hat, gloves and scarf.

'Oh my God, stop!' Arthur said, but his face was lit up with amusement as Teg picked up on the happiness and began to bound around Spike, her tail wagging and her tongue out.

Annie began to laugh and laugh, great big bellyfuls, going weak-kneed as she fought for breath. It wasn't just the sight of chocolate that gave her a buzz.

This, here in a kitchen with a father, son and dog, was sheer joy: what other people called domestic bliss. It was her first taste of it in a long, long time, perhaps ever in her grown-up life. This, she realised, if ever she dared to dream, would be what she'd wish for.

22

A wonderful stay in the shepherd's hut – it was the height of hut couture! Apologies for the misunderstanding. We misread the blurb 'perfect for naturalists' as 'perfect for naturists'.

Derek and Sheila Fleming, Reading
Campsite Visitors' Book

She was going to do it, she was going to do it. She was really going to do it.

Wanda chanted her tub-thumping mantra as she went up the high street on a mission to buy everything she needed for guests to light – and more importantly put out – the fires she was finally allowing from tonight.

Lew had volunteered to be with her, knowing she was as nervous as a sausage about to be put on the barbecue. The after-school half-term dash would be underway later as families arrived from all over for anything from a couple of nights to a seven-night stay. It was the same story over the weekend too and then there'd be campers coming and going all week. Every space was booked, motorhomes too, and the bell tent and shepherd's hut were a real draw for the 'too posh to pitch' set. Plus the caravan was going live! What a hit Dilys was! Since they'd revamped it and put photos on the website, Instagram and Facebook, Wanda had had record inquiries, attracted by the white bright space with retro kitchen and framed images of seventies and eighties icons such as Freddie Mercury, Madonna and George Michael. Carys had donated her smart speaker so people could get in the mood with tunes from back in the day and Mam had done a great job stitching covers and cushions with floral emblems and stripes.

It would be the first real test for Under A Starry Sky – and Wanda was ready. Well, almost. She needed to pop into Fork Handles for skewers, sand, kindling and logs. But first, she would pick up her order from Gobaith Gifts of branded brown paper bags stamped with the moon and stars which would make up the welcome packs stuffed with marshmallows and hot chocolate sachets from Blod's. Undeniably, campfires were part of the experience, she had to face up to it. And while the weather was forecast to be dry, it could still get nippy of an evening. Complaints about a ban on what was part and parcel of tent life would be a killer for the business. There was nothing to worry about, she told herself, she'd bought the safest fire pits going and had dotted them around the place on level patio blocks, away from over-hanging branches. Each would have a watering can of water and a bucket of sand beside them and there were plenty of extinguisher points around the site.

The door tinkled as Wanda went in to the gift shop. There was no sign of Sara, just Nisha, whom Wanda had known since she was knee-high through the girl's father Amir at Keep Calm and Curry On.

'Hi, lovely! Where's that boss of yours?' Wanda asked. 'Skiving off?'

Nisha looked shifty. 'Er … she'll be five minutes, she said. Running late.'

'Okay, I'll pop to Coffee on the Corner, then I'll be back. Want anything?'

'No, ta. I'll tell her you've been looking for her. Make it ten minutes, actually, she's tied up, she said. Well, not tied up literally, but you know …'

Wanda gave her a funny look. What was she on about? An espresso would make things clearer, so she left, but paused to look up at the windows of her flat. How she missed her own space. It was nice living with Mam and Carys, but sometimes she wanted to be alone on her own sofa. The curtains were closed – poor Bowen had probably been on call again.

On she went, to the corner, getting a coffee from Alis, who was working on the official flyer for the disco. She picked up her sheet of A4 and held it up for Wanda's opinion. It was amazing! Blod's idea had been picked as the theme; in bright bubble letters, it said: *Blast from the Past, Midsummer Night, 21 June, fancy dress, a fiver includes first drink and all profits to the fire service.*

'I thought I'd do cutting and pasting for real,' she said, pointing out the images of jivers, mods, hippies, glam rockers, punks, New Romantics and hip-hoppers which she'd stuck on with Pritt Stick. 'I wanted it to look authentic, with an old feel to it. Phil the Pill has a colour printer thing so he'll sort that, then a bunch of us can post them up, in the shops or in our cars. I'm thinking of going as Elvis.' She certainly had the hair for it – thick, black and short so she could easily quiff it up. 'Blod says she's got a white jumpsuit with gold fringing.'

Of course she'd have a spare one hanging about!

'What about you?' Alis asked her.

'No idea! I need a think!'

'While you're here, I'm wondering if you'd have a think about something else, too. You know my dad's old ice-cream van?' Wanda smiled, remembering the nursery-rhyme jingle and the taste of a Mr Whippy on a hot afternoon. Alis's dad would always give her a flake for free, too. 'It's just a thought, it's still in the garage at theirs, sitting there doing nothing. I could do a breakfast run at yours of a weekend. I'd pay you a cut, obviously, they're your customers after all. My husband reckons it'd be easy to install a griddle. He can hold the fort here while I come up.'

'I love it! You could do afternoon teas for tired trekkers too!'

'Yes! I've got my food hygiene certificates already so it'd be just a question of converting the van.'

It would be another string to the campsite's bow. 'Perfect. Let me know when you're ready to start.'

It was sunny outside, so Wanda decided to sit at a bistro table and wait for Sara to arrive. As she took her first sip, she almost choked when she saw a woman with a hood up coming out of Bowen's. *Oh God*, he'd clearly been shagging her in Wanda's bed! She hoped he had some Vanish. She'd have to get a new mattress when she moved back in.

Then a gust of wind exposed the woman's blonde head, and Wanda saw that it was Sara. Sara had been doing it on Wanda's bed in Wanda's flat! No wonder Nisha looked uncomfortable.

'SARA!' she shouted, running up to her. 'Please tell me you haven't been at it on my kitchen worktop!'

Sara inhaled and Wanda knew her so well, she could read her mind: she was considering whether to make something up but then she realised she'd been caught red-handed. So she just gave Wanda a big dopey smile.

'Oh, seriously?'

'I Dettoxed afterwards,' Sara said, lamely.

Wanda couldn't help but guffaw. 'That's something, I suppose. So anyway, you and Bowen! How long's it been going on for? Why didn't you tell me?'

'A few dates, it's very casual. Although he seems quite keen.' Sara blushed and Wanda was totally thrilled for her. 'He's so lovely. We just hit it off at Lew's dinner thing and ... you know ... I thought, *why not?* Even though he's a few years younger than me.'

'Get you!' Wanda said, taking her arm as they went to the shop, where she picked up her paper bags. There was even more love in the air at Spike's. As he helped her load the Land Rover, he sang Annie's praises for bringing Arthur out of himself.

On the drive home, a little self-indulgent voice in Wanda's head asked when it would be her turn. Romance seemed to be everywhere – Sara and Bowen were an item, Spike and Annie were inevitable, the reformed glamper wankers had got engaged in front of her and Wanda had caught the nudists gazing into each other's eyes over a flask of tea. She shuddered as she recalled turning the corner into the privacy of the shepherd's hut quarters to be confronted by the sight of the man's hairy bottom bent over a disposable barbecue as he flipped bacon. And Glanmor's latest blog rubbed it in, too – he and his wife had renewed their wedding vows on a Spanish beach in bikinis and bathers. Wanda, though, was sat on the shelf approaching her best-before date. But she wasn't going to think like that, she'd promised herself. No self-pity, she hadn't the time for it. Besides, a million jobs awaited her.

The day sped by in a slog of cleaning, check-ins, showing people to their plots and answering queries – but it was fantastic, especially when it came to taking payment for their stays, canoe cruises and bits and pieces of supplies she'd begun to sell in reception. Carys was manning the phones inside and popped out to cover loo breaks, while Mam made sure Wanda didn't go hungry or thirsty with regular deliveries.

At dusk, she shut the cabin, feeling tired out but happy, taking in the busy field of multicoloured tents, people sat out on camping chairs, tucking into their tea, drinking wine and beer, kids in the play area and climbing trees, a couple canoeing out on the lake. It was a sea of smiling faces, of guy ropes being adjusted, pans being washed up and all under the beginnings of a starry sky. But there was an anxiety building inside her: the fire pits were beginning to be lit, one by one orange flames were dancing – it would be all too easy to go inside and pull the curtains. Yet she would only fret all night if she did. Just tonight, for peace of mind, she needed to make sure the fires would be out by the 10 p.m. curfew. Even if she had to go round and douse them all herself.

With impeccable timing, Lew appeared next to her. 'Fire marshal reporting for duty!'

Wanda took a deep breath to steady herself: not just at the demons before her but at him, appearing yet again to help her. He'd made it obvious he had done so to speed up her departure, then he'd softened and said he wanted her to go for her own sake. Then there was Annie, who'd said he might want her to go because he couldn't be around her if they weren't friends. Yet here he was, reaching out to her. But when she thought about it, Wanda realised it all added up to the same thing: that he didn't want her to stay.

'Wow. Look at this!' he said, scanning the campsite.

'I know! It's like the old days.'

'But it's different, it's got you stamped all over it. Quirky, cool, warm ...'

Oh hell. He was killing her with kindness now. Ice-cold Lew would be much easier to deal with as far as her emotions went.

'Ready?' he said.

'Not really. But no point putting it off.'

They set off on patrol, wandering around, the circles of fire growing brighter as night fell. Some were well on the way, with flames licking bubbling marshmallows on sticks, while others were at the beginning, just a scrunch of newspaper and tiny wigwams of kindling, being fanned into life.

Every now and again, Lew would ask if she was okay – and surprisingly she was, because every pit they passed was under control. It was completely different to the raging wildfire fifteen years ago. But then he chucked her a curveball.

'Why don't we go and build one, by the last pit at the edge of the lake?'

'Really? Do we have to? I mean, is that necessary?'

'To truly get over something,' he said, his cheekbones

accentuated in the low light, 'you've got to be exposed to it, to get used to it.'

If only that worked as far as his company was concerned – these brief moments together only made her feel more for him.

'I've taught so many people who are frightened of heights and by the time I've finished with them they're abseiling like experts!'

At the lake, he took off his rucksack, emptying it of newspaper, kindling and wood before instructing her to get on with it. He was here, just on the log stool, she didn't have to worry. Fighting the tremble, she did her best and managed to get it going.

'There we are, safe as houses, well done!' Lew said.

It did look cosy. But then there was a crack and a hiss and she jumped.

'It's just me opening a can of lager, Wanda,' he said, handing it over. 'Brought a few tinnies for us. Don't panic.'

She took one, two, three big gulps of fizz and gave the appropriate *'aaah!'* 'Thank you for this.' She held up her can and then gestured at the fire. 'I never thought I'd get this close again.'

She realised the same went for being with him. The buzz of the beer and the cloak of darkness gave her the courage to address the moment. If she didn't raise it now, when would she?

'I'm sorry I didn't chase you up after the fire. Your calls and messages … I wasn't in the right place and then not seeing you at the funeral … I was a mess for a long time afterwards.'

Wanda took a little look at him, staring at the flames.

'I regret not coming. I wish I could've but it was ... difficult. Stuck where I was.'

'I don't suppose it was easy to get here when you were halfway up a Scottish mountain in crampons, days away from civilisation.'

'It did feel like I was marooned, yes. I think that's why I went to Norfolk after. I'd had enough of the mountains. The highest point there was roughly the height of a stepladder. It was good for what I needed at the time. Somewhere different.'

Wanda held her breath. This was what she had guessed – and this was the first time he'd properly opened up to her.

'After the fire, I thought there was nothing heroic about mountains. Being somewhere flat was straight-forward and open, like a blank canvas. I needed that. But then ... stuff happened ...'

She willed him on – there had to be a woman involved. But he didn't bite.

'The Bunkhouse was meant to be, that's the way I look at it.'

He looked up at her intently. They were definitely sharing a moment and she felt flustered, unsure what his eyes were saying.

'Even with me here,' she said, clumsily.

'Even with you here, yes,' he laughed. 'And I wouldn't want to be anywhere else.'

Wanda's insides went full mush – whether he was including her in that, she had no idea. Annoyed at her-self for reading what may or may not be into what he said, she changed tack. She had deliberately walked away whenever she heard anyone mentioning Belmira: Wanda didn't want to know if they'd turned The Bunkhouse into The Bonkhouse. And yet, she kind of did …

'Not even Portugal?' she said, with a slight arch of her brow.

Lew frowned, then the penny dropped and he tutted, with a playful twinkle in his eyes. 'Belmira has asked me if I'd like to go and visit.'

I bet she has! Wanda thought jealously, before calling his bluff in her very best calm and collected voice. 'I can sort you cheap flights, no problem.'

'I'll bear that in mind, thanks,' he said, getting up to throw the last log on the fire, crouching beside it, fanning it and generally indicating he wasn't going to tell her anything about his love life.

'I'll go after this,' he said. 'I'm fully booked on a climbing course tomorrow. Need my wits about me.'

'Do you enjoy teaching?'

'Yes. It's amazing watching people push themselves.' He stood up and went to sit back down again.

'Have you thought any more about doing that speaking thing at school? About the danger of fire? The one Bowen asked you about at your open house.'

'No time,' he said, quickly, deciding against joining her, distractedly patting his pockets.

'It won't take much! I think you'd be good at it. They'd listen to you, what with you being outdoorsy and local. They'd look up to you.'

He began to pack his rucksack and then he passed a watering can to Wanda and gestured she should put the fire out. But there was still time before the curfew.

'You're all capable and—'

'Leave it, Wanda.' His body had gone stiff.

'Okay, I was just—'

'You weren't the only one affected by the fire,' he said quietly over his shoulder. 'I'm not what people think I am.'

Before Wanda could analyse what he'd just said, he added with a laugh, 'I mean, what if they found out I take a hot water bottle to bed? Come on, pour the water.'

The flames immediately died and she received a face full of billowing steam and smoke, but there was neither panic nor the taste of the past. But her surprise was overtaken by confusion. She'd found out more about Lew tonight, yet she felt she knew him less. What had he meant about being affected by the fire, and not being who people thought he was? Maybe she ought to check he was okay. But by the time she'd decided to, once she'd triple-checked there really were no smouldering sparks left in the pit, there were only head torches and whispers to be seen and heard all around her. And Lew was already lost in the darkness.

23

'What a sick birthday!' Arthur said as he collapsed onto the back seat of his dad's van.

Teg leapt in beside him and, with a huge sigh, immediately laid her chin on the boy's thighs and conked out, the very definition of doggo.

'Looks like we're taking 'ome 'alf the beach with us!' Spike said, dusting himself down as he got behind the wheel, blasting the air con to cool them all down. He turned to Annie and smiled, making her feel warm inside. 'Of all the places we could've gone and we ended up beside the seaside, beside the sea!'

A regular visitor now to their home, Annie had been there when Spike had said Arthur could pick anywhere, within reason, to celebrate his big day. A tour of the Millennium Stadium in Cardiff? A go on Europe's longest zip wire in North Wales? Mountain biking? White-water rafting? But his main concern had been what they'd do with Teg. 'I'll have her!' she'd said as if it was obvious. 'But you're coming ... aren't you?' he'd said, as if it was even more obvious. 'Dad, Annie can come, can't she?'

Me? she'd thought, flattered, even if it was just a show of manners. Of course, she'd said she hadn't expected an invite, what did Arthur want her there for? Take a friend instead! And then it became clear that everyone was 'busy' – it could have been true, because his birthday was during half-term, yet it wasn't inconceivable that parents were making excuses. Annie knew that feeling. Once Spike had finished lying prostrate to convince her she was welcome, she agreed: 'I'd love to!' Immediately, Arthur had suggested the beach, somewhere fun which had something for everyone. That dog had unveiled Arthur's true nature – beneath the armour of his worries, he was thoughtful, generous and kind. Annie had known just the place: beautiful Barmouth beach, which had it all and was only a ninety-minute drive away.

And they'd had a right day of it in gorgeous sunshine. Candy floss, fairground rides, amusements, sandcastles, fish and chips and mooching round the tacky touristy shops, where they still sold clingfilmed plates of 'bacon and eggs' made of rock, which Annie remembered from childhood visits here with Nanna and Bampy. All three had ended up on trampolines while a tethered Teg drooled with envy at her mad humans. She got her chance to bounce on a dog-friendly stretch of sand, where she went giddy with excitement, splashing in the shallows and deeper, her tail poking up from the water like a submarine periscope. Enchanted by her contagious joy, their just-in-case swimsuits were whipped on and they ran together holding hands, Arthur in the middle, screaming as the freezing water hit their feet, stomachs, chests and shoulders. They'd dried off on towels for an hour or so, lazing drunk on the great outdoors, with salt crystals leaving their skin pleasingly tight, all in the shadow of Snowdonia, with the mountain of Cader Idris rising spectacularly behind them. Naturally, she had felt self-conscious at being half-naked in her sensible black one-piece, her scars and stretch marks, cellulite and corns on show. She had a functional relationship with her body: it was strong, it worked and she was thankful, but she hadn't considered herself a sensual person since ... well, ever. Spike was an absolute gent, never making her feel uncomfortable; but then why would he when he was so clearly out of her league? Only now, as Annie sank into her seat, did she allow herself to think how gorgeous he was. Muscly without being too like a bodybuilder, toned without the shouty six-pack, with a wide smooth chest and chunky thighs that tapered to elegant calves and perfect toenails. In other words, the opposite of Dean. She realised that this was the first time she'd thought of him all day. It was incredible because usually he haunted her twenty-four-seven. The silent calls continued, no doubt to intimidate her into dropping her challenge on his custody bid. She wouldn't think of him any more – she wouldn't let him spoil a wonderful day.

A happy tiredness settled on them as they began the drive home. In the mirror of the sun visor, she saw that despite a slathering of suncream, Arthur's face had become a dot-to-dot of lovely freckles. He must've got that from his mam; she'd been fairer than Spike, whose natural glow had become golden, making his eyes bluer and his teeth whiter. While he was sun-kissed, Annie, as usual, was sun-snogged – she'd have strap marks already. She got it from Bampy, who'd been dark until his hair turned white.

Look at yourself, she thought, seeing a deep furrow on her forehead, and the beginnings of what would be liver spots as she aged. Her hair, getting more silver with every examination, was dramatically waved and stiff with salt; her lips tasted of it, too. What a bloody state. Then again, if she started wearing make-up and fussing over her appearance in Spike's company, he might realise how she felt and as far as she was concerned she wouldn't even confess that under interrogation. Being friends, as ever, as she would stick to even if the sky caved in, was more than enough.

'Annie, say that place name again, the funny one!' Arthur called.

'What? Llanfairpwllgwyngyllgogerychwyrndrobwllllan-tysiliogogogoch?'

'Yes!'

'Known as Llanfair PG for short.'

'And what does it mean again?'

'St Mary's Church in the hollow of the white hazel near a rapid whirlpool and the church of St Tysilio of the red cave.'

'How do you remember it?' Spike said.

'No idea! I was obsessed with it as a kid; I've never been there, but I was so jealous if anyone brought back photos of themselves standing next to the sign at the railway station. I think it was because when I was growing up, Wales was kind of England's poor relation – it still is in many respects, but it was worse then and we had to look for things to be proud of, stuff that made us stand out.'

'We should go! Get that photo!' Arthur mimed a selfie – and then realised he'd gone at least six hours without technology. 'Dad! My phone! Can I have it?'

'Annie's got it. Do the honours, will you? Ta!'

She handed it to him with the juice pack she'd got

him as her gift. 'Thank you!' he sang, finding his earbuds, popping them in and switching himself off from the world.

'He's been a different boy since you've been around,' Spike said, quietly, giving her a quick glance of gratitude. 'Like he was before.'

'He's a great kid. That's Teg working her magic, that is, not me!'

'Partly, yes, but he's really fond of you.' He paused. 'When you walk in to the cottage, the mood lifts straight away. It's not like 'avin' a visitor, like we're on our best behaviour, we can be ourselves. You're a big part of our lives.'

Annie was so touched – he made it sound as if she was a rainbow when she had always felt like a black cloud. 'That means a lot to me, Spike. It works both ways though; you two let me in and I love coming over.'

'And today's been amazing, you didn't have to come but I appreciate it, that you did.'

'What? I was thrilled to be asked! You've given me the chance to enjoy some of your family time.' It was so easy to talk openly with Spike – even easier being side by side: you could be more open because you weren't face to face. 'Not having kids of my own, it's lovely to borrow Arthur.'

'You can borrow 'im anytime!' he laughed. 'You're on his wavelength, you don't talk down to 'im, you knew Barmouth would suit 'im down to the ground. The beach was a special place for Arthur and Lucy. She'd take 'im down to Brighton for the day sometimes or Camber Sands, Broadstairs. A right pair of beach bums, they were. Every 'oliday we'd book, I'd say, shall we go, I dunno, somewhere other than the beach – a city, the mountains, the jungle! I knew we'd never go but I'd get a kick out of them teamin' up against me, outraged at my suggestion.'

'He must miss her so much. You too.'

'Yeah, of course, and two years on it ain't any less heart-breaking. But finally I can see a way forwards. It was probably out of sheer desperation that I upped sticks and moved 'ere. I just couldn't be around the old places any longer. I needed it at first, it was a comfort to 'ave 'er there around us. Then I ended up feeling suffocated by it, it was just a different phase of grief. Had we stayed we'd have worked it out. I'm glad we came though and in time I think Arthur will be too, 'e's getting there. Loves the gardening club, Teg's everyfing to 'im and I even had a nice call from 'is teacher at the end of last week saying his behaviour has started to improve. You've played a part in that. I'm not saying you're a substitute mum, 'course not, but a female in the 'ouse, not just any female, natch, I mean you, yourself ...' he was gabbling now, in case he'd offended her, '... you soften the edges, you make us less sharp, if you get me?'

He needn't worry. 'I know exactly! You need balance. But also I get Arthur, I think, because I was the same as him. My mam walked out of my life and hasn't been in it since. It messed me up.'

'Do you ever see her?'

'She doesn't want to know me.' Her voice no longer caught when she told people this. She was used to it.

'How can a parent be like that?' Spike was incensed. 'I mean, I know dads walk away all the time, and it's much rarer for mums, but whoever is doing it, they must be really selfish or ill.'

'Or young. Or all three. I've let it go no[...]
at her for a long long time. It made me wa[...]
cepted, to belong, whether that was hanging aro[...]
corners to try to be in the cool gang or marrying[...]
thought it was my duty to please. But I've survive[...]

'What did I say? You're a healer! You need your[...]
surgery.'

'I've never told anyone this ...' she hesitated. Was
this too much of herself to give and to lay bare? She had
imagined if she had ever told anyone they'd be a very
trusted confidante, a soulmate. Yet she and Spike had
only known each other a few months. But it felt the most
natural thing to open up about hanging up her muddy
boots, having her own Aladdin's cave of organic herbal
this and that. She was a bit frightened he'd see her as
ridiculous though. But no.

'Wow, that sounds cool. I could see you doing that.
Annie's Apothecary!'

Could he be any more lovely?

'You could hire a corner of a shop to start with. Hey,
why not mine?'

He was only teasing. 'I've always thought there's a
market for airy fairy products for manly DIY types,' she
laughed.

'Ah, but it's nice to dream.'

'What's your dream then?' Annie wanted to know
everything about this man.

'I only 'ave 'em for Arthur. I don't have any for myself
any more. Losing Lucy took something away from me
that I'll never replace. It's all about 'im now.'

'Maybe you're just not there yet ...' Deep inside
she yearned for him to mention finding something or

meone again – to hint if he ever thought of love, that was a possibility she could hold on to.

'There's a lot to take on.'

She couldn't speak, not right now – she'd only blurt everything out. She pressed her lips together hard, to seal them, and looked out of her window and sat on her hands, because otherwise she'd place them on him and tell him he was her heart's desire. He was so special, Arthur too, the four of them including Teg would make a great bunch.

Whoa. It frightened her how quickly she'd put them all into one unit: it was impractical, unrealistic and downright stupid. Tiny steps would only ever be the way. Arthur was the most important thing in this equation. Her sudden realisation found her a way through. She had to park those feelings, it was that simple. The rest of the journey was quiet – the winding A470 and the breathtaking scenery of mountains and valleys deserved a bit of respect.

As they came to the outskirts of Gobaith, Arthur piped up slightly too loudly over whatever he was listening to. 'Dad! Are we having a birthday tea when we get in?'

''Course!' Spike said. 'Posh sarnies—'

'Cut in triangles?' Arthur took his earbuds out of one ear.

'Yep. Our special crisp mix – Monster Munch, Hula Hoops, Ready Salted—'

'And Wotsits!'

He might be heading towards adolescence but Arthur was still a small child at heart. *Weren't we all?* Annie loved a birthday tea too!

'Obviously!'

'A place for Mum?'

Spike nodded at him in the rear-view mirror. 'A tradition of ours,' he explained to Annie, 'done it every year ever since. Same food, same squash, same same.'

'Cake after?'

'Malteser one, mate!'

'He'll grow out of it one day,' Spike said to Annie. 'But I'll do it if he still wants it even when he's forty!'

'Why wouldn't you!'

'You'll come in for cake, won't you?' Spike said.

'You have to,' Arthur said, 'otherwise Teg will be sad if you go straight off.'

'In that case ...' Annie laughed, feeling back on track with this dynamic, taking it for what it was: a platonic friendship with a kid at the heart, a lovely mess of a thing with a stinking wet dog thrown in.

Arthur started to pump the air with his fist. 'Yeeees! You've fallen for my dastardly plan!'

She swivelled her head round, gasping, covering her open mouth with her hand, pretending to be in shock at being his fool.

'You both have!'

'Eh?' Spike said, as they pulled up outside the cottage.

'Well, Dad was going to say something to you, Annie, weren't you, Dad? And then he chickened out, and now he has to say it now you're coming in. Don't you, Dad! Doesn't he, Annie?'

Spike groaned and he was blushing and touching the tip of his nose in embarrassment. 'Arthur!'

His son was already out of his seat, having decided whatever was about to happen would be 'so cringe' that he couldn't bear to hear it. 'Just tell me what she says, Dad. Come on, Teg!'

'Oh, no. Has the dog got terrible farts?'

'Er, no. Not quite.' He took a breath and gave an awkward smile. 'Look, it was just a thing I said in passing and Arthur kind of got excited and um, you know I don't want to ruin this, but I wondered ... would you be up for going to the disco ... with me? It's fine if not ...'

'Oh! Right!' *OH YES!* She hadn't expected that. Was he asking her on a date? Surely not; he'd alluded to the fact that he wasn't in the zone. But then again he was fidgeting with nerves. She was all of a dither. Did it matter what his motive was? Not at all. 'Okay, yes. I'd love to!'

'Great. I was thinking of what we could go as. Like as a couple. Not that I mean we're a couple, ha, no, as in ... whatever ... I was thinking I could be Axl Rose and you could be Slash.'

He was the sweetest thing! 'Well, I wouldn't need a wig! Sounds brilliant.'

'Cool, lav-er-ly.' He rubbed his hands and his eyes twinkled at her. She was definitely getting some vibes off him. Well, she never! A shyness crept upon her at the prospect of what was possibly something there between them.

'Right, well, shall we ...?' she said, taking off her seat belt.

'Yes! There's birthday tea to be made! I'll butter and fill.'

'And I'll do the triangles!'

They got out of the van, him jangling his keys, and he gestured *ladies first* up the path with his hand. Arthur was looking shifty by the front door. As Spike unlocked it and let Annie in, she heard him whisper, 'She said yes, son.'

'Told you!' Arthur said. 'I'll go and set her a place at the table.'

And as he whipped past her to get to the kitchen, he gave a huge 'Wahoo!' which almost matched the elation in Annie's heart.

24

*We came on a recommendation of belting scenery and a
big Welsh welcome but were warned to expect no-frills
camping. So we were bowled over to find it had had
an upgrade! Super facilities yet not fancy-pants, with a
special charm of its own. Thank you, Wanda and Lyn, for
a wonderful stay – we left feeling like family.*

Audrey and Bob P., Lancashire
Campsite Visitors' Book

The sunshine of half-term week had continued into
June and Gobaith was roasting like a leg of lamb.

The scorching fortnight had turned the campsite grass
yellow and there'd been a run on tent pegs at reception
to replace bent ones because the earth was as hard as a
miner's hat.

But tomorrow, in the early hours, the weather would
break. This may have been their summer. And so locals
and tourists alike were spending Saturday night in the
beer garden of the Travellers' Rest, on a last hurrah to
soak up the final balmy evening.

Wanda had tried to resist but Mam and Carys had
ganged up on her to take the weekend off: she'd pulled

double shifts in the week because Carys had been laid up in bed with a cold. All but one of the pitches were occupied, from Friday to Monday, so nothing major would be required: for goodness' sake, the pair of them had said, they were more than capable of cleaning the bathroom, refilling loo roll, emptying bins, giving out directions, selling logs and whatever else came up.

She hadn't realised how knackered she was. With no 6 a.m. alarm to wake her, she'd got up this morning at the luxurious time of 9 a.m., stretching like a cat, taking her time to shower and dress. Then it was outside to join the queue for a breakfast bap and posh coffee at Sunny Side Up, the name of Alis's new venture. The ice cream van had been resprayed yellow, matching deckchairs were set out and from the speaker came not a grating twinkly chime but a background playlist of easy-listening tunes. Eavesdropping on the campers, Wanda learned they liked having a break from their frying pans – her friend had pulled it off. The rest of the day had been spent reading and resting and she could feel the benefits as she wandered back to the picnic table with a tray of drinks from the bar. Life was good: the campsite was earning again, Mam no longer needed walking aids and Carys was blooming. Just like the honeysuckle and jasmine, which gave off a heavenly scent.

'Cider for you two,' Wanda said to Annie and Spike, who had moved even closer in her absence. If they hadn't touched tongues yet it would only be a matter of time. Totally comfortable in each other's company, they both looked dazed when they returned every now and then to the group chat, self-conscious that they were only talking to each other but then sliding back into it, unable to stop themselves. She didn't blame them, though – they were dazzling together: Annie's tumbling glossy dark hair against her brown skin complementing Spike's blond hulking Scandinavian look. Fair play to them, they had to make the most of a babysitter for Arthur.

'G and T for you, Alis. Aperol Spritz for you, Sara.' The two ladies broke off from high street gossip – mostly centred on who was going as what to the disco – to give thanks before diving back in.

There was lager for Bowen, who was smiling dreamily at his lady, and that left a large glass of white wine for Wanda.

'Iechyd da!' they chorused. Cheers indeed!

Their celebration was interrupted by a flash of blue lights going past the pub. They just caught the red of the fire engine as it went down the lane and automatically they scanned the countryside. The mountain wasn't alight, Wanda saw, relieved, but Bowen made a call and he announced it was a grass fire just outside the village – kids. Again.

Eventually, everyone returned to their conversations and Wanda felt a right lemon. But that was preferable to being a sitting duck as Phil the Pill came at her with love-heart pupils.

'Mind if I join you?' he asked, very nicely. Still, she knew it would be half an hour of running talk, personal bests and Strava trophies.

''Course not!' she said, brightly, feeling bad about her snottiness. 'How are you?'

'Good, good. Very good. Although sore hamstrings, groin strain—'

'Jogger's nipple?'

'No. I ... uh ... tape them up.' His Adam's apple rose and fell as he tried to swallow the tension. It must take guts for him to approach her time after time. If only she could feel something for him. Yet he was as ginger as she was – she didn't go for that look, she hated her own fiery pubes, let alone having to get to know his. He wasn't unattractive: he was slim, he looked after himself, he had nice blue eyes, and he was intelligent, kind and ... There was just no damn chemistry.

'So ...' he said and she could feel herself squirming as he rubbed his thigh with his spare hand. The other held a bottle of mineral water. *Please don't ask me out again*, she prayed. *Because it's horrible for you and it's depressing for me.* It was the wine inside her and she started to say, 'It's fine, really,' but something shifted in him.

'Oh! No! I'm not doing that again,' he laughed. 'I'm actually with someone now.'

'Great!' she said, relieved and then feeling a thud inside. Ashamed, she realised it was her ego, crashing to her pelvic floor.

'Yeah,' he said, nodding over at a woman who gave a shy wave from a wholesome crowd. She was gorgeous. Amazonian, a natural beauty with long dark waves. Those love-heart pupils were for her, not Wanda. 'Third date! We met through the running club. She's a pharmacist too. But I didn't come over to tell you that.'

'No?' He was well within his rights, frankly.

'No, just that the extras I didn't have for your mam's prescription, they've arrived.' He got up. 'Shouldn't mix business with pleasure. Ha! Right, I'd better be—'

'Yes! Yes. Thanks. Well done!' she said as he left, cringing at her congratulations for copping off. Who on earth was she to say that to him when she hadn't in aeons – and he had. Was this what her love life had come to? She knocked back her glass and got up, not knowing where to go. Everyone was high on life here; she felt like a party pooper. 'Just nipping to the loo,' she said, picking up her bag, her skin clammy as the heat turned muggy. The feeling came at her from nowhere – one she hadn't had for a while: claustrophobia and the need to escape. Bugger this weekend off. She'd been all right being occupied, but now ...

'Wanda!'

She looked up and Lew was calling her from a group standing at the garden gate which led out to the lane.

'Save me,' he hissed in her ear. She shivered at the near-contact. 'They're discussing hiking socks. Moisture wicking and athlete's foot.'

On closer inspection, they were indeed old-school ramblers, with pints of real ale, beards, poles and backpacks.

'They're staying at The Bunkhouse. I need to have a breather!' His warm fingers grazed hers and her heart hit 100 m.p.h. Then to the crowd he said, 'Sorry, I have to go, I'm needed.'

He held his palm out for her to go first and they went out into the night.

'Freedom! Finally!' he said. 'There's only so much rambling talk I can handle.'

'Glad I could be of some use,' she said. 'I was going anyway.'

'Home?' he asked.

'No. I thought Las Vegas for a quick bit of blackjack before bed. Of course I'm going home!'

Lew hooted. 'Mind if I walk with you?'

'Go ahead.'

The chatter of the pub was soon behind them but the evening didn't feel over. It was one of those nights which could go on and on. Wanda felt heady with it, wanting now to make the most of her weekend off.

'I'm going to have a nightcap if you fancy one?' she said as they approached the campsite turning.

'Here? Or Las Vegas? Because I need to be up in the morning.'

Wanda giggled in the quiet of the dark and it set him off too, the moon making his eyes and teeth sparkle and the humidity shining on his skin. She put a finger over her lips and told him to wait outside the farmhouse while she made up two whiskies on the rocks. The hush was all around them and they tiptoed through the campsite. The firepits were out, a few people were murmuring as they packed up chairs, sleeping bags were being zipped up and torches flashed under canvas.

By the lake, it was as if they had the world to themselves. Utterly bewitched and before she'd known that she was going to do it, she had opened the bell tent and drawn back its curtains.

Silently, they pulled the double mattress to the edge so the lake, the mountain and the Milky Way were framed like a photograph. Lew sat, then lay down and put his arms behind his head so he could gaze in wonder. Magnetised to him, rooted to this land, she joined him, their bodies just inches apart, and she sighed at such beauty: ripples on the silvery water, the distant crack of twigs, of the night breathing, the majesty of the hillside, the ridge leading to the peak and the never-ending heavens pricked with millions of dots of lights.

'A shooting star!' she gasped, watching it trailing through the velvet like a comet, dazzling before it disappeared into nothing.

'Wow!' Lew said. 'I haven't seen one for years. I haven't been watching. Too busy, I s'pose.'

Wanda felt the sultriness of the night press on her chest. The banter had gone; in its place was something else. Intimacy and space to talk.

'It was all laid out for me,' Lew said quietly, as if he too sensed the moment. 'My ex, she wanted to settle down and have kids.'

Her heart curled up into a ball – he had virtually admitted he wanted to remain a bachelor.

'Not with Kirstine, anyway. I was stupid, I let it all happen; too much of a coward to leave. I didn't want to hurt her, but of course I did. Never again. Next time, if there is one, I'd make sure . . .' He exhaled heavily, clearly still feeling guilty.

'You saved her from worse in the long run,' Wanda said. 'I, however, do the total opposite. Leg it before the engine has even started running.'

'Never had a big relationship, then?' he asked her.

'Nope, not like you. Nowhere near that. The usual lasted three, six months or so, I made it to nine months once. I always thought that one would be enough to stop me wanting to leave, like that would be the test. No one ever did.'

'Where would you be now if you had left? If your Mam hadn't had her accident?'

She hadn't thought about it recently but the itinerary

of colour, spices, smells, heat and discovery was burned into her brain.

'On a South Pacific beach, snorkelling above a coral reef. I'd have left South America a champion tango dancer, fluent in Spanish, with a halo from some kind of voluntary project. I'd be chilling out before I went to Indonesia to become a yogi surf chick, then India to make proper curry, last stop Morocco for souvenir shopping.'

'Bring me back something, won't you?'

'Yes, don't worry, I do intend to go still. I'll be out of your hair eventually.' She side-eyed him and elbowed him for emphasis.

'Oi! About that ...' He cleared his throat. 'I just want you to do what you want to do. That's what I was going to say to you when Carys came over about the website booking, that time. I wanted to say I was glad we were friends again.'

It meant so much to Wanda to hear that. But there was a part of her that felt hollow that it was just friends he was talking about. It blew Annie's theory out of the water – he could obviously cope with being around her if he felt comfortable enough to say this now.

'How have we never met anyone, either of us?' She spoke her thoughts out loud, not caring because it was obvious – there was no one hanging off her now, was there? She heard his head move and felt his eyes on her. Unable to resist, she faced him and her stomach looped the loop. The wind had picked up and the tent was flapping.

'There was someone ...' Lew's eyes flicked back to the mountain.

Wanda's breathing went shallow. Was he referring to her? And then she let it go. Did it even matter if he was?

This was all history. They both knew she would be leaving and maybe the drinks had loosened his tongue. Nostalgia was intoxicating. But it didn't hold up when you asked it to be something real and workable, when you had crow's feet and utility bills. They might have a connection, but now Wanda wondered if it was simply because they'd had a past. And she wasn't looking backwards any more.

'Annie said to me to look up, not down; it made me change how I saw what was happening here, to feel the feelings and process them and act. I think you've got to be brave.'

He blinked slowly, his eyelashes fluttering. 'What if you're afraid?'

Drops of rain were starting to fall and the air had turned fresh.

'Well, then you either try or you don't, I guess.'

Lew swallowed and he raised a hand to her face, his fingertips tracing her cheek. He was talking about them, that was clear now, and her brain was struggling to piece together what was happening while her body was responding with desire.

'What if ...' he said. But he shut his eyes and pulled his hand away.

The ghost of his touch remained. Something was holding him back. But what? She saw a tear and her heart began to ache. Until she saw another and another – they weren't tears but droplets of rain. At the same time, they realised the tent was leaking. A gush of water began to run down the central pole that was holding it up. The plastic seal at the top had gone, Wanda saw as the sound of a deluge hammered down.

They jumped up as a gust of wind made the walls shake

and suddenly the pole was swaying and just in time, they grabbed at one another and made it out as the tent keeled to the left and collapsed like a half-hearted erection.

How lucky no one had been in there! Damage, injuries … it didn't bear thinking about, and to be honest there was no time to do so anyway because sheets of rain were drenching them both. They were already soaked through, their clothes stuck to their goose pimples. Her hair was instantly coiling drips of cold water and her feet were icy from rivers of water flooding from the field.

They began to run; there was no point trying to rescue the tent now, and Wanda thanked God everyone else's were holding up against the weather.

'Do you want to come in?' she shouted over the downpour as they reached the farmhouse.

'I'd better not,' he said, his face now blank. Just like the *what ifs* of tonight, his emotion had been washed away. The moment was lost. In turmoil, she watched him stalk off, asking herself if tonight had really happened. What was the point of that, though? Only the here and now mattered. And he had gone. All that was left was the knowledge that she'd have no lie-in tomorrow – this place was going to be an absolute mudbath by morning.

25

The opening bars of Madonna's 'Crazy For You' boomed out and Annie's heart exploded at Spike's strong arm around her waist.

How much she wanted his body against hers. He'd lit a flame inside of her. Desire, my God, she'd never known anything like this before: it was grown-up and elemental, not some little fleeting crush, nor jumbled up with poor self-esteem or duty. There was hope too that she was worthy. In another first, he inspired her confidence and his respect made her feel a queen at best and an equal at worst. Spike's touch signalled their friendship was tipping into something more; it had done ever since he'd asked her to come with him to tonight's midsummer Blast from the Past disco.

Yet she didn't want it played out in the community hall where there were eyes on them.

'Can we go outside?' she said, laying her hand on his chest, her pulse reacting urgently to his solid bank of muscle. Annie wanted to be alone with him: to cherish the happiness, to get it right, in what she hoped would be a film she'd play on repeat in her head.

'You okay?' he said, pulling his Axl Rose bandana off

his head, concerned for her rather than bristling with rejection.

'Yes, I just fancy some air.' She removed her top hat and shook out her corkscrewed hair. Being Slash from Guns N' Roses was hot work. In matching black faux-leather drainpipes, they slipped along the side of the dance floor packed with friendly faces in fancy dress of Tom Jones medallions and Madonnas in lacy gloves.

There was Blod Stewart, with spiked-up hair sprayed yellow, wearing wet-look leggings and a Scotland scarf round her shoulders, swaying with Lyn, who'd come as Scary Old Spice in leopardskin pyjamas. Elvis Alis was slow dancing with Pastor Pete, aka Adam Ant, and Bowen and Sara were smooching as David Bowie and Debbie Harry. There at the side, laughing their heads off were Lew and Wanda. She had straightened her hair and become the redhead from Abba, Anni-Frid, in a T-shirt dress cut to the thigh with wedges while he was Freddie Mercury with a stick-on tache, white vest, chest wig and a stuffed sock tied on to a broom handle for a microphone.

Released into the outdoors, Annie waited for the relief of the cool breeze. It did nothing but fan the fire inside her. This wonderful man didn't make her feel like a teenager – he made her feel like a woman and it came at her in waves. His warm hand slipped into hers, his hungry eyes reflected her own longing and without a word she led him away from the light towards the safety of a huge oak tree. Anticipation spilled over and they found one another gently in the darkness. His tender lips on hers, their chests and hips and legs sealed, their tongues tasting one another, losing themselves in the beauty of their perfect chemistry.

Annie instantly felt complete: as if Spike was who she'd been waiting for, as if everything that had gone before had been about monochrome survival on a hostile planet and this was the world righting itself, turning it into a burst of colour. Yes, she was leaping ahead of herself, yes, she was breathless with lust, but this abandonment of caution was like shedding a skin, of having the courage to demand that life be better. They were dragged back into consciousness by a wolf-whistle which made them both smile shyly. Their foreheads still touching, their eyes locked in, they were drunk on each other – and they obviously looked like they were to whoever had caught them. She looked over her shoulder to see who it might be but there were only shadows. Annie stared back up at Spike and he was drinking her in, his palms cradling her face as if she – *she!* – was heaven-sent. *I completely adore you*, she said to him in her head, *you've given me faith and this moment, I swear, is the most blissful of my entire life and nothing will ever sully it . . .*

'Didn't take you long, Annie.'

Her blood turned to ice. She knew that harsh, mocking voice. Having felt her tense up, Spike instinctively pulled her closer. 'Who's that?' he said, as she whipped her head round, searching for Dean Pincher's sickening presence.

'My ex,' she whispered, her stomach clamping up, her shoulders hunched, all desire replaced by fear and then a surge of anger that he had chosen this moment to crawl out from under his rock. How long had he been watching? Her skin crawled at his Peeping Tom act – and then she recoiled as he emerged from the road.

'What are you doing here?' Annie seethed, quaking,

but knowing she had to hide it. 'How did you know I was here?'

He smirked and then ignored her, speaking to Spike, trying to goad him. 'I wouldn't bother, mate, she's damaged goods. Bad fucking news.'

Annie froze. Spike would resist, she knew he would, that's why she felt so much for him, but still she had to wait a few beats to trust her instinct. It meant that Dean would try again, though.

'Poor dog, all alone in the house. She's nervous, isn't she? Doesn't like noise. No one next door to keep an eye out for intruders.'

'You've been up there?' she cried, nauseous that he must have been tailing her to know where Teg was.

'And the boy, well, he wouldn't put up much of a fight, would he?'

That meant Dean had been lurking more that once. Arthur wasn't there tonight – he had made a friend at last, Nathan from the gardening club, and was over his on a sleepover.

Spike stiffened at the mention of his son. This was too much. Teg was one thing but now, because Dean had cased Spike's joint, a child was involved. Arthur was absolutely not to come close to this.

'You are a nasty piece of work,' Annie said. 'Don't you ever go up there again. I'll call the police.'

Dean laughed. 'Dog'll be dead and rotted by the time the cops get there.'

Annie gasped at the threat, her brain scrabbling for words amid her horror. How she hated him. How she wanted him to curl up and die. Her breathing had become shallow and she felt herself losing her courage. Was this how it was always going to be? She'd believe she'd taken a step away from him and then he'd reappear, soiling her progress with reminders of where she'd come from.

'Good job I've got CCTV, ain't it?' Spike said in a low voice as if he'd sensed her desperation.

'Yeah, right, 'course you have,' Dean said, thrilled to have had a tug on his line.

'You going to risk it?' Spike pulled himself taller, towering above Dean's skinny frame, and he visibly shrank.

Annie hated the fact it had taken body language to make Dean stand down; for this physical power was something she would never have. That was the kind of neanderthal Dean was. But she realised she could deliver the final blow. Because he'd made a mistake in coming here – he'd got too big for his boots. He'd dropped the dog-custody nonsense but still felt it was his right to intimidate her.

'You come near me again and I'll refuse to divorce you.'

'So?'. He was having a go at a comeback. But she had him by the short and curlies.

'You'll have to wait for that money you need from the sale of the house … the money you need to repay the false expenses you claimed for, why you lost your job, that you only got to keep quiet about because you said you'd pay it back double.'

'Bitch.'

He started to retreat, but he wasn't finished.

'Comfy at Blod's, are you?'

Again, he was letting her know he was keeping tabs on her.

'You're too much of a coward to turn up there!'

'Am I?'

'I'd watch it,' Spike growled. 'I'm a witness now.'

Dean quickly turned away and his footsteps gradually faded until he was swallowed by the night.

Instantly, Spike was filling the air with expletives and what he'd like to do with him. And then the apologies began. 'Sorry I got involved, it's your battle to fight, I know I shouldn't have stepped in. I just wanted to back you up, give you some support.'

'It's fine,' she said, relieved the scene was over. 'I'm just glad he's gone. Do you have CCTV, by the way?'

'No! But first thing tomorrow I'll get some. Oh, come here, Annie,' he said, reaching for her. 'Talk about from the sublime to the ridiculous; what a night.'

But Annie couldn't accept that. Security cameras in a place like this were unnecessary, an abomination that she would be responsible for.

'Spike ...' she hugged herself instead of him. 'I can't do this.'

'What? What do you mean?' His eyes examined her fearfully.

'Arthur could be dragged into this.'

'So what are you saying?'

'I'm saying that we ... leave this ... for a while.' She felt her chin wobble as she said it. This was killing her. But too much was at stake – Arthur had to come first. And really, this was what she deserved. The scale of her joy was so huge that it couldn't be real. It wouldn't last. 'I just feel so attached to Arthur that if something happened to him ...'

'Don't you think I hadn't thought about that?' Spike's face was softer, imploring, telling her he would care for her.

'Well, yes, of course.' But things had changed. The world had gone back to monochrome. This was what she had to do to make sure Arthur was unharmed. Look what had happened to Ryan when his life had been messed up by a bad man. That was all she cared about.

'But if you feel it's too complicated, too risky, I understand.' He had agreed readily. Perhaps it had been too soon for him after all.

'We can still be friends, can't we?' But she would never forget his kiss, how it had transported her to a place she'd never been before and she knew she wouldn't go to again.

'Yes. Definitely. Arthur would never forgive me if we weren't.' Spike gave her a weak smile and she suggested with her eyebrows that they head back to the party.

'I think I'm going to call it a night,' he said, suddenly weary. 'Teg can keep me company.' *Instead of Annie? Was that what he had imagined?* Because Annie had as they'd touched. Yet now it would only ever happen in her dreams. She couldn't feel sorry for herself about it – this was what she was used to: she was a loner, to have proper friends like she had now was more than she'd dared expect.

'Can I take you home?' he asked.

'I ought to see if Blod wants to go back,' she said, reluctantly.

'Cool,' he said, shuffling his feet. Where there had been no air between them, there were acres of space now.

Her arms ached to hold him again. Had Dean not appeared then they might be leaving together. But better it ended now, before she really fell for him and her bad luck and baggage cast a bad spell on the most precious of fathers and sons. Spike was still standing there, and she wondered if he thought she might change her mind. She couldn't. And she wouldn't.

'I'd better go,' she said, nodding, squeezing her fists tight, keeping her fingers curled up in case they dared to unfurl.

But before she left him, she allowed herself one last gorgeous look at the man who'd been hers for one magical moment.

26

Sunrise on the mountain top – do it!

Chloe, Deb and Hazel, Cardiff
Campsite Visitors' Book

Wanda's alarm went off but it was pitch black around her.

Was this a nightmare? No. She was definitely awake. A joke, then? But what kind of an idiot would set a clock for 3.15 a.m. on a Sunday morning?

It took her a few seconds to remember: she was that kind of idiot. And she only had herself to blame.

Some campers had returned from a sunrise climb of the mountain this week and they'd shown her the most amazing photos. If only they'd been the walking-boots brigade then she could dismiss them as such. But they'd been three really nice women who'd been after an adventure on a mums' weekend away. 'You've never done it?' they said. Well, then, she'd felt not shamed exactly, but inspired. If only Wanda hadn't told Lew about it last night after they'd had a skinful at the disco. Drunk on the power of being international rock stars from Abba and Queen, they'd decided they'd do a super-group mash-up

dawn climb to the peak one day! 'Tell you what,' she now recalled saying with a groan, 'it's the longest day tomorrow! Let's get into the summer solstice vibe!' 'Yeah! Let's!' Freddie Mercury had postured, with a half-wonky moustache, which did nothing to curtail his good looks. Now she prayed Lew would have forgotten all about it. If she just lay here and didn't move and shut her eyes ...
Ping!

'Coming, dancing queen?' he said. 'Got stuff for brekkie and a flask! Be here by 3.45 at the latest.'

It had been her idea – what could she do? So with a flamboyant throw of the duvet, she managed to sit up, stagger out of bed, dress, clean her teeth, get down the stairs, grab a torch and stagger up the hill to the beat of her banging head. She flashed her light at him and snorted. Lew was looking as dishevelled as she was. Wordlessly, he handed her a swig of his water – she'd already necked two glasses before she left but hangover thirsts were unquenchable.

'This better be worth it,' she said, stumbling alongside him on the path as they set off, shivering from the coldest part of the night. 'It's actually quite nippy.'

'We'll warm up,' Lew said, 'out of sheer bloody exhaustion. My legs are aching already.'

'That'll be from you leaping off tables with your microphone broomstick.'

'Was that before or after you teamed up with Agnetha to do "Dancing Queen" – on the stage?'

'It makes a change from being a drama queen,' she said. 'Think yourself lucky I didn't come as Mick Hucknall – there aren't many gingers in rock and roll to choose from. Oh, why did we do shots with Blod?'

'I'd like to put it on record that you insisted on the tequila.'

'Just think of the smug factor when we get there,' she said, albeit unable to possibly imagine it when her sheets would still be warm.

'That's the only thing keeping me going.'

'And breakfast. What time's sunrise?'

'Four fifty-three a.m.' Just over an hour from now. Hopefully they'd have a brew going by the time they watched the sun peek over the horizon.

They fell silent, their feet and breathing making the only sounds. There were no birds, no car engines, planes or wildlife. The line of shrubs which chattered with life in the day was dormant, the stile barely visible, the woodland as dark as a cow's stomach.

They were probably the only ones up in the entire village. Ha! Apart from Spike and Annie, who had disappeared together and then she had no recollection of either of them returning. Tonight would definitely have been the night for them! As was becoming usual, Wanda and Lew had ended up hanging out all night together.

Somehow they always found themselves side by side in spite of the blurred boundaries that Wanda tried not to think about any more. If he had something to tell her, he'd do it in his own time: she wouldn't try to prise him open, she wasn't sure she'd like whatever it was he had to say. Whatever, they were drawn to one another, like an inevitability.

And here they were again. Under a starry sky. It made the slog worth it: with each step they climbed closer to the Milky Way, which was running like a river through the heavens, lighter in the middle, brighter with every gasp. A lurch, though, and they'd be done for. And the earth loomed black, slowing them down.

'This is actually quite scary,' she said, as she misjudged her footing and slipped on a scramble of scree. Lew was there to grab her.

'Try it with a backpack!' he said, panting as they stopped to clear their rising panic.

'Don't worry, I know someone in Mountain Rescue. Although he might be over the limit.'

'Not helpful,' he said. Just a few minutes into a mammoth climb and they were already blinded by the night. The bounce of the torchlight threw up creepy shapes. They were unable to see beyond their feet and hands. It was hard to judge direction because of the wind which blew from all angles. And this lack of perspective, this absence of a looming peak, robbed them of all their orientation.

'Should we turn back?' Lew said quietly, taking hold of her hand. Their pulses were in rhythm, out of fear, exertion and sheer stupidity. 'Imagine if we got lost. We'd never live it down. This is going to take forever.' They stood in silence, feeling terribly small in the universe. Wanda was on the verge of surrender. And then the universe must've known, because it sent them a sign.

'Look!' Wanda cried.

An ever-so-slight strip of orange had appeared where the mountain met the sky. It revealed they were at the bowl of the hill – they knew the rest of the ascent off by heart. And while it was obvious, it needed to be said to spur them on. Lew did the honours. 'It's getting light!'

He gave her hand a squeeze to gee them on. 'Let's just do this. Like you said, we just need to act and be brave.'

His eyes sparkled in the moonshine.

'Yeah?' she asked, wondering if this was his way of telling her he'd taken on board what she'd said the night the tent collapsed. Because that had been weeks ago and he hadn't shown any acknowledgement of it in their contact before now.

He nodded.

'All right then,' she smiled and he grinned back lopsidedly at her. Her insides fizzed. So on they went, hand in hand, slowly but surely, concentrating hard, pointing out rocks and stumbling blocks, as the lunar-like path zig-zagged upwards. Their climb was difficult but repaid by the ever-changing sky – it was as if a lighter had been put to a touchpaper, sending up slow motion flames of colour. Wanda would pause every now and again to photograph the view of deep navy hills against the orange, reds, pinks and purples. It was staggeringly beautiful and spurred them on to quicken up, to make up time; if they pushed hard they'd do it. They took off their jumpers, knowing they'd be bare-armed for the rest of this long day, and finally, the creamy top of dawn revealed the ridge, which was the toughest stretch. They navigated the narrowed corridor of earth and stone, aware of the abrupt edges which fell away mercilessly.

And just as they got to the top, slapping the trig point in a high-five of celebration and adding their own to a pyramid of stones left by climbers before them, the tip of the sun broke the skyline. They'd done it! Lew threw off his backpack and Wanda twirled around in a circle, blown away by the never-ending blue panorama of hills and heavens. She wasn't into crystals and all that stuff but there was definitely a higher power involved somewhere along the way.

'This has got to be an official mountain, Lew. It's just got to be.'

'And it will be, I'm sure of it. And soon.'

Lew's arms came at her and they embraced, laughing and gasping, and then he didn't let go, and she found she didn't want him to either. They had the land to themselves, miles and miles of it, as if they were explorers claiming discovery. Euphoria flowed back and forth in an infinite loop: they swayed from side to side, her head against his neck, her nose breathing in his salty scent, her mouth just touching his naked skin. Lew's hands were sweeping her back and a primal sensation seeped into the periphery of her mind. Once she'd felt it, she couldn't control it – heat swept over her, she could feel blood rushing to her lips, her nipples and between her thighs. *Oh God, he was delicious.*

'I think I'm still drunk,' she swooned, gazing into his eyes, feeling completely erotic, and then dropping her head because this couldn't be happening.

'Me too,' he whispered.

They'd only ever been this close once before: back in the shepherd's hut fifteen years ago. But he was different now, he'd filled out, the muscles of his back dipping into his spine and the padding of his chest more pronounced. He was a man now and she was a woman. The tempo had changed, his touch was firmer but slower, more sensual. She was lifting her chin, he was dropping his and their cheeks were touching. Millimetre by millimetre, they were moving their faces until their noses were together and their lips crept towards each other's until they found a symmetry. Their heads tilted and Lew's breath was mixed with hers and their mouths were seconds from finding each other. She had to feel his skin, she needed to put her hands on him to check he was really here – they went under his top and her fingertips touched his firm and soft sculpted back and he did the same, slipping his palms onto her, caressing and massaging, as they became lost in each other. Still they hadn't kissed, it was like they were saving themselves until they reached the point of explosion. As her confidence and desire grew, her hands rose from the small of his back, feeling the two indents of dimples that she had desired in her dreams – but what was this? A rough expanse, rippled with what had to be scars.

'No,' he said, suddenly pushing her off. The sun was completely up now and it seared her eyeballs.

Confusion swept through her – what had she done? What was wrong? They stood there speechless, staring, breathing hard. Wanda not understanding, Lew full of ... what? His eyes were wide; was that fear? Was she terrifying? Had she hurt him?

'What is it?' she said, imploring him to tell her what the Welsh cakes had just happened.

He gulped and looked down at his feet, his hands on his hips.

'Lew, tell me. I might be able to help. Lew, it's me. It's always been you and me.'

She'd said too much, she'd known it as soon as it had left her mouth – the guard would crash down again. But when he looked up at her, she saw he was close to tears. She reached out to him, her body pleading for him to explain.

'This is why we can't be together, Wanda.'

'What do you mean?'

'My back. The skin, it's an old burn injury.'

'So?' She'd want him if he was an old Yorkshire pudding charcoaled at the back of the oven. 'I don't care! You should see my stretch marks!'

'It's not about that ...' He rubbed his face with his hands. 'You're perfect.'

She was perfect! He'd just said it! But, of course, it hit her: this was the first slice of the dumping compliment sandwich. Say something nice, fill it with rejection, finish off with another slice of something kind.

'Don't tell me, "It's not you, it's me ... Right, well, it's been lovely getting to know you but after several decades I've realised it's not working out."'

'Listen, Wanda ...'

'What?' She bristled with irritation. 'I have wanted this ... you ... ever since we met. Even though you used to put snails in my school bag. There's not been one day when I haven't thought about you. You've got to be straight with me because I can't keep playing this game of getting close then having to step back again. If you don't feel the same about me, just tell me. I'll get drunk, cry, bore everyone senseless, pretend I'm absolutely fine when I bump into you, curse whoever you end up with, and then eventually I'll be all right, I'll meet someone, maybe, and if I don't I'll have gone travelling anyway to get away from you. So please, this has gone on for too long.'

'The burns,' he said. 'They were from the fire.'

'The fire. The "fire" fire, the one at the campsite?' she asked with trepidation. 'From fifteen years ago?'

'Yes. I was there when it started.' He looked very guilty, barely able to meet her eyes.

'You?'

'Yes.'

Suddenly the space between them multiplied as shock sent her reeling backwards, away from him, repelled by his presence. She felt sick at the sight of him.

'What exactly are you saying?' she said, not wanting to believe what she now suspected. But it all made sense. Lew leaving the village, Lew's lies about not finding Ryan, so he could put the blame on him. He'd let everyone believe it for so long. Was it him who'd started it? *Poor Ryan. Poor Annie. Her dad.* And she felt the old fury anew. She couldn't look at him. She didn't want to be in the same airspace as him. That was it. She snapped and began to walk away from him.

'Wanda!' he said. Then again and again as she picked up speed, scrambling down, feeling her heart in her throat, and he began to shout to call her back. 'Let me explain!'

All that crap about making amends, doing up the shepherd's hut, even teaching her to make a fire again! The gall of it! No wonder he'd wanted her to leave! Pretending that he was glad she was around. And then he'd forgotten himself, thinking with his dick. All because he felt guilty. Her legs worked harder to put more distance between them, and she looked back to see if he was chasing her.

Instead he was stood quite still, watching her. 'Go on then, Wanda, run! Run again! Like you always do!'

She had felt with her fingers the damage to his skin from that night – the connection, of touching the past, of touching his lies.

'I will not leave this place until I'm ready,' she yelled

back. 'But until then, I want nothing to do with you again. Nothing.'

They faced one another across the mountain – she waited to make sure he wouldn't move. And then once she was sure of it, she turned her back on him forever.

27

With an 'enough's enough', Blod had insisted Teg should come to stay.

Having a four-legged guest had never been specifically outlawed by her – she was simply too kind a person to do that. It was just that Annie hadn't wanted to impose another inconvenience on her.

Even though she paid rent – Blod would only take peanuts, admittedly – it weighed heavily on Annie that she'd been living with her since January. Blod never suggested she wasn't happy about the arrangement; in fact she was grateful, she said, for the company of an evening. But it felt to Annie as if she was taking advantage, putting on Blod, making her feel the force of her mistakes. She was a grown woman, she shouldn't be depending on a pensioner to put her up. When shame came calling, it either came in the night when the sunken velvet sofa was making her back ache or in the day when her back ached even more. Folding her sheet and duvet and stacking them with a pillow on top behind the chair each morning was always a reminder, too.

Annie tried to ease her guilt by making herself useful. Yet it was a fine line not to make Blod feel redundant: people had their own ways of doing things. She was the queen of her realm and Annie didn't want to dethrone her.

Add Teg into the mix and it wouldn't be something benign – it would be actual disruption. And so it had proven to be.

The house was a teeny-tiny thing anyway and Teg made it feel like it was bursting at the seams. Overnight the territory had become divided like Korea – the cats were confined to the kitchen, having access to the garden for their toilet business, and the dog was on a short lead in the sitting room with the front door her only way in and out. Should anyone make a break for it, they'd have to get past a baby gate first. It was hard enough for the humans, checking the coast was clear when going from one room to the other, especially with cups of tea and biscuits.

It was unsustainable. One wag of Teg's tail and bits went flying – she'd already taken out one of Blod's china figurines. Emotionally there was an effect, too. The cats no longer had the run of the two floors and were not only deprived of a lap of an evening but a snuggle with Blod at night. From Teg's absence, Annie knew only too well how big the gap was when the animal you were used to curling up beside you wasn't there. Teg had taken to refusing her bed so she'd have her enormous body on hers all night – Teg was feeling insecure and that also meant accidents, both wet and solid, plus barking at strange noises and the meows of the cats.

Mostly, though, she knew her upset was at being moved on yet again, particularly away from her best mate, Arthur. Annie had felt like the Wicked Witch of the East when she'd turned up at Spike's the day after the showdown with Dean at the disco.

Spike had opened the door and the joy on his face – the beautiful joy – told her he was hoping she'd come to tell him she'd made a mistake, that she would take this on with him, together. He'd quickly gathered not when she'd told him she'd come to get Teg. It was one of the hardest things she'd ever done in her life: resisting her heart's urge to be with Spike, to fall on him and never let him go. She'd had to feel the ground beneath her feet, stay firm and zone out to get through it.

'It'll break 'is heart,' Spike had said, not manipulatively, but stating the obvious.

'I can't risk something happening here in Arthur's home, where he feels safe.' She'd sounded robotic but the alternative was a breakdown.

'Teg is part of that.' He'd almost pleaded.

'But she'd also be the thing that caused trouble. I hate doing this, taking her away. But we can't take the gamble.'

'It feels like we're giving in to Dean.'

How easy it was for a man to say that: they had physical power when push came to shove. Women only looked for an exit or how to hunch into a ball to lessen the blows.

'I'm trying to protect Arthur.'

'Dean won't come back, we sorted 'im out.'

'I won't believe it until I'm divorced.' More silent calls had come that morning. She couldn't take it any more – she was going to have to change her number.

Spike acquiesced with a soul-deep sigh. But proving himself to be the good guy he was, he had put on a united front when they'd sat with Arthur to break the news. Without even discussing it, they'd said nothing about

Dean – just that it was time for Teg to be with Annie again. Arthur's high from staying the night at Nathan's was punctured and he'd cried and cried and clung onto his furry pal like a teddy bear, whispering goodbyes. Annie had had tears too: the last thing she wanted to do was to take this little boy's best mate away. But she'd be responsible if anything happened – who knew, Dean could be watching them right now. She'd left, promising walks together and invites for tea – but it'd be like inviting giants into a doll's house. That was the thing about any such relationship with Spike, too – how could she do it when she had nothing? She could hardly invite him for a night of passion under a crochet blanket with a dog in the audience. There were too many obstacles, and that told her she had made the right decision.

The weight of worrying about Arthur's safety might have lessened from her shoulders but her heart was still heavy. A couple of hours at the community garden after work in the days since had helped in terms of distraction. Teg could have some freedom and the cats could have a fuss off Blod.

Arriving there again tonight, she parked the van, shifted her wheelbarrow out of the boot and began to fill it with her tools, soaking up the gorgeous evening, which was warm, still, sunny and dry.

This was her happy place: where duty didn't come into it. Nearly two months in, it had gone from grassland to *Gardeners' World*. Thanks to the kids, the blank canvas was now full of colourful flowers, of violets and reds, blues and oranges. The borders buzzed with bees, the runner-bean teepee was actually being used as a chill-out spot and the veggies were well on their way. Spike had worked wonders with the pallets, creating an outside living room which the children had painted rainbow-style. All that was left to do was the barbecue area, which Spike would tackle next, and then christen it with burgers and bangers. Annie couldn't wait for that day, nor their produce sale – the Grow Up gang had already been able to harvest lettuce and broad beans to take home. Okay, they'd pulled yucky faces at the prospect of eating their greens but they'd admitted later that they'd tried them and quite liked them. That was what it was about: from farm to fork, having an end result and a sense of achievement. The frenzy of growth that came with mild weather and enough rain meant it required a lot of maintenance, which was lucky for her when she needed the escape.

She breathed in the greenery with zest and felt herself relaxing with every step. She saw someone was already there, and as she got closer, it became clear that it was Spike. The spin and stop of her stomach was inevitable; but this was the consequence of her decision and she would stick to it, so she put on a smile and called out a *hello*, expecting a wave in return. But she saw now he had his hands on his head and was looking around him with agitation. What was up? And then she saw it for herself and dropped the wheelbarrow dead, covering her mouth in distress.

The garden had been wrecked – completely and utterly destroyed. With horror she took in the plants ripped from their beds and trampled on; the teepee had been pulled down with force, judging by the broken canes, the pallets splintered by stomping feet and the vegetables disinterred from their compost.

'I just got 'ere,' Spike said, white as anything. 'I was

going to prepare the ground for the barbecue. I can't believe it.'

Rage consumed her. 'Now you see what he's capable of! Now you see it! I told you!'

The apologies came thick and fast then. 'I'm sorry, Spike,' she said, her shoulders shuddering with gulps of breath, 'I didn't mean to take it out on you. This is devastating, for the kids, for us, and all because of me. Dean Pincher will haunt me forever.'

Spike grabbed hold of her. 'Listen, we're going to make this bigger and better than it was before. I refuse to let that bastard do this to us.'

'He'll do it again.'

'I won't let 'im!'

'How? How are we going to stop him? We can't patrol it day and night!'

Another punch hit her between the eyes when she saw the smashed-in-two Grow Up Garden sign which the kids had designed by themselves, the letters made out of hand-drawn leaves, flowers, animals and vegetables on a wooden board.

'This could only have happened last night or this morning,' Annie said. 'Thank God Arthur isn't here to see this.'

'I know. This would be too much on top of ... everything.'

'Teg misses him so much,' Annie admitted. 'So do I.' She hadn't exactly avoided Arthur but she hadn't gone to visit since she took Teg away – she'd reasoned that it would make him feel worse. 'How is he?'

'All right,' Spike said in what would be an understatement. 'But I don't want you to feel bad, I see this now and you were right, I underestimated Dean.'

'Maybe I could pop round?' she suggested, wanting to make it all better.

'I dunno. He's off school at the moment.'

'What's wrong?'

'Stomach upset, 'e says. And don't get me wrong, he isn't eating and he's had a bit of a temperature, but he's still up and about. Well, I left 'im just now in front of the Xbox to be truthful. I was only going to be here an hour.'

Annie felt like torturer-in-chief. She'd done this to him by taking Teg.

'It's all my fault.'

'Kids get bugs all the time.' Spike had no need to appease her – but he still tried to, such was the gent he was.

'I wish I could see him.' It was self-indulgent of her and she immediately wished she could undo it.

'It's probably best you don't at the moment.' He winced, knowing that would cause Annie pain.

'Of course.' She'd only wanted to make sure Arthur wasn't involved in any of this nastiness, but it had bitten her on the arse.

'The fing is,' he scratched his stubble, and she knew he was about to deliver something which would pile on more torment, 'about the other night, he kind of asked me if you and me were ... you know ... more than friends. And I had to tell him the truth, that we'd decided to put things on hold for the moment. He's upset ...'

'Oh no,' Annie said, her posture collapsing, worry back on her shoulders.

'I think it's brought back the feelings of losing Lucy.'

That was understandable and he needed to know she

got it. 'I never wanted to replace her, Spike. How could I?'

'No, I know, Annie,' he said, putting his hands on his chest, 'but it seemed so easy the way you fitted into our lives. As if it was convenient ... no, that's the wrong word ...'

No matter. The damage was done. Annie blinked back her devastation and looked up at the sky.

'I mean, it felt right, you being wiv us.'

He could be backtracking because of her obvious upset. Whatever, the point was she couldn't take any meaning from it – he was all over the place.

'It's okay, Spike,' she said, staring at him now, her eyes probably communicating her broken heart, but she could only be true to herself: 'You don't need to explain any more.'

'I just can't let Arthur down, if it didn't work out. He adores you, we both do, but it's a whole other thing to take on a child and he would see you as a mother figure and—'

'Please ... it's okay.' Annie felt weak because actually, this was what she wanted: to be with Spike and Arthur as a package. She wasn't scared: motherhood was what she had wanted for so long. It wasn't that she had got involved with them to fulfil this need – she had come to terms with never being a mum. It had just grown as she'd become part of their lives.

Spike and Annie stared at one another. Before their kiss, before anything had happened romantically, a conversation between them like this would have ended in a hug. How very much she wanted to comfort him and herself in each other's arms. But there were new rules now. They had to learn new steps and that meant space. It was the cruellest conclusion of all.

'You go,' she said, holding herself to stop herself from falling apart. 'Arthur needs you. I can clear this lot up.'

She expected him to protest but he cleared his throat and nodded, leaving her to survey the mess of the garden and the wreckage of her heart.

28

We came here as 'mystery guests' for **Happy Campers**
magazine and we're delighted to say Under A Starry Sky
passed with flying colours! Our review will be in next
month's edition.

'Mr and Mrs Brown', Worcester
Campsite Visitors' Book

S ara and Wanda's weekly curry had been on ice lately.
Life had become incredibly busy after all – busier
for Sara though, nudge nudge, wink wink. So for Wanda
to have pinned her friend down for a long-overdue girls'
night in over wine and a takeaway was a treat. And a
necessity, such was the burden Wanda was carrying
around with her.

Adulthood gave you an insight into life's greys but
try as she might, Wanda felt like she'd regressed since
finding out Lew had been involved with the fire. He'd
admitted it. *Black.* Yet how could it be possible? *White.*
What other reasons, what greys, could there be to explain
how he'd been injured? Because if there were, surely
he would've been open about it right from that night?
Instead he'd left Gobaith and had never mentioned to

anyone that he'd been there with Ryan. It had to be guilt. It had to be. But marrying that with who she knew him to be – or had been – was impossible. Then there was the fact he had helped out on the campsite – was this out of conscience? Yet why had he come back at all to rebuild The Bunkhouse if he was responsible? Wouldn't it be foolish to return to the scene of your crime?

She could ask Lew, obviously. As soon as her shock and rage had subsided to below volcano level, she'd realised she hadn't asked him anything about it all. It had been too much for her to bear his company. Going to him now to ask 'why?' and 'how?' was out of the question. She wouldn't be able to look him squarely in the eyes she'd surrendered to during their sexy hug on the mountain at sunrise. He made her feel so much stuff – and whatever it was, whether frustration, anger or love, it was at top volume and full heat. Her fingers could still feel his damaged skin and the way he'd recoiled.

Wanda couldn't confide in her mother, she'd go marching up to Lew with bells on without question. Carys was out of bounds too. On the verge of entering the third trimester, she needed no excitement: the consultant had warned her the twins could be born at any moment from now on. Annie didn't even know Lew had been with Ryan that night – hearing that her substitute brother had been in cahoots with Ryan would be devastating on top of the community garden being vandalised by her ex. It was all too premature to raise. That left Sara, and Wanda knew she could trust her. Even if they hadn't had any decent one-on-one time lately, they always picked up as if they were carrying on a conversation from five minutes ago. There was such comfort in that while things changed, their friendship never did. Neither did their little routines.

Sara had turned her lounge into an Indian restaurant – as she always did. And the set-up was the same: her round coffee table was spread with a gorgeous multicoloured silk throw Wanda had given her after she received it in a tourist-board promotion of India. Waiting were two candles, napkins, glasses, a bottle on chill, bowls, cutlery and side plates and an Indian playlist off Spotify set the scene. By the delicious spicy smell of it, Amir from Keep Calm and Curry On had delivered their usual – all they had to do was ring up, announce their names and he'd know what they wanted. And in came Sara with a tray laden with steaming-hot chicken biryani, veggie balti and naan, plus poppadoms and mango chutney. To finish off they'd have After Eights from Blod's and microwaved flannels for the old face rub. Once they'd laid it all out, they sat cross-legged on the floor, their eyes smiling at each other and the grub and they tucked in with big spoonfuls of one another's dishes.

'Bloody lush!' Sara said, threatening to spray rice all over the place.

'God, this is so good!' Wanda replied in ecstasy through stuffed chops.

'Ha, listen to us, groaning over food!'

'Closest I'll get to groaning, let me tell you. Unlike you!' Wanda raised her eyebrows suggestively.

'Shuddup!' Sara giggled. 'It's love, not lust!'

'Oh, really?' Wanda gasped. This was how it was though – no warm-up was required between them. 'Have you said that to each other, then?'

'Bowen has!' Wanda caught a very cute and coy flutter of Sara's eyelashes. 'But I'm not there yet.'

'But you're close?'

Sara nodded. Her inner glow had transformed her: she resembled an angel in soft focus. Wanda understood her reluctance to spell it out – she didn't want to jinx it by saying it aloud.

'Ah! There's lovely!'

'Yeah. But I've got to be careful.'

'Deffo.'

'My first marriage fell apart as soon as the honeymoon was over. I need to make sure this is the real thing.'

'Wake up and smell the coffee, you mean?'

'And his socks! I've got to see him warts and all, once the initial thrill has kind of calmed down. Because at the moment he puts the loo seat down but that might change.'

'Glad to hear he's treating my toilet well!'

'It is weird going up there when it's yours. But then it felt like a second home anyway. What's the plan with it? Are you going to move back in soon? Not that I'm thinking of Bo, I wouldn't be moving him in with me. Too soon.'

Wanda saw this as her chance to fill Sara in on the conclusion she'd reached. 'I'm going to let it out for another six months. Maybe longer. I've decided. I'm going to go travelling as soon as I can. Once the babies are born and everything's settled down. I've enjoyed getting the site back on its feet but ...'

'What is it? Are you okay?' Sara had spotted the undercurrent.

Wanda laid down her fork. 'I almost snogged Lew the other day.'

'Whaaaaat?' Sara leaned in over the table and topped up Wanda's glass.

'There isn't a happy ending. Don't get excited.'

Wanda told the tale, feeling everything she had felt afresh: the excitement, the wonder, the sensuality. How she had seen him not as Lew the teenager but Lew the man, the old infatuation changing into something more grown up. Sara started apologising for being so wrapped up in her own stuff that she hadn't even realised Wanda was sweet on Lew again. But Wanda hadn't wanted to admit it to anyone until now. Then she got to the blow.

'You think he started the fire?' Sara said, agog.

'I don't know. I can't believe he would've but why else did he flee?'

'But what would his motive have been?'

'No idea. Maybe it was a game that went wrong. Maybe Ryan pushed him into it. I've gone over it and over it but it doesn't make sense. Yet the scars were there, the way he jumped back, he was acting guiltily. It's made me think this is something that can't be worked out.'

'And that's why you want to leave?'

'Yes.'

'I don't blame you, to be honest. But can you go, not knowing what happened? Why Lew was up there?'

'Maybe I'll have to. Because Lew hasn't come to me to explain. And I'm not going to ask. It's up to him. I'll only be accused of making a drama out of it.'

'Hardly! This is justified!'

'And do I really want to know? I can't possibly ever see his point of view about this. My dad ... the site ... it was like the end of my innocence. It was all over the news, everywhere we turned for months, there was so much damage.'

'God, yes.'

'Do you know, I had a feeling Lew was hiding something. I assumed it was just that he'd had his fingers burned by his ex and life in general. Never did I imagine it was actual burns. I thought me and him might ... we were getting close. To think I even told him how I felt about him up there on the mountain. I'm heartbroken. I've lost him all over again, yet I wouldn't want him anywhere near me.'

Sara crawled round the table to give Wanda a cuddle. 'I totally get why you're going to leave. But I think it's important you try to find out more. Because if you don't, you might never come back. It'll get bigger and bigger until you can't face it. And, being totally selfish, I couldn't bear that. Who would I have my curry with then?'

Wanda gave her a little smile. 'Thanks, mate,' she said. 'But your world is changing already. You've got a guy on the go. But for me, it's like I'm standing still. I've got to move on. Nothing will change for me here. I've climbed that bloody mountain – I've sorted the campsite pretty much. The phone doesn't stop ringing, we're booked solid through to the end of September. Word of mouth is going far and wide, we've even had enquiries from abroad. I had a camping journalist contact me the other day, they want to feature us in a UK top ten coolest campsites feature. It's fab, but what else can I achieve here?'

Sara's silence, so rare it was nearly extinct, shouted out what Wanda knew: it would soon be time to get packing. She had chased the dream of Lew for so long but she'd never really known him at all. Too much time had been wasted: she wouldn't make the same mistake again.

29

So the destruction of the community garden had been Dean's last act of fury.

His humiliation at the disco night dressing-down by Spike and Annie had had to be cancelled out – Dean had always needed to have the last word.

But finally it was over. She'd had a letter from his solicitor saying he had given up his claim on Teg and had agreed terms. There'd been an offer on the house, lower than what she knew it was worth, but he had obviously trashed the place. Still, it'd be enough for her to buy something. And that was what mattered – a safe haven for her with a garden of her own. Small plots could be as beautiful as the biggest: she imagined hers would be a square of stone surrounded by luscious borders of greenery where she could sit of a weekend with a cup of coffee, cocooned by nature. Just the thought of that stilled her – imagine how she'd feel when it happened! The realisation that she had arrived at the 'when' of her life, leaving behind the 'if', came to her as she made her way to the high school to drop in a proposal.

A head-of-year teacher had heard about the community garden and had asked her to come in last week to talk about doing a project with the kids. A piece of land at the back of the school had been set alight last week by arsonists; the little sods had torched an old shed too, but the school had decided to make something positive out of it and turn it into a garden. There'd be a bit of money in it for Annie but that wasn't why she'd jumped at the offer. It was a measure of how far she'd come – to be invited back to the school where she had failed so miserably was reward in itself. It would also distract her from the gaping hole inside of her at having lost Spike and Arthur. She'd seen them at Grow Up but there had been no chance to make a special effort because she'd had to really rally the kids, some of them in tears after the vandalism. Teg had made up for it, bounding at Arthur and Annie had had to take a deep breath when they were reunited in licks and cuddles. Spike had been friendly but there was a wall between them now and the politeness of their encounter, asking for tools, please, and fake bright smiles had hurt her deeply. But that was how it had to be.

The timing of the school job was perfect in that sense. And she hoped so much that Arthur might sign up for it when it started. She'd caught herself searching crowds of pupils when she'd come in before and she was doing it now, scanning the shirts and trousers in the corridors for his fair head and freckles. It was so strange to be walking them again: being offered a seat in an office where she had once been told to stand up straight and explain herself in a bollocking over late homework or the wrong uniform had felt like an out-of-body experience. Yet it had really happened, and Mrs 'call me Sue' Harrison had been thoroughly engaged with Annie's off-the-top-of-her-head ideas, thanking her profusely for her time at the end. That sentiment remained: the secretary had told her to go on up to the year group area to personally hand over her fat A4 envelope outlining the project. Again, Annie picked up on an entirely different ethos in the school compared to the harsh environment of her days in the classroom. The buildings had been updated: there was a bright cafeteria smelling of basil and garlic in place of the gloomy prison-style hall that had stunk of cabbage; and all sorts of activities and clubs and trips and achievements were postered up on the walls. Who'd have thought she of all people would be treated like a valued pillar of the community. Her younger self would never have believed it! It was so ridiculous she felt a smile spread across her face. And there was Mrs Harrison waiting for her as if Annie was a VIP.

'Annie! Hi!' she said, holding out a hand and shaking hers enthusiastically. 'Are these the plans? I've been looking forward to getting them!'

'They're rough in terms of measurements but you'll get the gist and I hope they don't disappoint you, Mrs Harrison.' This woman, in her trendy khaki shirt dress and cool pink pumps, may not have been anything like the old dragons who'd once taught her, but even so, Annie would never call her Sue.

'I'm sure they won't! You're a breath of fresh air. The total opposite of the gardening type, if you get me, you're young, exciting and "can do". The other two I approached were not quite what we were looking for.' Ha! Annie knew what she meant – her rivals were generally older men who took sharp intakes of breath at anything other than a mow and a trim. 'Gardening doesn't have to be fuddy-duddy. And the way the planet's going, it's important for the children to get close to it to see it's worth looking after.'

'I completely agree! My proposal is all about that … the eco benefits as well as the psychological boost of getting your hands dirty, nurturing something from seed to plant.' Annie was gushing like a bottle of pop. 'I've tried to think of ways to draw them in – we could do plant murals and chill-out zones, make a greenhouse out of plastic bottles …' Mrs Harrison beamed. 'I can introduce maths into it too: there's this thing called the Fibonacci sequence which you find in plant spirals such as sunflowers and fern fronds. Learning outdoors is always more fun. And if that fails then I'll sell them the celebrity cool angle – loads of them are into gardening these days, Instagram is full of floral influencers, it's crazy!'

'Well, I can't wait to read this!' Mrs Harrison waved the envelope in the air as if it was a trophy. 'Thanks for bringing it up here.' A buzzer went and classes started pouring pupils. 'Do you need me to show you out, or—'

'No! Don't worry, I know where I'm going.'

God, it was such a thrill to meet people on your wavelength. It was as if her soul had been given a dose of Miracle-Gro plant food. Her self-esteem was back up off the floor, she was dizzy with pride and so she found herself sucked into the flow of students, swept along the corridors, down the stairs and back towards the school entrance. But then there was a bottleneck as a load of kids queued to get into the hall and as she got closer to the door she thought she saw someone familiar sat on the stage. It couldn't be Lew. But it was. What was he doing here? And there was Bowen beside him in his fire service T-shirt. Lew must've come round to the idea of giving a talk at the school. *Good on him!*

They were too far away to wave to, but if she just stood

here with the door ajar could give them a thumbs up if they looked her way. But suddenly, the room of chattering children was being shushed by a teacher who was introducing Bowen and Lew. Bowen began to speak about the danger of fire but had trouble getting their attention; there were a lot of fidgeting bodies and wide yawns. He sensed their staring into space and cut his losses, making way for somebody, he said, who had suffered first-hand in the biggest fire in Gobaith's history. That got their attention. For Lew wasn't some old git who would give them a lecture – he was one of the village's good guys, relatable and handsome, down to earth and cooler than the average bloke around here. As he got up, he looked nervously around the hall and Annie sent him all the vibes she could over the sea of heads to wish him luck.

'Hi everyone,' he said, 'I'm Lew Jones, this is my old school. I've been sat here like you lot, bored out of my brains, wondering how long it is till lunch.' The kids laughed and he looked at his watch. 'Fifteen minutes. But I'll make it quick and then you can have more free time, yeah? That all right?' He asked the teacher, who made a show of thinking about it before he nodded.

Cheers broke out and just like that Lew had won them over.

'I'm not going to tell you all the stuff you know. Arson's a crime … it's a huge risk to life not just at the fire itself but because it takes firefighters away from other incidents … it costs millions of quid every year … blah blah blah. That doesn't mean anything, does it? It goes in one ear and out the other.' He performed a shrug, which sent a ripple of confusion around the room. If he wasn't going to talk about that, what was he going to say?

'No, I think it's more powerful to show you something instead.'

There was utter silence.

'We've all seen the line of fire on the mountain top, at a distance it's mesmerising, quite pretty too. It's not harming anyone, is it?'

Every face was focused on him wondering what he was going to do next.

'But if you're close enough ...'

Lew began to pull at his T-shirt. What was he doing? He wasn't getting undressed, was he? Whispers went up and the kids swapped looks of disbelief. He took off his top and slowly turned around – and gasps went up from everyone, Annie included. His back was covered in scarring, pink and mottled, uneven and scrammed. Annie was reeling – she hadn't known anything about this. He had never told her that he'd been injured that night.

He turned to face them again and put his T-shirt back on.

'I was involved. I had to go to a specialist burns unit. I told everyone I'd gone to Scotland for a course. I was too frightened to say anything. And then I left the village because I felt responsible for the fire ...'

Sickened and enraged, Annie stepped backwards, holding her hand over her mouth. Lew had been involved? And all this time he had allowed Ryan to take the blame? The shock sent her flying away from the door, she could still hear his voice but his words had turned to gobbledygook. She had to get out of this place before she threw up. Somehow she managed to find her way out, her stomach heaving, her head hot, her fingers cold. Scrabbling for her keys, she ran to the car park and made it to the hedgerow just in time to relieve her sickness. The adrenalin got her inside her van and away and then the pounding came to her head as she drove on, towards home, and as she got to Blod's, the weakness came and she staggered limply inside, needing to process what the hell had just happened.

'Annie!' Blod came to her, her arm catching hers just as she dropped onto the sofa and Teg jumped up. 'What is it?'

'I can't believe it ... I've just seen something that changes everything. Ryan wasn't alone.'

'What?' Blod was shaking her head.

'Lew's back, he was scarred.' She shut her eyes and could still see the welts – and to think she'd made him potions for burns and he'd have used them on that. 'He was there with Ryan. That night. Lew always told me he'd never found him up there.'

'Lew? No!' Blod said.

'I saw it with my own eyes, I heard him say it.'

What should she do with this information? What could she say to him? Why hadn't he spoken to her about this? No wonder he had avoided giving a talk at the school. Something must have happened to twist his arm. None of it made sense, though. She needed to talk to Wanda. That's what she had to do. And then she remembered that Wanda had been virtually absent from village life for days now. Annie had knocked for her after discovering the vandalism but Carys was the one who'd come – she'd said Wanda was up to her eyes with work and when Annie had messaged her she'd either send back a rushed 'Sorry, busy' or nothing at all. Could the two things be related? But how? Because now she understood the last thing she wanted to do was to leave this house and face people. Had Wanda been burdened with the same knowledge? But surely she would have said something to her. And yet was it Wanda's job to do that? Perhaps Lew had said he'd talk to Annie. Yet to do a big reveal like that in public without telling Annie first showed a serious lack of judgement. She felt completely let down by him: perplexed and betrayed, and then her shoulders were rising and falling as she began to cry, her mind a mess of questions, her heart in so much pain it was like losing Ryan all over again. A huge lie had been told, a cover-up of some kind. She needed to speak to Lew. But the thought of him made her retch. All she could do, and all she'd be capable of for the foreseeable hours, was to curl up and nurse her wounds.

30

One of the main charms of Under A Starry Sky is it being family-run. We were on the receiving end of home-style hospitality and we hope the next generation of Williamses arrive safely and continue the good work!

Mr and Mrs Dempsey, Portsmouth
Campsite Visitors' Book

Wanda's finger hovered on the confirm button.

There before her on her screen was the itinerary she'd had to cancel but was now ready to rebook, departing on October the first. Today was July the sixth; that gave her eighty-seven days until launch.

She did a mental check of her dates – for the millionth time, because she was paranoid she'd get it wrong. While their due date was towards the end of September, the twins would be here by hook or by C-section when they hit week thirty-seven, which was the beginning of the month. It would mean Wanda was there to help Carys settle into motherhood and she'd get to bond with the babies herself. Yes, she was right, as she finished her calculations. All that remained was a countdown of 3-2-1 and …

There was a knock at her bedroom door and Carys appeared, enormous stomach first, looking white as a sheep.

'You okay?' Wanda said, putting her laptop down and examining her face. It was pinched with fright. She got up and went to her sister, who suddenly froze.

'There it is again, I can feel something moving,' she said. 'I felt it before but thought it was just a twinge.'

'It's not Rock and Roll having a mosh?' It was a stupid question but she needed to ask it.

'No. It's different. My bump, it's all tensed up.'

Wanda could see the anxiety in her hands which swept across her bump, trying to detect what was going on.

'Do you think you're going into labour?' Wanda said, trying to hide the fear which was rising in her chest. The babies were twenty-nine weeks. Their chances of survival were good, but they'd be in an intensive care unit, tube-fed and on oxygen. Wanda had read up on everything but didn't like to let Carys know she knew the score: she didn't want her thinking she was worried.

'I hope not. Please, God, stay in there, you two,' she said to her tummy.

'Maybe they're those practice contractions? The Branston Pickles.' Their name for Braxton Hicks, which Mam had misheard. 'Have you timed them?'

'Yes, they're random, I was just having a nap and they woke me up.'

'That's good.' Proper contractions were regular.

'But I dunno ... I'm scared. My back aches and that's meant to be a sign.' She bit her lip and Wanda could see the anguish in her eyes. 'If it wasn't twins, I don't know if I'd want to be checked out. But there's so much stuff that can go wrong here, I'm just terrified.'

'Right, I'll take you now to the hospital. No arguments.'

Carys gave a massive sigh of relief. The poor thing, having to shoulder all of the concern alone. By taking charge, it meant Wanda had allowed her sister to admit that was what she had wanted all along. And she could always say she'd been forced to go with Wanda if she felt silly if it turned out to be nothing.

'Better bring your bag,' Wanda said. 'Just in case. You go down, tell Mam, I'll get your stuff then meet me in the Land Rover.'

Carys waddled off slowly at the speed of – and, to be honest, the size of – an oil tanker. Pregnancy was wonderful, obviously, but there were definitely draw-backs. Shiny hair and strong nails Carys might have but Wanda's rose-tinted view of it had been ripped away by her sister's plight of constipation, exhaustion, swollen ankles, overheating in the sunshine and sleepless, uncomfortable nights.

Wanda fought Mam off, who was desperate to come but someone needed to hold the fort, and lugged Carys's bulging bag of newborn nappies, tiny babygros, maternity pads and huge knickers outside.

'Let's look at this as a test run, eh?' Wanda said at the wheel as they sped off.

'Yes, good plan. Thanks, Wanda, I don't know what I'd do without you.' Carys was never far from tears these days.

'Well, how chuffed do you think I am that I'm your birth partner?' The less said about that absent father the better. It was irrational to blame him when he knew nothing of the situation. The chances of a one-night stand ending like this were slim, yet Wanda wished he'd been the nice guy he'd seemed when he got together with Carys. It was all so disappointing. That was men for you. It was crushing that Lew fitted into that category too.

Two weeks it'd been since his big reveal to her on the mountain top and he'd gone to ground, only rising up to perform his frankly puzzling topless strip on the high-school stage. What had he been thinking? Was he losing the plot? It was erratic behaviour. Or maybe it was a release after all these years of denial, as if once he'd lanced the boil with her he needed to do it again and again to prove his remorse. His ears had to be burning – Gobaith was on fire with questions: what had he had to do with it? Were the police involved? Did it count as a guilty plea? What happened to him to get all those scars? For the meantime, there'd be no answers. Lew had disappeared on some residential training course in the Peak District – talk about convenient timing; an old mate of his had stepped in to run The Bunkhouse – and Wanda was glad of his absence. But still his confession had reopened the village's wounds. Mam and Carys were of the opinion that there had to be a reason for all of it – Lew just wasn't like that. They refused to believe it, more like. While Wanda felt wretched, she couldn't imagine how Annie was feeling. To find out her brother had taken all the blame must've been horrendous, especially when Lew had been so close to Ryan and her. Wanda had knocked on Annie a couple of times but Blod had said she was either at work or feeling unwell: it was clear she wanted to avoid people. Even her messages had gone unanswered. It had made Wanda's decision to leave all the clearer. She wondered if she'd ever come back ...

Another wince from Carys and Wanda shoved

everything back in its box. This was what mattered – this was perspective. She parked up and escorted Carys to the maternity unit, where she was ushered in by a calm midwife, whose kind hand on Carys's arm emphasised her words: 'It's probably nothing, don't worry.' But how could they not? Wanda tried her best to reassure her as the medics buzzed around finding a bed, strapping her to a monitor and taking her blood pressure. Yet when the midwife furrowed her brow and announced the results were a little high, Wanda could feel panic rising. A cold feeling crept up her spine when Carys nodded *yes* to the question did she have a headache or slightly blurred vision. The contractions had gone, *that was good, wasn't it?* Wanda said as positively as she could but that wasn't the reason for their investigations. They were looking at pre-eclampsia, which affected the flow of blood to the placenta.

'That's dangerous,' Carys gasped. 'For the babies and me.'

'It depends on the severity. We'll do bloods and a urine test,' the midwife explained.

'They'll fix it, Caz, it'll be fine,' Wanda said, smoothing her sister's hair.

'I'm afraid it's about managing it,' the midwife said. 'The only way to cure it is to deliver the babies. But we need to keep them in there for as long as we can to avoid further complications.'

Carys nodded bravely but she was fighting tears when the news came: she had a moderate case of pre-eclampsia and would be kept in until they had her blood pressure under control. Best case, she could go home after that; worst, she'd have to stay there on bed rest until the twins were delivered – the risk otherwise was possible disability and brain damage to mother and suffocation in the babies.

'That'd be at least two months in here!' Carys had cried into Wanda's shoulder as she rocked her in her arms.

'Whatever it takes, we'll do it, you and me, eh?'

'I'm so scared,' she whispered.

You and me both, kid, Wanda thought.

Saying goodbye was torture. Carys looked so young lying there but it was better she was under observation than at home. Wanda had never imagined she would be leaving the hospital without her sister and her fear echoed in her footsteps as she walked the corridor to the exit shortly after 9 p.m. At the steering wheel, she allowed herself a little cry – she'd have to let this out before she put a brave face on for Mam. Back home, Carys's absence hit them hard and Wanda caught Mam staring at her spot on the sofa, empty but for the dent left in the cushion by her body. As much as they tried to reassure themselves it would all be fine, Mam's wringing hands gave her away. And Wanda's cup of tea went untouched. She sent Mam to bed; she'd follow in a bit but really she had no idea how she would sleep. Maybe some air might help.

Wanda went to the lake and sat back against a rock, her knees up, waiting for her eyes to adjust to see the stars in all their glory.

'Please keep her and the babies safe,' she said to the night sky, weary with worry but her brain working away on something she wasn't quite sure of. It was a niggling feeling related to seeing her sister there all alone in the ward when other mums-to-be were being fussed and loved by their other halves. If only there was a way she could find this Danny Platt. If only she could work out a way to do it without causing an international manhunt, which Carys had explicitly vetoed. No Facebook results, no online luck. How could this be allowed to happen? This bloke, whether or not he was interested in Carys, had a right to know he was going to be a dad. Whether it was for the first time or not, that didn't matter. Two babies were coming into the world without a father. If she had to bloody well go up to Manchester herself and break her way into every call centre and demand to talk to every Daniel in a headset ... But then she had a Google alert whenever the combination of call centre plus Manchester was mentioned on the web and it had thrown up nothing that included a man called Daniel. A while back, she'd started to email a few of the largest call centres out of desperation, admitting that yes, this does sound crazy but do you have a Daniel Platt working for you? Obviously she was either ignored or given the standard – and quite bastard right – 'unable to help due to confidentiality' reply. It was utterly hopeless. Manchester had the largest office-based work sector in the country outside of London – her hunt was akin to the needle-and-haystack combo, like trying to find a Jones in Wales ...

And then she saw a shooting star and the niggle was transformed into a puff of magic of sheer utter lunacy that couldn't possibly lead anywhere – and yet it was worth a go. A shot of the longest proportions, the equivalent of that American tourist who once asked her if she knew Tom Jones. But what other lead did she have? So Wanda jumped up and legged it back through the tents to the farmhouse, on a mission to see if that funny feeling inside of her could possibly come to anything.

31

Annie's coping mechanism had kicked in – once a loner, always a loner.

That was her default and it had gradually returned as the ashes settled after Lew's bombshell.

Her *oomph* had gone, she was detached, but she wasn't dead. She still had a life to live and should that be on autopilot, so be it. What had she always said about great expectations? They came to no good. She'd be grateful for the money in her pocket and the roof over her head. It still felt like she was in a fug though, even here under the cool canopy of the woods at the base of the mountain, where Teg whipped through trees in pursuit of a rustle in the branches, for there could be a squirrel to chase up some bark if she was lucky. In fact, this feeling inside, that she was sleepwalking through her days, was here in the dappled dancing light on leaves and the striped beams of sunshine which broke through, projecting like torchlight. There was an ethereal, other-worldly quality to it, which matched how she saw the world. She took a seat on a stump and tried to ground herself, but still she was floating. What would it take to bring her back to earth? There was the sound of a crack underfoot and she turned, looking through the green air dotted with flies and midges, seeing a figure who she'd known would eventually track her down.

She'd been the artful dodger in Gobaith of late, keeping away from people, shopping outside the village, rising early for work, making the most of the long sunny days and evenings and returning late just to eat, then sleep. Lew's business would be dominating the tittle-tattle and there would be eyes on her to see what she thought of his confession. She didn't want to get dragged into it: she needed to tend to her own pain in private and deal with the injustice of Ryan being blamed all this time. She had rebuffed Wanda so many times she doubted there'd be a friendship at the end of it. Wanda had more important things on her mind too, with Carys in hospital. Whatever Annie was going through, whatever Wanda was suffering, their problems couldn't compare to the tightrope of those babies' survival.

Inevitably, she knew the answers would lie with Lew, but she hadn't been ready to face him. She'd known it would come, though. And here he was. She'd wondered how she'd feel when she set eyes on him. Enraged? Distressed? Violent? But there was none of that when he came closer and closer, his eyes wary, wanting to give her the room to do whatever she pleased. Instead Annie was in a kind of trance, as if her emotions were in a vacuum; she felt still, prepared to hear what he had to say before she reacted. To give in to the hatred that lurked at the distant edges of her mind would be something she could never return from. Perhaps it was because she still didn't believe it, that Lew was responsible. If he was, if he told her, if she heard it from his mouth, then that would be final.

'I thought I'd find you here,' Lew said, from across the clearing, getting down on his haunches so he was physically lower than her in an act of submission. Poor Teg didn't get it – she was the lowest in the hierarchy here, so she rolled onto her back, exposed her belly and throat and crooked her paws until Lew gave her a rub.

Annie picked up a twig and ran her finger along its rough yellow lichen, a sign they were in the purest of airspace: how long would that last? How long would it be before Lew soiled it with whatever he had to say?

'I've been away,' he said, trying again, 'on a course, just got back. I came looking for you straight away.'

If she was the cynical type, she'd have said, 'And what? Do you want a medal?' She said nothing, waiting.

'I should've told you, Annie. I'm sorry. With all my heart, I'm sorry.'

She nodded slowly. This was the first step towards the thumping agony which was waiting in the wings.

'What happened?' She was giving him permission to tell it from his side before she considered whether to accept his apology.

He ran his hands across his face and then down, as if he was trying to cleanse himself.

'I went to find him,' he said, staring into the woods. 'You'd said Ryan had gone off on one, so I went. It took forever. He wasn't where we all usually went, by the cave. He was further on, much further; it was dark, too, so I had to be careful. I was shouting his name over and over and then I saw him.' His voice had cracked and he dropped his head.

So it was true, he had lied. He'd always said he'd never found him. She found herself jumping to conclusions

290

and it took every inch of her to rein them in. She needed to take in anything he had to give her on Ryan. She'd always thought she was the last one to see him alive: this was precious information which she wanted to hug to her heart. She was holding her breath and her questions so Lew could continue.

'He was wrecked, Annie,' he said, his brown eyes full of remorse for telling her this truth rather than something sweet. 'He was really drunk, there were a few cans around him.'

Her head fell down because of course it wouldn't be anything other than devastating. There would be no happy twist – the last she'd seen of him had been red-hot anger after a row with his dad. Lew paused until she had collected herself, or what she could gather together from the rubble inside of her.

'He'd built a fire and was trying to light it as I got there. I asked him what he was in a strop about, why he had his arse in his hand, something along those lines, that's how we spoke to each other.'

She could imagine it, their banter.

'He was kind of laughing and swearing but not easily, there was a bitterness there. I tried to coax it out of him but he had his lighter and he was all fingers and thumbs, making sparks, and I was praying there'd be no lighter fuel left. Then it worked and I was gauging what to do, but he started crying. He said he'd made the fire because he was lost, he'd tried to find the path but he was so pissed he kept going round in circles. If he'd been sober then he'd have been fine. But he'd got scared and thought if he made a fire someone would see him and he'd get back down again.'

Her poor, desperate brother – and she felt so sorry for Lew for having to break all of this to her. Was this why he hadn't said?

'I said to him to put it out, I was there now, I'd take him down, but he wouldn't act rational, you know how people get when they're rat-arsed?' *Yes, she'd seen that in her own mother.* 'So I sat down with him then and thought if I could talk to him he'd calm down or sober up. He started rambling about things ... he said his father was an arse ...' *Oh, Ryan, how awful it had been for him.* 'They'd argued over a missing fiver from the kitchen pot. Ryan said he was as bad as his dad for drinking, he was going to end up like him and he ... didn't want to be alive anymore. He wished he was dead.'

Annie swallowed back the lump in her throat and put her hand there to keep it down.

'I didn't like the sound of it at all. Meanwhile the fire was getting bigger and higher and I was thinking this was bad news, I tried to stamp it out and then Ryan was pulling at me, because my shorts had got a spark on them, he was trying to help.' Lew's voice was shaky now and he wiped a tear from his cheek. 'I turned my back to the fire to pat my shorts and I lost my footing ...'

That image, she could see it in her mind, in slow motion – the tumble, the danger.

'I fell back into the fire ... only briefly but it was enough to burn me, I was rolling on the ground then, making sure I wasn't still alight and then I saw the flames darting off away from me, there was a wind up there, it was so dry it zipped across as far as I could see and beyond, heading down. It was furious, that fire. I was in terrible pain, disorientated, and I called to Ryan.'

Annie's chin was wobbling and then they were both in tears.

'I saw blue lights coming and I panicked, we had to get out of there. I looked everywhere to find him but he'd gone ... that was the last I saw of him. The fire by now was raging. It was totally out of control – the noise, the roar of it, I'll never forget that.'

He was reliving it before her – how many times he must've seen this in his nightmares. That insomnia of his, this was why.

'I decided to split, it was an adrenalin thing, it was all just a terrible accident and I was in agony too then, I had to get back to Mam, being a nurse, she'd know what to do. I ended up at the burns unit, I couldn't come back here after that, how could I?'

No. She understood. 'And this is why you kept it to yourself?' she asked.

'I thought if I said I'd seen him start it, I'd send him to prison. I thought if I disappeared, didn't admit I'd found him, he might have got away. I couldn't believe it when they found his body. I wanted to protect you, Annie, that's all I wanted to do.'

'Oh, Lew! I'm so sorry I thought wrongly of you.' He'd acted out of kindness to her, carrying this load alone for years.

Her legs took her over to him and they stood and hugged, united in their grief.

'I should've put that fire out straight away,' he sobbed into her hair. 'But I lost everything that night. My best mate. The girl I loved. My self respect. I came back, I thought I'd try to do some good here, maybe that'd make me happy. Instead I've just hurt everyone all over again.

I went to do the talk because Wanda and me got close, she felt my scars ... it tipped me over the edge, like I had to absolve myself, show these stupid kids what they're up against. I didn't go into all this at the school, I kept it brief, I didn't mention Ryan. I said it was just an accident that went disastrously wrong.'

'How could I ever have thought you'd let him take the blame? I actually thought that of you. I'm sorry,' she said, over and over, holding on to him so tightly because he was threatening to buckle.

'It's okay,' he whispered.

'You have to tell Wanda all of this.'

'I know, but I can't. She hates me. We got close again, we climbed the mountain together and I let myself get carried away, she felt my scars, she ran and I've given up on her ever wanting to see me again.'

'But she'll understand!'

'What if she doesn't believe me? She knows I've lied about Ryan, I'll have to tell her I lied about going to Scotland. She won't be able to trust me.'

'Come on, Lew, come on. You have to try.'

'No.'

'No more secrets, Lew, no more.'

He pulled back with red eyes which said there was something else.

'Knock a woman while she's down,' she said, with a small smile. Because what else could there possibly be? Now was as good a time as any, get it out the way whatever it was.

'There's something I need to tell you, Annie.' He looked even more drained, if that was possible.

'Go on,' she said, steeling herself.

'It's about the vandalism at the community garden.'

32

*Oh, the romance of this place! My husband of fifteen
years and I came here for a 'date weekend' and we fell
in love again Under A Starry Sky! We'll never forget the
magic of gazing up at stars that had travelled for millions
of years to reach our eyes – an enchanting place!*

Mr and Mrs James, Liverpool
Campsite Visitors' Book

With her hand down a blocked shower drain, Wanda
was discovering it wasn't always easy keeping the
illusion of glamping alive.

Most of the time, she kept it together, a swan, com-
posed on the surface, projecting deluxe relaxation while
her legs paddled furiously below. But as her yellow
Marigolds fished out pubes and head hair, she unleashed
a quiet torrent of swearing. This was why she wasn't
tempted to go down the hot tub route – they were very
en vogue. Yet in her mind they were basically giant pools
of human DNA. It'd be just her luck to get one and then
get an STD while she was cleaning it.

She shuddered at the thought, peeling off her rubber
gloves, giving herself a 'job done' tick, the eighth so far

this Tuesday morning with hundreds more to do.

Campsite life had gone crazy. The madness of the pretty much fully booked school holidays hadn't even started yet and already she was knackered from the rush of campers who wanted a bit of summer before the site was crawling with kids. She'd made life even harder for herself by putting together a timetable of family-friendly activities for the six weeks, thinking there might be a bit of interest in yoga by the lake, den-building and cookouts. The reaction was like she'd just announced she was selling tickets for the last gulp of air on planet Earth. Her trouble was, her brain whirred and she reacted without thinking of the consequences.

She shouldn't moan – talk about hashtag success problems. This was what she'd wanted to do, what she'd had to do for Mam and Carys. But she was absolutely frazzled with the long days, the paperwork, the physical back-and-forth of maintenance and problem-solving, from anything to do with hook-ups to complaints about 'over-enthusiastic' neighbours performing drunken karaoke at bedtime. That reminded her, she needed to stock up on earplugs at reception. There was also bedding to change in the caravan, shepherd's hut and bell tent. And she had diarised starting to look for a part-time campsite manager to cover autumn and spring because – *yes!* – she'd finally managed to click 'confirm' on her travels.

There was a long way to go before she could think about that though. Operation Find Danny Platt was underway – she couldn't mention it to Carys for fear of raising her hopes. Mam was back on the spreadsheets and reporting a massive turnaround in income, so much so that she could begin to start paying back Wanda. The bottom line was, Wanda had created something bigger than she had expected and now she had the task of keeping it going when she was gone. Nothing would stop her this time – she was absolutely determined to go. It kept her mind occupied, away from Lew. She simply didn't have the mental space for him and his Jekyll and Hyde act. Her priority was family.

On cue, the Land Rover rolled into the driveway and Wanda dropped everything.

'How was the scan, Caz?' she asked, helping her out of her seat. She'd been released from hospital after three long nights once her blood pressure had reduced, but she had to have scans every other day to check blood flow through the placenta and measure the babies' growth. The risk of pre-eclampsia still lurked and so when she wasn't being lubed up with ultrasound gel, she was on strict bed rest.

'All fine,' Carys cried, levering herself from the car. Each time she returned, she was cheery but then once the relief had passed, the countdown to the next check-up built up again. It was a cruel circle to be in.

'Back to the sofa, my girl,' Mam said with a stiff finger and a slam of the driver's door.

'How was it?' Wanda asked her mother, who'd driven today for the first time since her operation.

'Twenty miles per hour all the way,' Carys said, rolling her eyes.

'That was for your benefit, young lady. Now in!' Mam tutted.

Carys almost filled the door as she was ushered inside and into the lounge to her 'don't you dare move' station. The coffee table was groaning with baby magazines, snacks, water and TV remotes and there was a footstool to deter more ankle swelling.

'You okay?' Wanda said, feeling for her on this warm day.

'Yeah … and no. I'm just sad that I can't enjoy this last bit. I was having a healthy pregnancy and now it feels like I've lost something. But you can't help trouble, eh?' That's what Dad would say when life didn't go according to plan.

'Tell you what, tonight we'll sort that lot out, yeah?' Wanda nodded at the branch of Mothercare in the corner of the room. Two car seats, a moses basket and a double buggy were boxed and brand new; everything else, such as the baby bath and changing mat, was borrowed or bought second-hand and needed a wash or a wipe.

Carys's eyes lit up – that was more like it. 'Fab! It'll feel like I'm actually doing something of use.'

Wanda's heart was breaking for her. 'But you are! You're keeping those twins going.'

Mam shouted through, announcing 'Someone to see you' for Wanda.

Lew? her heart yelled with hope. Her head replied with a *damn you!* In the kitchen, Mam mouthed 'Annie' and jerked her thumb to the back door.

Lovely! Wanda had given up on her lately – well, not given up exactly. She'd accepted Annie wanted to be alone to recover and, on a practical level, this was her busiest season and she needed to use all the daylight hours going to make hay. So she was chuffed to bits she'd come out the other side – they had so much to catch up on. Apparently something had happened with Spike, she'd heard it on the grapevine but hadn't poked her nose in to ask. But she'd get the chance now. She'd get them a drink and they could sit in the garden and take five.

'Hiya!' Wanda said to Annie, who was just as pleased to see her, and they had a funny jiggy hug.

'It's been ages. Sorry. Been through the mill a bit.'

'Same here. Got time for some lemonade? Mam's cloudy one.' Wanda opened the fridge and found the jug and held it up for Annie to inspect.

'I haven't had that for years!'

'Come on then,' Wanda said, pouring two glasses, 'let's go into the back garden. Pretend we're ladies of leisure.'

They both let out a loud groan of ecstasy as they planted their bums on deckchairs. Mid-July and they were already done in.

'We're old before our time!' Wanda laughed.

'That's hard graft for you.'

'To think I used to moan about sitting down all day every day in an office. I dream of a nice sit down these days.'

'Cheers!' Annie said, swigging away, making the same appreciative noises as Wanda at the bitter-sweet on their tongues.

'What's up then?' Wanda asked, stretching out, letting her mock Crocs fall off her tired feet so she could feel the cool grass on her bare toes.

'Oh, you know, not much. Falling in love with someone, putting the brakes on a relationship with an adoring man who then thanked me because the rejection made him see he'd gone too fast. Breaking a little boy's heart by taking my dog away from him. Plus I'm responsible for Blod's cats being under kitchen arrest.'

'Not much at all then.'

'No. Quite quiet, actually.' By Annie making light of what had happened with Spike rather than crying over it, it showed she was in a better place than she had been. 'What about you?'

'Just as dull. The love of my life – yes, you were right, I admit it – turned out to be a lying bastard. Not just to me but to you too.'

'That's the thing …' Annie took a sip and fixed her eyes on Wanda over the rim.

'Oh, no. Don't tell me you've come over to defend Lew. After what he's done! He hasn't had the guts to come over. He told the world before he told me. He virtually confessed to the fire.'

'It wasn't like that.' Annie said it quietly but firmly.

'How was it, then?' Wanda said, feeling sour. But as Annie explained Lew's version of the night's terrible events, Wanda held her heart. She could imagine him trying to reason with Ryan, to stamp out the fire Ryan started. Her eyes shut with the pain of hearing how he'd fallen into the flames, then carried the torture all alone for fifteen years. How could she have thought badly of him? It all made sense: his disappearance and his absence at the funerals. Why hadn't she chased him up? Why had she thought the worst, that he was off living his life? That's what he'd meant when he'd said Wanda wasn't the only one affected by the fire. But there was so much love for him too: the horror he'd been through, the strength he'd found to confess it all. It didn't matter who he'd told first – it only mattered that he'd found a way through the agony at all. She wanted to get up and find him and hold him and say how sorry she was. Yet something was holding her back.

'He doesn't know I'm here, Wanda. He doesn't know I'm telling you.'

'Why hasn't he come to me himself? He must think I'll hate him ...' she said, distressed at the thought.

'No. It's exactly the opposite. He respects you too much to come and bother you. He wants to stay out of your way. He thinks he'll be rejected, he's ashamed of the lies.'

'Oh, Lew,' she whispered.

Annie leaned forward and stared into Wanda's eyes. 'It's not too late. You both adore each other. You're made for each other.'

'I know,' Wanda confessed. 'I felt it the morning we hugged on the mountain top. It's never felt more right.'

'There you go!' Annie smiled. But it dropped when she saw Wanda's shaking head.

'It can't happen. I've decided – I'm going travelling in October. I can't start something with him. I can't not leave. Not again. And there's no chance of anything happening before I go. There's too much to do. Not enough hours in the day. And if I was chucked an extra one or two, I'd either go to sleep or spend it with Carys and Mam. I need to be on the ball before I go. I need to make sure those two – or four – are set up for good.'

'Are you not coming back, then?'

'Who knows? That thing about doing all the things I wanted to do away but doing them here, I've done them – you made me see what I needed to do was here under my nose all along. Now though, I feel I've reached an end point.'

'What about Lew? Wouldn't you come back for him?'

'The thing is, I have to go away, right. If I was going to start something with him, I'd have to stay.'

'Not necessarily, you could still go off.'

'But I'd be choosing something over him. Everything could change for me if I left. Like, my life could take another turn. I might find somewhere else to live, be bitten by the travel bug. Run off and join a remote community in the wilds of Mexico!'

'I see what you mean; your perspective might change as a result of your experiences.'

'Exactly. And staying here for a man goes against everything I kind of believe in, in terms of being in charge of my own destiny. And who's to say he's part of it? Maybe he was always destined to be the one who got away or the one who got me to go away?'

'I know it's not the same, but with Dean, I only realised things would change if I made a change happen.' Annie drained her lemonade and heaved herself up out of the deckchair. 'But that doesn't mean Lew can't be part of it.'

'I dunno. I can't see a way round it.'

Wanda followed her out, praising her for not letting Dean get the better of the community garden.

'It's looking good again though, you've worked so hard on it.'

A cloud crossed Annie's face as they stepped outside.

'Don't say anything,' she said in a low voice. 'But it wasn't Dean who did it.'

'Eh?'

'Lew was filming from his drone to catch the sunset over the mountain. He's showed it to me and I saw who did it.' Annie cut eye contact – there was clearly something very difficult going on.

'What? Who was it?' Wanda reached out to touch her arm in case she wanted to talk.

Annie sighed and shook her head. 'I can't say. I'm going to have to speak to them. But I'm not sure how to handle it.'

'Shouldn't you tell the police?'

'It's not that straightforward,' Annie said, jangling her keys and taking her secret with her.

When was anything straightforward?

33

Well, this was awkward.

Full of trepidation, Annie had arrived at Spike's with a four-pack of warm cider, a big bag of value cheese balls and a defrosting Viennetta from Blod's Shop. But when he'd shown her to the garden where they'd be eating al fresco, she saw she'd got the mood all wrong.

She'd assumed his invitation to join him and Arthur for a Friday night bite to eat would be casual to the point of fish fingers and chips. After all, it was about getting the three of them together for Arthur's benefit – he was playing up at school again, which didn't surprise Annie at all. She felt a responsibility for the impact her almost-relationship with Spike had had on him – and hadn't she said she would still be part of his life even if it wasn't as a substitute mum? Seeing Teg would help him, too. It wouldn't be a biggie, there was no need to posh it up, was there?

Instead, Spike had gone to town with his patch of countryside. A square wooden table had been laid for three – and a dog. The humans each had a tea-light candle flickering away in a jam jar set above their cutlery, which was entwined in ivy, while Teg had a bowl of biscuits. Spike immediately explained he'd move it to the grass when they actually sat down. He wasn't that mad, he'd winked and Annie had laughed in spite of her nerves. Jolly multicoloured outdoor lights were strung across the boughs of trees, there were throws on the backs of the chairs for when the night set in and a milk jug contained a posy of freshly picked blue hydrangea blooms. It was beautiful and sweet, magical even, but it wasn't appropriate – it was as if he was over-compensating. And it revealed that Spike wasn't on the same page as Annie.

As she took a seat and the muggy air settled on her, he nipped inside for a bottle of chilled rosé. Her toes were curling. There were so many reasons for it.

She'd misjudged tonight with her low-key offerings, which of course, being the man he was, he had accepted with grace. They had kissed one another's cheeks hello, stiffly entering each other's personal space, which, along with his delicious clean smell, brought her unwelcome longing scrambling up to the surface. The chit-chat of 'Come in!' and 'How are you?' was so far from the natural intimacy of the relationship they'd had before Spike had abandoned ship, for entirely valid reasons. She had agonised about even going. There were things that needed to be confronted. But to rebuff this chance to see Arthur would cause everyone pain. Annie had had to come. It was all so delicate and excruciating – and yet still she felt herself warm at the sight of him as he came through the back to join her.

'Just a few nibbles to keep us going,' Spike said, unloading a tray. 'Olives, hummus, pitta strips and a minty bean and courgette thing I whipped up from the community garden spoils.'

'I'm having courgette with everything too.' The plants

had become octopus arms, giving a prolific crop already. 'Courgetti, roasted courgette, courgette pesto. I've even made a courgette cake. It was nice but Blod said she'd rather have a doughnut.' She was babbling to fill the space. 'This looks amazing.'

'Eat up!' he smiled, completely unruffled, pouring them wine. 'Homemade pizzas for the main course. Viennetta for afters. The only thing better is Arctic Roll.'

She should be hungry – her lunch of a sweaty sandwich shovelled in during a job had been a long time ago. But her stomach was full of apprehension and it was an effort to eat what on any other occasion would've sent her taste buds on a feeding frenzy. How was she going to say what she had to? She sipped her wine and then as it hit the back of her throat the heat of alcohol on an empty tummy warned her to go easy.

'Arthur won't be long,' Spike said to Teg, whose ears pricked up and head tilted at the mention of her friend. Annie felt her emotions whirling at his name. Then to her, he said, 'He's just popped to Blod's to get some cheese.'

'Oh, you should've said, I'd have brought some with me. Rather than cheese balls.' She rolled her eyes to show her embarrassment.

'I love cheese balls! I'm saving them for when Arthur gets here or I'd scoff the lot.'

Putting people at ease was so natural to him. But tonight he seemed uncharacteristically out of tune with the atmosphere. Maybe he was as nervous as she was? Yet how different their reasons were. She couldn't stand it any more.

'Thanks for inviting me. I ... er ...' she said, breaking into the speech she'd planned in her head.

But he leaped in. He was out of sync and didn't catch the tone of her voice. It was so unlike him.

'Thanks for coming. I know it's ... strange. This is new for both of us, it's not easy trying to navigate, is it?'

'No,' she admitted. 'But it's about him, isn't it?' Would he take the hint now? 'How is he? He must be doing better if he agreed to this.'

She prayed Arthur had bounced back.

'Erm, it's a surprise. He doesn't know.' Spike shifted uncomfortably in his seat.

'Oh. Right.' *Oh dear, more like.* The stakes seemed even higher now. But Spike was a great dad, he knew his son best, didn't he?

'Yeah.' He scratched his stubble, as if he was doubting himself. 'I've done the wrong thing, 'aven't I?'

'No, no, no one knows him like you do, you'd have weighed it up ...' Spike raised his eyebrows at her. He knew she was trying to be supportive. 'All right, all right. I must admit, I don't think secrets and surprises are maybe the best way with Arthur right now. But I'm not a parent, don't listen to me. In fact, it might—' She had been going to say it might be a good opportunity to talk without him here but Spike was reaching out to her, just stopping his hand before it touched her.

'Annie, you're one of those people who's instinctive with kids. I trust your opinion. You'd make a great mum.'

He had got her wrong – he now thought she was acting weirdly because she was sensitive about not having children. That was a whole other conversation and certainly not one for tonight.

Still he ploughed on. 'You know, I never wanted you to feel that I was thrusting Arthur on you. And I never even asked you about parenthood ... whether you wanted it or not.'

This was veering off on a tangent, a painful one. Because now they weren't involved, did he have the right to know her most innermost loss? It was private. Not to be shared with him. But she felt she had to give him something.

'Look, yes, I did, very much, but it didn't happen for me. That's not what this is about.'

'No? Oh Gawd, I'm so sorry, I didn't mean to pry.' His shoulders sagged and he rubbed his face. She felt guilty then, for had she sounded harsh?

'Listen, Spike.' She tugged on her messy plait to give herself a second to explain.

Again he pre-empted her. 'Honestly, you don't need to say anyfing. This is what I meant about new rules.'

He got up and looked around for something to justify it, deciding on adjusting Arthur's tumbler. She felt her chance slipping away.

'Where is 'e, actually?' He looked at his watch. 'He should be back by now.'

'Where would he have gone?' Annie asked.

'He's been running off.' Spike sighed.

'He might just have got distracted. Met someone on the way. You know what Blod's like, she's probably ...' And it hit her. 'I told Blod I was coming here. You don't think he's found out and legged it, knowing I'm here?'

'That sounds about right. I should've told 'im. I've fucked up.'

'Do you want to go and look for him? Take Teg with you?'

'I don't know. He's been so unsettled lately.' Spike looked in physical pain. 'Maybe he doesn't need me chasing 'im? I thought we were getting somewhere but all of this just makes me feel useless. Lucy was good at this stuff. I can't get it right.'

It was heartbreaking and she knew she had to tell him, even though it'd be pouring misery onto misery. If not now, when? It might explain a lot to Spike.

'Sit down a minute, Spike,' she said, taking control. 'We'll look for him in a bit, he probably just needs to get his head together.'

Following orders and nodding, he seemed grateful for the direction. But she felt sick with what he saw as a helping hand. She was merely preparing him for worse.

'I need to tell you something,' she said, her heart thumping. 'About Arthur.'

'Yeah?' She saw a flash of worry in his eyes – she could only imagine the fear that would be escalating inside of him as his mind raced for answers. 'What is it?'

'It's nothing too awful.' She felt she had to cushion him. 'But the community garden, the vandalism. He was involved. It wasn't Dean.'

'What?' His eyes were confused, incredulous and begging her to go on.

'Lew had been filming from his drone the night it happened. He was editing it and saw Arthur there.'

'What? So he was there? That doesn't mean it was 'im.' She didn't blame him for his instinctive defence of his son. She'd thought that too when Lew had told her.

'I've seen it with my own eyes.' Over and over, watching this little boy wrecking everything the group had achieved. That he had been a part of.

Spike immediately held up his hands. 'Of course, sorry, I didn't mean to think ...'

'I get it, Spike. I was as gutted as you are. I wanted it to be Dean, it made sense in my head that he'd wanted one last act of revenge on me. But it was Arthur.'

'That little ... I'm going to march 'im down the police station.'

She understood his anger but she had to defuse it. 'You'd have a job doing that, the nearest one is miles away.'

He shut his eyes and tried to control his breathing, which was hard and fast.

'Spike, you said you trusted me, yes?'

He opened his eyes, stared into hers and nodded. 'Yes. Absolutely.'

It all came out – she'd had days to react and process Arthur's cry for help.

'Right, so I've thought about this. He did it because of us. The garden represented something we'd all made together, it represented stability and safety, and then when things didn't work out, he felt let down. It's part of his grief. It's part of all these confusing emotions going on in his head, there's hormones kicking in too, there's the old "boys don't cry". I saw it all with my brother. The absolute worst thing to do with Arthur is to go mental at him. It'll teach him nothing. He was just unable to express himself in any other way. This poor little dab needs love, not a police caution.'

Spike had tears rolling down his face. 'I don't deserve you, Annie. You're heaven-sent. I'd 'ave done exactly what you told me not to do. What an idiot. Me, not 'im.'

'No, you're not. It's natural to feel shocked and sickened.'

'I did, I do.'

310

'But he's twelve. He hasn't hurt anyone. The only person he's hurt here really is himself. He needs help, Spike. Love. It might help you understand, if you watch it ...'

'You've got it on you?' he asked, wiping his face dry with his waiter's tea towel over his shoulder.

'Lew emailed it to me. I must've watched it hundreds of times. It's not nice when you see it at the beginning ...' She handed her phone over, hearing the buzz of the drone, hovering here and there, knowing it frame by frame.

She could tell Spike recognised the boy's lope right from the off by the way he winced. The ripping at plants, the uprooting of veg, the lashing out on the sign. Quickly, she pointed out to watch for when Arthur's fury ran out, when regret hurtled in, how he'd crumpled to his knees and fallen into the foetal position – this was hurting in action.

'What are we going to do about this? If you want to go to the police then I'm one 'undred per cent be'ind you.'

'No. There's no point. Do what I said, be gentle with him. Show him you're there for him.'

Teg began to bark and then ran through the garden towards the house.

Could that be Arthur? The two of them exchanged quizzical looks. If he knew Annie was here, then it was a good sign he'd come home. She crossed her fingers, hoping that he did know. But if not, then the sight of Teg's wagging tail and excitement would lessen the blow of the surprise. Spike got up but Annie told him to sit. 'Let him come to you, be calm.'

He appeared at the back door, his eyes wary. Teg was in full bounce mode, pawing Arthur's thigh, trying to get his attention.

'Blod said you were here.'

Annie gave him a smile which she hoped conveyed how much she loved this little boy.

He was hiding behind his fringe but Teg was having none of it. In a last desperate bid for a smooth, she lay down on her back and waited for a rub. Which way was he going to go? Annie and Spike were waiting.

'It's nice to see you,' he said, shyly, unsure, and he dived onto Teg for a quick wrestle.

'You too,' she said, allowing herself a huge beam.

Then he saw his dad. 'Have you been crying?' It was how children always said that sentence to a parent. With disbelief because parents never cried. With terror that something unimaginable had happened. Annie instinctively saw Arthur associating it with his mother's long death.

Annie willed Spike to open up, to show it was okay to be emotional.

'Yes,' Spike said. 'I missed you, that's all.'

Arthur looked utterly perplexed. He'd only been gone a while.

'I've let you down,' Spike added. 'Come here, son, I need a chat.'

Arthur looked unsure. 'Are you drunk?'

'No! Come here!' he laughed. 'Give your old man a hug.'

Somehow Arthur sensed this was important and made his way to him.

Annie got up. She didn't need to be here for this conversation.

'I'm just going to turn the oven on. Your dad said he'll be in to do the pizzas in a bit.'

'You'll stay, won't you?' Spike said to her.

Of course she would, if that was okay with them – the answer lay in Arthur's shining eyes.

As she left the table, she told herself not to look, it wasn't her business to see what was going to be a difficult heart-to-heart. But when she went in the door, she couldn't help it – she glanced back and there they were, father and son, hugging the lives out of each other.

34

*The worst staycation we've ever had. The welcome pack
was rather more unwelcome with its strange fruit cake,
processed marshmallows – have you heard of sugar-free?
– and cheap star-spotting map. The thread count on the
sheets was woefully low, we were disgusted there was
no coffee machine, smart TV or butler service. Next year,
we'll be back to luxury safaris in Kenya. We don't expect
to see this review on the website!*

The Bowler-Parker-Smyths, Buckinghamshire
Campsite Visitors' Book

A mass of weirdy-beardies had descended upon
Gobaith as if it was hosting an anorak convention.
Wanda was being harsh – these ladies and gentlemen
who were swarming the village for the official Ordnance
Survey measurement of the hill were harmless, re-
sembling retired maths teachers. She hadn't realised the
earth's lumps and bumps were so fascinating to people.
It turned out that where trains had spotters, peaks had
baggers who lived to tick off climbs on their lists.

So when word had spread among the elite geeks that
the gods of mapping were at work, they'd come mainly

as one in a crowd of beige utility shorts, woolly socks and sturdy boots. The exception was a niche bunch of cool young things in Patagonia T-shirts with wraparound bug-eyed sunglasses and watches that she suspected talked to the International Space Station.

Gobaith had reacted quickly: Spike had set out trekking poles, base layers and hydration systems on the pavement, Blod had a rush on protein bars and Sara had taken a punt on 'Born To Climb' mugs and stacked them up in a mountain-shaped pyramid in the front window. Up here, Alis had brought her Sunny Side Up van to the campsite to flog cream-peaked 'snowy mountain' coffees and themed baps, including the Snowdon roll of egg and bacon and the Everest of sausage, tomato and black pudding. Carys had been permitted to sit at a trestle table to sell mint cake-flavoured bara brith, made under her daughter's orders by Mam, who had been sceptical of her tampered-with recipe until she'd tasted some and mischievously declared it 'not bad'.

In the gorgeous summer sunshine, the visitors were keen to share their excitement. As she went about her business, Wanda merely had to catch someone's eye – or be trapped by theirs, to be more precise – and she was being informed about the differences between the Nuttalls, Hewitts, Marilyns, Munros and P600s. This one had the potential to join the elevated ranks of the Nuttalls, of which there were almost two hundred in Wales, if it hit two thousand feet – or six-hundred-and-nine-point-six metres if she preferred metric.

It was fascinating. To a point. But there was no denying that their enthusiasm was contagious. The school holidays were here and a mixture of locals and campers gathered in the lane as the surveyors unpacked their gadgets.

'I hope they've got a tape measure in there,' Wanda said to Alis, as she took the chance to grab an elevensies coffee.

'Actually,' a voice said behind her in the queue, 'measuring mountains has come a long way from traditional trigonometry and the calculation of angles.'

Wanda eyeballed Alis then turned around to announce she was only taking the piss. Never mind mansplaining, this was mountainsplaining. But an earnest face was peering up at her through wrinkles as craggy as Kilimanjaro.

'These days it's far more sophisticated,' he said, gently, poking his glasses up the arch of his nose. 'They'll be using global positioning technology devices to communicate data to satellites. They'll need to be in position at the top for several hours, taking thousands of readings, for accuracy. There is another way, photogrammetry, where images are taken from above and then loaded to a computer which puts together a 3D model. Of course, there is the debate over whether any measurement can be truly accurate.'

Wanda smiled. He was only enjoying his moment. And she hadn't known about the specifics if she was being honest.

'How long will it take for the decision to be made? Whether it's a hill or a mountain?'

'It'll have to verified back at HQ. Won't be long. Then if it's in the club, you'll see more like me here. You won't believe what a difference it will make. I've come from Cumbria just for this.' Wanda wanted to pat him on the head, he was so endearing. She stepped aside to let him order. 'I think I'll have the Mont Blanc cheese on toast, please. I'll be going up behind the OS team. I'm sixty-four, so I need all the energy I can get!'

'Well, in that case,' Carys said, 'I'll chuck you some bara brith in for free!'

'It looks like fruit cake but it's moister, a kind of tea bread,' Wanda said, unable to resist a bit of woman-splaining. It was also because the nightmare of the posh family from Bucks lingered – she'd tried to tell them it was a Welsh thing, but they accused her of racism against the English. Remove their comment from the website? Hardly! People would have a right laugh at it, plus they'd know by the snotty tone that the site would be perfect for the genuine campers out there. It had been a shock to get a bad rating because they'd become a rarity. You couldn't please all the people all of the time, that was just the way it went. Under A Starry Sky had found its place – 'cwtchy cool' had even become a thing in glamping circles after the brilliant write-up in *Happy Campers* magazine.

Wanda took a sip of her latte and inspected the crowd – anticipation was mounting and then a silence fell. The professionals were putting on their backpacks and in-specting gadgets, discussing what had to be very technical things. And there was someone else with them, deep in conversation. She'd know the back of his dark head any-where. Lew, his hands talking, gesturing upwards, then he was looking around and damn her laser eyes – they must've been burning through him. Her throat went dry and everyone disappeared from her view: it was as if there was only him in the world. Whenever she'd seen him lately, it was the same – her radar always picked him out. Whether it was across the road, driving past or in the village, she couldn't help but see him – and only him.

They hadn't been alone in each other's company since the sunrise climb. Four weeks had passed and with it the developments of his school talk, his absence on a course, his return and revelation of what had really happened that night. In turn, she had been through a perspective-changing time – the twins' scare, the pressure of work and the decision to leave in October. The sequence of events had opened a chasm between her and Lew. It wasn't out of anger or distress any more since Wanda had learned the truth. Gobaith too had settled once they'd learned that Lew was in fact a hero rather than the perpetrator. The community's narrative had also changed: the fire was no longer regarded as arson; it had been an accident and Annie had received no end of sympathy and apologies about Ryan. No more grass fires had happened since. But Lew and Wanda's own resolution was yet to come. They performed a kind of dance if they were in the same airspace: they kept a safe distance, exchanging stares and brief smiles. There wasn't time for any deep and meaningfuls anyway: Lew was off on daily treks and abseiling jumps and scuba dives at reservoirs with his Bunkhouse guests. Wanda was either asleep or on duty. Nights out when the tourists were having fun were out of the question. Wanda did want to talk to Lew – she yearned to, actually. But as time ticked by there was an awkward edge to it all too: the longer you left it, the harder it would become. If one of them didn't make a move then it might never happen.

She saw Lew saying something to one of the surveyors, holding a finger up, which she guessed meant he wanted one minute. And then he was heading her way and she gulped, mesmerised by him, a whirl of nervous emotion, wondering if he was really doing this now. But then perhaps there was safety amid the drama going on around them. Or he felt this was a good moment to seize because he had to be quick.

'Hi,' he said, softly. 'I've been meaning to—'

'Me too,' she said, close to a palpitation.

'We need to talk,' he said.

He'd made the first move and gratitude flooded through her veins.

'I'm sorry I never told you the truth about the fire.' He held her eyes in an act of taking full responsibility.

'It's okay, I understand why. I'm sorry you went through such agony. I'm sorry I thought the worst of you.'

'I'm sorry it's taken me this long to say sorry.' His eyes were still on her. But instead of wanting to lose herself in them, she found herself breaking contact.

'We seem to do a lot of this. Apologising,' she said, feeling the start of a dull ache of doubt about how they would move forward.

'We've just got history, that's all.'

Was that it? Or was there more to it? Was there an immovable, insurmountable object in their way? Because she didn't feel closure from this exchange. Lew, though, looked visibly lighter and was smiling at her when she faced him again. She didn't know exactly what the next link was in her chain of thought and how she could explore it here. That would be for another time. The hill was waiting.

Lew looked up at the peak, which was majestic against

the baby-blue sky. Wanda said, 'You'd better go' just as he said he ought to.

'Be safe,' she said, with intensity, which she immediately saw as ridiculous and hilarious. He was only going up a flaming hill – he wasn't about to be launched into space.

'If I don't return ...' he said, heavily, 'tell Blod she can cancel my milk.'

They both guffawed and it was the most wonderful thing. Their connection was effortless again. And he was gone, back with the crew who moved off as a sea of kids and parents left a respectful distance before marching behind them.

She watched with admiration as he led the way, understanding now why this had been so crucial for him: it was his redemption for the fire, he wanted to make Gobaith famous for something beyond that, to give people a point of pride and to push them into the future. He was a truly beautiful human being. But why did she feel as if there was something heavy in her heart?

'Wanda! You coming up?' Annie said, glowing with happiness. 'Join Arthur and me?'

The little boy grinned. 'And Teg! Teg's coming too! She's living with me again!'

Instinctively, Wanda knew that when Annie had texted to say the garden vandalism had been sorted, this was what it had all been about. Second chances for a kid like Arthur made the difference. Wanda would never speak of it to another person in her life. Too much good was going on to dwell on the bad.

'I'd love to,' she said, 'but we've a load of check-outs and arrivals.'

She waved them off and went back to the farmhouse to attend first to the sheets out on the line in all their woefully low-thread-count glory. Then there was the bell tent to tidy up, the prosecco to put on chill, plus a million other jobs. Not least the latest with Danny Platt.

Because her intuition – or should that be wild stab in the dark – had paid off. In early June, the site had had a lovely couple from up north come to stay and they'd left a lush review in the comments' book. So far, so nothing. But they'd said they'd visited on a recommendation and were prepared to accept 'no-frills' conditions in return for the 'belting scenery and a big Welsh welcome'. That had meant the recommendation had come from before the revamp. The husband and wife were from Lancashire and had signed their review 'Audrey and Bob P.' and upon inspection in the bookings record that P stood for Platt.

Yes, it was ludicrous, yes, it was unlikely, but their nature had been like Danny's; it might've been the accent but there was something about the warmth of their ways. And how they'd felt like family – okay, maybe that was stretching it. Why hadn't it occurred to Wanda before that it was them, like at the flaming time? But Carys had been bed-bound with a cold and it had been when the site was just taking off. She'd have missed Ryan Gosling with a throbber, she'd been that tired.

So with no other plan, Wanda had written to them, asking the impossible.

She was probably barking up the wrong tree – probably the wrong forest – but they didn't happen to know a Daniel Platt? They had written back after a while: sorry, they'd been off trying to find a better campsite than Under A Starry Sky but they'd failed so far.

'We do know a Daniel Platt. He's our nephew and over a family roast, we got talking about camping and he mentioned that he'd come to your site in December. He loved it there, said it was very special. May we ask what it's regarding?'

She'd replied, saying it was a 'personal matter' and would it be possible to have his address. Obviously, it wasn't. 'You understand, we want to help but ...' They suggested if she gave them a bit more info then they'd contact Daniel, who was 'working away'.

Wanda had casually asked Carys if he'd mentioned that when they'd met, but no. Did 'working away' mean they were covering for him in that case? He could've buggered off somewhere, though; maybe he was into travel. What if he had gone because Carys had never rung him? Wanda was being dramatic, as ever, imagining him as a heartbroken soul.

It left her with a quandary: what more did she dare say? She could hardly divulge he'd put two buns in her sister's oven, she was thirty-one weeks gone, ready to drop any minute and, by the way, did they know if he was married or with someone?

Wanda knew she'd be chewing her biro tonight into the early hours. But she didn't have those hours spare. She had to get this done – and there were five minutes left on the tumble dryer. Wanda got out her notepad. She was very sorry she couldn't say any more, she wrote, but please if they could tell him Wanda at the campsite in Wales needed to speak to him, could they possibly pass the message on?

She'd have to speak to him first just in case it was bad news. She'd work out if or what she'd tell Carys if or when she got there. Wanda signed the letter, popped it into an envelope, ran down to the postbox in the lane and kissed it goodbye, wishing it good luck.

What right did she have to wish for fortune? She'd had more than her fair share in this manhunt and she feared she'd just about run out.

35

Elbow-deep in pond slime, this had to be in Annie's top five worst jobs.

Gloves were pointless, the gloopy water would only spill over the tops, so when it came to clearing blanket-weed, you were better off going commando. But it meant you felt things brushing up against your hands – you couldn't see what, it was so murky – that sent your imagination into grotesque overdrive. And the stink! It was proper buzzing.

Yet Annie had never been happier. The clue was in the 'top five' list, which her new work assistant had brought with him in the fortnight he'd been helping her out. Not a day went past when he didn't ask her for her 'top five' of something.

Annie suspected it was Spike's suggestion, but Arthur had asked if perhaps he could lend a hand to make up for what he'd done to the community garden. She'd been thrilled – this was peak summer when she worked all the hours she could to cope with all the jobs she had. He had fallen into her stride as if he'd been born with green fingers, learning quickly what needed to be done and always checking he wasn't about to hack someone's prize roses. The company, too, when you were used to lonely days, was a treat. And he brought fresh eyes with him. Like now, when she pulled the weeds out of the depths of Blod's water feature with a huge grimace.

'It's like toxic nuclear mermaid hair!' Arthur cried from where he was deadheading bedding plants, taking absolute delight in her disgust.

She laughed at his description. He had such a funny way of seeing things and it tickled her every time he came up with some 'Arthurism'.

'Is it time for *sglods* yet?'

She smiled up at his request for chips spoken like a true local. Wanda had helped him so much.

'We'll get them in a minute,' Annie said. 'Let's just tidy up, then we'll hit the road.'

But not before Blod was out of her back door offering yet another cup of tea and squash for the lad.

'I think three mugs is my limit,' Annie told her.

'All right, well don't say I never offer,' Blod jostled, in her matronly way, her bosom rising beneath today's pink camo kaftan which matched the tips of her hair. 'Here's something for you, Arthur.'

She pressed 'just a little bit of pocket money' into his hand.

He looked at Annie with uncertainty.

'Take it. If you feel bad, spend it in Blod's shop!'

His face broke out into sunshine. It was only a couple of quid but it was as if Blod had given him gold. What a woman she was. A small token, but to him it was appreciation and acceptance – Annie knew the value of that.

'*Diolch!* Thank you, Blod,' he said, putting it away in his shorts pocket, which Teg instantly went to sniff in case it was food.

'Lovely job, the pair of you, fair do's. Got a visitor later ...' Blod made big eyes at Annie. She couldn't keep a secret if her life depended on it. Especially if it was her own. 'A gentleman.'

'Never!'

'There's life in the old cow yet!'

'Well, have fun!'

'Oh, we will!' Blod cackled and, with a wink, she began to whistle 'When I'm Sixty-Four' by The Beatles.

And then they were back in the van, stopping at Oh My Cod – which Arthur wanted to pay for, bless him. But Annie insisted. Wages wouldn't be part of the deal, Spike had ruled that out as soon as she'd had a word. He wanted Arthur to learn about actions and consequences. That night when Spike had learned Arthur was responsible for the vandalism had been emotional. She hadn't seen or heard whatever he'd said to his boy, but there were no raised voices and when she'd returned from putting the oven on, they were cuddling and in tears. Arthur was devastated and remorseful but once he'd apologised and Annie had told him about her brother, they moved on to his grief. The little poppet had said he'd trashed the Grow Up garden because he'd lost Annie like he'd lost his mother. All three made a deal that they'd never tell a soul – Dean deserved to have the blame on him – as long as Arthur promised to talk his feelings out. Ever since, he hadn't stopped.

'Annie,' he said in the passenger seat, blowing on a hot chip to give to Teg. The tone of his voice told her he was about to ask her something deep.

Her *mmm* at the delicious taste of vinegar and salt became a hum of encouragement to go on.

'Would you rather ...' Ah, his favourite dilemma game. 'A cold fried egg or hot jelly?'

'Yuck. Neither. But if I had to ... hot jelly.'

'Cat food or a dog biscuit?'

'Dog biscuit.'

'A really rich man or ... my dad?'

She looked at him out of the corner of her eye. He was examining a chip to see if it had any green bits. The windscreen was fogged up, so she gave it a wipe and rolled down the window. Was it her or had it just got very warm in the van? His question was a no-brainer, obvs, but she didn't want to give him any romantic hopes. God, how she wanted Spike, more than ever. But it was just not going to happen. She was thankful their relationship was back to how it had been – easy, fun, yet solid, and Arthur was benefiting too. They'd talked about Lucy, the three of them, how Annie was an aunty and she wasn't going to replace Lucy. No one ever would. She realised he was waiting. She remembered he was twelve and it was just a simple question.

'Your dad.'

'Really?' He pretended to be appalled. 'But he's got really bad toenails.'

She laughed.

'Think of what you could buy if you went with the rich man.'

'But your dad is the richest man in the world. He's got you, for starters. And so much heart.' *Genuine, funny, open, handsome, sexy*, she could go on and on.

'Why aren't you together then?' he said, as if it was that easy.

327

'We're friends. We like it that way.' He did, she didn't, to be truthful.

'Dad told me yesterday, well, he admitted it actually, we were wrestling and I wouldn't let him up till he told me, that he ... likes you, likes you.'

Her silly heart jumped for joy but it was just him playing about. 'That sounds like a forced confession to me.'

'I asked him again at bedtime.'

How she wanted to quiz him on this, but that was unethical. Yet she had to say something. 'Were you sat on him at the time?' Then quickly, before he could answer, she started the ignition and ordered 'belt up!' The next stop was Mrs Jenkins, definitely top of her worst jobs.

'He said it again, Annie.'

Still on about that, was he? Did that mean it was actually true? She couldn't let herself go down that road though – it'd damage what they had worked hard to get back to. Annie stood to lose this lovely set-up if she asked Spike to consider anything more than mates.

'I said he had to choose. Would you rather one of those posh ladies, all dressed up and that, or you.'

Charming! To think that was how Arthur saw her! It was right, of course, she wasn't one to glam up, but people didn't usually say it with such bracing honesty. She almost giggled before the next thought was of Spike with someone else and she felt sick as a dog.

'He said you.'

Hang on ... he hadn't had to say that, now, had he? But then maybe he was thinking better the devil you know. She'd go with that.

'Take care lest you buy a cat in a sack. Or, as the English say, you don't want to end up with a pig in a poke.'

'I have no idea what you're on about. Cats? Pigs?' He started meowing and snorting and Annie sighed with relief, because that meant that was that. She made sure of it by giving him a briefing on what they'd be doing next. 'She's a bit of a misery, so we won't knock. Okay?'

''Kay.'

On the way, Annie kept an eye out for any 'for sale' signs. With the house going through, it wouldn't be long before she could have her own place again. She'd had a look online and there was very little going for what she'd have. Her price bracket was in the one-bed terrace or dilapidated cottage range. She'd rather have somewhere to do up, though, if she had the choice. Somewhere with a garden, an open fire for her and Teg to snuggle up in front of over the winter and a desk – because she had plans for the future, not least for the high school plot which Mrs Harrison had approved with bells on. Never had she thought she'd be where she was! And it got her through the slog of an hour at Mrs Jenkins's.

Once they'd done, Annie picked up the usual envelope on the doorstep and collected the recycling. The plastic bag snapped just as she was sticking it in the back of the van – empty litres of gin, whisky and vodka toppled with a clatter, along with some receipts. Being a light drinker, Annie gasped at how much Mrs Jenkins had spent. How on earth could she afford this much each week? But then addicts would find a way. She lodged the bottles inside one of her tote bags to stop them rolling around and jumped in the van.

'I've been thinking,' Arthur said in *that* voice as he climbed into his seat.

'Not again?' she groaned, ruffling his hair playfully.

'I think you should add me in to your business name. Just for the summer.'

What a sweetie! 'Any ideas?'

'How about … The Lady Boy Gardener?'

Goodness knows how, but she managed not to snort. It was bad enough being asked if she did waxes – what on earth would people expect if she became The Lady Boy Gardener?

She gave a noncommittal 'maybe' before slamming the door and announcing a definitive 'not!' into the air. There was no way she was going to let this chat continue.

So she climbed in her side and asked him if he fancied an ice cream. It was a cheap distraction, but at least the subject of ladyboys would be dropped in favour of his top five flavours.

36

This campsite should come with a weather warning. It was raining when we got here, it has rained non-stop for five whole days and we're so fed up we're leaving early. Utterly miserable. Wanda was nice but not very apologetic. Rude!

Anonymous, Thank God we don't live in Wales
Campsite Visitors' Book

'So these stuck-up people ... they actually wanted me to take responsibility for the weather and give them a refund!' Wanda cried at the kitchen table after she'd been dragged into Mam and Blod's so-called quiet drink. 'Maybe I should put a disclaimer on the website,' she scoffed. 'You know, *please note, the weather is beyond our control*. How I kept my cool, I don't know!'

'You should've told them to go play with their gran!' Mam said, which was as close as she got to swearing. She was of the old school; it was the same with bodily functions: she'd do silent ones, known around here as 'chapel farts'.

In a stream of ear-piercing expletives, Blod suggested all manner of things they could go and do to themselves.

Thanks to the potency of her own blackberry wine, she had got louder and merrier in the hour since they'd started gassing. No wonder Carys had taken her thirty-three-weeks of bump to bed with a herbal tea. The poor love was in limbo, living from scan to scan, but she'd been told that only a month of this at most remained. Once their lungs were developed, the babies would be delivered at thirty-seven weeks, so at least Carys had an end in sight.

'Some people, eh? The arrogance of it!' Mam tutted through a Joker-style Ribena smile.

'There's always a bad potato in the sack,' Blod said.

'And they can't wait to pull a wasp's nest on your head,' Mam added.

It was almost a competition to see who could crowbar the most obscure idioms into their conversation.

'Although not all tourists, of course. Some can be quite charming.' Blod simpered behind her jazzy new specs, black-rimmed circles that reminded her of someone. But who? Something was afoot and Mam was straight in there.

'Who is he? And has he got a brother?'

Oh dear God, Mother, Wanda thought. Blod and Mam were cackling like hyenas, smacking one another's arms like they were a couple of ... well, randy mature ladies.

'The first to the mill can grind!' Blod leered suggestively.

First come, first served? This was appalling! They were talking about a person here, not an object.

'Look at your face, Wanda! Look at her face, Blod!'

'Oh get over yourself, are the old not allowed to love?' Blod boomed. 'We'll have to get you signed up to internet dating, Lyn! Find you a shining clean Welshman like mine except he's from the Lake District. We met the day the mountain was measured.'

The mansplainer! Wanda remembered him. Blod had bought matching specs. But he seemed so un-Blod.

'He came in for mint cake and we got talking and there was just something there. I mean, it's a mystery, he's shorter than me and a former mountaineer, and you know me, I'm more kitten heels than walking boots. He's younger too, only by a few years but it counts at our age, Lyn! But we just clicked. I never thought I'd meet anyone again.'

It was truly heart-warming. And then it took a mind-boggling turn.

'I tell you something, my Malcolm, he's got stamina. He calls these,' Blod said, looking down her nose at her chest and flapping her floaty purple tunic, 'my peaks of Snowdonia!'

More hooting ensued.

Dearie me, it was a sad state when Wanda's love life was the dinosaur next to Blod's.

'Right, well, that's my cue to leave before you start going into the … ins and out, so to speak.'

'Suit yourself, Wanda. Just a word for you, my Belmira, she's still on his tail. That's the polite word for it, anyway.'

How did she know that was where she was off to?

'As much as I'd love to see her find a man, I wouldn't want her to steal him from you.'

Wanda gasped. 'Is that why you got him to take her on a date? To make me jealous? I was so upset about that!'

'There you go, Lyn. You owe me a fiver, she does fancy him. I knew it!'

Wanda's jaw dropped.

'She's not denying it either!' Blod already had her hand out and Mam, Mam! She was in her purse too. They were incorrigible.

'I'm on my phone if Carys needs anything.'

She grabbed her mac and went out into the evening and found, at last, the wind and showers had stopped. August had come back to Gobaith. The sky was a bag of cotton wool and early-evening blue – it'd mean layers of sunset, a real belter of one. It'd be even more spectacular at Lew's, where she was heading up the lane.

The weather really had been as awful as the unhappy campers had said. Her week had been spent sweating in wellies and waterproofs because even though it was wet, it was still warm. Make-up hadn't touched her skin for days and it had felt strange getting a little bit dressed up to-night. Nothing over the top, just a floaty green summery dress she'd bought for her travels which brought out the red of her hair. She'd tied it back, it was long overdue a cut but when had she had the time? Even though she'd had cancellations because of the conditions and a few people had packed up before the end of their stay, she'd been kept busy laying down chipping paths on mud, dismantling abandoned soaking collapsed tents some had left behind and endless bathroom-block cleaning.

At least it distracted her from her worries. She hadn't heard a squeak from Danny Platt and she was beginning to lose hope. Her own position needed to be kept at bay too. Because she'd worked out why she and Lew could never be. Tonight she would tell him. Adrenalin instantly kicked in when she reached the driveway of

The Bunkhouse. Finally they had found a slot to see one another to have The Chat.

But as soon as she turned the corner to Lew's bungalow she was disarmed. As a speaker played chill-out tunes, Lew was lying back on one of two giant orange lobster lilos which he'd set out on his patch of garden. There was an upside-down crate behind them with a coconut wearing a scuba mask, two glasses, each sporting a mini umbrella, and on the grass was a bucket of water filled with bottles and cans.

'Welcome to Club Tropicana!' he said, his arms aloft, his eyes twinkling. 'Thought we could pretend to be on holiday. It's the closest we'll get for a while.'

On cue, the sun came out, making the earth steam, and he produced two pairs of comedy pineapple shades, which they instantly put on and giggled. Talk about touched! It was like he'd peered into her soul, seen what she needed and came up quite rightly with a good lie-down, a drink and a few lols. More than that though, it showed he knew her dreams. And it broke her nervousness completely.

'This is genius, Lew,' she said, gingerly settling down on her lilo.

He sat up effortlessly – she knew she'd be rolling off her lobster when it came to it – and began to rummage in the bucket, which chimed with clinks and clunks. 'There's prosecco, a few tins of cheesy cocktails, lager, cider ... what you fancy?'

Er, you, she thought, drinking in his smooth brown arms, his long eyelashes, neat stubble, ninety per cent dark chocolate eyes, that mop of curls and the suggestion of muscles under his T-shirt. All that turmoil and look at her, quite the walkover. She wanted to have a look at the cans, but she daren't move because knowing her there'd be a dubious squelch and she'd have to say it wasn't her.

'There's G and T, cosmo and mojito ... how about a cosmo? It's like a bit of liquid sunset.'

He passed a cold one over to her, pulling the ring, which sounded the hiss of bubbles, and chose one for himself.

'Perfect!'

'At your service,' he said, his lovely straight teeth displayed in a smile on those tempting lips.

Wanda sank back into the comfy claws of her lobster and took in the view. The sun was dropping ever nearer to the horizon, matching the colour of her drink, while the mountain had become a silhouette of navy blue. The lake below sparkled, like a palm full of jewels, and the clouds were streaks of pink and purple. It was beautiful in its simplicity – the opposite of the complexity of her relationship with Lew. Her spirits began to fade as she considered it. Yes, they had a natural rhythm of their own, but her conclusion about their compatibility was painful: when the going got tough, they didn't have a good track record. It was as if they'd unravelled the past only to find there was a knot at the very heart of them.

'So ...' Lew said softly into the dusk. Wanda tensed up at the weight of this one word. What hope did they have? 'Having a good holiday?'

His lilo squeaked as he turned his body to face her and she felt terrible for not returning his smile.

'Oh ... is this all ...' Lew looked embarrassed and dropped his eyelashes.

'No, no. Lew, it's lovely, it's just that it reminds me I'm going away.' And he couldn't be a part of that.

'But that's good, isn't it? What you want?'

'It is, yes. It's just I feel …' How she wanted to be able to be in the moment and throw herself at him, at them. '… sad.'

'How so?' he asked, forgetting his feelings, showing concern for hers.

'Because I thought when I went, we'd be okay.'

'We aren't?' He seemed genuinely surprised. 'I've apologised, I'll say it as much as you need to hear it.'

'I know you're sorry, I know you did it to protect Annie. It's the most courageous thing and—'

'But it all came out too late, is that it?'

'No, Lew. I get that, I get why you avoided it all. I did exactly the same. It's just … I wish we could've met without all the past being part of it.'

'How do you mean?' Lew frowned.

'Like, we can do real life as individuals, but together … somehow we always make a pig's ear out of it.'

He looked crushed and the sparkle in his eyes went out as the sun disappeared.

'So it'll never happen, between us?' He gulped.

'I just don't have faith in us as a couple.' Her voice cracked as she confessed what she wished she didn't believe.

'But we've never tried.'

'We did. That night in the shepherd's hut.'

'But we were kids!' he said gently.

'We're not the same as then.'

'That's good. No more lies, we can start afresh.'

'But I'm going away in October, aren't I? We can't start something then ask each other to wait. If it was going to work, wouldn't it have happened already?'

He put his hand out and she reached for his, their fingers entwined. 'No. I think we had a load of stuff to deal with and we buried it for so long and it was going to take a while to fix. That's why I came back. To find you. I didn't know if you'd be here, but I thought it was the best place to start. And then here you were, and okay, we had a rocky start but this can work. I know it. And I'll wait for you, if you'll let me.'

Wanda hadn't factored this in. She'd expected him to take it on the chin as a no. Desire swooped in, she desperately wanted to place her lips on his. Her heart was thudding so loudly in her ears as if it was echoing back at her off the mountain. But with this sorrow she was feeling too ...

'What if I don't come back? How can I come back? I'll have no job and a mortgage needing paying.'

Lew nodded. 'But I can help.'

'I can't make any promises and I can't let you make me any either. We'll just be setting ourselves up for another separation and this time, we're older, it's more serious.'

He looked at her and she saw his loss reflecting her own.

'I accept it, but I don't understand why we can't try. We don't know what's around the corner. Didn't you say you had to be brave?'

It would be so easy to shut her eyes on all of it and give in to him. But when their bodies had parted the same truth would remain.

'Lew, if this happened, tonight, if it happened now, I don't think I could ever be apart from you ever again.' A tear rolled down her cheek and his eyes were glistening too.

'This feels like goodbye,' he said, squeezing her hand. Her throat was aching as the emotion swelled up.

Just once she'd allow herself to touch him. She pulled him to her, he did the same, and then they were side by side, his arm around her, her head on his shoulder, her face tucked in his chin as if they'd been made for this moment.

'I mean it, Wanda, I'll wait,' he whispered, caressing her back.

She shut her eyes and breathed him in and wished she could stay there forever.

37

A hush fell as Pastor Pete began to deliberate just who would win the title of Wonkiest Veg in show.

With forensic expertise, he was handling curly courgettes and scrutinising bum-shaped potatoes, while the crowd at the community garden suffered an agonising wait under the beating August sunshine.

Finally, after an adjustment of his collar and a dab of his top lip with a hanky, he laid a gold rosette next to Arthur's two-legged carrot – and the Grow Up kids went wild, hoisting Arthur up into the air to celebrate to a round of enthusiastic applause.

Annie was overwhelmed by the turnout. The event was never intended to be this big – just a couple of stalls of veg and flowers to help pay for some seeds and tools next year. But when word had got round, it mushroomed. The village wanted to get behind it and offers came flooding in. Annie had been here late last night putting up a marquee that Wanda had rustled up. Then back again first thing to set up tables and checked tablecloths, to receive tombola goodies, raffle prizes and donations of treble-tiered Victoria sponges. And Gobaith hadn't let anyone down. There were smiles everywhere; campers were mixing with locals, people were having impromptu picnics and Sunny Side Up was doing a roaring trade in cold drinks. It was the most blissful scene.

'You did this, Annie,' Spike said, giving her an elbow and then passing her an ice lolly while he tucked into his. Lately, he seemed to be close whenever she needed him, eager to support her and fulfil any wish she desired. 'You got the Xbox generation off their screens and into gardening. Look at them!'

Their gang was busy helping kids up onto hay bales brought by a farmer for some seating, teaching little ones how to make daisy-chain crowns and giving tours of the garden.

'It wasn't just me.'

'Come off it. It's you responsible for this. You! Arthur didn't know 'is arse from 'is elderflower before you came along.'

With heat rising inside of her from pride and his attention, she needed to cool down.

'Ooh, it's fizzy!' she said, as the bubbles hit her tongue.

'Alis's homemade prosecco ones.'

'Delicious ...'

'Stop changing the subject anyway. You have a special talent, Annie.'

He gave her the loveliest smile. It was so easy to get carried away when she was with Spike. Alone, she would be able to square the circle of feelings she had for him – they were friends, nothing more. But in his company, it was a different story. She couldn't help it: was he giving her vibes? Had Arthur been right when he'd said his father '*liked* her liked her'? Her body temperature remained hot despite the refreshing ice pop. She made a decision to believe she was blushing at his praise because otherwise she'd end up frustrated and sad.

'Thanks,' she said, 'I've really enjoyed this project. And the school one will start in September. It makes me think that maybe the dream of having an apothecary shop isn't what I really want to do. Like, it's a fluffy marshmallow of a thing, my own little potions on the shelves, crystals and organics. I'm not sure it'd be right for me.'

'You could keep that up as a hobby. Teaching is an extension of your healing powers. It's your real calling, I reckon.'

'Do you?' That was funny, she'd been thinking about investigating something along those lines. But she had no qualifications. Then again, a tentative search online had shown her she could study as well as work. If she could combine what she loved and take it into the classroom . . .

'Yes!' he laughed. 'Isn't it obvious? You get through to the kids, you've got something about you. Something sort of . . . magical.'

Now he was blushing. She waited for him to backtrack, to say he hadn't quite meant magical but something else. Instead he repeated it as if he was in a daze.

'I . . . er . . . well, I just want you to know how much you mean to me. And Arthur.'

Was he trying to say something to her? Something she'd wanted him to say increasingly in the days since her reason for breaking off their relationship had disappeared? For Dean's threat had retreated. A new number meant no silent calls and the divorce was going through. Now she could see he'd been all bark and no bite. Hope climbed inside of her like a wave – until it collapsed when she realised that Arthur had achieved an equilibrium, making friends, settling in, and that was because there had been no more change. This was the best it would be with Spike and she had to be grateful. But he was still looking at her with more than platonic affection and he was searching for words.

'I was wondering ...'

Annie felt ever so flustered. Her lolly had dripped over her fingers. She began to rummage for a tissue in her tote bag but instead she pulled out a screwed-up piece of paper. That'd have to do. She unfolded it and found it was the receipt from Mrs Jenkins's from the time the carrier bag full of her bottles had split. Just as she was about to wipe the stickiness off with it, she scanned the address of the shop on the receipt – and her heart jolted.

Her eyes began to swim as she checked herself, to make sure she'd read it right. Blinking hard to stop the letters moving, she read them again, and again, trying to put together their meaning. Because it couldn't be true, it absolutely couldn't be.

Annie was reeling, the receipt was trembling. This couldn't be right. Yet what else would explain it? The truth was here, in its cold precision, like the serrated edge of a blade. She was gasping for air, her legs were buckling and she began to stagger.

'Annie, are you okay?'

Spike's voice came from a million miles away and then boomed in her ears.

'Oh my God,' she heard herself saying out loud. Her eyes tried to focus, looking to make sense of everything, but it was all too bright.

'Annie, speak to me,' he said, his arms around her, his hand gently on her cheek.

'I've got to go,' she said. 'Now.'

'Like this? I'll come with you.'

Maybe it was a good idea to have him with her, in case something happened to her at the wheel.

'Don't make a scene,' she whispered, dropping her gaze to the floor, avoiding eye contact with anyone.

With his hand at the back of her left arm, he steered her through the crowd, stopping only to tell Arthur to look after Teg, to stick with his mates, to find Wanda if he needed anything and to ring if there was a problem. He wouldn't be long. In his van, Annie mechanically did up her seat belt and stuttered instructions to Spike to follow the road out of Gobaith and into the country-side. Rather than a seamless flow, the journey seemed like a photo reel of familiar trees, postboxes, houses and signposts interspersed with snatches of the letter swirling through her head. He didn't press her for any details, any information. Instead he was reassuring her softly, telling her she was fine, she was okay and she was here with him. And when they pulled up, he simply said, 'I'll be here, Annie.'

She looked into his face, wanting to explain, except there were no words. They were all jumbled up. She couldn't speak of something she didn't understand. Only by doing this would she be capable of processing it all.

She nodded and got out, still clutching the piece of paper, which was now grey with sweat. A deep breath and she stood with the van door between her and Mrs Jenkins's unblinking windows, which stared her out, defiant.

Something possessed Annie then. Years of rage spilled over. She slammed the door shut and walked slowly towards the pink and red-brick speckled terrace, squaring up to the silent net curtains, vowing she wouldn't leave until she knew everything.

Up to the front door, with its shining knocker as if this woman was respectable. As if. She couldn't even bring herself to touch it. She was breaking the rules by even standing at the doorstep. Her fist was clenching, raising and knocking the wood with her knuckles, not feeling the contact at all. It was like an out-of-body experience but she had to make it real – so this time she used the base of her hand and sounded a thud, and another, and then another, until the boom of her hand matched the boom in her head and in her heart.

There was no answer. She bent over and flipped up the letterbox, parting the brushes to see into the gloomy hallway.

'Hello?' she shouted. 'Are you there?'

Annie's eyes searched the gloomy hallway for a hint of a shadow.

'I'm not leaving!'

And there was the sound of a shuffle of slippers on lino. A clink of ice against a glass which was shaking in the woman's hand. A waft of cigarette smoke. A cleaning housecoat over her clothes. Long grey hair hanging life-lessly around her haggard face.

Annie hadn't seen her for years. Not because she hadn't wanted to, but because this woman wanted it this way. The only contact they had was through the garden and that was because Annie insisted on doing it. Hatred swelled up inside of her. How many times had she been watched, killing herself to try to make this place decent?

Like a warning, pain, anger and devastation seared

through Annie – but the need to know was more powerful.

'Has Dean been here?' Annie yelled at her as sobs broke free. 'Just tell me, Mam, tell me the truth.'

38

We had such a great time we wanted to stay on for bank holiday but it's all booked out. We'll definitely be back! Thanks for an amazing stay!

Cathy and Dave Saunders, Herts
Campsite Visitors' Book

Wanda collapsed into her father's comfy armchair, kicked off her flip-flops and let off an extravagant groan as she fell back against the headrest.

It was the final Friday of August – summer's crescendo of bank holiday weekend was staring her in the face. Today had already been an absolute nightmare of change-overs, scrubbing and queries for both her and Mam. The site was as full as an egg. She just wanted to sleep. But it was only lunchtime. She had the rest of the day to get through, then tomorrow Under A Starry Sky was hosting a huge barbecue for campers and the community – why had she done this to herself? Stupidly, she'd come up with it the night she'd torn herself away from Lew's Club Tropicana. Her groin growled at the memory of what she'd given up – *not now, thank you*. He was the one who'd said it was like a goodbye on the lobster lilos: she'd done the sensible thing and gone home. She wished she hadn't: although she knew it was better all round she had. That saying, *it's better to regret something you have done than something you haven't* was all right if you didn't have a round-the-world trip at stake. Wanda knew herself too well: to kiss Lew, to stay the night, would've conflicted her even more. It was too dangerous. The thank-you barbecue to the people of Gobaith was the preamble to her departure.

Even so, Lew was still under her skin. She had a horrible feeling he would be until she got on the plane. That meant there were thirty-three days to get through. And that prospect was a slap in the face on top of her exhaustion. Because now they had both acknowledged the chemistry between them, they were at the stage of exchanging heated glances – maybe she needed to wear science goggles and a boiler suit, that'd be a turn off. If she could just keep it together until October the first ... then again, to be quite honest, if he came in here now butt naked, she was so tired she'd turn him down. Five minutes, that's what she needed, she thought, sinking into velvet, her limbs heavy. But just as she was dropping off, she came to with an instinctive jolt. She'd sensed a change in the light in the lounge – not to be rude but Carys was so big she was capable of a total eclipse of the sun. Her sister was stood in front of her with a look on her face. There was excitement, fear and now a grimace. Wanda shot up out of her seat.

'Is it happening, Caz?' she cried before realising that excitement wasn't helpful. She repeated it this time softly, her hand going to Carys's back as her sister took hold of the chair's arm and gurned.

'I ... think ... so,' she said, puffing her way through pain.

'How long has this been going on? You poor thing!'

'A ... couple ... of ... hours.' She began to pant. 'Been ... bouncing ... on ... my ... ball ... *nyeargh!*'

At the crest now, Carys was breathing deep and slow. Once it had passed, she said, 'Because I thought they were Branston's.'

Carys handed her phone over – she had a contraction app on the go and it was looking like they were regular and getting closer.

'Any other signs?'

She nodded. 'You don't want to know, bowel-related, down-there stuff.'

'Do you want to go to the hospital?'

Carys's eyes widened and then she tried to look at her feet. 'I think my waters have just broken.'

'Right, come on, let's go then. I'll tell Mam to ring ahead. They did say to go in if this happened.' Not just because they lived a good drive away but because it was twins.

'Maybe Mam should go with me? What about the campsite?'

'Shut up! I'm not missing this! I'm your birthing partner!'

'You sure?' Carys looked so young and vulnerable. She couldn't imagine how she would be feeling, about to bring two babies into the world without the father. Still no word from him and it had broken Wanda's heart. Thank goodness she hadn't told Carys about her efforts to track him down.

'There's plenty of people Mam can call on if she needs

help. I've done all the hard stuff, she just needs to book people in. Honestly. And if anyone moans then they can do one. Let's get in the car, I'll get your bag.'

And then, as Carys waddled off, Wanda gave a prayer – first of thanks for letting the twins get to almost thirty-seven weeks and then another asking for them to be delivered safely. One thing was for certain, if this came to nothing then Carys would probably end up being induced. Trying to keep herself calm was going to be hard until they got to the maternity unit. As she went around gathering what Carys needed, she could feel her dramatic tendencies battering to be released but for once, Wanda would refuse to entertain them. She found Mam, who offered to go instead because it was a messy business, giving birth.

'I want to do this, I need to, for her,' Wanda said meaningfully, communicating what they had discussed between them on many occasions: Wanda would play the part of the dad if it came to it.

'Of course,' Mam said, close to tears. 'And put a towel on the seat, will you? I've only just had the Land Rover cleaned.'

That was why Wanda had to be with Carys. Mam would only say something totes inappropes when push came to shove. Wanda was glad to report Mam's valeting concerns to Carys as she reversed out of the campsite. It gave them some light relief until the next contraction came along. And the next. At the hospital, the midwives were waiting for them, and Wanda had never felt more relieved for Carys and for her own worry: being in the hands of the professionals – and their latex gloves, monitors and soothing voices – meant Wanda could concentrate on her job. While Carys was examined and the delivery suite buzzed with staff, she set about doing what she could to match the birth plan, producing Carys's requested extra-large Nirvana T-shirt, cueing up the playlist of indie classics, lining up snacks on the side and rubbing Annie's herbal massage oil between her hands to warm it up. It was all progressing nicely, the first baby was head down, there seemed to be no issues preventing a vaginal birth. This would go swimmingly!

Except hours later, when the gas and air had come out, Carys was told she was still only in the early stages of labour. Wanda had to control her shock. Carys was in so much agony – to think there were potentially hours and hours to go until she had dilated enough. An epidural would only be given when labour was established. No doubt if Mam had been here she'd have said, 'No pain, no gain.' Not even that made Carys laugh this time. She was too busy being sick. The language around them began to change, the comings and goings of nurses and doctors increased, a drip was on stand-by, there were mentions of forceps, C-sections and emergencies. The twins' bag of tiny nappies, babygros and hats and mitts remained unzipped in the corner and Wanda began to feel frightened. Out of that came anger at Danny flaming Platt. If he could see what he'd caused, if he could see what Carys was going through ... she'd like to show him some forceps, right in the trouser department.

'Why don't you go and get something to eat?' one of the midwives, Sam, said around nine after she suggested a bath for Carys to tide her over until she was ready for a visit from the anaesthetist.

'I don't want to leave her,' Wanda said quietly.

'We'll look after her.' Sam said it kindly and it made Wanda feel ridiculous.

'I'm sorry, I'm just scared.'

'We're here for your sister. You need to look after you. It's going to be a long night. Now, don't worry, she's in the best hands. We'll get her through it.'

She was right. 'Caz, I'm just popping to the canteen,' she said brightly. 'Want anything?'

With tired eyes, Carys said, 'Vodka and tonic?'

'There's champers in the bag for after, all right?' Wanda blew her a kiss and waved cheerily. 'I won't be long.'

As soon as she'd got out of the room, though, she slumped against the wall and put her head in her hands. This was all so unfair! If she could swap places with Carys, she would. It was quite the most terrifying thing she'd ever seen. How had human life continued? Why did women have to go through this? She felt helpless – she knew it was self-indulgent but she began to cry. Wanda had to get away from the door in case Carys heard, so she made her way out of the maternity department, catching night falling through a window. She had to ring Mam but she'd left her phone in the room. She couldn't go back. No way. A strong cup of coffee and a sandwich was what she needed to pull herself together. Tears were still falling and she berated herself for being so weak. 'For God's sake,' she said under her breath; if only she had some back-up. But Mam would be in bed by now – okay, she wouldn't be sleeping, but how would she get here? There was no one else who could help. Cursing, she let herself out of the department and was stomping down the corridor angrily when she got to the swing door – only for it to suddenly fly open at her. Incensed and ready to give a 'watch where you're going', she fell mute. He was here! Danny Platt was here!

'I've been ringing!' he cried, breathless with urgency. 'Your mum gave me your number. Where is she?'

'It's you!' she said, clasping her hands to her face.

'Yes! Where's Carys? How is she, how are the babies? I can't believe I'm saying babies, I'm going to be a dad!' Anxious, in shock and then joy, he was going through the emotions like he was chain-smoking a pack of fags.

'I never ever thought you'd come! This is beyond!' she sang, hugging him, her spirits soaring at his arrival. 'Follow me.' She swivelled on the spot and they began a quick march. Then something awful occurred to her. 'Oh God, my mother must've broken it to you.'

'She did give me a bit of a telling off,' he said, grinning, his teeth looking pearly up against his tanned skin.

'You haven't been in prison then? I did wonder.'

'What?'

'You disappeared. Your aunt wouldn't say where you were. Where've you been? You haven't got a wife and kids have you? I better check before you see her.'

'No! Don't be daft! I explained this to Lyn. I tried to ring Carys after I'd left in December – but there was no answerphone. I thought Carys had my number so I gave up, I thought she was playing hard to get. Then as the days passed, I thought about a letter – but when she didn't call, I just assumed she wasn't interested. I was gutted. The office had an opportunity in India, to get some call centre training. I thought, why not. I got back this morning. There was a note from my aunty waiting for me – to call you. I didn't want to risk it ringing out again so I got in the camper van and came down. I thought, what the 'eck, and now I'm going to be a dad of twins!'

'Not for a while, I'm afraid.' She filled him in and once she'd verified to reception he was who he said he was, Wanda went back in to see Carys alone. But she wasn't there and her mind began to spiral out of control. She dashed out and the midwife caught sight of her from another door. 'She's in here.'

Wanda peered round and saw her sister finally looking less peaky. The bath was like a cocoon; her sister had always loved the water, and Carys seemed to have bounced back a little.

'The drugs are good!' she smiled, holding the gas and air mouthpiece aloft, looking like the winner of the Miss Wet T-Shirt While Pregnant competition.

'Listen, before the next contraction comes, I've got something to tell you. Danny's here, he's waiting outside, I found him, and he's just turned up. If you want me to tell him to wait, that's f—'

'You what?' Carys's jaw dropped. 'Get him in here now, I need someone to shout at! And you go home. I mean it, I couldn't have got this far without you. But go, see Mam. Get some sleep.'

'Sure?'

'Positive,' she said, her eyebrows starting to lower as the rollercoaster of pain ploughed on.

Wanda leaned down to give her a peck with an 'I love you', then ushered in the father, who dropped to his knees and kissed Carys over and over, sending them both weeping.

'My God, you're beautiful,' he said.

She took his hand, then a breath of gas and air, moaning as agony consumed her.

'Oh Danny,' she said tenderly as she came around, putting her forehead to his, 'you absolute wanker! Where the hell have you been?'

Wanda stepped back and left them to it, retreating from their reunion in the most bizarre of circumstances. What a day, what an almost-nine months. What a turn-up! She felt guilty that she could leave but then this was right, this was how it should be. She went to Carys's room, found her bag and her phone, which had been on silent. There were millions of missed calls. Messages galore. Voicemails: Mam asking what was happening, Mam shouting Danny had come, Mam telling her off for not picking up. Then one from Lew.

'We've done it!' he said, with a busy background, 'it's official! The mountain! It really is a mountain. Just by an inch. They got back to me!'

Wanda punched the air as she left the hospital.

'We're in the Travellers' Rest, celebrating.'

So that's what the noise was.

'Come down if you can. If you see Annie, let her know. I've been trying to get hold of her for days now but haven't heard anything.'

Oh, yes, Annie had gone quiet. She'd left the community garden produce sale quickly, Wanda remembered seeing her leave with Spike. Wanda hadn't given it a thought at the time but now she was puzzled. Because she hadn't turned up to do the grass this week. And Annie was like clockwork.

'Anyway, if you get a chance, come and see me!' he finished off as she got to the car.

Wanda would've liked nothing more than to fall into his embrace. But she couldn't go partying when Carys was in the wars. She had to be on stand-by throughout the night. It was all too emotional to go and get drunk. The mountain had been given an inch. Wanda knew herself too well – she didn't trust herself not to go over the top and take a mile.

39

Annie had never insisted on anything from her mother, ever.

Why would you when you'd been handed over at birth to be brought up by someone else without a backwards glance?

In a way, it made things simpler: knowing reconciliation and apology and declarations of love were simply not on the cards. One question had always remained: why had her mother chosen to keep Ryan but not her? As a girl, Annie had asked that of Nanna – Annie's dad had legged it, her mother was young and incapable. Asking her mother herself, though, it had been on the tip of her tongue many times. She'd been too afraid to hear what she'd say.

But now, sat in this house, where cigarette smoke hung and clung to everything, clasping her hands to her lap to stop the tremors, Annie realised there was no point in knowing. Instead she saw she'd been blessed to have escaped the day-in, day-out neglect that her brother had endured, which had set him off on a doomed path to death.

Annie couldn't change her past, but she could be master of her future: so for the first and only time she was

357

demanding something of her. It had to be early, of course, before the drinking began; maybe there was even whisky in her mother's cup of coffee? Yet both of their mugs were untouched, cooling as the pine wall clock ticked its way to ten o'clock. Now they waited, Annie perched on the edge of the threadbare settee, her mother hovering by the door leading to the kitchen, uncomfortable in each other's company.

Ten days had passed since Annie had come here for answers. The scene then had been an emotional mess of tears and shouting, quite different to how the atmosphere was today: the same went for the room, which had been littered with bottles and fag ends but was now empty of sin. Appalled by her mother's confession, she had been in a daze. Spike had waited for her, scooping her up, taking her back to his, collecting Teg and arranging for Arthur to have a sleepover at Nathan's. Then he'd held her for hours on his sofa until she had cried herself out. He'd slept in Arthur's bed, while she'd had his and had woken to the smell of breakfast and coffee, the sound of him humming along to the radio and the pleasure of receiving a morning hug. He'd given her everything she'd needed: care, concern and love.

Annie had struggled with what to do. Turn the other cheek? For that was what was expected of women, to step away from danger. And she had done that her entire life. Yet this injustice, Annie couldn't let it go. Women weren't supposed to take up space, they didn't spread their legs when they took a seat. But this was about standing her ground. Spike had offered to come, he backed her whatever choice she'd make. She'd refused, though – she wanted to do this by herself to assert her worth and strength.

An engine coughed up the street and spluttered to a stop outside. A white van, the one she now knew had followed her that day when she had put it down to paranoia. Annie stood up, staking out her position, as Mrs Jenkins shuffled to let Dean in.

His shadow in the hall, a clink of glass inside a rustling carrier bag, and then in he came.

'What the hell is she doing here?' Dean said, furious, glaring at Annie.

Mrs Jenkins shrank and Annie saw in an instant the reason why her mother had betrayed her. Not just now but all her life, abused by bad men.

'You've set me up!' Dean hissed. 'You bitch. That's where you get it from, Leanne.'

Annie registered the use of her full name, designed to remind her of the father who had gone, whose name, Lee, had been attached to her in what could only be her mother's way of trying to please him, to stamp him on his child. But the blow fell short of Annie.

'I know what you've been doing. I know you've been bribing her. Bringing booze here, getting her drunk to get information out of her, getting her to call you if I show up so you can follow me.'

That's how he'd found out where Teg was. While her mother had never spoken to her when Annie had come to do her garden, she had been watching her after all, even reporting the flyer for the Blast from the Past disco in Annie's van window.

'Some mother she is, grassing you up for gut-rot gin, grassing me up too so it appears,' he snarled, his fingers turning white as he gripped the handles of the bag which contained his latest delivery. Mrs Jenkins had stepped back behind the sofa, shielding herself. Annie stepped forward to seize territory.

'Oh no. It was your own stupid fault I found out,' Annie said, with steel. 'You left a receipt in the bag. A receipt from the shop next door to our house.'

Dean's jaw clenched. She'd got him. But slippery as ever, he would try to wriggle out of it. He began by dropping his shoulders, making himself smaller. 'I only did it because I cared, I wanted you back. I said that to your mother, didn't I?' He darted his eyes to Mrs Jenkins.

'Leave her alone. This is between you and me. And this is where it ends. I'll contact the police, get you done for harassment.'

'Listen, I've left you alone since that night at the hall, the disco, haven't I?' His voice was softer, his eyes pleading – she'd fallen for that too many times.

'Yet you've still been coming. The receipt was recent. And you're here now. Why's that?' She knew why, but she wanted to draw out his discomfort.

'I wanted to look out for you.'

'Hardly. You're just biding your time. I won't stand for it. I won't have you coming back into my life.'

Dean sized her up, looking her up and down, searching for a weakness. But he wouldn't find one: he had been her rock bottom, she couldn't go any lower. He knew he'd been out-played. Suddenly he swung the bag high and roared, baring his teeth, in a display of physicality, the only power he had over her. Annie gasped involuntarily, but that was from shock, because she wasn't afraid.

'Everyone knows I'm here,' she said, strangely calm, while her mother cowered. 'Everyone knows I'm meeting you. You do something to hurt me or her, you'll be the one who suffers.'

This trump card, of a community she'd once fled but which now rallied around her, finally silenced him. He dropped the bag and the old carpet swallowed the impact.

He was panting, but he was outmanoeuvred. Dean dropped his head and then went to go.

'No more following me, no more turning up and no more calls,' she warned his back.

'The calls? I never made those.' He shrugged and left, slamming the door behind him.

'It was me,' her mother said with gravel in her throat.

'You?' Annie said, turning to her.

'I wanted to warn you what Dean was doing but I ...' Her shaking hand went to her chest and her bottom lip quivered.

A wave of sorrow hit Annie. This woman was in a prison of fear and suffering. Life had gone spectacularly wrong for her, off the rails, into bad relationships with a dead son and an estranged daughter. She had tried to contact her but she hadn't had the courage to see it through. So there had been some loyalty from her mother, just not enough.

'I'm going to the graveyard,' Annie said, wondering if she could build on that loyalty, 'to see Ryan. If you wanted to go?'

Mrs Jenkins's eyes moved to the bag of alcohol on the floor. Would this be the moment she freed herself? But no. She was on her knees, peering to check that nothing was broken or wasted. There was no point in picking her mother apart: she didn't care about herself, how could she care about anyone else? She'd written herself off a long time ago.

But Annie wasn't like her. And she was glad, she thought, as she shut the door quietly behind her.

40

Smoke was rising over the lake but this time Wanda didn't even think of fire.

With Spike helping out, her hands were flipping sausages and burgers, filling baps and spooning relish as her mind kept asking, *when would those babies be born?*

More than twenty-four hours in labour and poor Carys was still waiting to deliver them. The epidural had come along at midnight, Danny had rung this morning to say Carys had managed to get some sleep while the pain relief did its thing. Having run out of fidgeting, Mam had gone up there to see if she could boss them out. That left Wanda jumping every time her phone buzzed, but it was always friends and family asking, 'Are they here yet?'

Under blue skies and sunshine, Saturday afternoon's barbecue in the community garden was packed out, heads and dinghies were bobbing in the water and the mountain was lush with green. Not long and her Wandalust account on Instagram would change for good: there'd be palm trees, Colombian coffees and shots of rum in salsa bars. Wanda felt a nostalgia for this place now as the days were passing – where there had been fear of leaving back in the winter, now she felt she was ready. Under A Starry Sky was a top-rated campsite, nominated for an award and booked up for next summer already. Mam was fitter than a fiddle. And the sooner she got away from lovely Lew, the better.

Diolch Gobaith, read the banner by the barbecue: this was her thank you – and the start of her goodbye. September would gallop along in a blur of nappies, finalising arrangements for her travels and finding the right person to take over the campsite – no one suitable had appeared as yet. Everyone who mattered to her was here. Apart from Carys and Rock and Roll. The mountain – *the official bloody mountain!* – was getting national coverage announcing the world's newest mountain and the phone hadn't stopped. At dawn, campers had raced up, excited by the timing to be the first to conquer it before the rush of ramblers and serious climbers. She looked up at its peak and she swore its jagged edges were curled in a smile ...

'Extra onions, please!'

'Annie! Hiya!' Wanda hadn't seen her for a while. She looked different somehow, relaxed and rested. 'Where've you been?'

'Seeing off Dean Pincher. For good.' Annie beamed. 'It's all going to be coming up roses from now on!'

Wanda returned her smile. Then it dawned on her – in

all likelihood she wouldn't be here to see it all work out for Annie, and it caught her in the throat. And of course that was when her phone went.

'It's Carys!' Wanda said.

'Let me take over at the barbie,' Annie said.

Shaking, Wanda answered and waited.

'They're here! Rock and Roll are here!' Carys sounded groggy but elated, on a high, and no wonder!

She took the phone away from her mouth and bellowed. 'Carys has had the twins!'

A cheer went up and there was Blod, waving her arms madly, shouting, 'What has she had then?'

'Oh yes!' She could finally make the big reveal. 'Boys!'

There was more celebration, but Wanda could have said 'kittens' or 'pork pies' and everyone would have reacted the same.

'Caz,' Wanda said back into the phone, 'did you hear that? We're so blinking happy!'

'I did! Oh, Wanda, they can't wait to meet you.'

'I can't wait to meet them! When shall I come? Now? Tomorrow? How are you? How was it? You're a hero. You did it!'

'It was long,' Carys sounded so tired. 'But they're beautiful. I can't stop looking at them. I'd love you to come as soon as, but I need a rest, so later?'

'Completely. I can wait. What about their names? Are you going to call them what you wanted to?' With the father there, he might have different ideas.

'Danny said since I'd done all the work and the worrying, I could choose. So yes. Will came first, five pounds seven, then ten minutes later there was Liam, five pounds five.' Will and Liam, named after the sisters' father William Williams. The tears started then between them. 'Danny cut the cord and I'm having a large glass of that champagne you put in my bag.'

'And they're healthy? And you're okay?'

'They're perfect. I'm exhausted, I've got more stitches than a race of marathon runners. I need a shower and sleep, but this is the best thing that's ever happened to me.'

'To us,' Wanda said. 'To us.'

And she felt her feet spreading and her toes gripping the soles of her flip-flops as if to root herself to the land. *Oh no.* This wasn't supposed to be happening: she was just being emotional, surely?

A photo pinged through immediately after the call ended and there was Mam cradling a baby in the crook of each arm. Wanda's fingers expanded the image and her heart surged at Will on the left and Liam on the right, both swaddled in blue blankets covered with little lambs, their noses like buttons, their lips cherubic, both topped with fluffy dark hair. Her nephews, named after her father, who had made Mam a granny. The glow inside met the wobbles travelling up her legs.

Annie was taking the tongs out of Wanda's hands and telling her to go and show everyone the adorable bundles who had made her an aunty. Like a bolt, Wanda knew she loved them more than anything in the world. It was instant and all-consuming, primal and deep. Instantly Wanda knew she was done for. All that stuff about leaving and finding herself, her true calling – now they were as flaky as pastry.

'Let me see!' Blod had elbowed her way first to the queue and a chorus of 'Aah!' went up as her phone was passed down the queue.

Lew was the last in the line – and he was there wait-ing for a *cwtch*. Her arms went round him and felt the muscled sinew of his back. Her face was against his neck, her cheek pressed against his warm bare skin, her chest sucked against his. He had one hand circling her waist while the other was stroking her hair. She had shut her eyes, she realised, and it felt like heaven to be this close to him. She found she wanted to stay like this forever. What was wrong with her? Even worse, she didn't even want to be right.

The latest testimonial in the visitors' book, written by a couple their age and asking why you'd go anywhere else in the world when you had this, had struck a chord when she'd first read it and now it was like hearing the bongs of Big Ben. A series of TV-news-style headlines ran through her mind: *Bong!* Wanda Williams wanted to see the world. *Bong!* But now she's having second thoughts. *Bong!* She's in love with this bloke. *Bong!* And she's pretty sure he loves her too. *Bong!* Oh dear.

Quickly, she pulled away from him and started chat-tering, anything to drown out the exclusive bulletins.

'They're so cute! I can't believe it! Carys is a mam, her Danny turned up!'

'Want me to take you up there? I can drive you.' Lew was already searching his pockets for his keys.

'No, Carys is so tired. I can see them tomorrow, her and Danny need to do some bonding too.'

'Yeah, good call. You'll have a month with them, won't you, before you go.'

Wanda gave a faint whimper. Four weeks, that's all she'd have with them. Four weeks, that's all she had left with Lew. She couldn't do it. She couldn't leave. It was rising up inside and cantering up her throat and onto her tongue.

'I'm not going,' she blurted out. 'I'm not going.'

'No, I know!' he laughed. 'I can take you to the hospital tomorrow.'

'No. I mean I'm not going going. Leaving. I want to stay.' She looked into his eyes, her chest heaving.

His face fell. 'What?'

'I can't bear to leave you,' she said with every bit of her body and soul. 'I love you.'

Lew's mouth fell open and his head went back as if she'd punched him one. He looked confused and shocked.

What the hell had she just said?

Wanda stepped away and backed off. His hand went out to her, his eyes were wide. She had massively misjudged this moment – it was simply the relief and joy that the twins had arrived safely. That's what she needed to say to him: the emotion of it all, the beginning of two new lives, well, that's why she'd said something so ridiculous.

Yet the truth was quite different: their birth hadn't caused it, their birth had just unlocked what she had always known. Now that she'd said it out loud, what on earth was she going to do with it?

41

'I stink of onions, sausages and smoke,' Annie said, plonking herself on a hay bale just in time to watch the sun setting behind the mountain. 'But it's been the best day.'

'I like a woman who's easily pleased,' Spike laughed, joining her with a thud which sent stray pieces of straw into the air.

Knackered from cleaning the barbecue grill until it shone, she managed to find the energy to elbow him in the ribs. Spike fell backwards, pretending to be mortally wounded. And while he was down there, his arm rustled inside his rucksack on the ground and he came up with a bottle of fizz.

'Still cold,' he said, triumphantly, popping the cork, releasing foam, which he quickly poured into two plastic glasses. 'I stuck it in the freezer last night and it's been in a cooler all day, just in case.'

'For what?'

'For you! For today. Obviously I didn't know how it was going to go with Dean or your mum, but I thought I'd 'ave some on ice if it'd gone well. In fact I thought it might help if it 'adn't too.'

Touched by his thoughtfulness, Annie held her glass

to Spike's and thanked him with her hand on her heart. A waterfall of bubbles cascaded down her throat, cutting through the dust of the barbecue, which she had ended up running with Spike for the rest of the day. Once Wanda had come down from the high of the twins' safe arrival, she'd checked if Annie was okay to stick to the burgers then thrown herself into collecting rubbish around the campsite. She was still going, alone in the distance by the lake. It had been heaving but the locals had trekked off to the pub to continue the party and the campers were in semi-circles of chairs, an audience for nature's evening show of splendour. Wispy clouds were turning pink against the deepening blue sky as birds flew around in their swooping bedtime ritual.

A peace had settled – just as it had in Annie's life. Nanna Perl had given her childhood some security, but unrest had never been far away. There'd been her mother's neglect, Ryan's death and Dean's cruelty, which had conspired to make her believe that that was what she deserved. Then the rock bottom of January, of being homeless, of fearing for Teg's life, sleeping rough and being penniless. But seven months later, she had a future as a free woman, a homeowner and a teacher.

'I never thought I'd see this day,' Annie said, 'I owe it all to coming home to Gobaith. If you'd told me years ago that I'd be saying that then I'd have thought you were mad. I finally feel like I belong here.'

'Me too,' Spike said. 'Arthur's settled, 'e's made friends. Look at 'im!' He gestured to his son, who was building a den in the distance with the Grow Up gang while Teg lay closely keeping guard. 'He used to be a right townie! This place has been part of 'is healing. And mine.'

'He's blossomed, Spike. You've done a great job.'

'Only thanks to you.'

'I think the dog did more than me! They give you a reason to get up, animals. Oh, nothing will beat this feeling, Spike. I feel complete.' She turned to him and smiled.

'Do you?' His eyes searched hers meaningfully, then he went back to taking in the lake, which was still and calm. 'Nothing else missing?'

Annie sensed a change in the air between them: perhaps he wanted to acknowledge their almost getting together. That was fair enough, it had been part of their short history.

'It's okay, Spike. You don't have to go through it again.' Annie had come to the conclusion they would be friends and nothing more. She had licked her wounds and reached acceptance. 'I've got so much going for me. Honestly, you don't need to feel bad about things.'

Spike dropped his head and then looked up at her beneath his fair eyelashes.

'The thing is ... I've been thinking ...'

Her heart stood up to attention with hope. But she pushed it back down with a deep breath. Spike had made it clear how he felt about her.

'I love Lucy, I always will.'

She didn't want him to feel his agony anew. And really, she didn't want to hear again the reasons why they couldn't be together. But he was twisting his body towards her to open up to her. She did the same, mirroring him, to show she was on his wavelength.

'I know, Spike, it's okay.' She put her hand on his knee to reassure him.

'I don't fink you do ... I've wanted to say it for a while, ever since I backed off. I 'ad to, to make sure, I couldn't risk messing you about.'

It sounded as if there was a 'but' coming. Well, this wasn't what she'd expected to be in the script.

'Right.' His hand had gone to hers – not on top of it in a commanding way, but underneath it, to cushion hers.

'But I didn't want to say anything while you've been going through all this stuff with your mum and Dean. I don't want to 'ijack the moment or take advantage or—'

'No, of course not.' Spike was a measured man, not prone to ups and downs, he was a constant of kindness. She could hardly dare to breathe with where this was going.

'And I don't want you finking that what I want to say is because of 'ow you've been there for Arthur. I mean, you're brilliant with him, but that's not why ...'

His fingers curled round hers and Annie knew then and there what he meant and her heart began to flutter.

'I just wasn't ready. But I am now. If you'll 'ave me.'

'Oh!' she whispered.

'I understand completely if you want to stay friends; whatever 'appens, I'll always be there for you.' He nodded, emphasising his words.

Annie was unsure this was actually happening to her. He saw it as hesitation.

'You don't have to decide now, take all the time you need. But if it's a no, then that's okay, we've made it work so far and—'

'Enough,' she said.

He shut his eyes in disappointment and resignation and she felt a smile on her lips, in her cheeks and all the way to her eyes. When he opened them again, she caught his surprise and his dawning realisation that she might not be about to dash his dreams. He went to open his mouth.

'Shhh! You've done enough talking!' she said, softly, putting a finger on his cupid's bow. To think he was waiting for her, this wonderful person who had made her believe men could be good. More than good, a perfect fit. 'The answer's yes, Spike.'

Tears glistened in their eyes as they allowed their longing and their love to come to the surface.

'Being with you, Annie, it's like I've come 'ome.'

She knew exactly what he meant and their gaze was loaded with anticipation, but that'd have to wait.

'Home, did you say?' Arthur called, running up with Teg and then stopping dead, catching his dad holding hands with Annie. 'Are you two ...?'

'If that's okay?' Spike said shyly.

'Sick!' Arthur cried. 'Although no snogging, not in front of me.'

Annie laughed at the boy's grimace. She realised she and Spike hadn't sealed this with a kiss yet. But it didn't matter – it would happen, it was a certainty.

'Let's go then,' Spike said, pulling Annie up, their palms entwined. 'Let's go home.'

'I'm starving,' Arthur said. 'Shall we do pizzas? Home-made ones?'

'You and your stomach,' Spike tutted as they crossed the field and made their way to the lane.

'But I haven't eaten for a couple of hours. Three hot dogs wasn't enough. By the way, Dad, Annie, we could all have a sleepover tonight, couldn't we? Like, Annie can stay now, can't she?'

The innocence of him was delightful.

'Yeah, if she wants to.' A lesser man might have been tempted to play up the innuendo but Spike matched his son's straightforwardness.

'I'd love to.' Annie's smile was cheesier than a bag of this little boy's favourite Wotsits.

'We can watch a film! Shall we stay up as late as we can? See who's the last to fall asleep?' He was chattering with excitement, swinging his arms as the four of them walked side by side. 'And I've had an idea, the house next door, Annie can buy that, then we can have a giant house and we can all live together. Maybe you can have a baby and I'll have a brother!'

'Steady on, mate! She'll run a mile.' Spike was blushing from the simplicity of his son's vision.

'Nah, she won't,' Arthur chimed. 'You won't, will you, Annie?'

'Run? You'd have to drag me away!'

'See? See, Dad!'

Spike raised his eyebrows to give her a way out.

'I'm afraid you're stuck with me,' she said. 'This is where I'm meant to be. Forever.'

42

We were only here for Friday night but by luck, we'd just arrived when the hill officially became a mountain! There was a right party on! This morning we were among the first up there. In the words of Sir Edmund Hillary, it is not the mountain we conquer, but ourselves – particularly when you've got a hangover the size of Everest.

Sam and Vic, Bristol
Campsite Visitors' Book

Only now in the darkness was it safe for Wanda to face it.

Alone at the edge of the lake, away from the campsite, she had reached the point of no return. Telling Lew she loved him and she was prepared to sacrifice her dream for him had been too much, too sudden, not just for him but for her. Because it was crunch time.

Hugging her knees, she accepted what she'd held at bay during the rest of the barbecue. Thinking of the twins had been her salvation – what was there to worry about when they had been born healthy and they had a mam and dad to love them? Litter picking for the last few hours had helped, too, looking down at the ground so she didn't have to engage with anyone. And of course, catching Annie leaving hand in hand with Spike had given her so much joy; those two were made for each other. But here, where the lake was as black as her heart, she had to make up her mind.

What was it that she wanted? To travel, to fulfil her lifelong ambition to see the world, just as she'd told her father she'd do? Or to be with Lew? Where she was sat, her eyes stinging, she couldn't see a compromise.

Soft steps came from behind her. Wanda turned to see Lew's shape advancing slowly and she quickly wiped her face.

'Hi,' she said, controlling the wobble in her voice and trying to smile.

'I've been looking for you,' he said, sitting beside her, his eyes twinkling in the moonlight. 'What you said earlier ...'

'I should go. It's obvious. I was just all over the place earlier.'

'Wanda, you are doing my head in.'

His exasperation met her own and combusted.

'I'm doing *my* head in,' she cried.

'You have to go, Wanda. For you, for your dad ... for me. You can't not go because of me.'

'I know that.' He was infuriatingly lovely. 'I'm just so torn.'

'I told you, I'll wait for you.' He grabbed her hand and she turned to see him at her mercy. She took it back and crossed her arms, feeling as if she was in a straitjacket.

'We've been through this. I can't hold you to it, what if you go off the idea and I come back and you've met someone else?'

'Wanda, I don't want anyone else!' He almost laughed and it made her cross. He made it sound so easy. Since when had things between them ever been like that? Inside, she was building up to something – there was frustration and confusion and then the bloody obvious ...

'Things happen when I go away, Lew. You know that.'

He shook his head. 'So that's it. You're still carrying that around with you. After everything we've been through. When are you going to stop it? You're not some kind of jinx on your own happiness. Can't you see? You make things work whatever's happening around you. You're not responsible for everything and everyone! All you have to do is go, keep in touch: there's this thing called FaceTime, you know, then come back and I'll be here. And we can work out what happens next then.'

He was knocking down her defences one by one. She flung her hands out into the night. 'All right, all right. I admit it. I'm scared, Lew.'

'What of?'

'Like, I go away thinking it's going to be the best thing and what if I hate it? It's the same with you, what if I've waited so long to be with you and then it happens and it doesn't work?'

She dipped her head, not wanting to see him smirking at her. Instead she felt his arm go round her.

'Well then, why don't we try before you go?' he said, gently. 'Then, if it does crash and burn, which it won't, you can leave.'

Wanda looked up. His eyes were so warm and true she felt herself coming round.

'But if it works ...' Then she felt the shudder of fear again. 'Maybe I won't want to go.'

'I'll make you!'

She laughed at the romance of it: this man she loved telling her he'd pack her off if things worked out between them.

'I owe it to you – you made me face up to the night of the fire, you did that! It changed my life.'

'I dunno ...' she said quietly. She needed something more to convince her it was worth a go.

'I'll visit you, then. The Bunkhouse will close for a month or so in the winter. I'll come, just like I was always going to the first time you were supposed to travel.'

'Really?' That would be a game-changer if they could commit to meeting up.

'Yes! Although can I do the beach bit? I don't fancy the adventurous part. I get my kicks here, in this land. And in you. In all your ridiculous behaviour.'

Her eyes searched his and she began to process what he'd said and offered. She turned her face to the lake and then it came to her, the latest comment in the visitors' book.

'It is not the mountain we conquer, but ourselves,' she said, softly. 'That's what I need to do.'

'Maybe you've almost done it? Look at what you've done here, to this place. You've given your mam, your sister and those babies a future. You made me deal with the past, you saved me, Wanda. Isn't it time you thought about yourself? Your dad, he'd want that too.'

She began to nod slowly, looking up for inspiration and then gasping when she realised. 'This weekend it's the sixteenth anniversary of the fire, I'd forgotten.'

'Maybe that means something.'

'That I'm ready? To move on?'

The heavens answered her questions. High up, there was a flash of light. A shooting star was streaking across the sky. She gasped again and pointed. There was another one. And another!

'Yes. All of this, Wanda, it's just the beginning. Of you and me.'

She turned to Lew and where there had always been resistance and barriers there were none. In their place was love – and desire. She caressed his cheek with her fingers and then slid her hand back to his neck. She moved in to his body and placed her lips on his, where they were always meant to be. As they kissed, everything made sense. Fifteen, no, sixteen years in the making, she finally felt complete. She was drunk on him and all of the possibilities which lay ahead of them, convinced now she had conquered herself. Her soul was bursting – and then suddenly she jolted back.

'What?' he said, fearful. 'You haven't changed your mind, have you?'

'No!' she sang. 'It's just ... I've had an idea!'

Lew rolled his eyes and groaned. 'Oh no, not another one.'

Wanda guffawed.

'Can you tell me about it tomorrow?' he said. 'Can we just enjoy this for a bit? We've waited long enough.'

'All right then,' she sighed.

And then together they lay back on the earth and snuggled up into one another under a starry sky.

Epilogue

Four Months Later ...

Wanda had finally found what she'd been dreaming of.

The sand was whiter than she had ever imagined possible, the sea was a mass of sparkling emeralds and the sky was the truest of blues.

She took a few seconds to breathe it all in, her toes wriggling into the soft powder, before she waded into the bath-warm water and let herself fall back to float face up to the baking sunshine. A blissful piece of paradise was hers here on New Year's Day on an off-the-beaten-track Indonesian island beach where a gentle breeze caressed the palm trees.

Oh, the irony that she could take as many photos as she liked but there was no wifi to whack them up on @WandaLust. That was part of the experience, though – of hugging this all to herself until she rejoined civilisation. For now, it was pure present-in-the-moment bliss.

Until a goddamn jet ski roared past and she got a mouthful of wave. She spluttered and gagged, her arms flailing around, temporarily disoriented, her vision a blur. Choking, her feet hit the sand and she felt something brush up against her leg – a sea snake?

Argh, she shot off screaming, her legs making *kerplunk*

noises through the water that reminded her of an unfortunate diarrhoea episode in the South Pacific.

Back on land, the salt was making her mosquito bites sting – she'd been eaten alive. And the skin on her shoulders was sore. No matter how much factor 50 she put on, the UV somehow always got through. Insta tits-and-teeth travel influencer, she was definitely not.

This, she'd found out, was the reality of travelling. Yes, there were jaw-dropping sights and life-affirming adventures but more often there were the humdrum, normal life inconveniences, irritations and downright disgusting discoveries. Long hot traffic jams in Cartagena; her heel snapping mid-tango-class in Buenos Aires; suffering unbearably earnest paid-for-by-daddy gap-year students on a street-kid project in Chile and a bug-infested hostel in Tahiti. The main problem, wherever she'd been, was avoiding idiots who seemed to latch on to her, always banging on about wanting to find themselves, a quest that usually involved a bar.

She didn't want to sound ungrateful so she didn't tell anyone on FaceTime calls how much she missed a home-made cup of tea with proper milk or *cwtchy* winter nights in front of a fire. She only admitted that to Glanmor in España, when she called him to show off her Spanish. He knew exactly what she meant regarding the milk, but as for the cold, he didn't miss that at all.

Instead she started to work on her idea, the one she'd had the moment she'd kissed Lew when she'd decided she could leave Gobaith. If she travelled with that in mind, then she began to enjoy herself much more. And it helped distract her from the lamest thing of all – how much she missed Lew. Obviously, he had been completely right:

they were sickeningly loved-up, with no hiccups. They hadn't had a night apart and the village had dined out on their relationship: *We knew it! We knew you were in love!* But once she'd got past the initial embarrassment of people giving them gooey – and smug – smiles when they held hands in public, she'd moved on to not even remembering what it had felt like to not be with him. Secretly, it *had* made it harder to leave; she felt there was so much to lose. But that was part of the deal she'd made with herself. And she had no regrets – even if she'd just made the least graceful exit from the sea. Looking around, though, no one appeared to have noticed. She pulled her sunbed into the shade and started the seventh SPF application of the morning, happy she'd got away with making an idiot of herself. But an enormous grin of laughing gear in pale blue shorts and ripped six-pack coming towards her from the bar told her otherwise.

'All right, Ursula Andress?' Lew said, before launching into a rendition of the James Bond theme music.

'Oh, if it isn't Daniel bloody Craig in his budgie smugglers!' she said, full of sarcasm, which was really hard to do actually, because he looked better than Daniel bloody Craig in his budgie smugglers. Lew had only been here a week and already he was mahogany. She looked like a pint of semi-skimmed next to him.

'I love your freckles,' he said, as if he'd read her insecurity, planting a big kiss on her lips. 'Here, got you one of these.'

He handed her a chilled coconut with a straw.

'It better not be one of those cleansing turmeric ones, they're vile,' she said. 'Or laced with rum. I'm still a bit fragile from last night.'

'Nope. Just coconut water.'

Phew! The tourist side of Indonesia was a place of extremes, either party central or hippy heaven. So it was a welcome relief to arrive on the Togean islands yesterday. Lew had flown in to Bali on Christmas Eve and their Christmas Day had been spent mostly in bed in a fancy hotel as a treat for their reunion. Wanda had been so excited to see him; apprehensive, too, because she was still haunted by 'what ifs'. Yet as soon as he'd stepped out of arrivals, they'd clung to one another like the soulmates they were. She'd been proud to negotiate the crowds, to get them back to the hotel and then out the next day for a simple but delicious seafood meal. But the heaving hustle of Bali had been too much for them: Wanda suggested the Togean islands, having heard they were relatively unspoiled. She flaming well hoped so after she broke it to Lew that it would take an overnight eighteen-hour ferry journey to get there. She remembered what he'd said about not wanting adventure. But he let her take control and God, was it worth it. New Year's Eve was riotous back on Bali, with fireworks, twenty-four-hour open-air beach clubbing and champagne. Here it had been more low-key, with sundowners, drinks and dinner on the sand and local musicians drumming in midnight before they'd returned to their bungalow for some fireworks of their own.

'What do you fancy doing, then?' Wanda asked, stretching out with a sigh. 'A boat trip? A dive? The coral reef is spectacular, apparently. Or there's a lake where you can swim with stingless jellyfish.'

'Whatever you want to do, my little mermaid,' Lew said.

'To be honest, I'm happy to just chill today.'

'Me too. We've got bags of time. Another three weeks, I make it.'

That reminded her.

'Lew,' she said, turning to face him as he did the same and reached out for her hand. 'I've been thinking.'

'Not again. Does your brain ever stop?'

'Listen, this is important. I think I'm ready to go home.'

'Now? We've only just got here!'

'No. After. Once we've left here and travelled around. When you go, I mean.'

'Really?' He pushed up his sunglasses and his eyes were even more beautiful, matching his tanned skin.

'Yeah. I'm done with it. I've had a good time and I've done what I wanted to do and no one died and I just think I've reached the end point. Is that rubbish of me?'

'No. It's up to you, you don't have to prove anything to anyone.'

'I'll rearrange my flights, then. I can do India and Morocco another time.'

'Yeah?' He was beaming unashamedly.

'Yeah!' She took a slurp of her coconut water. 'It's all part of the plan.'

'It's a goer, you reckon then?' Lew got up and sat on the side of her bed, parking himself next to her so his thigh touched hers. He was the most touchy-feely man she'd ever known, as if he was making up for their lost years.

'There's definitely a gap in the market for me to organise itineraries for women travellers my age and upwards. I've found some brilliant spots, more upmarket than budget backpacking but not stuffy. I met lots of women who wished they'd had some kind of insight, or that there was a way you could match solo travellers together. I can do that for them. I can do it from home. I just need to take it online. While it builds, I can do some shifts at the campsite—'

'You can help at The Bunkhouse if you'd like, too. And,' he said, beneath those thick eyelashes, 'you know, you could always … stay with me, for nothing …'

Wanda almost squealed. 'As in kind of … move in?' Bowen was still renting her flat and Sara loved the short commute to work.

'Well, your toothbrush is still there. We were practically living together anyway. So why not?'

'I'd love to,' she said. 'It's not as though we have to wait to get to know each other, is it?'

Lew laughed. 'You know me, scars and all. Talking of which …'

He handed her his sunblock and asked her to do the honours. And it *was* an honour to touch the part of him that was part of them. She dotted the cream on her fingertips and began to massage it in to protect the damage. And then she kissed his shoulder blades one by one, smelling the salt and sun on him.

'I miss smelling Will and Liam,' she said, laying her cheek on his back, wrapping her arms round his downy waist. 'Their little fluffy duck hair. It's almost painful seeing them on FaceTime and not being able to sniff them.'

This was another reason why she felt the call of home.

'Four months old now. I missed their first smiles.'

'Oh, Wanda, don't beat yourself up about it. They don't know anyone at the moment apart from Mam, Dad and Nanny!'

'I want to go home, Lew. I want to see my nephews growing up.'

Lew turned to hug her and his embrace squeezed out more of her hidden feelings.

'I want to make sure Mam isn't overdoing it, keep an eye on the campsite.'

'I told you, Danny is doing a fantastic job.'

As luck would have it, when they were wetting the babies' heads, Danny had told Wanda how much he hated working nine to five in an office. He'd always wanted to do something outdoorsy and vocational. She'd talked it over with Carys, who'd loved the suggestion: Danny was hands-on with the twins, determined to give this unexpected family unit everything to make it work. And Mam was delighted when he agreed to manage Under A Starry Sky.

'I need to make sure Mam isn't dating the wrong type either on those websites.'

'She's just having fun!'

'I miss Sara. And Blod.'

'They're both in la-la-loved-up land so I wouldn't worry about it.'

'I miss Annie, too.'

'She misses you. But she's got so much on with her teacher training and doing up the house.' She'd bought the cottage next door to Spike and Arthur and they were living happily side by side. The first thing she'd done when she moved in was tear down the fence between them and Teg was free to wander back and forth between their back doors. On the quiet, Annie had told her Spike wanted to try for a baby with her – and they were giving it their best shot.

'And you make me want to go home again too. I miss you,' her voice wobbled. '*Te echo de menos.*' Once she'd got to grips with finding out where the toilets were and how much a coffee was, that was the first phrase that really stuck when she'd learned Spanish.

'Now you're just being dramatic,' he said, rubbing her back, and she could hear the smile in his voice. She gave him a pretend shove and then broke off from their hug so she could stare into his eyes. 'But that's why I love you, Wanda Williams,' he said.

'To the stars and back?' she asked.

'More. To the Welsh stars and back.'

To that night sky in Gobaith, specifically. That was what she missed most of all: the land of her father, the mountain protecting the village, her home, the place of her birth. She'd gone away to find out that the place she loved most was where she had started. But she'd had to go through this to find that out. A sigh came from her lips. As usual she was getting caught up in it all.

'Right,' she said, slapping her thighs, 'I'm not sure I've made enough of a fool of myself so far today.' She threw Lew's snorkel at him and put on her own, laughing at their giant goggles. 'Let's go and see what we can find. I wonder if we could get snorkelling masks for the lake at the campsite? That'd be good!'

Lew rolled his eyes at her. 'Just forget about Gobaith for once! Let's enjoy the rest of the holiday.'

'Okay, okay,' she huffed.

'Good! We'll be home before we know it,' he said.

'I know, I know!' Wanda said as she took his hand and led him to the sea, 'I can't bloody wait!'

Acknowledgements

It all started in 2018 when my friend and I decided to drag our boys off their screens and into the great Welsh outdoors.

We jokingly called it Rambling Club, we being very much not ramblers, possessing neither walking poles nor beards. Just two mums making gags about how 'extreme' we were, taking packed lunches and sweets for our sons' flagging limbs, getting overtaken by the pros in hardcore outdoorsy walking gear.

Our first hike was ambitious – Pen y Fan, the highest mountain in South Wales. But the screaming of my thighs was drowned out by the joy of reaching the top and seeing the wilderness of the beautiful Brecon Beacons stretch out beneath us. It had us hooked, even the kids, especially Ollie, my dog aka The Secretary.

Since then we have walked behind the waterfall of Sgwd yr Eira, trekked to the tidal island of Worm's Head, encountered wild horses on lonely roads, conquered The Skirrid and The Blorenge and sighed at beaches and forests and bluebells. Most wonderful of all, we had a freezing and very remote wild swim in Llyn y Fan Fach, the inspiration behind the lake in this book. (Apologies if you happened to see my exposed backside that day while I was getting changed, there is a helpline available.) Please note, I used artistic licence to relocate its Lady of the Lake legend to my fictional village of Gobaith, I hope she doesn't mind.

Every adventure always includes a cry of 'let's get ready to raaaaamble' (spoken like the boxing MC Michael Buffer and then sang like Ant and Dec), getting lost, taking ridiculous short cuts up and down sheer hillsides and wet feet – but that's all part of it, life too. What stays with us though is the magic of the landscape and the awe it inspires. Laughter, lots of that, with my dear friend Ceri and pride in our boys, Reuben and Paddy. So it's to them I say my first thank you. Rambling is the new raving!

Next is the coolest gardener in the world @girlinthegarden77, who let me shadow her for a few weeks so I got to experience Annie's back-breaking work for myself. It's the toughest job I've done - thorns, sunburn, getting drenched, clearing ponds with bare hands and blisters from digging in all weathers - but there's no satisfaction like it when you're done. Chloe, you're an inspiration.

A huge *diolch* to Angharad Rhys, my wonderful Welsh-speaking friend who answers my ignorant questions on the language and its meaning. Any errors are obviously mine.

Thanks also to one of the best humans I've never met – @hoskas who once tweeted the advice she gave her sons growing up which I loved, admired, pinched for this book and also dish out to my son: Don't Be A Dick.

Nick Machin, how we miss you, Fork Handles is for you and Sufia.

To my soundboard JC, who claims superstition as

the reason why he's never read a word I've written, and Pillow the cat who tries to change them by stalking across my keyboard.

Then there's one of my earliest and loyal readers June Bolt, for her lush bara brith.

Friends and family – I love you, gang.

Now to the fabulous book people...

Lizzy Kremer, my agent, who is my queen and I adore her. Everyone at David Higham, especially Maddalena Cavaciuti, for doing the maths and contracts and stuff that I have no idea about.

My editor, former Orion publishing director, Clare 'Steel' Hey, for her infinite genius and for making me better.

Sally Partington once again delivered a magnificent edit, saving me from grammar jail and educated me in the process, you have the very best eye.

Plus Alainna, Babs, Britt, sales, audio and all at Orion – my name is on the book but you guys do the real work. Artist Robyn Neild is a mind-reader because her covers always match what I imagine in my head.

Retailers, it's a dream come true to see my books on your shelves. Special thanks to marvellous Mel and the team at Griffin Books – I am very lucky to have such a busy and bright bookshop down the road.

My author pals are The Best – thank you for keeping me going when the words are difficult to find, especially Miranda Dickinson this time for giving me lots of support when the going got tough. Pro-reviewers, you're so very wonderful and your opinions matter so much.

Bloggers, you're unsung heroes, giving up your time for nothing for the sheer love of books.

I always thank my Twitter and Facebook pals too, you brighten my day and help when I'm limping along at my desk.

Finally, you, the reader. (I have readers! I still can't get over it.) Your messages and your reviews make my heart burst. Thank you so very much for everything, lovelies.

By the way, should you ever be in Annie's position, the Dogs Trust runs the Freedom Project, which helps owners escape domestic abuse by providing safe temporary foster homes for their dogs. Please give them a call and set yourself and your dog free.

Credits

Orion Fiction would like to thank everyone at Orion who worked on the publication of *Under A Starry Sky* in the UK.

Editorial
Charlotte Mursell
Clare Hey
Olivia Barber

Copy editor
Sally Partington

Proof reader
Jade Craddock

Audio
Paul Stark
Amber Bates

Contracts
Anne Goddard
Paul Bulos
Jake Alderson

Design
Rabab Adams

Joanna Ridley
Nick May

Production
Ruth Sharvell

Editorial Management
Charlie Panayiotou
Jane Hughes
Alice Davis

Finance
Jasdip Nandra
Afeera Ahmed
Elizabeth Beaumont
Sue Baker

Marketing
Brittany Sankey

Publicity
Alainna Hadjigeorgiou

Sales

Laura Fletcher
Esther Waters
Victoria Laws
Rachael Hum
Ellie Kyrke-Smith
Frances Doyle

Georgina Cutler

Operations

Jo Jacobs
Sharon Willis
Lisa Pryde
Lucy Brem